In the House of Dark Music

In the House of Dark Music

by

FRANCES LYNCH

The Leisure Circle

British Library Cataloguing in Publication Data
Lynch, Frances
   In the house of dark music.
   I. Title
   823'.9'1F   PR6063.0451/

   ISBN 0–340–23440–7

Part One

1

THE YEAR WAS 1856, the season early March, the time twenty minutes after midnight. And the place was Goodwin's Court, a narrow London alleyway, heavily shadowed, lit only by the wavering gas lamps outside the archways at either end. A thin, unpleasant rain had been falling for most of the previous evening, blown almost horizontal by the bitter wind. Now the rain had stopped, and only the wind remained, gusting cruelly.

The red-headed boy sleeping in one of the alley's dark doorways shivered at its icy touch, but did not wake. He was dreaming, and uttered small frightened cries, held fast in the sinister grip of his nightmare. His jaw quivered and his eyelids fluttered, his hands clutching feverishly at the sawn-off handle of the stiff-bristled broom lying between his knees. He twisted his tousled, carroty head from side to side. But still he did not wake.

One side of Goodwin's Court was bounded by a high blank wall. On the other there stood a row of tall, narrow houses, once elegant and respectable. Now they were neither. For the alley lay to the east of Leicester Square, on the Covent Garden side—that is to say, the disreputable side.

The boy's name at that time was Midge. This was not his Christened name, but it served him very well. He was small and thin, yet by no means weakly. Though he could not himself have told you how old he was, he had in fact been discovered some ten years before, very new and wrinkled, wrapped in a shabby blanket on the nearby steps of St Martin-in-the-Fields. And now he was a crossing-sweeper, with a stand in St Martin's Lane.

Faring better than the majority of foundlings, he had been

taken in by the vicar's wife and farmed out shortly afterwards to one of her husband's parishioners, a man called Meiklejohn. Mrs Meiklejohn, only recently brought to bed of her fifth still-born infant, had welcomed the boy, calling him Reuben, sentimentally, after her deported brother.

Mr Meiklejohn's welcome, however, had been rather more worldly, for the boy brought with him two shillings weekly, paid by the vicar's wife. Thus, when the vicar was moved to another parish a few years later and the allowance terminated, Mr Meiklejohn's welcome terminated also. By then the child was nearing five years of age and, so Mr Meiklejohn considered, well able to make his own way in the world. He contrived therefore to lose Reuben shortly afterwards, somewhere during a long Sunday afternoon walk in Hyde Park. And Mrs Meiklejohn, by then with two demanding children of her own, was for all her protestations secretly relieved to see her husband return without him.

Now, at the age of ten, young Reuben had indeed made his own way in the world, for he had won himself an established profession. And his only notable loss along the road had been that of the name his adopted mother had chosen for him. But he was not a large child, and Midge suited him a great deal better. He slept in Goodwin's Court because it was only a stone's throw from his crossing on St Martin's Lane and he needed to be close at hand, in case some flash lad turned up early one morning, planning to half-inch it.

Besides, he liked the girls who worked in the houses there. Sometimes at night they gave him pennies as they passed, or peppermints in little screws of scented paper . . .

Again, trapped still in his nightmare, he cried out. His carroty head jerked, and his bare feet scrabbled on the doorstep. And then, suddenly, mysteriously, he managed somehow to break the dream's eerie possession of his mind. With a final convulsive shudder he woke, cold sweat upon his brow, and stared wildly about him.

No one can know another's dreams, certainly not a child's.

Even he can only know them confusedly, perceived through the warped glass of the window of memory. Midge crouched in his doorway, aware simply that he had been terribly afraid. There had been a great darkness, and a figure even darker than the darkness. And *music* ... He knew the music, remembered it as a tinkling melody he had heard played long ago by a hurdy-gurdy man in a coat covered with brightly-coloured patches. A sad little melody, not at all frightening. Why, then, had it seemed so in his dreams?

But already the horror was fading. Midge felt the thick, strong handle of the broom between his knees, and was reassured. It was a good broom, his most important possession. And it was safe.

He forgot his fear. Two large brown rats, disturbed in their scavenging, sat up on their hind legs to peer at him where he sat, huddled in the shadows. He shoo'd them away and they sidled off, twittering angrily. He wrapped his man's reefer jacket more tightly about himself, and settled back to sleep.

It was at that moment that approaching footsteps caught his attention. He looked up, saw the fiddler enter the far end of the alley, the Bedford Broadway end, where the gas lamp flickered on the wall by the arch. Midge knew the man was a fiddler from the fiddle-shaped box he was carrying. He was used to musicians —they often came and went along the alley. They played either in Drury Lane or at the Italian Opera House in Covent Garden.

The fiddler came towards him, picking his way between the muddy puddles. He interrupted a group of cats squabbling over a mouldy rabbit skin. Distantly a late cab clattered by on cobbles. One of the windows above his head screeched open, a square of light slanted out across the opposite wall, and a young woman shouted something down. But the fiddler took no notice, and the light died abruptly as the window was closed again, to the accompaniment of mocking laughter.

Suddenly, just as the man came abreast of the place where Midge sat crouched in the shadows, a second, bulkier man

11

appeared beneath the archway behind him. He stood beneath the street lamp, watching the fiddler walk away from him. And then he began to whistle.

Instantly Midge's body stiffened, every muscle locked in a sudden spasm of horror. For the tune the man whistled was from his nightmare. The very same tune, it came to him softly, caressingly, out of the very same darkness. Simple, innocent, childlike, it crept into the most secret parts of his mind, filling them with incomprehensible terror. He would have fled, but could not. Incapable of even the smallest movement, he stayed in his doorway, eyes wide and unblinking.

The whistling ceased. In front of Midge the fiddler had paused, intrigued, not certain where the sound was coming from. Behind him the man beneath the street lamp raised his hand and called.

"Herr Falconer ... A moment of your time, if you please, Herr Falconer."

Midge could see him clearly, the figure from his nightmare: tall black hat, high-buttoned coat with a curly fur collar, one hand raised, the other holding a slender walking stick with a silvery band that gleamed in the lamplight.

The fiddler turned warily. "My name is Falconer. Who wants me?"

"A friend, Herr Falconer. Just an old friend."

The other, larger man started slowly forward, nearer and nearer. Midge began to tremble convulsively. Here, in the figure of this smooth, black-garbed foreigner, was all the nameless horror of his dream. He cowered away, struck dumb with childish fears. He struggled to speak, to warn the fiddler, but the words stuck fast in his throat. He watched, agonised, as the fiddler took a fatal pace back along the alley.

"I know that voice," the fiddler said. "Is it not—?"

But the question died on his lips. For in an instant the other had quickened his steps to a lumbering run. And in his hand there was now no longer a walking stick but rather the glancing blade of a sword. Its steel seemed to shimmer like the light of a thousand stars. He came at the fiddler, thrusting wickedly.

His victim had no time to flee. Watchfully, in silent concentration he stepped back against the wall and parried the sword with his instrument case. Midge was weeping now, the sobs wrung from him with terrible, soundless intensity. The fiddler's instrument case was struck from his hand. He grappled with his opponent. The two men staggered back and forth, grunting desperately, their feet slithering on the wet pavement. Midge gazed up at them from the safe shadows of his doorway. Strangely, the worst of his fear was passing. His weeping ceased. He had seen men fight before. This was real, human, no longer dream-like.

The larger man had his left hand at the other's face, gouging for the eyes. Midge had a brief glimpse of gold glinting on his finger. Then the fiddler bit the hand and for an instant, fatally, the two men parted. And in that instant the attacker wrenched his right arm free and drove his sword into the fiddler's body. It grated hideously on the wall behind.

The fiddler cried out then, a single piercing cry that faded quickly to a whisper, then to silence. And Midge knew, with absolute certainty, that the fiddler was dead.

Once again curtains were drawn above him and a square of light slanted down as a window was opened. And once again a woman shouted, though this time more in anger than enticement. Across the alleyway the murderer had his victim propped up against the wall, one arm now in friendly fashion about the corpse's shoulders. And his voice was friendly too, as he shouted back.

"A thousand pardons, *gnädiges Fräulein*. My companion has taken too much wine, I fear. But you may depend on me—I'll see he doesn't trouble you any more."

He laughed then, cheerfully. But Midge saw how he kept his head studiously averted all the while.

There was muttering overhead, then the window was closed and darkness returned to Goodwin's Court. At once the murderer stepped back, letting the body of his victim sag and tumble slowly forward on to the stones. In haste he stooped and lifted the fiddler's wrist, holding it between finger and thumb and glancing anxiously up and down the alley as he waited, his head tilted as if listening. Then, satisfied, he nodded to himself.

"*Gut. Gut . . .*" he murmured."*Ohne Zweifel ist der Schwein jetzt tot.*"

He let the dead man's hand fall. Picking up instead the instrument case from the pavement where it had fallen, he hurried off with it down the alley, back the way he had come.

Suddenly Goodwin's Court was uncomfortably silent, deserted save for the crumpled body of the man called Falconer, its arms flung out, its head lying in a muddy puddle not two yards from the doorway where Midge still cowered. For a moment the boy watched and waited, reminded of his dream, its darkness, its nameless horror. Then, farther down the alleyway, a man emerged from one of the houses. Turning up his coat collar, he hurried towards Midge, looking neither to right nor left. At the fiddler's body he paused, peered briefly down, then stepped round it and hurried on, disappearing into St Martin's Lane without a backward glance.

His going dispelled Midge's uneasiness. It too had been real, human, no part of his dream. He ventured out into the alley, leaving his broom on the step behind him. The dead held no fears for him: he'd seen dead men before, had touched them too. Once he'd filched a pair of boots their owner had no further use for. He'd sold the boots for twopence to a rag man with a barrow.

Midge stood by the corpse, pushed at it tentatively with his bare foot. There'd be money in its pockets, perhaps even a watch on a golden chain. And the shoes—so shiny black, they'd be worth a tanner at the very least.

A tiny sound disturbed him, and he looked round fearfully. The murderer—what if he returned? But it was only the cats, tussling again at their rabbit skin. Midge summoned his courage, squatted down, and began to fumble with trembling fingers at the buttons of the dead man's coat. They were horribly stiff, and the yielding warmth of the body made his stomach heave. But the boy persevered. Wealth was within his grasp. Security . . .

Suddenly a man's voice rang out down the alley, high-pitched and angry. Midge froze. It was the murderer come back, he had no doubt of it. Another second and his own lifeless body would join that of the fiddler. He ducked away and fled, half on all-fours, whimpering with terror, away from the shrill, insistent shouting. Blindly he scuttled the length of Goodwin's Court and was gone.

Behind him a tall, slender figure in dove-grey cloak and tight, elegant trousers, stepped gingerly down the alleyway. Peering about him, his stout malacca cane with its weighted head hefted ready in his right hand, the man came at last to the body of the dead fiddler. As the boy had done, he pushed at it tentatively with his foot. The body rolled over and its coat, loosened by Midge, fell open to reveal a white shirt-front ominously darkened with a stain above the heart, about the size of a baby's hand.

"A deader, by Gad. And within the hour . . ."

The man raised his eyebrows in cool surprise. Then he turned and fastidiously retraced his steps. Only when he was clear of the alley, under the gas lamp in the relative safety of St Martin's Lane, did he fumble beneath his cloak and produce, on a long bright chain, a silver police whistle which he put to his lips and blew, piercingly and repeatedly.

At that moment, far away in a broad-eaved house high on a Bavarian cliff above a snowy valley, a toothless old woman was sitting up in bed, a smile on her wizened lips, staring with unseeing eyes at the flame of the scented nightlight in its saucer beside her. Her sleep, like that of the boy's, had been restless that night, as if disturbed by dreams. She had twisted and turned, and once she too had cried out. But there had been no terror in her cry—rather a strange exultation. As if what she

15

had dreamed had brought her a fierce, malignant pleasure.

Her cry had aroused the younger woman, thick-limbed and ugly, sleeping in the next room. She had lain motionless, not breathing, listening to the snow-laden silence of the night, ready on an instant to hurry to the old woman's side. But the cry had not been repeated, and the younger woman had breathed again, turned over in her narrow bed, and gone thankfully back to sleep.

Now the old woman was awake. She had hauled herself laboriously up till she was sitting, propped awkwardly against her fine, lace-edged pillows. Normally, once fully roused, she would at once have rung the bell on the table beside her. She was not, in the usual course of events, one to suffer sleeplessness gladly, or to show undue consideration for the rest of others.

Tonight, however, the old woman smiled, and the silver bell on her side table remained silent. The dream—if dream it was— had left her elated. She stared entranced at the tranquil flame of her night-light. She thought of her son in far-off London. Soon now, his tasks completed, he would be returning to her. She smiled.

Somewhere out in the frozen night an owl hooted. She heard it and shifted her thin, crippled body, picturing its flight among the moonlit pine trees. And smiled again. She too, that night, had gone hunting.

After a while she stretched an arm down beside her bed and brought up a fine leather violin case. She placed it upon her knees, opened it, and took the instrument out. The dim light shone softly on its reddish flowing curves. The old woman rested then, half-dreaming again as she plucked absently at its strings, the sound no more than a faint ticking in the vast black stillness of her room. Then, when she was ready, she lifted the bow from its velvet cradle within the case's lid, tucked the fiddle beneath her chin, and began to play. Her hands jerked and trembled, so that she could scarcely find the notes she wanted.

16

The younger woman stirred again in the adjoining room, woke, listened to the thin, uneven scraping. But she made no move to leave her bed, for she recognised the melody. It was a song from a music box, a children's song, ages-old, innocent and sweetly sad.

Always the old woman hated to be interrupted when she was playing, but never more so than when she was playing this tune. It had been her daughter's favourite. Her dead daughter's favourite.

So the younger woman lay quietly in the lonely darkness of her room. And, as she listened to the music, she wept. For no proper reason that she could understand, save that the song was so hauntingly pretty, and played so badly, with such crabbed, uncertain fingers.

> *Ach, du lieber Augustin,*
> *Augustin, Augustin. . .*
> *Ach, du lieber Augustin,*
> *Alles ist hin.*

In London, in Mattie Falconer's little basement kitchen, the clock on the wall struck one. Mattie looked up from her patch-work and frowned. Surely the clock must be wrong? Even allowing for more curtain calls than usual, Albert should have got away from the theatre by twelve-fifteen. And it wasn't more than a twenty-minute walk from Covent Garden to their home in Bacon Street, one of the narrow grey streets behind Waterloo Station.

But the clock was never wrong. It was an American clock, oblong, with a large glass door and a painting of the Rocky Mountains on the glass below the face. It had kept excellent time, ever since Albert had brought it home from the market on the Lambeth Road six years before, just after they were married.

Mattie laid aside her needlework. Albert was late. Something bad must have happened. She got up, went to the outside door and opened it, letting in a blast of cold night air. She shivered

17

slightly, and went back for her shawl. She was an upright, graceful young woman, with a slim waist and a fullness of figure that not even her simple brown worsted dress and white apron could conceal. Neither could the workmanlike set of her hair, its thick dark tresses parted in the middle and drawn back over her ears into a bun at the nape of her neck, detract from the hint of passion in her full mouth and finely curved brows. Her face was heart-shaped, her eyes wide apart and of a russet brown colour in which, when she was laughing, flecks of bright gold danced.

Now, however, her broad, high forehead was furrowed. She stood for a moment in the open doorway, listening. The street above was silent, save for the distant, night-long clatter of the railway. Behind her she heard the rocking chair creak slowly back and forth, then stop. Pinning her shawl tightly across her chest, she closed the door and went up the steep area steps. She stood for a long time, staring down Bacon Street, certain that at any second Albert would appear, his coat tails flapping in the wind. She'd wave to him and he'd wave back. And when he reached her he'd kiss her forehead in his tired, absent-minded fashion, and tell her what a goose she was to worry.

There could well be, she knew, several perfectly harmless reasons why Albert might be late. He played his fiddle in the band at the Italian Opera House on Covent Garden. The following night there was to be a Masked Ball at the theatre, so the conductor, Mr Costa, might easily have delayed the musicians, handing out new band parts. Or Albert might just have lingered, chatting with the actors.

But Mattie believed neither reason. Today had been Professor Anderson's Gala Benefit, offering a long and difficult programme, and Albert had been at the theatre since noon. He'd be anxious to get home to his bed.

For a long time she stood, shivering in the bitter March wind. Then she turned and went back down the steps to her warm kitchen. She crossed to the range and poked up the coals in the black-leaded grate. She gazed about her. The oil lamp cast a tranquil glow over everything—her sewing on the table, all the scraps of bright fabric lying tumbled where she had left them. But she drew no comfort from the calm, safe little room. Something bad had happened. And she didn't know what to do.

There was, in fact, nothing that she *could* do. Except wait. She daren't leave little Victoria alone in the house. Neither, at that hour of the morning, dare she rouse her friendly neighbour, Aggie Templeton, and ask her help. Aggie's man was a demon where his sleep was concerned.

Thinking of her child, Mattie was filled with a sudden, unreasonable panic. She snatched up the lamp and hurried to their bedroom, with its big iron bedstead, and the mahogany wardrobe her mother had given her, and the cot with its white starched frills. She held the lamp high, gazed down at her small, flaxen-haired daughter, sleeping peacefully beneath her snug counterpane.

The sight filled her heart with such a passion of relief and love that she pressed a hand tightly to her breast, simply to still its beating. Her husband was a good man, and unfailingly kind, but it was her daughter to whom she gave her profoundest devotion. And Vickie was safe. The child made a small sleepy sound, disturbed perhaps by the brightness of the light on her face, and turned over, burrowing deeper, like a mouse, beneath the bedclothes.

Mattie left the room, closed the door softly behind her. She replaced the lamp on the kitchen table, settled herself again in her rocking chair, and picked up her needlework. It was her custom always to wait up for Albert, his supper keeping warm in the oven. It was the very least she could do. He worked long, hard hours, and brought his wages home to her, every penny, and a man had the right to expect a little thoughtfulness in return. She always waited up, so she would wait up now. Even if—

But she could not bear to think of it. Cruelly the picture came into her mind of his journey home on foot through the dark London streets. She put it from her. Certainly there were thieves, violent, wicked men. But it was the rich they preyed on, with sovereigns in their purses and gold watch-chains across their ample waistcoats. What would they want with a poor, shabby musician? Determinedly she bent to her work, cutting the neat paper shapes, tacking the scraps of material over them.

At two o'clock she was still working. And at three o'clock also. While the child slept on, innocently unaware. It was with the coming of three o'clock that Mattie, remembering Albert's dinner still warming in the oven, paused in her work to take it out. It was dried up, ruined, so she put it outside on the kitchen windowsill for the cats. Then she returned again to her assiduous stitching.

By the time the American clock struck four, however, Mattie's hands were still, her eyes closed, her head fallen awkwardly forward upon her chest. The coals in the grate settled and died. The lamp faded also, its wick charred now and trailing wisps of sour smoke. The room grew steadily colder. Five o'clock came, and six, and seven on that drear March day, and still Mattie slept on in the old rocking chair, safe for a while from the bitter reality of her situation.

It was nearly eight o'clock when the scrape of hob-nailed boots on the area steps roused her. She lifted her head, saw the grey light of day filtering in through the curtains, and was instantly wide awake. Heavy knuckles rapped on the door. In a flash she was across the room, dragging the door open, staring beseechingly out at the two men who stood there, squashed together in the tiny space at the bottom of the steps. Only one of them wore uniform, but she had no doubt at all that they were both policemen.

"Tell me he's not dead. Dear God, please tell me Albert's not dead."

But she knew from their faces that he was.

"Mrs Falconer? Mrs Albert Falconer?"

She nodded, biting her lip. Behind her she could hear little Victoria, disturbed by the sudden racket, calling to her.

"Could we come in, please?" The policeman's thin face was

as grey as the morning "Inspector Gradbolt, ma'am. I'm afraid I have bad news for you."

She stepped back a pace. "Yes. Yes, of course ..." She gestured vaguely. "I ... I was expecting you. But I've been asleep, you see. And now the fire's gone out, and I ... I don't seem to—"

"She's going to faint, Sergeant Griffin. Catch her, you fool."

But she didn't faint. It was just that she was confused. Events seemed to be repeating themselves. Bent over her needlework she'd already lived through this moment a hundred times, the solemn policemen, their hugeness in her tiny, cold kitchen. She walked calmly away to the window and drew back the curtains. This too had happened before, the clatter of the curtain rings, and the two men shifting their feet in the doorway.

"Come in," she said. "Sit down. Make yourselves comfortable." She fumbled with the strings of her apron. It wasn't right for these strange, important men to see her wearing her apron. "I'm afraid you must excuse me while I go and see to my little girl. Your knocking on the door—I think it's frightened her."

She left them without another glance, taking off her apron as she went and rolling it into a tight ball. Victoria was sitting up in bed, not yet worried, simply curious. Mattie fetched the child's doll from the mantelpiece and gave it to her.

"Tell 'Melia there's no need to fret, will you, dearest? You know how quickly she gets into one of her states." The doll's waxen face looked up at her unblinkingly. "There's two nice gentlemen come to see Mama. Tell her if she's quiet and good she can have a boiled egg for breakfast when they're gone."

Victoria hugged the doll defensively. " 'Melia's always good, if I tell her so."

Mattie straightened her back. "That's my best girl," she murmured, turning away. Across the passage, in the kitchen, the clock on the wall began to strike eight. She put the rolled-up apron down on the bed and paused in front of the wardrobe mirror to pin up stray wisps of hair.

21

She was almost through the door when her daughter called after her. "Have the horrid gentlemen come to see Papa too?" she asked.

Mattie looked back. "They're not horrid gentlemen," she said firmly. "They're nice. Very nice. Sometimes I don't think you listen to a word I say."

She closed the door then and leaned for a moment against the wall, examining its purple roses, gathering the strength necessary to return to the nice gentlemen. Up to the moment of Vickie's question she had been safe, protected by her sense of unreality, by the feeling that everything had happened before. Now, suddenly, the world was real. Even the roses on the wallpaper were real. And she was horribly afraid.

Back in the kitchen the police sergeant was on his knees in front of the grate. He had emptied it of cinders and was busy laying a new fire. He had even found her bundle of kindling sticks where she kept them in the bottom oven. She wondered if his wife also had a bottom oven that was good for nothing except drying sticks.

Inspector Gradbolt had taken off his heavy green tweed ulster and hung it on the back of the door. Now he was seated at the table. Mattie's sewing things were pushed to one side, and the inspector was rolling to and fro a small metallic object that glinted in the growing daylight.

He rose as Mattie came into the room and stood, quite still, looking sombrely down at her. He was not, she thought, at the best of times a cheerful person. His clean-shaven face was long, with hollow cheeks below high cheek-bones, and thin, almost colourless hair recently sleeked down with pungent bay rum. The knuckles of his bony hands were painfully chapped.

He cleared his throat. "Mrs Falconer," he began, "I'm afraid we have serious news for you concerning your husband. He—"

"He's dead." She walked calmly to the table, sat down in her rocking chair. "Albert's dead. I realise that. Otherwise you wouldn't be here ..."

Her voice tailed off. She shrugged her shoulders then, sud-

22

denly, leaned forward and hid her face in her hands. She needed to think. There were plans to be made. And she was so tired.

She felt the inspector's hand upon her shoulder. "Perhaps you have a neighbour, Mrs Falconer," he said gently. "Someone who could come in and . . . and be with you."

Looking up at him, she saw that he cared. In his eyes there was knowledge of all the petty ugliness of the world. But there was compassion also. His work had not embittered him, had not armoured him against the suffering of others.

"Please tell me what happened," she said. "I must know, you see. I won't make a fuss, I promise. But you must tell me."

Down on the floor beside her the police sergeant struck a match and held it to the paper and sticks he had laid in the grate. He was a solid man, broad and dependable, with a heavy black moustache, and he watched the fire as if it were the most important thing in all the world. Mattie felt that she was among friends.

Inspector Gradbolt sat down opposite her. "Your husband's body was found in the early hours of the morning, ma'am. In Goodwin's Court. You may know the place."

She shook her head, stared down at her hands. "How did Albert . . . how did my husband die?"

The inspector produced small oval eyeglasses, breathed on them, and began to polish them on a large, very white handkerchief. "You must have had a long and worrying night, ma'am. For which I'm profoundly sorry. But there was the management of the theatre to be consulted, concerning next of kin. And these matters take time, I fear."

"How did my husband die?"

She saw the inspector's glance flick sideways to his sergeant, then back again. Poor man, she thought, I wouldn't like his job.

"It's the doctor's opinion, ma'am, that Mr Falconer can have suffered very little. Death would have been virtually instantaneous."

"But *how*—?"

23

"Mr Falconer was stabbed, ma'am. Through the heart."

"I see." Suddenly it didn't seem important. Indeed, she wondered why she had thought it so vital that she should know. Albert was dead—*that* was what mattered. "I see," she said again, very softly.

Inspector Gradbolt nodded to his sergeant, who rose from the fire and moved away to the outside door. Already the flames in the grate were crackling loudly. "You're very brave, Mrs Falconer. I admire that. But perhaps if we were to come back later . . ."

"No!" Convulsively she leaned forward, clutched his arm. "The man who killed him—have you caught him? Do you know who he was?"

"Not yet, Mrs Falconer. But we will. We will."

She believed him. His voice was quiet, but coldly determined. Come what may, sooner or later, he would find the murderer. "You must tell me everything you know," she said. "Please."

Her hand was still on his arm. He placed his own gently over it. "There's really very little, ma'am. So far, that is. A gentleman was passing in St Martin's Lane. He chanced to look up Goodwin's Court, saw a boy bending over your husband's body. A boy with red hair. He shouted and the boy ran off. When he reached the place, your husband was dead."

Mattie frowned. "A boy? Then it was a *boy* who killed—"

"That's hardly likely, ma'am. It was a very small boy, according to the eye-witness. Hardly the strength . . ."

Mattie nodded. Albert wasn't a big man, but he was strong. She glanced at the pine dresser against the back wall, remembering how he had carried it down the area steps unaided. He wouldn't have let himself be killed—not by a little street boy.

"We're looking for the boy, mind," the inspector went on. "We know he is a crossing-sweeper. Ten years old or so—mostly spends his nights in a doorway close by where your husband's body was found. Left his broom there, as a matter of fact. We think he probably saw the attack. May even be able to identify the murderer."

24

Ten years old. A crossing-sweeper, only ten years old, spending his nights in a comfortless doorway . . . Mattie thought of her own child, and shuddered. What a sad, terrible world it was.

"Poor little boy—actually to see the murder."

"I shouldn't let it worry you, ma'am. These lads are tough—they have to be or they wouldn't last long on the streets."

He carefully lifted her hand off his arm, and rested it on the table. Then he turned to his sergeant. "Fire's burning nicely now, Griffin. What about a splash of tea?"

Mattie half rose. "Let me—"

"You leave it to Sergeant Griffin, ma'am." For the first time Inspector Gradbolt smiled. Briefly it made his thin grey face seem almost young again. "He has unexpected talents, Sergeant Griffin has."

The sergeant picked up the kettle from the side of the range and went to fill it at the tap out in the area. Mattie watched his quiet competence. Remembering the sticks, she thought perhaps she'd been wrong. Perhaps there wasn't a Mrs Griffin. Perhaps he was used to doing for himself.

She turned back to the inspector. "This Goodwin's Court," she said. "Do not people live there? Are there not houses? I do not wish to teach you your business, Inspector, but might not someone living there have seen something? Or heard something?"

"Certainly there are houses, ma'am. But of the disreputable sort, if you take my meaning."

She did. With another man, the mention of such places would have caused her acute embarrassment. But not with the inspector. He knew so much of life. If he was not embarrassed, then why should she be?

"Naturally we have enquired," he went on. "But such folk are seldom helpful. It's a question of sides, Mrs Falconer—us on one side, them on the other. I suppose you can hardly blame them."

He spoke thoughtfully, sadly, playing again with the small

25

metallic object, rolling it backwards and forwards on the table. Mattie saw now that it was a gold signet ring.

For a moment silence fell in the tiny kitchen. Then the inspector gathered his thoughts. "Your husband would have been carrying his violin, I understand. Was it a particularly valuable instrument?"

She knew then that the violin had been stolen. She sighed. "Not valuable the way some violins are. It was modern—a Becker. Albert worked for the makers once, as their English agent. But it had a very pretty tone. And it was valuable to us. We . . . we don't have very much money, you see."

Instantly she felt ashamed. She hadn't meant to sound sorry for herself. And besides, the inspector must know for himself that they weren't rich, just by looking round her kitchen. Not rich—but not poor either.

Inspector Gradbolt was rummaging in the pockets of his Norfolk jacket. If he had noticed her confusion, he gave no sign. "Which reminds me, ma'am—we found some money in your husband's pocket. Not strictly according to regulations, ma'am, but I brought it along. Sad time like this, I thought you might have some use for it."

He stacked a small pile of coins on the table beside the gold signet ring. "Interesting, wouldn't you say? That the murderer should go off with the violin, I mean, and not bother with these. Are you *sure* it wasn't a valuable instrument?"

She shook her head. "I told you. It was a Becker. They're made in some factory in Bavaria. My father has a music shop in Greenwich—he sells Beckers to students all the time." Which wasn't quite true. If her father sold two of his cheapest violins a month he thought himself lucky.

Beside her on the fire the kettle began to sing. Sergeant Griffin had found the tea caddy on the fringed mantelshelf and had brought across her second best teapot from the dresser. He poured hot water into the pot and swirled it round and round.

"Your husband was a brave man," the inspector told her. "There are signs that he fought for his life, and fought hard."

26

Mattie tried to concentrate. There was so much she didn't understand. Suddenly she'd had enough. She felt utterly weary, and the whole room seemed to be slipping away from her.

"This ring now, Mrs Falconer. It was found on the pavement close by your husband's body. Must have been torn off in the struggle—not to put too fine a point on it, there's traces of blood, you see." He held the ring up. "The question is, ma'am, have you seen it before? Is it your husband's?"

She focused her eyes with difficulty. "There's a little bird on it," she whispered.

"Quite right, ma'am. A golden oriole, so they tell me. But the question is, was this ring your husband's, or did it belong to the murderer?"

She peered at the heavy gold signet ring, and at the bright little bird engraved on it. Then, as understanding dawned, she shrank away in horror. "Albert never had a ring," she said. "Never. Not in all the years I knew him. He never had a ring, I tell you ..."

There was a roaring in her ears. And Inspector Gradbolt's voice, strangely hollow and far, far away. "Now she really *is* going to faint, Sergeant. Lord save us, man, haven't you got that tea ready *yet*?"

2

MATTIE'S RECOLLECTIONS of the next few hours were confused. She remembered weeping, and her shame that she should do so in front of two strange men, and the rough feel of Inspector Gradbolt's green Norfolk jacket against her cheek. Her husband was dead, murdered, and the two policemen were there on account of that. One of them, a sergeant with a heavy black moustache, was trying to give her a cup of tea.

A gap followed. Then Aggie Templeton stroking her hair, and her little daughter Victoria, still in her nightdress, looking up at her. The kindest soul, Aggie was, and Victoria thought the world of her. The policemen seemed to have gone away, and Aggie was making faces at someone over her head, and little hurry-up movements with the hand that wasn't stroking her hair. Mattie turned towards the door in time to see the departing figure of Bashford Scroggs, who was simple, and ran errands for everyone on Bacon Street.

Next Mattie remembered being in bed, with Vickie tucked up beside her, and they were looking at the pictures in *Shock-headed Peter*. They couldn't read the words, for they were all in German. The book was Albert's—a memento of one of his journeys to Bavaria, before he'd met her. She loved his stories about all the places he'd seen . . . the snowy mountains, the houses like cuckoo clocks, the brightly-painted sledges, the horses with plumes, and bells on their harness. And suddenly she was crying again, and Aggie had come and taken the child away, and played with her in the kitchen "till Mama was better".

And then, astonishingly, her own Mama was in the bedroom. But not the mama she was used to, the mama with the handker-

28

chief drenched in lavender water spread across her forehead, reclining in the crowded little parlour above the music shop in Greenwich, the curtains drawn, her voice a querulous whisper. No, this was a new mama, an organising mama in her outdoor clothes, briskly taking off her hat, full of firm good sense.

"Goodness gracious, Matilda, you can't just lie there. There's a deal of important matters to be attended to. You've lost your man, child, but you're not the first and you won't be the last. Life goes on. And you've got little Vickie to consider."

Her mother was rummaging in the wardrobe, taking out clothes. She paused, looked back over her shoulder. "Which reminds me—what have you told your little girl about her poor dear Papa?"

Close to tears again, Mattie shrugged helplessly.

Her mother returned to her curious task. "Heavens child, you must tell her *something*. She's not a baby—she knows something's happened. My advice is to say her papa has had to go away on a long journey. It's true, in a way ..."

She emerged with a final armful of clothes, kicked the wardrobe door shut behind her, and stood staring at Mattie. Suddenly she allowed her voice to soften. "He's not coming back, child. He was a dear, kind man, and you had the joy of him for six good years. That's a deal more than many of us women can say."

She put the clothes down and came forward to sit on the bed. She put an arm round Mattie's shoulders. "The time for grieving will be later, my dear. Good gracious, just now I doubt if you even understand properly what's happened."

She kissed Mattie's forehead lightly, gave her a squeeze, and then was up on her feet again, bustling about the room. Mattie watched her in utter bewilderment. Finally she asked her what she was doing.

"Doing, child? Why, I'm getting you ready. You have a portmanteau, I imagine. No arguments, now. You and Victoria are coming to stay with us, just for a while. Your father's getting your old room cleared out this very minute."

29

It had been, Mattie was afterwards to realise, the very best treatment she could have received. Sympathy would have undermined her completely. Calm good sense, however, and the removal of all personal responsibility for the immediate future, gave her exactly the breathing space she needed. For just a few hours, she could be a child again.

And, moreover, the sort of child, dependent and trusting, she had not been for ten years at least, not since her mother had taken to the chaise longue in the darkened, lavender-smelling upstairs Greenwich parlour. While her father, the irrepressible Towzer Skipkin, stayed downstairs in the shop, squeezing the waists of such female customers under the age of eighty who would permit the liberty, selling concertinas on credit to villainous-looking sailors who were never seen or heard of again, and so muddling the records of his piano-roll lending library (which was their only regular source of income) that the suppliers were continually threatening to take it away from him altogether. One grew up quickly in such a household.

Meekly, obediently Mattie got out of bed and dressed herself. Then she went out into the kitchen where Victoria, wearing her best blue dress and frilled pinafore, was eating one of Mrs Skipkin's strange, delicious meals, consisting of anything that happened that moment to be in the food cupboard—in this case porridge, and kippers, and apples baked in their skins.

Mattie ate the porridge and the kippers. But she left her apple—her mother had forgotten to sugar them, and anyway she wasn't hungry.

She was still sitting at the table, absent-mindedly stroking Vickie's hair—which her mother had somehow found time to put up in curl papers—when Aggie Templeton appeared in the doorway, backed up by Bashford Scroggs and seemingly half the street, to announce that the cab was waiting.

Just at that moment her mother entered the room, carrying the bulging portmanteau and several large brown paper parcels. And at once all was bustle. Coats and mufflers were put on, paper curlers taken out. The cabbie was called to carry up the

30

portmanteau and the parcels. The doll 'Melia was fetched, and thrust into Victoria's anxious arms. The fire was doused in the grate and one last circuit was made to check the fastenings on all the windows. And then, almost before Mattie was aware of it, she had been bundled up the area steps and into the cab. Victoria was plumped in beside her. There was a brief consultation outside on the pavement between her mother and an over-awed Aggie Templeton, during which a discreet amount of money changed hands in return for a watchful eye being kept on the premises. And finally, after giving the most particular instructions to the cabby both as to his destination and as to the precise route he should take in order to get there, Mrs Skipkin climbed into the cab and seated herself with a satisfied sigh.

As the four-wheeler rattled off down Bacon Street, Mattie peeped out through the tiny oval rear window. Quite a crowd of neighbours had gathered to wave. Only yesterday she had been one of their number, secure and quietly content. Now, in her sudden bereavement, she felt a stranger to them all. A faint chill gripped her as she wondered if she would ever return to those dear, damp basement rooms where she had first come as Albert's eighteen-year-old bride, full of joyful expectation, six short years before.

Seated at the plain deal desk in his office up on the second, attic floor of the building that overlooked the quiet, grassy quadrangle of Great Scotland Yard, Inspector Gradbolt was dutifully eating the jellied eels and pickle brought to him by Sergeant Griffin from the stall on Parliament Square. He ate with care, a napkin tucked into his loosened shirt collar. And as he ate he read yet again the police doctor's report on the injuries sustained by the late Albert Falconer.

His sergeant waited, his thumbs tucked smartly into his uniform belt. Other CID sergeants wore plain clothes, but not Inspector Gradbolt's assistant. With the CID still only fourteen years old and regarded by many people as hardly better than government spies, the inspector preferred a uniformed man at his elbow. It was Inspector Gradbolt's contention that the calming influence of a uniform should not be underestimated.

Unobtrusively Sergeant Griffin warmed the backs of his legs at the few niggardly lumps of coal that smouldered in the grate. It was also Inspector Gradbolt's contention that the human brain worked best in a low ambient temperature. Accordingly he rationed out the official coal like a miser, and frequently sat at his desk muffled up in his outdoor clothes.

At long last the inspector laid down the report. He used a crust of bread to mop up the last of the pickle. Then he sighed deeply.

"A wretched business," he murmured. "And what's to become of that poor young woman now, I wonder?"

Sergeant Griffin didn't answer. He had worked with the inspector long enough to know when to speak, and when to hold his peace. But he discreetly moved a few paces forward, away from the fire.

The inspector sighed again. "Widowed," he said. "Cruelly widowed—and to what purpose?"

Still Sergeant Griffin remained silent.

"Robbery, perhaps? The theft of that fiddle?" Inspector Gradbolt looked up at the sergeant over the tops of his eyeglasses. "Talk to me, friend Griffin. Confide your thoughts."

Sergeant Griffin blew out his cheeks. "The fiddle wasn't worth much—not according to the young lady."

"But would the murderer know that? To the uninformed eye one fiddle must surely look very like another. And it certainly seems that the criminal went off with it."

"Unless it was the boy as took it, sir."

"No ..." Inspector Gradbolt hunted for a moment among the papers on the desk in front of him, then resignedly gave up the search. "I recall the man who found the body saying most positively that the boy carried nothing away with him. He ran, according to our informant, almost on hands and knees, just like a monkey."

32

Sergeant Griffin subsided. The eye-witness's phrase was vivid enough to carry conviction.

The inspector sat back thoughtfully. "No, friend Griffin, I think we may assume that the murderer took the fiddle away with him. The question is, was this theft his main purpose in committing the murder, or was it, as it were, simply an after-thought?"

"An afterthought, sir?"

"Put in to confuse, perhaps."

"I wouldn't know about that, Inspector."

His superior shook his head impatiently. "If theft were truly the motive, Sergeant, then why did he leave the sovereigns?"

"What if he was disturbed, sir? Disturbed by the boy—Midge I think he's called."

"Then he'd have killed him too. Just as he'd killed the fiddler. What man who has just committed one murder baulks at a second?"

Sergeant Griffin hesitated. Surely the killing of an innocent child was scarcely the same as ... Then, suddenly, he saw what was really being asked of him. It had happened before, often. Clearly the inspector had in fact already arrived at some final and positive conclusion. What he needed now was not arguments to the contrary, but rather his sergeant's support and encouragement. Which Sergeant Griffin felt it was principally his position to provide.

"You're right, sir, of course," he said. "I see it all now."

"Do you, Sergeant? Do you really?" For some seconds Inspector Gradbolt eyed him shrewdly. The sergeant held his breath, belatedly aware of a certain crudity in his response. But the crisis passed, and his superior lowered his gaze. Casually he fingered the doctor's report. "Stabbed through the heart, this says, friend Griffin." He cleared his throat. "*Stabbed*—the word suggests a dagger, does it not?"

Wisely the sergeant waited to be told exactly what the word in fact suggested.

"But a dagger long enough," the inspector continued, "to

33

penetrate in a horizontal line straight through the poor wretch's body and out at the back. Hm?"

Sergeant Griffin hedged warily. "It *is* possible, sir. Downstairs they picked up an Italian only last week, sir—stiletto on him ten inches at least."

"Certainly ten inches would be sufficient ..." Inspector Gradbolt lifted a foot-rule from his desk and held it experimentally, dagger-like, in his fist. "But it would have needed to be an extremely small Italian, would it not?"

When pressed, the sergeant was capable of thinking quickly. "You mean, sir, on account of the angle?"

"Precisely so. This dagger, if dagger it be, entered the body in a horizontal line, deviating neither to right nor left. Therefore the man using it must have been striking roughly on a level with his head."

Sergeant Griffin stared doubtfully at the foot-rule. He *had* seen daggers held differently, and pushed straight into people. But he wasn't going to say so. "In that case, sir, discounting a child as wouldn't have the strength, either the weapon wasn't no dagger, or we're looking for an Italian midget."

Inspector Gradbolt glared at him. "I'm afraid I don't share your sense of humour, Sergeant. This is a murder enquiry, not a turn at the Palace of Varieties."

"I'm very sorry, sir." The sergeant blushed. Sometimes he couldn't win, no matter what. "What you're saying, sir, is that the weapon wasn't no dagger."

The inspector took off his glasses and massaged the bridge of his nose. He frowned wearily. "I'm in a bad mood, Sergeant —you must forgive me. But I can't help thinking of that poor young woman ..." He turned his head away, looked down at the papers littering his desk. With an effort he regained his former businesslike manner. "Clearly the weapon was no dagger, but rather a sword. And almost certainly a sword usually concealed within a stick. They're common enough these days, I fear, on the streets of the city."

The sergeant watched in careful silence as Inspector Gradbolt removed the napkin from his shirt collar and began folding it into a small neat oblong.

"He's a gentleman, this murderer of ours, if he carries a sword-stick. A man of means, I'd say. And therefore obviously no common robber."

At last the conclusion, final and positive. Sergeant Griffin relaxed. "Very true, sir. So he took the fiddle simply to confuse."

For Inspector Gradbolt, however, the arrival at his conclusion seemed to bring him little comfort. "The net result of which, friend Griffin, is that we are, in short, confused." He put the napkin on the desk, and his eyeglasses squarely on top of it. "What, then, are we left with? No motive, certainly. A murderer who is a gentleman. A missing violin, probably irrelevant. A few muddy footprints too blurred to be of any value. And a possible witness, the boy Midge, now mysteriously gone missing."

"We've got the signet ring, sir, engraved with that bird." Sergeant Griffin tried to sound hopeful. He hated to see the inspector so low. "If we was to find the shop what sold it, then maybe they'd know the gent as they sold it to."

"You're right, of course." Inspector Gradbolt brightened. "A golden oriole—it shouldn't be hard to trace."

"Neither should the boy, sir. Word's gone round all the stations—we'll pull him in, sir—no time at all."

But the inspector wasn't listening. "And I'll tell you another thing, Sergeant. If I was a criminal, and I lost my signet ring at the scene of my crime, I'd get myself another. Waste no time about it. Just in case somebody started asking awkward questions. And *that's* when our man will have to show himself."

He looked up, his jaw hardening. "We'll get to him, Griffin. If I have to call on every jeweller's shop in London myself, we'll get to him. Perhaps not today, perhaps not tomorrow. But I swear we'll get to him."

Sergeant Griffin experienced a moment's unease. Tomorrow? What made the inspector think they'd still be on the case tomorrow? After all, to the Police Commissioners, just how important was the murder of one unknown musician—in a city where crimes of violence were a daily occurrence? The Commissioners not having met the young widow in the case, poor young thing . . .

These too, he knew, were sentiments best kept to himself. Sufficient unto the day was the evil thereof. And anyway, the inspector had already leapt to his feet, filled with his new determination. "There's work for us both, friend Griffin," he announced. "You, my dear fellow, must have another talk with the ladies of Goodwin's Court. Daylight, so I'm told, finds the poor creatures at a certain disadvantage."

He hurried to the door. "For myself, I intend to follow up in the matter of the ring. Both rings. Trace the design on the old and institute enquiries concerning the new . . . Between you and me, though, I'm pinning my best hopes on finding the boy. Lord save us, he can't just *vanish*. Not with every peeler in London on the look-out for him!"

Midge was tired out. And very hungry. He sat on the steps outside St Paul's and nursed his empty, aching stomach. Wretchedly he remembered yesterday afternoon, and the three whole pennies he'd had in his pocket. He'd spent the lot—on hot tea and winkles. The tea he'd needed against the cold March wind. And, as for the winkles, well, he'd reckoned a lad with a broom and a crossing of his own could afford a few luxuries once in a while.

Now, only half a day later, he'd lost his broom. And therefore his crossing also. And his pockets were empty.

Running away from Goodwin's Court the previous night, he'd taken refuge in the fruit and vegetable market at the far end of Floral Street, where there were bright naptha flares burning, and big friendly men with baskets on their heads. He'd stayed there a long time, watching the wagons come in from the country, before he suddenly realised he didn't have his broom any more. The discovery threw him into total panic. He'd left his broom behind him in the Court, and it was a serious thing to lose it. But he daren't go back, not back into his dream, not back in the dark between those echoing, death-filled walls. With the murderer still waiting, like as not, ready to jump out on him.

So he tried not to worry, and told himself he'd go back for it first thing in the morning, soon as it was light. Nobody'd get on to it before then—except maybe one of the girls who worked upstairs, and they were his friends. They'd keep it safe for him.

But when he went back for his broom in the morning, it wasn't there.

And the dead body of the fiddler wasn't there either. Only a faint red smudge on the stones to tell him it hadn't all been just a part of his nightmare.

There was a constable though, out on St Martin's Lane, who saw him and shouted, and blew his whistle, and chased after him. So he had to run away again, and gave up all hope of ever getting his precious broom back.

First he hid in an empty cab shelter. There was a crust lying on the floor under the cabbies' bench. It was rock-hard, and had been nibbled by mice, and normally he'd never have touched it. But now, without his broom, he couldn't afford to be fussy. He chewed it disconsolately, and wondered what to do next.

If things went on like this he'd have to go back to thieving. He didn't like thieving—not since his friend Cruncher Billings had got himself caught, and they'd sent him to the boot-brush factory. He could think of nothing in the world worse than the boot-brush factory.

After a while a cabbie arrived in a shocking temper, and chased Midge out into the street. So he begged a bit on Kingsway, and tried to hold a gentleman's horse, and received nothing but angry words for his pains. There'd been a constable too, on point duty on High Holborn, who had shouted out, then left his post to come after him. But Midge had dodged away across the street, narrowly escaping the wheels of a horse-bus, and scuttled off into Lincoln's Inn Fields. Policemen were no friends of his—he ran from them more or less on principle.

Midday found him on Shoe Lane, hunting in dustbins until an angry man in a leather apron chased him away with a chopper. He wandered on, munching the few old brussels sprouts he'd found. They left him, if anything, hungrier than ever.

When he came to St Paul's he sat down on the broad stone steps. In his experience people were at their most generous coming out of church. But no one came. So he sat and nursed his empty, aching stomach, and decided at last to go in search of Mr Stumpy Miller. You could usually find Mr Stumpy Miller, strapped to his trolley, somewhere around the Strand or the Aldwych. Mr Stumpy Miller kept himself clean, and played the spoons. He had no legs, but he did all right. And Mr Stumpy Miller was Midge's friend.

All the way to Greenwich Mattie's mother kept up a constant flow of chatter, principally for the benefit of little Victoria. The room Vickie'd have at the back, her mama's old room, over Grandpa's workshop . . . the park she could go and play in . . . and the tall sailing ships out on the river, and the lights that shone on them at night, reflected in the water like stars . . .

Sadly Mattie wondered when her mother had last seen either the park or the sailing ships. For many years now she had lacked energy for more than the briefest of excursions, either to church or down for a gossip in Mrs Wassnidge's cluttered little shop on the corner of Ship Road, smelling of cheeses and turpentine. Really, it seemed to Mattie that Albert's death had been just the very thing her mother had needed to shake her out of her querulous torpor.

And Mattie herself, what of her own reaction to her sudden, terrible loss? Albert had been a *good* man, a quiet man . . . dependable . . . affectionate . . . Tears sprang again in her eyes at the thought of the emptiness his going would leave in her life. Yet this was hardly the distraction of grief she might have

38

expected of herself. Indeed, now that she had a chance to collect her wits, she had to admit that at least a part of her sorrow was caused by regret—shame even—that she was not more deeply moved by the death of her husband.

She should have been devastated. They had loved each other, had they not? And he always so kind and gentle ... She reminded herself of how much he had given up for her sake: the footloose days of his bachelorhood, the jaunts to Bavaria, his travels the length and breadth of England, encumbered by no more than his case of violins and his order book. For he had been a man without responsibilities or family ties, the only child of parents who had died when he was barely out of his teens. And, on account of his constant travelling, a man without any real friends. But it was a way of life that had appealed to him, she knew. He'd been good at selling, and in the course of his journeys there were often bands he could help out in, by way of some extra income on the side. But he'd given it all up, and settled down, without a murmur. Six years they'd had, and never a truly cross word between them.

She sighed, staring out at the shabby shop-fronts on Jamaica Road. Perhaps that was half the trouble. Never a cross word, and never a really joyful one either ...

Not that he hadn't courted her eagerly enough. He always said, from the very first moment he came into her father's shop and saw her serving behind the counter, there had been no other woman he wanted, no other woman he could love. And those early days together, those summer afternoons watching the cricket on Blackheath or taking the ferry across to see the big tea ships unload in the India Docks, they'd been joyful enough, hadn't they?

She sighed again. No, it was after their wedding, after their honeymoon really, that the change had come about. Three days they'd had, at Southend: three rainy days trudging up and down the mile-long pier, and three unhappy nights ... Mattie closed her eyes and rested her head against the fusty velvet of the cab lining. She'd never understood why those nights were so unhappy. She'd done everything he'd expected of her. Everything. And in the fullness of time little Vickie had been born, which was what it was all for, wasn't it? And yet . . . She rocked her head sadly to and fro, hearing again the unbearable sound of Albert crying in the darkness beside her.

And afterwards, though he smiled often, and ruffled her hair, and called her his little Muffin, all the joy seemed somehow to have quite slipped away. And now he was dead . . . Mattie turned away from the others in the cab and wept, very softly and gently, not letting her mother or her daughter see. She wept, not for Albert, nor for herself, but for what might have been.

Her father's shop, T. Skipkin and Partners, stood on Copperas Street, just off Creek Road, sandwiched tightly between a rag-and-bone man's yard and a dusty dealer in Naval Necessities. Matilda knew that the 'T' in her father's name stood in fact for Theodore. For some reason lost in history, however, Towzer was the name he was invariably known by. Except in the case of her mother, who referred to him always as Mr Skipkin—in the hope, possibly, that a certain old-world decorum might thereby attach itself to him. Sadly for her, the hope was vain. Towzer Skipkin had been born indecorous, and would remain indecorous until the day he died. In view of which obvious fact, it was all the more remarkable that Mattie's mother should ever have married him.

As for the 'Partners' emblazoned above the murky window of his shop, they were simply an indication of Towzer Skipkin's unquenchable optimism. One day, he maintained, they would undoubtedly materialise, bringing with them that magical commodity called *Capital* . . . which would result, equally magically, in boundless prosperity for all. And for which happy day he thought it reasonable to make every possible preparation.

When the four-wheeler arrived, Towzer Skipkin was waiting, mop and duster in hand, in the shop's open doorway. "Mattie . . . my dearest . . . my poor child . . . welcome!"

He advanced magnificently across the narrow pavement. He

40

was a small man, thin as a wisp. Nevertheless his words, so Mattie feared, could have been heard down river as far as Gravesend. They rose and fell, *molto espressivo*. Not for nothing had Towzer Skipkin once taught singing and elocution in Marylebone.

He wrenched open the carriage door. "Your elegant boudoir awaits you, my pet. No effort has been spared. Your father, I dare claim, has laboured mightily. Dust and dinginess, the accumulated detritus of six long years, all has been banished!"

Mattie alighted, was engulfed at once in a tender embrace. Her mother followed, leading Victoria, a trifle awe-struck, by the hand. "Hot bricks in the beds, I trust, Mr Skipkin?"

"Naturally, Maud my dear. Naturally . . ."

From which over-smooth reply Mattie rightly deduced that the bricks in question had quite escaped his memory.

He hurried on. "And here's Victoria—here's Grandpapa's very bestest little girl. And what do you think Grandpapa has in his pocket? A peppermint, perhaps, for his only bestest?"

He hunted, produced eventually a crumpled paper bag, quite empty. "Dear me, dear me—now, isn't that the strangest thing? But never mind, my bestest. Never mind . . ."

And he lifted Victoria, planting on her cheek a whiskery kiss that Mattie knew from recent experience would well-nigh suffocate the child with pepperminty vapours.

Her mother tapped him on the shoulder. "If you do not mind, Mr Skipkin, we will go on in while you settle with the cabman." She leaned closer. "A little generosity would be suitable. He drove us admirably. And was most obliging in the matter of our baggage."

Mattie rescued Victoria, then reluctantly followed her mother inside, leaving a deflated Towzer Skipkin to hunt again in his shapeless, unpromising pockets. They were scoring off each other still, she observed with a further lowering of her spirits.

Maud Skipkin led the way through the shop. Little had changed since Mattie was last there, certainly not the shabby

41

chaos of the shelves. As they went by, Toby Grimble, who had been twelve when he replaced Mattie behind the counter, bent his head even closer to the pile of score sheets he was pretending to catalogue. He too seemed very much the same, both in his shyness and in the unfortunate fit of his celluloid collar.

Behind the shop there was a musty store room, with a door that gave on to the workshop out at the back, and a crooked, decaying staircase to the living quarters above. On the window-less landing at the top of these stairs Mattie was suddenly stopped dead. She let Vickie go on ahead with her mother. It was as if a trap were closing inexorably about her. This was what her former life had been, this landing, this threadbare oilcloth, this faint pervasive smell of gas, this gloom . . . No wonder then that she had married the first man who asked her. She'd have done anything in the world just to get away, to be able to breathe. And now she was returning.

Her Sunday afternoon visits down the last six years had been different. Then she'd been bringing little Vickie for tea with her grandparents. She'd been a married woman, separate, safe, with a husband and a life of her own. Now she was none of these things. She was back where she started.

Panic possessed her. She fought with it, reminding herself to be grateful for her parents' generosity. They could hardly welcome this disruption in their lives, yet they'd taken her and Vickie in without a moment's hesitation. And she *was* grateful. Truly grateful. A widow now, and penniless, she must learn to trim her expectations accordingly.

She squared her shoulders and went on forward bravely into the small back bedroom, the *elegant boudoir*, her father had prepared for her. It was, in fact, as poor and shabby as it had always been, shabbier even. Six years shabbier. Yet she greeted it with affection and true gratitude.

A battle had been fought and won, first of the many battles over the pain of her bereavement that she must fight and win.

Elsewhere, on a gleaming cliff-top in Bavaria, far from London's gritty, wind-scoured streets, the sun was shining. And on a balcony, sheltered beneath wide eaves, an old woman was sitting in a wheel-chair, swathed in vivid shawls. Before her there stretched a breath-taking prospect: the snow-laden roofs of the town spread out in the valley below, the quaint green dome of the church, and beyond, the darkly flowing river Isar and the towering crags of the Karwendelgebirge.

Yet the old woman, her mittened hands ever restless in her lap, saw none of it. Her eyes were open, yet blank, turned inward. For she was thinking of her son. Soon, his tasks completed, Bruno would be returning to her. Soon. Very soon.

Suddenly it was as if she could hear the chink of his sleigh-bells, his stamping feet in the house below, his voice calling for Günther to stable the horse. In a moment he'd be on the stairs. He'd be by her side, big and strong, kissing her fondly, laughing, describing his journey, warming her with his love and the reckless vigour of his youth. Warming her . . .

Slowly her waking dream faded. The house behind her was silent and she shivered, wondering if she'd ever be warm again. He'd been away so long. Mittens . . . shawls . . . what substitute were they for the living presence of her son?

All at once, unmistakably, she smelt smoke. Not wood-smoke from the handsome tiled stove in the upstairs parlour behind her, safe and familiar. Bitter smoke, sickly and cloying . . . Where had she smelt such smoke before? The carpet? Could it be that the room behind her was burning?

Desperately she tore at the wheels of her chair. But they wouldn't move. She rocked to and fro, choking, beating the air. "Liesl," she cried. "*Liesl—save me.*"

A younger woman, thick-bodied, plain, appeared on the balcony, standing in the doorway at the far end. "Don't be afraid," she said. But she came no closer.

The old woman lurched half out of the chair towards her. "Liesl . . . where is Liesl? The house is afire. I smell smoke. Burning . . ."

"There is no smoke." The woman came forward slowly, dispassionately. "And Liesl is dead."

"Don't say that. Don't ever say that." The old woman covered her face with her hands. "And send for Günther. The house is afire, I tell you . . . Smoke—everywhere smoke."

Her companion settled the old woman back into the wheel-chair, evaded her wildly clawing hands. "There is no smoke." She picked up a shawl that had slipped to the floor. "You've been having one of your dreams."

"The carpet—everything's burning. And screams. Terrible, terrible screams . . ." The fretful cries continued, gradually subsiding. Then the old woman stopped, looked up at her companion. "Trude? Is that you?"

"Who else would it be?" Briefly the younger woman's expression softened. "Who else would it be but faithful Trude?" Then the veil of indifference descended again. "Faithful Trude," she repeated. "Ugly Trude."

The old woman was still confused, and did not hear her properly. Or, if she did hear, chose not to admit it. "Trude? I wasn't dreaming, you know. It had been . . . such a beautiful dream. But not then. Not when I smelt the burning." Her fingers picked restlessly at the blanket round her legs. "That was no dream, I swear it."

"It must have been." Her companion sniffed the sharp air. "All I can smell is the pine trees."

The old woman grunted. Suddenly she held out a crabbed, pleading hand. "If the house had really been afire, Trude, you would have rescued me, wouldn't you? You would have rescued me?"

The companion hated her name. Trude or Gertrude, neither made any difference. It was, she thought, as ugly as herself. So she inflicted a moment's doubt, a moment's insecurity on her employer as she stooped and released the wheel-chair's brake. "You must come inside," she said evasively, "now that the sun has gone down behind the mountains." Then she tilted the chair, and turned it. "Of course I would have rescued you," she told the old woman.

44

She wheeled her away then, into the house, leaving the balcony silent and deserted. While down in the valley the lights of the town came on one by one, as bright as stars in the frosty evening air.

That night, Tuesday, March 4th, 1856, a Grand Masked Ball was taking place in the Italian Opera House in Covent Garden. In general such balls were vulgar affairs and, to begin with, the theatre's owner, Mr Gye, had been reluctant to give his permission. His lessee however, Professor Anderson, claimed to have suffered such losses during the previous six weeks of his tenancy as to make the ball an absolute commercial necessity. And Mr Gye, after a brief, horrified examination of his tenant's accounts, had been forced to agree with him.

The ball was well attended. From eight o'clock onwards Londoners began to arrive in their hundreds: knights in armour, devils and dustmen, pierrots and columbines, Cyrano de Bergeracs in monstrous false noses . . . and also many Robin Hoods, in neat Lincoln green. And among these last, kitted out by chance in identical costumes, two Bavarian gentlemen. They were not together, though both were visitors to the city. Both, also, were without partners, but drawn to the occasion by the relief it represented from the usual dismal round of the London winter. For they were sociable enough people, in their own very different ways.

They met, quite by accident, shortly before nine o'clock, on the pavement outside the theatre, beneath the unsteady gas lamps. One had come in an elegant carriage and happened to alight from it just as the other was approaching on foot. Beneath their cloaks their costumes were identical. In their hats, however, one wore a long green feather, while the other had none.

Not yet wearing their green dominoes, they recognised each other immediately. And clearly with little pleasure.

Bowing stiffly, they addressed each other in German.

"Herr Becker—what a coincidence to meet a fellow-townsman."

45

"A coincidence indeed, Baron Rudolph."

"And so far from home, too."

"Very far, Baron Rudolph."

They cleared their throats and shifted their feet.

"It is a cold evening."

"London is a cold city."

Then, as if by common agreement that enough had been said, they bowed again.

"It was good to see you, Herr Becker. My respects to your mother."

"And mine to your sister, Baron Rudolph." .

"*Aufwieders'n*, Herr Becker."

"*Aufwieders'n*, Baron Rudolph."

They parted then, both evidently feeling the other's company to be unwelcome, and carefully made their separate ways into the theatre, where dancing was already well in progress. And if one or other of them was aware that the orchestra that night lacked its principal fiddler, he wisely made mention of the fact to no one at all. Not even to the partner he quickly acquired from among the professional ladies decorating the foyer.

Behind the two men, however, in the crowd of spectators outside the Opera House, a small barefoot red-headed boy stood rooted to the spot, staring after them with horror imprinted on his thin, pinched features.

Earlier that evening, down on the Strand, where Midge had searched in vain for his friend Stumpy Miller, it had seemed that everyone was gravitating towards Covent Garden. There was, so the word went, a rare sight to be seen: the gentry, dressed up in all manner of outrageous costumes, making fools of themselves. So he went along too, just for the fun, following all the idlers, the laughing soldiers and their girls, the opportunist pickpockets, up Bow Street to the pavement outside the Italian Opera House.

Once there he quickly wormed his way between all the legs, finding himself a place right at the very front, where he could see inside the building, through the big open doors, to the footmen with their powdered wigs and the brilliant chandeliers. He stood there, jostled on all sides, cheering and jeering at each gaudy new arrival, blissfully happy. He wasn't even hungry any more—just as darkness was falling he'd seen a monkey in a bright red jacket escape from its organ grinder master, and helped to recapture the little animal, and been rewarded with sixpence from the organ grinder's hat. Sixpence for a hot pie and peas. And a cup of sweet tea too.

Suddenly, however, with the arrival of two gentlemen dressed as Robin Hood upon the pavement in front of him, he had fallen curiously silent. At first he hadn't been quite certain. He watched them converse, awkwardly shifting their feet. Then, as they parted, and the taller one turned briefly in his direction, he froze, horror-struck. For he knew, without the smallest shadow of doubt, that he was looking upon the fiddler's murderer.

The man bowed slightly, said a few further words, and then walked away into the Opera House. And a moment later the second man followed him.

After that, for Midge all the excitement had gone out of the evening. Soon he crept away, found himself a dark alley sheltered from the wind, and huddled down in a corner of it. Sleep was a long while coming. Each time, just as he was dozing off, the murderer's face would appear before him. The murderer's face as he had first seen it, deathly pale in the light from the street lamp, with shadows like bottomless pits beneath the wide brow, its nose sharply outlined, its sinister mouth smiling, always smiling ... He would jerk back then to full wakefulness, stare fearfully out into the silent street. Was the murderer not waiting there somewhere, lurking in the shadows, waiting for the tiniest movement that would betray him?

At last, his terror conquered by sheer exhaustion, Midge slept. And did not wake again until after five the next morning, when he was rudely disturbed by the harsh jangling of bells, and distant screams, and a sharp, unpleasant smell of burning.

He ventured forth, drawn by the clash of horses' hooves as

47

a fire engine thundered past the end of his alley. Out on the street all was confusion, men shouting, everyone running hither and thither. Only one thing was certain: the Italian Opera House was afire. Nothing could be saved ... And by the time dawn came up, yellow and threatening, all that remained of the theatre was a smouldering, smoke-blackened ruin.

3

THAT MORNING, Wednesday, Mattie Falconer was awake early. Little had changed on Copperas Street since the days before her marriage. The victualling wagons for the Royal Naval College still clattered noisily by at crack of dawn. And the rag-and-bone man in his yard next door still harnessed up his horse, with much slapping and swearing, the moment there was light enough for him to see his way on to the streets . . .

Her daughter was awake too, and out of bed in her night-dress at the window, peeping out between the familiar curtains. How many times, Mattie wondered, had she herself stared down upon that same dismal scene?

Vickie was disconsolate. "Why does that man shout so, Mama? Is he cross? Mama, I don't like this place. When will Papa come back from his long journey and take us away?"

Mattie moved sideways, making a space in the narrow bed. "You'll be cold, my pet. Come in here beside me. Bring 'Melia too, if you wish."

She waited while her daughter fetched the doll, then climbed into the bed, feet icy cold against her. She waited, knowing that no matter how long she might do so, Vickie's questions would still eventually need answers.

"It's really not such a bad place," she said at last. "This was Mama's room when she was a little girl. And Grandmama and Grandpapa are being very kind and nice to let us use it. And I expect the man's cross because he doesn't want to have to go to work." Briskly she rubbed her daughter's feet. "And Papa won't be coming back. Not for a long, long time." She kept her voice level. "Perhaps not ever."

49

It was, she realised, not so much Vickie she was protecting as herself. From the words that needed to be spoken, and their bitter finality.

The little girl was thoughtful a moment, wriggling her toes. "Is Papa dead?" she asked abruptly.

Mattie caught her breath. "Why do you say that?"

"My friend Betty's Gran—they said she'd gone away on a long journey too. But Betty peeped into the room, and saw her Gran lying there, dead as dead. So then they said her Gran was with Jesus. But she wasn't with Jesus. She was lying there in her room, dead as dead."

It had been a long speech, breathlessly delivered. Now Vickie looked up at her mother. "I don't want Papa to be dead," she whispered.

"Neither do I, my pet." Mattie hugged her close, rocking to and fro. "Neither do I . . ."

They cried a little then, the two of them together, that sad grey morning. And clung to each other for comfort, and warmth against the coldness of the world outside. And somehow Mattie's answer had been enough, for Victoria never once asked again about her father. And, although when questioned by strangers she would still tell them that he had gone away on a long, long journey, it was always with the kindly air of someone humouring poor silly people who didn't know any better.

They breakfasted with Mrs Skipkin in the smoky upstairs kitchen. The cooking range—Towzer Skipkin's unwelcome responsibility since his daughter had left to get married—wasn't drawing properly on account of the wind, and Mrs Skipkin's only solution was to flap pointlessly at the fumes with a folded copy of last August's *Illustrated London News*. While her husband remained discreetly absent, busy downstairs in the shop.

The talk, however, went briskly and cheerfully enough, all about finding work for Matilda, and the possibility of a school for Vickie, and of the shopping that must be done that very afternoon . . . and here her mother paused.

"B—l—a—c—k," she spelled out carefully. Then murmured,

50

"Pas devant les enfants, tu sais."

In the face of such heavy-handed discretion Mattie came near to telling her mother crossly that she was wasting her time —Vickie was no fool, and she'd worked out for herself the painful truth about her father. And besides, left to herself, Mattie would have preferred to mourn her husband in her own way, quietly and privately, without the baroque splendour of sombre veiling.

But she controlled herself, for the day had only just begun, and promised to be long. And already Mattie could see her mother's front of calm good sense was wearing thin. For Towzer Skipkin, in the shop downstairs, had begun to bang about and sing his favourite tenor arias. His top notes made the floorboards buzz, and caused Maud Skipkin to wince and ominously hold her head.

Suddenly, beneath them, the shop bell jangled, and there were sounds of loud, excited conversation. A moment later Mattie's father appeared in the kitchen doorway. His face was flushed, his wiry grey hair sticking out like a pan cleaner.

"Such news, my dears," he exclaimed. "A veritable miracle —the Opera House burnt to the ground, and not one single soul injured!"

Mrs Skipkin gasped protestingly, and closed her eyes. "Heavens, Mr Skipkin—it is scarcely eight-thirty. Could we not be spared such immoderate revelations until a more suitable hour?"

"But my treasure ..." He gestured dramatically. "It's the fire of the century. Engines were called from all over the city. And they were quite powerless. The fire had such a hold, you see. It was a leak of gas, they're saying, that caused the conflagration. And—"

"Mr Skipkin—I refuse, I positively refuse to listen to another word." Tried beyond all human endurance, his wife rose theatrically to her feet, a napkin pressed to her brow. "Mattie, I pray you explain to your father. Tell him the sensibilities of the gentler sex are not so lightly to be treated." She proceeded in fits and starts towards the door to the parlour. "Death and destruction . . . destruction and death—and at the breakfast table too!"

"But Mama," Mattie protested, "Papa expressly told us that not one single soul was even injured."

"Not another word. Already my poor head is splitting. Convey my respects to Mr Skipkin. I am sure it was not his purpose knowingly to distress me . . ."

She stumbled from the room, closing the door upon all further argument.

In consternation Mr Skipkin clapped both hands to his mouth. "Oh. Oh, I am ashamed. Mortified. I would cut out my tongue—I swear I would."

Mattie banged the table crossly. "Don't be ridiculous, Papa. You know as well as I do that Mama is . . ."

She tailed off. Mama was . . . well, precisely what was Mama? Difficult? An inadequate word. Intolerable? Clearly an inaccurate word, since Papa had been tolerating her successfully for the last twenty-four years.

Her father regarded her thoughtfully over the tops of his fingers. "Your mama, my dear, is somewhat at the mercy of the moon," he whispered, tiptoeing into the room and seating himself on the very edge of the chair beside her. "I can say this to you, Matilda, now that you are a grown woman and will understand. Allowances must be made, you see."

Mattie didn't answer. As far as she knew, there had never been any variation in her mother's behaviour from one month's end till the next. And one could hardly be in a permanent state of monthly disturbance. . .Still, if it comforted her dear Papa to believe otherwise she wouldn't contradict him. People came to terms with the difficulties of life as best they could.

"And we're none of us perfect," he went on. "In my own way I am a sore trial to her. I know I am."

Which was true enough, Mattie thought. Suddenly remembering her daughter, she glanced across the table, was relieved to see little Victoria untroubled, watching the dramatic proceedings with calm interest.

Mattie patted her father's hand. "Well, now that Mama is no longer present, I'm sure Vickie and I would love to hear whatever else you have to tell us."

"Well ..." Towzer Skipkin eyed them doubtfully. But the exciting news he bore was bubbling inside him and could be contained no longer. "I got it from young Toby, y'see. And *he* got it from a carrier passing down on Creek Road. The man was actually there, it seems. He saw the moment when the flames burst through the roof. All of London was illuminated, as far as the Surrey hills. The firemen pumped, but it was quite hopeless."

Excitedly he lifted his wife's half-finished cup of tea and drained it at a gulp. "People were pouring from the building, their fancy dresses smeared with soot and grime. And they were saved, thank the Heavens, every one. And the proceeds of the night were saved also—carried out in an opera hat, so the rumour goes, by a secretary ..."

By now his whisper was quite forgotten. He grabbed a piece of bread and began to butter it enthusiastically. "All the scenery is gone, of course. And the music—who knows what priceless gems, all utterly consumed ..."

He paused then, suddenly thoughtful. "Remind me, my dear, to look out our stocks of Donizetti. There may be a market for them yet."

Jigging up and down, he stuffed bread-and-butter into his mouth, spoke round it. "By six o'clock it was all over. The roof fell in in a shower of sparks, a positive volcano. And to think, Matilda, that I myself once sang upon those hallowed boards!"

The performance, often alluded to, had been before Mattie was born, in a musical entertainment entitled *The Feast of Neptune*. And, as her mother would have been quick to point out, had she been present, for one night only. And in the back row of the chorus, at that ... All the same, Mattie understood her father's mentioning it. His glimpse of greatness. And now, a special poignancy to the great theatre's sudden, tragic passing.

She thought sadly of Albert. Of the anxiety, had he lived,

53

that would be theirs today, with the theatre gone, and his liveli-hood with it. At least, she thought wryly, Job's comforter, she was spared that.

At that moment a further jangling of the shop bell below re-minded Towzer Skipkin of his duties. He rose from the table, hesitated, glanced shamefacedly at the closed, reproachful door to the parlour.

"A . . . cup of tea for your mother, perhaps? I'd take it myself, you understand, except that . . ." He sidled away in the opposite direction, running anxious buttery fingers through his grey, golliwog hair.

"Of course, Papa." Mattie reached for the kettle and moved it over the flames. "I'll see to it at once."

"Dearest Mattie." His smile was instant, full of childlike innocence and joy. "Dear Mattie—how *nice* it is to have you with us."

He escaped then, clattering cheerfully away down the crooked staircase. Nice it might indeed be, but she wished it was for a happier reason. He was downstairs now, and entering the shop. She heard his voice distinctly. "Why, Miss Fairbairn—aren't you the early one! And what can we do for you today, Miss Fairbairn? A love song perhaps? A sentimental ditty?"

Wearily Mattie glanced about her, caught sight of little Victoria.

"Don't just sit there, child," she said sharply, needing to vent her feelings on *someone*. "Eat up your porridge at once, there's a good girl."

And was immediately ashamed, and hugged her daughter, and took the cold, joyless porridge away without another word.

Maud Skipkin was reclining, in semi-darkness, on the chaise longue in the front parlour. The reek of lavender water almost took Mattie's breath away. Her mother accepted the cup of tea with a languid sigh.

"How thoughtful of you, my dear. What a burden I am . . . But you should not be waiting on me—not with poor dear Albert scarcely—"

54

Briskly Mattie interrupted her. "Nonsense, Mama. Now that I'm here I should certainly make myself useful."

Mrs Skipkin sighed again, and sipped her tea in silence. She seemed restless, however, and finally her curiosity got the better of her. She peered at Mattie obliquely, across the steaming rim of her cup.

"This . . . this fire at the Opera House. Naturally I do not share in your father's morbid preoccupations. But, now that I feel a trifle restored, perhaps you could tell me—was it really so terrible?"

Restored? Restored by what? By having managed to make life difficult for the entire household? Mattie held her breath, counted slowly to ten, released it slowly. A well-worn device, but it always worked.

"Terrible indeed, Mama," she said patiently. And went on to tell her mother all that she knew.

While from the shop below, up through the thin floorboards, there came faint masculine murmurs and sounds of innocent girlish giggling, punctuated by the occasional outraged squeak. Towzer Skipkin had been quite right. In his own way he was indeed a sore trial.

Later in the morning, her mother's curiosity satisfied, Mattie left her and, bundling Victoria up in hat and coat and muffler, took the child for a walk down by the river. She needed to think. Also, she told herself, she would enquire at the haberdasher's on Greenwich High Road whether they had need of a female assistant . . . In the event, however, she did neither. Her mind seemed frozen, incapable of positive thought or action. Instead she bought stale buns for a penny, and stood with her daughter on the river-front, throwing pieces of bun to the seagulls.

When the buns were all finished they wandered on together, leaning into the wind. Left to herself, she felt she could have wandered on that way for ever and ever, through the mean grey streets, among the shabby dock workers and the coarsely shouting sailors. She was a part of none of them. She scarcely saw them. She was a part of nothing.

55

But it began to rain. And Vickie dragged further and further behind, her little face blue with the cold. So Mattie turned, and they made their way slowly back to the shop on Copperas Street.

Toby Grimble was alone in the shop, clearly waiting for them. He darted forward the moment they opened the door. His shyness was forgotten. His eyes were very wide, and his adam's-apple bobbed excitedly above his gaping celluloid collar.

"Mrs Mattie ... Mrs Mattie ..." He flailed his arms disjointedly, showing six inches of bony wrist beyond his coat sleeves. "Mrs Mattie—there's a . . . there's a gennlemn to see you."

"A gentleman?" It was so dark inside the shop that the gas lamps were burning. But there was no sign of any gentleman. Calmly Mattie began taking off her gloves and bonnet. "What sort of gentleman, Toby?"

"Proper toff. C-came in a carriage."

"I see." She unwrapped Vickie's muffler, took off her knitted hat. Certainly it would be the policeman, Inspector Gradbolt. There was nobody else she knew who might run to a carriage. "And where is this gentleman? Where have you put him, Toby?"

The boy gaped at her, appalled. "I ain't put him nowhere, Mrs Mattie. 'Twas your pa. Took him up to the parlour. Straight on up to the parlour."

Which was remarkable indeed, the parlour being in general Mrs Skipkin's undisputed territory. She gave Victoria a slight push, followed her on past the high mahogany counter. "Then I shall just have to go up and see what this gentleman wants, shan't I, Toby?"

Behind her Toby Grimble's face shone as pale as wax in the sickly gas light. "A proper toff, Mrs Mattie," he repeated, awestruck. "Came in a carriage. Told it to be back in half an hour."

As she climbed the stairs she could hear ahead of her Towzer Skipkin in earnest conversation, voice rising and falling in his very best, most impressive manner. She smiled to herself, re-

56

membering nice Inspector Gradbolt and feeling slightly sorry for him.

In the kitchen she took off Victoria's coat, and her own. They lingered for a moment by the fire, warming themselves. Then Mattie straightened her back. Nice as he was, she didn't want to see the inspector. She didn't want to see anybody. But she went forward, nevertheless, and opened the parlour door.

". . . on the other hand," Towzer Skipkin was saying, "if a gentleman such as yourself were seeking a profitable outlet for a modicum of surplus capital, then . . ." Hearing the door, he broke off, turned. Mattie looked past him, saw her mother, somewhat flustered, sitting very stiff and straight upon the chaise longue. And beside her, very much at his ease, not Inspector Gradbolt at all, but a total stranger . . .

A broad-shouldered man, perhaps thirty years of age, and undeniably handsome, with a square jaw, closely-cropped blond hair, generous moustache, and a fresh, agreeable complexion, he rose at her entrance and stood, toying with his silver-mounted walking stick, smiling politely down at her.

Towzer Skipkin flung out his arms in a passionate welcome. "Ah, Matilda . . ." He hastened to her side. "Matilda, my pet, you have a visitor. This is Herr Becker, my treasure, all the way from Bavaria."

He led her forward, Victoria following close behind. "Herr Becker—my daughter Matilda. . .my grand-daughter Victoria."

The stranger bowed stiffly, thrust out his hand. Mattie took it, felt at once the strange, carefully controlled power of the man, and glanced up, involuntarily, into his eyes. They were of the brightest blue she had ever seen, their gaze so intense as to bring her heart up into her mouth, penetrating, acutely interested in all that they saw, and yet at the same time disconcertingly remote.

She stood, for what seemed an eternity, quite without movement, fixed like a butterfly beneath his unrelenting scrutiny.

In point of fact, the man Mattie Falconer had expected her

57

visitor to be was at that moment standing outside a ramshackle tarpaper shack on the Whitechapel Road, his sergeant beside him, patiently listening to the evidence of a cheerful, red-faced woman in frilled cap and greasy apron. Inspector Gradbolt himself was depressed, tired out and exceedingly wet. Already he had been on duty longer than he cared to think about, called from his bed before six that morning to attend the fire at the Italian Opera House. Not even his preciously-guarded CID status protected him from ordinary police work in the face of such disasters. Sergeant Griffin, subdued after a long, embarrassing and unsuccessful session with the ladies of Goodwin's Court the previous afternoon, had been there also, helping to direct the constables controlling the unseemly crowds of sightseers. Much of the building was in imminent danger of collapse, yet the people still pressed forward, morbidly eager for a sight of the still-smouldering ruins.

And then, when at last the inspector and his sergeant had been relieved at shortly after ten, and had returned thankfully to Great Scotland Yard, there had been a message waiting for them. A message so urgent as to take them out again at once, without even a warming cup of tea. And still no word of the boy, Midge. Nor of the missing violin.

So it was that the two tired policemen, smuts and dead embers still clinging to their damp clothes, found themselves less than an hour later on the Whitechapel Road, standing in the rain outside a shabby tarpaper shack bearing the legend: *T. Jackson Eqs. Knife Grinding. Sissors Sharpened. Engraving Undertook.*

They were talking to one Mrs Fodger, seller of pigs' trotters, owner of the stall next door. It was she who, early that morning, had entered the booth of the knife grinder, a hunchback, and had discovered his body, dead, slumped forward across his work bench. Although uneducated, Mrs Fodger was a sensible woman, and well accustomed to dead flesh of one kind or another. And anyway, so she said, finding the man in such a condition did not altogether surprise her: he had been elderly,

58

in failing health, and greatly over-fond of the gin.

She had not screamed, therefore, or carried on. Instead, for decency's sake, she had attempted to straighten him out—as much as he could ever be straightened out, poor crooked creature. And it was then that she had seen the blood—a wound directly above his heart and, upon further investigation, a second, smaller wound in his back, just below the hump. And said to herself that this was police business, without a doubt. So she'd touched the man's hump just one last time, for luck, and then gone in search of a constable.

Up to this point Inspector Gradbolt had learned nothing not already in the constable's report, which he had read back at Great Scotland Yard. Clearly the man was no fool. In the normal run of events Inspector Gradbolt knew only too well that the murder of some alcoholic and hunchbacked knife grinder would have been dealt with more or less on the spot. Sadly the long arm of the law had better things to do than waste its time on such unpropertied persons as T. Jackson *Eqs.* In this case, however, the constable had used his wits, recalling the hunt that was on for a street boy answering to the name of Midge, and in connection with a virtually identical despatching only two nights before. The constable considered, and his sergeant agreed with him, that the coincidence was too great to be ignored. Hence the presence now of Inspector Gradbolt and Sergeant Griffin.

The inspector examined his notes, already wet and getting wetter. At least this second murder had strengthened his position with Police Commissioner Mayne, who had been on the point of taking him off the Falconer case altogether. Two connected murders, even though both of unpropertied persons, could not so easily be swept under the carpet.

Inspector Gradbolt's notes told him it was the local police doctor's opinion that the knife grinder had been dead for several hours, possibly as many as twelve. The inspector turned back to Mrs Fodger.

"I see, ma'am, that you discovered the body at eight this

59

morning. May I ask what it was that took you in to see him at such an early hour?"

"I allus looked in, sir, first thing when I got here. There was mornings, y'see, when poor Mr Jackson needed a bit of help, sir—with his dressing and that."

Inspector Gradbolt had seen the dead man's body: its pathetic ugliness, its ingrained filth. He looked at Mrs Fodger with new respect. "You're saying, ma'am, that there were nights when Mr Jackson stayed here, when he didn't go home?"

"An' it please you, sir, Mr Jackson didn't have no home. That is to say, sir, this was his home." And she jerked a large red thumb at the ramshackle booth.

The inspector followed her thumb's direction, and suppressed a shudder. One hefty shove, and the entire structure would collapse in a heap of rotting timbers. What, dear God, could possibly be the motive for the murder of the poor wretch to whom such a noisome hovel was *home*?

He sighed. "You've been uncommonly helpful, ma'am. I wonder if you could tell us now roughly when you last saw the murdered man alive?"

Mrs Fodger considered. "He was fine, sir, when I went home to the kiddies. And that'd be six of the evening, sir, give or take a bit. He was standing in his doorway, sir, and we passed the time of day. Very civil, Mr Jackson was, when as the gin let him."

"Alive, and sober, at six o'clock." Inspector Gradbolt shielded his papers, and made a note. "Now then, Mrs Fodger, from what you know of his habits, for how much longer after you left him do you imagine Mr Jackson would have stayed open for business?"

Mrs Fodger smiled, possibly at the foolishness of such a question. "Why, sir, for as long as there was business worth a-staying open for." She leaned a little closer. Unpleasantly greasy odours leaned closer also. "Mr Jackson wasn't in a very big line of business, if you takes my meaning. If the work come his way, and he was capable, he saw to it."

The inspector retreated a pace. "So if a customer had arrived last night at seven, or eight, or even nine o'clock, Mr Jackson would have welcomed him in?"

"You have it in a nut-shell, sir. Not that it's all that likely, though. I mean, night like last night, who wants their knives a-grinding?"

"Very true, Mrs Fodger." The inspector glanced sideways at his sergeant, then summoned a pale sort of smile for his witness. "Well, ma'am, thank you. You've been most helpful . . ." Fixing his smile he waited, hopefully, for her to go away.

She stayed. "You wouldn't be of the Hebrew persuasion, would you, sir?" she said.

He raised his eyebrows. "*Hebrew*, ma'am? I think not."

"No more did I, sir." Mrs Fodger paused to blow her nose copiously upon her apron. "But I allus likes to ask, sir—seeing as it's the pork, sir, the trotters as I deals in. And seeing, sir, as you've said yourself how helpful I been." She smiled and gave him a seductive sideways glance. "Very tasty they is, sir. Though I says it as shouldn't."

Inspector Gradbolt took her meaning. And wished he hadn't. Uneasily he peered past her ample bulk, over the tops of his rain-blurred eyeglasses, at the gelatinous trotters laid out on the counter of her stall, yellowish and hairy. His stomach heaved. The district, however, was one where the cooperation of its residents should not lightly go unrewarded.

He averted his gaze. "An excellent idea, Mrs Fodger," he said with as much enthusiasm as he could muster. And added, traitorously, "My sergeant shall do the necessary."

He turned then, and sought relative safety in the interior of the knife grinder's hovel.

The floor of the booth was the cobbled street, on which stood various buckets of milky water, a cluttered work bench, a stool, many empty gin bottles, and, against the back wall, a pile of rags, presumably the knife grinder's bed. A grindstone and several other wheels and drills were all connected to a clumsy wooden treadle. And the whole windowless structure was lit

61

by a storm lantern, cleaned and refilled by the police constable, hanging from the tarpaper roof through which the morning's fine rain insidiously seeped.

Firmly Inspector Gradbolt put from his mind all thoughts of Mrs Fodger and her trotters. He moved to the work bench, and stooped over it. It was a pity, he thought, that the constable, after removing the knife grinder's body, had conscientiously tidied the bench, laying out the tools in neat, unhelpful rows. It would have been nice, he thought, to know exactly what the poor man had been working on at the moment of his death. There might even in that have been some clue as to the murderer's identity. Or at least as to the reason for his visit.

But the inspector wasn't one to complain. Conscientiousness in the man on the beat should be encouraged . . . Hidden behind an oilcan at the back of the bench there was a rusty tea caddy. And in it, clearly unnoticed by the constable and thus lowering Inspector Gradbolt's former high opinion of him, a curious assortment of not unvaluable jewelry. A cameo pendant, a decent enough silver watch, a costume brooch, a gold ring or two . . . all in significant contrast to the surrounding abject poverty.

The inspector was intrigued. So what, then, did this make T. Jackson *Eqs.*? A fence undoubtedly, though indeed in as small a line of business as Mrs Fodger had suggested. And the contents of the caddy left untouched, thus proving that the motive for the killing, as with that of the musician, had surely not been robbery.

Inspector Gradbolt poked sadly in the tin with one bony finger. Petty . . . petty . . . the petty gains of a petty thief, pettily disposed of. A cameo pendant, a decent enough silver watch, a costume brooch, a gold ring or two . . . The inspector grunted, suddenly intent.

Moving along the bench, he came to a small metal vice. Over this he bent even lower, whistling thoughtfully between his teeth. At last, a satisfactory conclusion arrived at, he straightened his back, removed his eyeglasses, and began to dry them carefully on his handkerchief. As he was doing so Sergeant Griffin came into the booth, carrying a greasy newspaper parcel which the inspector affected not to notice.

"You've been a long time," he observed. His own discoveries he had decided to save for a more dramatic moment. He would lead up to them slowly. "What more did the excellent Mrs Fodger have to tell you?"

The sergeant, however, had his own preoccupations. "Sevenpence halfpenny, sir," he said accusingly, placing his parcel firmly on the work bench.

Inspector Gradbolt flapped impatiently. "Money well spent, Sergeant Griffin. And we'll take it out of petty cash."

Mollified, the sergeant removed his high black hat and wiped raindrops off his forehead. "I did ascertain, sir, that the stall next door, on the other side to Mrs Fodger's, is unoccupied. And that, according to her, nobody in the neighbourhood saw nothing untoward the whole evening. Nor heard it, neither."

The inspector shrugged. "She would know if they had," he murmured. "The Mrs Fodgers of this world always do."

He paused, then replaced his eyeglasses and stooped again, lovingly, over the small metal vice. "So now we have two killings, friend Griffin—both using the identical method, both utterly ruthless, and both marked by an apparently identical lack of motive."

He allowed his voice the smallest rising inflection, inviting his sergeant to comment. Sergeant Griffin, however, wisely refused to be drawn.

The inspector leaned forward. "After all," he purred, "what motive could our gentleman with the sword-stick possibly have had for doing to death a wretched, penniless old knife grinder?"

Forced into some kind of reply, the sergeant cleared his throat. "I wouldn't know, Inspector Gradbolt. But I reckon as you're going to tell me."

The inspector tilted his head. "Am I really so transparent?" He considered the point. "Yes . . . yes, evidently I am."

"We been together a long time, sir," his sergeant told him.

Inspector Gradbolt gained the impression that he was being faintly patronised. If so, he told himself, then it was his own fault. "This vice," he said briskly, "has a tiny powdering of gold dust upon it. Which suggests, I believe, the third of the occupations on the dead man's sign board. Engraving, Sergeant Griffin. The engraving of something made of gold."

The sergeant was pleasantly impressed. "A ring, sir," he said excitedly. "Our man's got hisself another ring, like you said. And that's why the old hunchback had to die, sir. Because he'd seen him. Because he might of told on him."

"Exactly so, friend Griffin. A motive, clear as day." The inspector rubbed his hands. "Furthermore, Sergeant, we can arrive at a fair guess as to where this second ring was obtained." He thrust the tea caddy forward, with the air of a magician producing a rabbit from a hat. "Man of parts, our Mr Jackson was."

Sergeant Griffin looked inside, stirred the contents. "Can't say as I'm surprised, sir. There's so many of these little men at it, it's a wonder the big ones can make ends meet."

"My heart bleeds for them. It really does." Inspector Gradbolt offered one of his rare smiles. Then he checked. "But the thing is, Griffin, would our murderer know that?"

"Wouldn't take him long to find out, Inspector. Not if he put his mind to it. A few discreet questions, a greased palm or two . . . And he'd be needing someone a bit out of the way, sir."

A bit out of the way . . . Inspector Gradbolt looked round the dismal shack. His sergeant's words seemed something of an understatement. He sighed. "We've been out-thought, Sergeant. Our man's no fool. We do not advance, I fear. In fact, since we cannot know the design upon this new ring, we may even have taken a small step backwards."

"It won't be no golden oriole, sir, that's for certain."

The inspector acknowledged the truth of this. "Which is not to say, however, that the first ring may not still lead us to our man. Either that or the boy. If only we had more men, Sergeant. If only we had more men . . ." He turned away, thoughtfully touched the top of the vice. Then he lifted his finger and stared at the particles of gold adhering to it. "A motive, then, for the second killing. But still none whatsoever for the first. It worries me, Griffin. It worries me . . ."

But Sergeant Griffin's attention had been attracted elsewhere and he was no longer listening. He had bent down, and now appeared to be groping about on the cobbles. After a moment he rose again, and held out to the inspector what he had found. It was a feather, long and pointed, and bright green.

"Funny sort of thing to find in a place like this," he suggested.

Inspector Gradbolt took it, turned it over in his hand. "A feather . . . clearly dyed . . . the sort of thing a woman might wear in her hat."

"A woman, sir? I'd of thought as the ladies went in for something a bit more fluffy these days, sir. Ostriches and that."

"You're hardly suggesting it was worn by a man, are you?"

"I . . . I suppose not." The sergeant pondered. "Not unless it was on some sort of fancy outfit, sir."

"Fancy outfit, Griffin? On the Whitechapel Road?"

But Sergeant Griffin wasn't one to give up easily. "He could of had it hidden, sir. Under a cloak or some such . . . don't you think?"

Inspector Gradbolt hesitated. He had no wish to discourage his sergeant. But one did have to be realistic. "Exactly what sort of 'fancy outfit' did you have in mind, Griffin?"

The sergeant fingered his moustache. "I . . . wouldn't know, sir. Some kind of uniform, maybe."

Gently the inspector handed the feather back. "It's my experience, friend Griffin, that the simplest explanations are usually the best. After all, this *is* a knife grinder's—women must be in and out all the time. Tell you what—one of them was standing just where you are, caught her hat on the lantern. That's how she came to lose the feather."

Faced with such circumstantial certainties, Sergeant Griffin reluctantly abandoned his trophy. It fell quickly, straight as an arrow, and he kicked it away, under the work bench.

65

"What now, sir?" he said.

"What now?" Inspector Gradbolt straightened his back. He had indulged himself in speculations long enough. Weary as he was, there was work to be done. "We must take to the streets, Sergeant. Our best leads are the first ring and the boy Midge. Shop by shop and alley by alley—it's the only way."

He snatched up the tea caddy and hurried out into the street. Behind him, on the knife grinder's work bench, the parcel of pigs' trotters lay forgotten, to be dragged away by rats a few minutes later. Suddenly the inspector was possessed by a terrible urgency. A vicious, calculating, cold-blooded murderer was at large. And he must be tracked down before circumstances forced him to strike again.

Herr Becker released Mattie's hand, and stepped back a pace. Her first impression of him, she saw, had been correct. He was indeed an impressive, well-built man, the breadth of his power- ful shoulders played down by the trim lapels and conservative cut of his warm loden jacket. Also, save for the eerie remote- ness of his eyes, he was undeniably handsome. Something stirred within her and for a brief, unworthy moment, she forgot her widowhood and thought simply of the shockingly wind- swept sight she must present, fresh from her walk with Vickie down by the river.

Then, remembering and ashamed, she lowered her gaze.

Herr Becker addressed her firmly, his voice big and resonant. "I ask you, Mrs Falconer, not to look on my presence here as an intrusion." He spoke in flawless English, only slightly accented. "I come to offer my sincere condolences. I knew your husband well. He was a good man . . . and a fine musician."

She nodded dumbly. It pained her to be told of her dead husband's qualities, almost as if she didn't herself acknowledge them. A good man indeed—a good husband, and a good father . . .

Suddenly her mother was speaking, patting the seat of the chaise longue. "Bring Victoria, my dear—come and sit here beside me. Herr Becker felt he had to come. He is here in London on business and he read in the newspaper only this morning of poor Albert's ..." She broke off in confusion, eyeing the little girl. ". . . Read of the long journey poor Albert has been forced to go on."

Mattie led her daughter across. They seated themselves. How foolish it was, this game they must play for the sake of her mother's sensibilities. Gently she took Vickie's hand in hers.

"Victoria knows the truth, Mama. Her papa is dead. It is better, I think, that we should all be honest about it." Her voice, usually low and musical, held now an unmistakable note of authority.

Maud Skipkin winced, put two pale fingers to her forehead. "Well, Matilda, I suppose you know best . . ."

It was abundantly clear, however, that she supposed nothing of the sort. Moreover, Mattie realised, she was being forced to come to terms with a daughter who, although recently widowed and therefore supposedly meek and biddable, was nevertheless choosing to ignore her advice.

Mattie was aware of her father, hovering ineffectually in the background. But it was Herr Becker who came to her rescue. "I am sure you need not distress yourself, Mrs Skipkin," he said, calmly seating himself uninvited in the high wing-backed chair by the parlour piano. "Children are often wiser than we think. And often more courageous. It is we adults who are the cowardly ones."

He stared about him, his eyebrows raised, smiling urbanely, as if slightly astonished at his own perspicacity. Mattie dared a smile also, tiny, in mute gratitude.

"Very true. *Very* true . . ." Towzer Skipkin, once given a lead, was seldom slow to follow it. "Haven't I always said, dear Maud, that Victoria is my bestest, bravest girl?"

He darted forward, kissed the unprotesting child with passionate tenderness upon her forehead. Then he turned to Mattie. "Herr Becker comes from Mittenwald, my dear. In Bavaria, you know. The famous violin factory—he is its *proprietor*."

The word, so emphasised, was a warning, so it seemed, for her to be on her best behaviour in the presence of such an important person. "I had guessed it might be so," she said gently. Then, to Herr Becker, "My husband often spoke of you, and in the warmest terms."

"I'm truly glad to hear it, ma'am. It was a sad day for *die Familie Becker* when your husband ceased to work for us. An excellent agent. And, so fine a musician, such an advertisement for our product."

He leaned forward in the chair, his chin on the head of his walking stick, regarding her speculatively for some seconds in silence. Then, his mind evidently made up, he went on. "It is for this reason, Mrs Falconer, and not simply to offer sympathy, that I am here today. My firm owes a great deal to your husband. A debt that I fear we never fully discharged in his lifetime."

Mattie straightened her back. "Indeed, that is not so, Herr Becker. My husband was always most sensible of your generosity."

"A measure of the man, Mrs Falconer. I would have expected nothing less. Nevertheless—"

"No, Herr Becker." He was, she felt sure, sincere. But she had her parents, and she had her own health and strength. His charity she could never accept. Never. "It is fully six years, sir, since Albert left your employ. I cannot believe that any debt still fairly exists between you."

Herr Becker nodded. He sat back, wisely content. The offer had been discreetly made; the offer had been discreetly refused; between decent people there was no more to be said.

Towzer Skipkin, however, thought differently. "You're right, Matilda. Quite right. Perfectly right." His hands were everywhere, straightening his cravat, pulling at the flaps of his pockets, kneading each other until the knuckles cracked. "Absolutely right . . . A debt, no. A gift, certainly not . . . There might, though, be something to be said for a small *investment*, properly secured, of course. *Capital,* my dear. The chance to expand ones—"

68

Quietly Mattie reached up and touched her father's arm. "Papa . . . dearest Papa, if Herr Becker required an interest in a shop I have no doubt that he would open one himself. And almost certainly not in a district so unmusical as Greenwich."

"Eh? What's that?" Suddenly her father's hands were still. "Yes. Yes, of course . . ." He cleared his throat, intently regarded his frayed cuffs. "One does have to admit that the area is somewhat against one . . ." he said sadly.

Mattie gave his arm a tender squeeze. How she wished she could embrace him, comfort him. Seldom had she loved her father more. She turned to Herr Becker, anxiously sought some new, less embarrassing topic.

Again, his tact finely tuned, he saved her. "Speaking of music," he said, daring anyone present to deny it, "I imagine you will all have heard of last night's terrible disaster at the Italian Opera House." He spread his arms dramatically. "It so happens that I myself was present!"

Mrs Skipkin, who had been out of things for much too long, closed her eyes and uttered a faint shriek. "Death and destruction, Herr Becker—I cannot endure to hear of it."

But their Bavarian visitor would not be put down. He leaned forward and touched Mrs Skipkin's foot almost playfully with the tip of his silver-mounted stick. "Destruction certainly, ma'am. But no death, I promise you. I was there, and I can promise you that not a single person was even injured."

Towzer Skipkin saw a chance to rehabilitate himself. "I told them, Herr Becker. A positive miracle, I said."

"Forgive me, Mr Skipkin, but I cannot agree." Herr Becker leaned back in his chair. "No miracle at all, but the excellent work of your magnificent policemen. At once, I must tell you, at the very first sign of the fire they took possession of all the doors, prevented all entrance, and conducted all of us safely out. It was they who saved our lives, Herr Skipkin. I could wish that my own King Ludwig had such a fine body of men. I shall be grateful to them always."

Mrs Skipkin sniffed, torn between patriotic pride and her

inclination to disparage. In the end she saw her way to a bit of both. "A fine body of men they are indeed, Herr Becker. It must be said, however, that nearly two days have elapsed since my son-in-law's death, and they appear to have made no progress at all towards discovering the culprit."

Mattie frowned. "Little pitchers have long ears, Mama," she murmured. For Vickie to know that her father was dead, was one thing. To be told that he had been cruelly murdered was quite another. "And anyway, Mama, we have no idea of their progress. Why, we haven't even seen Inspector Gradbolt since yesterday morning."

But Maud Skipkin was unrepentant. "Which proves, in my opinion, that he has failed utterly. Otherwise we would have been sure to hear."

Herr Becker coughed apologetically. "I believe you do them an injustice, ma'am. These things take time, you understand. Naturally I know no details of this particular investigation. But if, as is so often the case, there were no witnesses, then—"

"But there *was* a witness, Herr Becker. The inspector told my daughter most explicitly. There was a boy. A boy with red hair, hiding in a doorway. Some little crossing-sweeper . . ."

Her visitor took out his watch, studied it calmly. "Then the problem, ma'am, is surely as good as solved. If the good inspector knows what manner of man he is seeking, then he will surely find him." He snapped his watch shut, replaced it in his pocket. "And now, if you will excuse me, I must—"

"But the boy has disappeared, Herr Becker. The wretched police have allowed him to slip through their fingers."

"They'll find him, Mrs Skipkin. A red-headed child should present little difficulty. They'll find him." He spoke with easy assurance, then rose and moved to the window. "Ah, as I thought. My carriage has returned for me . . ."

He turned to Mattie, fixed her with the powerful intensity of his gaze. "Mrs Falconer, it has been an honour to make your acquaintance. Believe me, ma'am, in my own small way I share in your sorrow."

70

"You are very kind." She rose also. "Let me show you out."

Her father fetched Herr Becker's capacious black overcoat, helped him into it, and gave him his hat. Then Mattie led him out. On their way down the stairs he politely enquired the time and the place of her husband's funeral. She faltered, remembering the previous afternoon's dismal caller, his hushed, sepulchral tones as he showed her his black-edged brochure and discreetly outlined the arrangements he had made with the Bow Street police. She hadn't wanted to see him, but her mother had insisted. Which had turned out to be for the best, since at least it had enabled her to spare poor Albert the full panoply of black-plumed horses her mother would otherwise have run to. It was all, anyway, completely unreal, a fantasy devised by others, nothing whatever to do with her . . .

But now, with this stranger's question, it became suddenly no fantasy at all, but a real event, at a real time, in the real world.

"Albert's funeral will be held at ten o'clock tomorrow morning," she said, her words formal, her voice carefully flat and unemotional. "At my mother's local church, Christchurch, on Trafalgar Road."

Down in the shop Herr Becker paused, and she waited while he made a note in his neat, leather-bound pocket diary. The shop was quite deserted, still and silent beneath the dimly sallow gas lamps. The street outside was dim also, lashed with rain, and empty save for the blurred outline of Herr Becker's waiting carriage.

He put his diary away, moved a few paces towards the door, looked out. Then he turned back to her and stood, thoughtfully tapping one trouser leg with his slender, silver-mounted stick.

"One little thing more, Mrs Falconer. Your husband had a violin, I believe. One of ours. A Becker."

She nodded. "He had it with him when . . . when he died."

"Where is it now, please?"

"It was stolen. The police think the murderer took it."

"Ah. So the violin was stolen. I see." Herr Becker hesitated, looking down at her, his stick now motionless.

71

At that moment there was a commotion in the back of the shop and Toby Grimble blundered in, almost invisible behind a tottering pile of music albums. Herr Becker watched him till he had safely reached the counter and laid his perilous burden down, then turned reluctantly away.

"So the violin was stolen. It is no matter."

Mattie hurried after him. "It doesn't really matter, does it? I mean, Albert loved the violin, but it was of no great value, was it?"

He opened the door to the shop, then waited for her. "My dear Mrs Falconer, I do not delude myself. Becker violins are excellent instruments of their kind—but assuredly of no great value."

Solemnly he shook her hand. "*Aufwieders'n*, Mrs Falconer."

Putting on his tall black hat, he walked slowly away across the rain-drenched pavement. His coachman jumped down, opened the carriage door. Herr Becker got in without a backward glance.

Up in the parlour again, Maud Skipkin greeted her daughter with a watchful smile. "Such a charming gentleman," she murmured. Then offered a hasty emendation. "For a foreigner, that is."

Mattie didn't answer. She was remembering Herr Becker's enquiry about Albert's funeral. Did he intend to be present, she wondered. And found herself hoping that he did. The funeral was something she dreaded profoundly. It comforted her, therefore, to think that Herr Becker might attend. He was indeed charming. But, more than that, he was strong. He radiated an impressive inner power. Nothing upset him. Nothing disturbed his magnificent self assurance. He was a man to be leaned upon in one's hour of greatest need.

4

THE FOLLOWING DAY, Thursday, the day of Albert Falconer's funeral, saw the boy Midge in full flight across the city. With the excitement of the fire in Covent Garden, and the pickings to be had at it, Midge had forgotten his quest for his friend Mr Miller until well on into the previous afternoon. A store room next to the Opera House kitchens had been found relatively undamaged, the food within it ruined however, by water from the fire hoses. A distribution to the poor had therefore been organised, and Midge had scrimmaged with the rest, triumphantly emerging with a half-sodden loaf, some moist cheese, three bruised apples, a grimy ham-bone, and six sooty oysters that he had no means of opening and subsequently threw away.

He'd have won more too, if he hadn't sensed a policeman's suspicious eye upon him and scuttled away through the rain before he could be told that he was taking too much. The policeman had even chased after him, and blown his whistle. But the crowds had been thick, and he'd got away easily. Clutching his booty, he'd retired to a safe dry place he knew, under a bandstand in the Savoy Gardens. A couple of tramps had been there before him, but once they'd slapped him about, and made sure he possessed neither money nor spirits, they hadn't bothered him. He'd sat by the wall, gnawing his ham-bone and staring out through a crack at the great blocks of stone arriving on wagons for the building of the new Victoria Embankment. And then, all the food gone and his stomach luxuriously distended, he'd dozed off.

When he awoke, hungry again, it was almost evening and the rain had stopped. So he set off once more in search of Mr Miller.

And found him, this time, after scarcely more than an hour.

He was sidling watchfully along Gracechurch Street when a sharp rhythmic clatter alerted him. He followed his ears, coming quickly to a broad stone archway under which Stumpy had trundled his trolley and was now busily bashing his spoons, the sound loud and clear above the rattle of the passing traffic. Midge joined him, squatting down on the pavement. He always squatted down to talk to Stumpy. Little as he was, Midge was taller than the legless spoon-player. And it couldn't be nice, Midge thought, always to be looking up at people. He got sick of it himself sometimes, and he was only a boy.

Stumpy nodded to him, not breaking his rhythm for an instant. "Mean lot of perishers we got here today, Midge boy," he said.

Midge looked at Stumpy's cap, lying on the pavement in front of him. It contained three pennies and a sixpence. Only ninepence. And ninepence was what Stumpy called his 'float', what he himself always put in his cap, just to encourage passers-by. "Nobody likes ter be the first," he'd say. "That's why it's important not ter put yer cap out empty."

Midge shivered in the wind that blew up from the river. "Like me to bottle for you, Mr Miller?"

Stumpy shook his head. "Not with this lot, boy. Spit in yer eye, like as not."

Midge was disappointed. Bottling meant going round with the cap, joshing the customers. A good bottle man was worth his weight in gold. Got a percentage, a good bottle man did. And Midge knew from past experience that he *was* good.

Snap-rattle-snap went the spoons. Snap-rattle-snap ... "Tell yer what, boy," Stumpy said after a long pause. "Best thing yer could do is make yerself scarce, that's what. Like in the Indian rope trick. Do a crafty scarper. Pfffft."

But Midge had only just found his friend so he sat on, fascinatedly watching the spoons flash and clatter. Up and down Stumpy's body they went, two in each hand, snap-rattle-snap, like castanets. Up against his jaw too, and the side of his head.

74

Making different notes, good as a symphony orchestra. Or so Stumpy Miller would claim. And Midge, never having heard a symphony orchestra, believed him.

It was doubtful, anyway, whether Stumpy Miller had ever heard a symphony orchestra either.

Now he looked sideways at the boy, past his flashing spoons. "Thing is, Midge boy, way I sees it, yer in trouble. I don't arst no questions, mind, but the signs is there. And they says trouble."

Midge screwed up his thin little face. "Trouble, Mr Miller?"

"That's what I said, boy. That's what I said."

Suddenly Stumpy Miller craned forward, looked carefully up and down the busy street. Then, apparently satisfied, he stopped playing, pocketed his spoons, slipped on a grimy pair of worn leather gloves and, pushing sharply upon the wet pavement, propelled the trolley on which he was strapped backwards into the shelter of a couple of old packing cases at the extreme rear of his archway. Midge prudently took up his cap, then joined him.

Stumpy grabbed his arm in a gloved, iron-hard fist. "I'm yer friend, boy. And I don't arst what yer done 'cause it don't matter a row of beans. But when the peelers is out lookin' for yer, boy, then what I says is it's time yer made yerself scarce."

Midge's heart missed a beat. "Lookin' for me, Mr Miller?"

"Took the words right out o' me mouth, boy. Lookin' for yer. Arstin' questions. Comin' round, nice as pie, arstin' questions." Stumpy released Midge's arm and his voice took on a curious sing-song tone, presumably representing the hated constabulary. "Good mornin', Mr Miller. Nice ter see yer, Mr Miller. We're heverso sorry to bother yer, Mr Miller, but you wouldn't of seed the boy Midge by any chance, would yer? Lad wiv the carroty top-knot—yer wouldn't know where 'e was by any chance, would yer?"

Instinctively Midge's hands went up to his hair. "What did you tell them, Mr Miller?"

"The truth, Midge boy. My advice is, always tell the peelers

75

the truth. Larst time I seed 'im, I says, 'e was 'eading out of town. Goin' north, I says. Goin' to see 'is auntie in 'ighgate, I says."

"But I ain't got no auntie up in Highgate, Mr Miller."

"Yer 'as now, boy. She's all writ down in the peeler's little book."

Midge thought about this, wondered if he really did have an auntie, gave up the effort in hopeless bewilderment. "But I ain't done nothink, Mr Miller. Honest I ain't."

Stumpy held up a large warning hand. "I arsts no questions, boy. That way I don't get told no lies." He leaned forward, lowered his voice. "Thing is, boy, the peelers now reckon yer gone north. So if yer takes my advice yer'll 'op it south. Take my meaning?"

Midge sat very still, his mind refusing to work. He licked his lips. "I'm 'ungry," he whispered, near to tears.

"Thought yer was, boy. Thought yer was." A glove came off, and the huge hand rummaged in one pocket of the chopped-off trousers. "One friend ter another, boy. No need 'o thanks. An' push off south, boy, fast as yer like. Better still, jump a ship. Sail off inter the big blue yonder. Them carrots'll be the death o' yer, else."

Numbly Midge took the coins Stumpy Miller thrust at him. Go south, boy . . . jump a ship . . . his friend was thrusting ideas at him also, and his thoughts were too confused to grapple with them.

Outside on the pavement people passed to and fro, smart people, rich people, full of prospects and promises, unaware of the advice being offered among dusty packing cases at the back of the archway. Go south, boy . . . jump a ship . . . Ever since Midge had lost his broom nothing had gone right for him. Now the very foundations of his world were falling away.

Suddenly their already shadowy retreat grew even darker. And at the same time a voice spoke, a man's voice high above him, god-like, using words Midge didn't understand, didn't

76

hear. He looked up, saw two men blocking the wide archway. One was in policeman's uniform. The other, the taller one who had spoken, wore a heavy green tweed ulster.

Now he smiled rustily, and spoke again, penetrating the boy's curtain of terror. "Don't be afraid, Midge. We only want to talk to you. Don't be afraid . . ."

Midge cowered away as the man stooped and held out his hand. And then, in a flash, inexplicably, all was confusion. Stumpy Miller cannoned forward on his trolley, hitting the policeman's knees, bringing him down, and his taller companion with him. For a moment Midge crouched, utterly dazed, watching the three men mill and tumble. Then he saw his chance, and slipped out past them.

"He's getting away, Griffin. For God's sake, man, stop him. He's getting away . . ."

Behind him there were shouts, and angry scuffling. And Stumpy Miller's voice raised clear above the uproar. "Remember what I said, Midge boy. Remember what I said—"

And Midge remembered, and ran south, ran without stopping, ran till he thought he was going to die, ran and ran, down Gracechurch Street and away across the bridge into the mazed and crowded thoroughfares of Bermondsey . . .

And Thursday morning, after an uneasy night spent under some straw in a disused stable in New Cross, found him still running. Go south, boy . . . jump a ship . . . Totally lost, Midge hurried on through the unfamiliar streets. Obedient to Stumpy's words, he was looking for a ship, and that meant finding the river. He had missed the Rotherhythe docks altogether, lying as they did on the great promontary of land where the Thames swung across by Stepney and Limehouse. But he kept on going, spurred forward by a recurring mental picture of the terrible smiling man in the green tweed ulster.

It was nearly ten o'clock when, on the outskirts of Deptford, the first tendrils of mist began to gather in the streets, bringing with them the mournful sound of foghorns on the river. Orientated now, he quickened his pace, and arrived in Greenwich just as the clock on the Royal Naval College was striking the hour.

The cemetery lay at an angle to Trafalgar Road, behind high black railings. Mattie Falconer shivered as she accepted her father's hand and descended from the carriage. The air was icy still, and damp now so that droplets of moisture gathered almost instantly upon her heavy veiling. But, more than that, she shivered at the prospect before her: black cinder paths and sooty gravestones, hemmed in by the identical backs of countless tiny black brick houses, beneath a lowering pall of dense river fog. And this, she thought, was where poor Albert must find his last resting place.

She turned and helped her mother out, and then little Victoria. The child moved very quietly, staring dry-eyed about her, her face white as paper within its rustling frame of black. Mrs Skipkin, however, was weeping, but unobtrusively, and Mattie did not blame her. She would have wept herself, had she been able.

The hearse had stopped ahead of their carriage, and already the coffin, Albert's coffin, was being lifted out. While away to the left, out on the road, leaning against the railings, an old blind beggar was piping mournfully on an ill-tuned penny whistle. Mattie thought of asking her father to pay him to go away, then changed her mind. She recognised the tune, an old Austrian folk-song, a sweet sad sound, touchingly simple. Albert would have appreciated it ... She moved forward, uncertainly, on her father's arm. Her voluminous blacks were unfamiliar, and ill-fitting. One simply did the best one could.

She had asked for the funeral service to be held entirely at the graveside: she hoped it would be over more quickly that way, and she dreaded the chilly emptiness of the church's interior, echoing round their tiny party. She was surprised, therefore, to see the considerable crowd waiting ahead of her, standing quietly by the newly-dug grave. A dozen or more, and all of them come to honour her husband's memory.

Many of them, she realised as she drew nearer, were from the Covent Garden orchestra. Even Mr Costa was there, the conductor, an impressive figure, standing a little apart, the damp air silvering his long, darkly curling hair. She recognised Inspector Gradbolt also, and was touched that he should have taken time off from his arduous duties to be present. He caught her eye, and bowed his head respectfully.

And then a late-comer striding through the gathering fog, removing his high black hat as he came. Herr Becker, a wreath of pale arum lilies held quietly by his side, which he gave discreetly to one of the undertaker's men as soon as he was able. Mattie watched him out of the corner of her eye, and was strangely comforted. Somehow, on the arm of her father, with her mother by her side, and her little daughter also, in the company of so many of her husband's friends, his coming made her feel less alone.

The vicar began to read the service. He was an old man, his beard long and grey, his eyesight poor, his voice thin and quavery, but he read the words clearly, and with great feeling. Mattie listened to them, was aware of their noble magic. Surely the strongest man, hearing them, must have wept. And yet she, a woman, of no strength at all, remained dry-eyed. She felt that she would never weep again.

Man that is born of a woman hath but a short time to live, and is full of misery . . .

Faintly there came the mournful braying of foghorns on the river. And, from behind her, still the husky piping of the beggar's penny whistle.

He cometh up, and is cut down, like a flower; he fleeth as it were a shadow, and never continueth in one stay . . .

The men were making ready to lower the coffin. She reached for her daughter's hand, held it tightly. Victoria was crying now: she could feel the child's noiseless sobbing. And still her own grief was frozen within her. She closed her eyes, listened to the creak of the ropes, and the soft grating of the earth on the sides of the coffin as it descended. Soon it would be for her to scatter the first clammy sods, to bury for all eternity the body of her husband . . .

And then, at last, mercifully, it was over. She turned away, waited while her father spoke a few decent words with the vicar. Towzer Skipkin, subdued for once, doing his duty quietly. While her mother abandoned herself to the moment's emotion, and her daughter shuddered silently . . . Mattie caught herself observing, as from a long way off, and judging. She shook her head. Dear God, she thought, why may I not simply *feel*?

Then Inspector Gradbolt was at her side, his hand on her arm. "You're a brave woman, Mrs Falconer."

She shook her head again, more vehemently. He'd said that once before, and it had been no truer then than it was now. She looked at him through heavy swags of fog-laden veiling.

"Your investigations are going well, I hope?" she said, her voice hard. And wondered why she'd asked, for she didn't care a jot for his investigations. Whatever their outcome, Albert would still be unequivocally dead.

The inspector hunched his shoulders. "The boy, ma'am—yesterday we almost had him, then he got away. I blame myself entirely."

"Got away, Inspector? Why should he wish to do such a thing?"

"These street lads, ma'am, they live as it were outside the law. I fear that they look on the police as their enemy." He stamped his feet on the gritty gravel. "But we'll get him, ma'am. You may depend on that."

From behind her came the cold, metallic clash of shovels. When she spoke again it was principally to cover this joyless sound. "Are there then no new developments in the case?"

Briefly he hesitated. Then, "None for you to trouble yourself with, Mrs Falconer. But we do have certain other useful leads . . ." He glanced over his shoulder. "Forgive me, ma'am—I'm keeping you from your friends. Perhaps I could call upon you. Tomorrow morning, perhaps, when—"

"My time is yours, Inspector." How *old,* she thought. How *old* I sound. It is this place—in such a place, at such a time, to be young would be a violation.

The inspector bowed, solemnly raised his hat. Then he walked quickly away down the black cinder path.

There were others waiting to speak to her, all with a kind word, praise for her dead husband, good wishes . . . She listened, and nodded, and scarcely heard them. She did not wish to seem ungrateful, but—

Her mother tugged at her sleeve. "All these good people," she whispered. "We should have prepared something—some small repast. But how was I to know?"

Mattie patted her hand. "We made no invitations, Mama. They're here for Albert's sake, not ours. Don't worry."

And then, suddenly, the churchyard was deserted, and only the two grave-diggers remained, diligent at the scrape and thud of their labour. And the tall figure of Herr Becker, standing diffidently at a distance.

Mattie turned to face him. He raised his tall black hat. Then he came slowly towards her across the worn, wintry grass.

"Mrs Falconer." He towered over her, gazing intently down. His voice was soft, and magically calm. "It is time, Mrs Falconer. You have been somewhere else, I think." He smiled gently. "I am a stranger, so I can say these things. You have seen your husband buried, and you have been absent. It is understandable. But enough is enough, Mrs Falconer."

And suddenly she knew that he was right. Now, at last, there was no longer any need. And the spring of her desolation was unlocked. The tears flowed, and she could not stop them, did not want to. Her sorrow was for herself, and for all the bereaved of the world, all the lonely, all the frightened. While plaintively, lost in the fog now, the old blind beggar played his pipe, a little children's dance tune, sprightly yet inexpressively sad . . .

The lake was frozen, its milky surface sparkling coldly in the sunlight. And the craggy, snow-streaked mountain above it seemed to tingle in the high, diamantine air.

The old woman, swathed in bright blankets, sat in her wheel-chair on the icy shore, her head tilted up towards the cloudless, dazzling blue of the sky. But her eyes were blind, and her hands moved ceaselessly beneath their covers, and her crooked body twitched in secret torment.

"No!" she cried, her voice no more than a faint scraping of boughs. And again, *"No!"*

Her companion shook the handles of the wheel-chair impatiently. "Frau Becker—wake up, Frau Becker. Wake up. You're dreaming again, Frau Becker. It is not good for you to dream so."

And still the old woman twisted and whimpered.

Behind them a path had been cleared, the snow sliced through and stacked in steep, spade-sized ledges on either side, back down through the woods to the house. And every morning, when the weather was fine, the man Günther would push Frau Becker up the path to the edge of the lake and leave her there with ugly, big-boned Trude. Trude of the low brow and the perceptible moustache. The two of them would stay by the lake for perhaps twenty minutes, Trude stamping her feet and flapping her arms, Frau Becker staring out across the frozen water, motionless, thinking God knows what.

But then, Trude grumbled to herself, what did the old fool ever think?

And then, when the twenty minutes were up, it was Trude's responsibility to get Frau Becker back down the path to the house. And a risky business that was too, for all that there was fresh grit thrown out daily. She'd have insisted on Günther dealing with this return journey also, except that she really preferred not to have him around. The great oaf looked at her in ways she didn't like.

Not lustfully, *Sie versteh'n.* That she could have dealt with. And besides, she didn't delude herself—no man had ever lusted after her, and no man ever would. No, he looked at her as if

82

he thought he knew what she was up to, and was secretly laughing at her . . .

Suddenly Frau Becker's hands fought free of their restraining blankets. One groped upwards, behind her, and caught hold of Trude's arm, while the other pointed tremulously out across the frozen water. The old woman's gaze was lowered now, her head jerking spasmodically.

"She comes, Trude. See, Trude—see how she comes!"

Unwillingly Trude's eyes followed the direction of Frau Becker's pointing finger. She looked, and saw, and it was instantly as if she had been turned to stone. She would have wrenched her gaze away, but could not. Every muscle in her body was rigid with the sheer horror of the moment. For the ice of the lake had parted, silkily, like oil, and through it the head and shoulders of a young woman had emerged. The shoulders, and then the arms, the breasts, the waist, dressed all in clinging black. The hands came through the ice, chalk-white, and were stretched imploringly towards the watchers on the shore. The face too was white, the eyes closed, a half-smile on its lips, the fair hair falling lankly on either side. And still the young woman came blindly on, rising from the lake, her hands outstretched, the ice closing silently, smoothly behind her as she came.

For a moment outside time Trude's heart stopped beating. The face, the smile, the long fair hair, she recognised Liesl's every feature. Liesl who was five years dead. Drowned on a moonlit summer's night, her body discovered at dawn, drifting among the vivid yellow irises at the water's edge. Liesl, whose troubled spirit had no longer been able to endure the pain of living.

And still the figure came towards them, moving now across the steel-smooth surface of the lake, the train of its dress dragging blackly behind it. It neither opened its eyes nor attempted to speak. Simply came blindly forward, its hands held out in silent supplication.

Trude shuddered, drew in a convulsive breath. "Liesl is

83

dead," she whispered. And then again, louder and louder, exerting the full, terrible force of her certainty, till her words echoed and re-echoed between the surrounding crags, "Liesl is dead, I tell you. Liesl is dead."

She wrenched her arm from the old woman's grasp, and stepped forward, round the side of the wheel-chair, making for the frozen edge of the water. "Liesl is dead," she cried.

And the figure on the surface of the lake was no more. The ice stretched milky white and uninterrupted to the farthest shore, sparkling brilliantly in the sunlight. Trude turned then. and saw the old woman, sitting strangely erect in her bright huddle of blankets, her eyes bright, her arms folded triumphantly across her sunken chest.

"You saw her," she said softly. "You saw my beloved Liesl."

Carefully Trude smoothed her dress, her suitable, ugly companion's dress, with the palms of her hands. "I saw nothing. The sun on the lake. The mountains. I saw nothing."

She returned to her place behind the wheel-chair. "It's time we were getting back," she said harshly. "The manager will be up from the factory at eleven. There is business to discuss. And I must make you ready."

Her 'make you ready' was to remind Frau Becker of the distressing intimacies in store. The old woman, in her evil triumph, deserved no better. But for once she was not to be shamed. As Trude began to turn the wheel-chair she twisted round and looked mockingly up at her.

"Dear Trude . . . dearest Trude, you needn't be afraid. My Liesl means us no harm, you know. Not if we keep faith with her."

Trude didn't answer. Savagely she kicked off the wheel-chair's brake and started back down the track. Mad, she thought. The old fool's mad as a hatter. It was a trick of the light, a passing shadow. I saw nothing.

She glanced back scornfully over her shoulder. The lake lay frozen, without movement, a blinding emptiness. And in front of her, at the bottom of the track, stood the house, wide brown balconies beneath overhanging eaves, firewood stacked comfortably against its walls, its warm rooms smelling of resin and hot spiced wine. And jolly Herr Zunderer arriving soon, up from the valley, his sleigh-bells jingling. He was fat, and laughed a lot. These days, with young Herr Bruno away in England, the factory manager's weekly visits were like a breath of fresh air.

The London headquarters of the General Post Office were on Lombard Street, a new and imposing building with a handsome paved courtyard, and stabling for horses behind. A structure suitable in every way to Mr Rowland Hill's great enterprise, the operation of the penny post, still only sixteen years old.

Unfortunately for Inspector Gradbolt and his sergeant, they arrived in Lombard Street at a few minutes before post time that afternoon. The courtyard was thronged, and the foggy streets around echoed to the jangle of letter bells as postmen in their fiery red uniforms hurried in with leather letter bags from all over the city. Bags with slots in their long wooden tops, through which even now people were still thrusting their last-minute mail. While cabs and post chaises, horses in a positive lather, tore into the street just in time to deliver some important despatch.

Clearly the inspector would get no sense out of any Post Office official until the rush was over. He drew Sergeant Griffin to one side, therefore, and they waited in the shelter of a convenient doorway. Across the end of Lombard Street lay Gracechurch Street, where only twenty-four hours earlier he and his sergeant had come so near to laying hands upon the boy Midge. Inspector Gradbolt sighed. His present errand aside, he still believed the boy to be his best hope of a lead. But since yesterday afternoon Midge seemed to have disappeared from the face of the earth. And that confounded spoon-player no help at all, with his talk of an aunt in Highgate when Inspector Gradbolt knew for certain that the boy was an orphan.

Gone northwards Midge had, so Stumpy Miller claimed.

And the inspector therefore wisely concentrating the Force's best efforts in the south. In Bermondsey and even as far across as Rotherhythe. But it was a huge area ...

Inspector Gradbolt coughed dismally. He was depressed. Fog always lowered his spirits—and the dead musician's funeral that morning hadn't helped. He was glad he'd gone, though. To the bereaved these things mattered. And the poor young widow, Mrs Falconer, could do with all the support she could get.

He hunched his shoulders in a gesture peculiarly his own. "Talk to me, Griffin. Confide your thoughts."

Sergeant Griffin blew out his cheeks and slapped his night stick in a reassuringly businesslike manner. "I was thinking, sir, how lucky it was I happened to overhear Constable Higgins, sir. We'd of missed Mr Bastman else, sure as eggs is eggs."

Inspector Gradbolt hid a smile. His sergeant was fishing for praise. Well, he deserved it. "You're my eyes and ears, Sergeant. I don't know what I'd do without you."

That morning, around lunch time, Sergeant Griffin had paid one of his occasional visits to the constables' rest room for a spare cup of tea. He'd been just on his way out again when he'd overheard one young peeler laughing about a disturbance he'd been called to the previous day, at the General Post Office. Some foreign geezer who thought he was being swindled. Nothing for the incident book though—the foreign geezer had pushed off in double quick time when the police arrived ... Nothing for Sergeant Griffin's own private incident book either, and he was more than halfway out through the rest room door when the constable had laughed again. Odd thing was, this foreign geezer had been trying to post a violin, he said. All the way to some place in Germany ...

The sergeant stared modestly at his boots. "Bit of luck, sir. Nothing more," he murmured, discreetly stroking his moustache. "Just back from conducting His Royal Highness, I was, sir. Him and the Princess Royal. Very civil they was, too."

This time Inspector Gradbolt allowed his amusement to show. Prince Albert had been inspecting the ruins of the Italian Opera

86

House, choosing a secure vantage point for Her Majesty, who would arrive at four. "Conducting the Prince Consort were you, friend Griffin? You and who else?"

Sergeant Griffin had the grace to blush. "Well sir, there *was* certain other high-ranking officers present, sir." He hesitated. "But they wasn't as acquainted with the condition of the building as I was, Inspector."

Inspector Gradbolt allowed this as a fair distinction. Who was he to question his sergeant's brief moment of glory? Besides, the street was clearing now, so they could get on with the job that had brought them there. A forlorn hope, almost certainly, though it wouldn't do to say as much to the excellent sergeant. And anyway, they had precious few other clues to go on . . . But as to why this sensitive foreign gentleman—even assuming that he was the murderer—should be so noticeably determined to entrust the violin he had stolen to the vagaries of Her Majesty's postal service, that was another matter altogether.

They found Mr Bastman at the far end of the long counter. The clerk who had dealt with the angry foreign gentleman was a sour-faced, fusty person, with snuff on his jacket and inky-stained fingers. He remembered the foreign gentleman very well.

"One of them gents as is trouble right from the word go, Commissioner. You sees 'em coming, and straight off you gets a nasty feeling in your water." He tweaked resentfully at his grubby sleeve protectors. "I speaks as I finds, Commissioner. Some gents is like that."

"My rank is Inspector, Mr Bastman."

"What's that?"

Inspector Gradbolt raised his voice. He had introduced himself perfectly clearly in the first place. "*Inspector*, Mr Bastman. Not Commissioner—Inspector."

The other glared at him. "That's what I said, innit?"

The inspector let it pass. It occurred to him that the foreign gentleman might not be the only troublesome person in the world. "Could you give us a description of the man, please, Mr Bastman?"

87

"Description?" Mr Bastman screwed up his eyes. "Big . . . That's it, Commissioner. He was big."

Inspector Gradbolt had heard fuller descriptions. "What of his face?" he prompted. "Was it fat or thin? Bushy eyebrows, perhaps? Heavy moustache?"

"Didn't have no face." Mr Bastman was enjoying himself. "Leastways, precious little, what with his muffler, and his hat down over his ears."

In spite of himself, the inspector's interest quickened. "You're saying that the man had concealed his face behind a muffler?"

"Don't know about *concealed*, Commissioner. Bitter wind there was, yesterday arternoon. And rain and that . . . Not that you'd know, o' course, snug in your peelers' palace, feet up on the table in front of a roaring fire."

Sergeant Griffin took a sharp pace forward. "Now just you mind what you say, Mr Bastman. We could just as well have this little talk of ours along at the station, if you'd rather."

Mr Bastman retreated a pace, tittered nervously. "Just my joke, Commissioner. You mustn't mind my little joke . . ."

The two policemen continued to regard him stonily. Mr Bastman licked his lips. "Big feller, the gent was. Well dressed, like, in a long dark coat. Carried a walking stick. Foreign accent—German, I'd say. Tall black hat. And when he took off his gloves, signet ring on his little finger."

Inspector Gradbolt wrote busily in his note book. Walking stick, signet ring—perhaps their visit hadn't been a waste of time after all. Funny thing, though, how observant folk got if you suggested a trip to the station. What, he wondered, did they imagine went on inside? Thumb screws? The Spanish Inquisition?

He looked up from his note book. "I suppose you didn't get the man's name by any chance?" he demanded fiercely.

Mr Bastman chewed his grimy fingernails. "No call to, Commissioner . . ." He swallowed painfully. "I knows the parcel's addressee, though—him what it was addressed to, like. Gent spelled it out for me—thought I couldn't read, I reckon."

He tittered again. Neither policeman joined in his mirth. "I'm waiting for the addressee's name, Mr Bastman," the inspector murmured.

"Going to one of them Barons, it was. House of a Baron von Kronstadt. Baron Rudolph von Kronstadt. Place called Mitten-wald. That's in Bavaria."

The inspector was writing again. "You did say 'the house of', didn't you?"

"That's it. People puts that when the party's not in residence, y'see . . . And I told him—you can't send no parcels, I said, not to Bavaria, I said, not via Her Majesty's Mail."

"And what did he say to that, Mr Bastman?"

"He said as it wasn't no ordinary parcel. A violin it was— as if that made any difference."

Certainly the foreign gentleman had been surprisingly forth-coming. "And what happened then?"

"Well, I got out my tariff book. Tell you what, I said, I can get it on the steam packet as far as Boulogne. Then it'll have to take its chance by Continental Carrier. Cost you a pretty penny too, I said."

"And what did he say to that, eh?"

"Started losing his hair, Commissioner. Money wasn't no object, he said. Flinging sov'reins about, he was. So I weighed the parcel. Wasn't easy, mind, working it out. Ounces in Eng-land, y'see. Grams in France. Then there's them loths, Com-missioner, what the Germans use. Just under half an ounce, they are . . . And all the time him banging the counter, shouting for me to hurry up as he didn't have all day."

"But you weren't to be hurried."

"Well, Commissioner, would you be?" Mr Bastman was regaining his confidence, heartened by the technicalities of his trade. "I got my job to do, same as anybody else . . . So what does he do next, so help me, but lean across and grab me by the coat collar. Shaking me, he was. Shaking me and shouting as I was making him wait on purpose."

"And were you?"

"Well now, Commissioner ..." Mr Bastman massaged his neck, remembering. "A person has his pride now," he admitted, not uncomplacently.

Inspector Gradbolt closed his note book. "And what happened then?"

Mr Bastman dusted himself down, reliving the drama. "By then, y'see, one of the others had sent the boy out for a peeler. A constable, that is. Course, the moment a uniform appears the foreign gent turns sweet as honey. Sov'reins on the counter. Saying as I can keep the change. Hurries off. Couldn't see him for dust, you couldn't."

"I see ... And you have this violin still, I presume?"

"Then you presumes wrong, Commissioner." But his bravado was short-lived, quelled instantly by a small movement from the watchful Sergeant Griffin. Mr Bastman spread his hands. "Wouldn't do, Commissioner, tampering with Her Majesty's Mail and that ... Went off last night, the parcel did. Halfway to France by now, I shouldn't wonder."

There was pride in his voice. And also an unmistakable triumph. Clearly Sergeant Griffin's threat still rankled.

The inspector frowned, discovering just how much he did not like Mr Bastman. "And what became of the change from the foreigner's money?" he asked silkily.

But the other was too quick for him. "We've a box, Commissioner, for the Postmen's Orphans. Perhaps you'd like to see it."

Inspector Gradbolt gritted his teeth. "There are only two Police Commissioners, Mr Bastman, and you can thank your lucky stars I am not one of them. My rank is Inspector, sir. Inspector, plain and simple."

Which did not prevent the box being brought, and a contribution levied ...

It wasn't as if Inspector Gradbolt grudged the Postmen's Orphans their sixpence. But, as he told his sergeant on the way back to Great Scotland Yard, it was the sight of that slimy toad's self-righteousness that really stuck in his gullet.

Back in his office Inspector Gradbolt sat down at the desk and took out his note book. "It seems, friend Griffin, that we're moving in elevated circles. Baron Rudolph von Kronstadt—now who would he be, I wonder?"

"Bavarian Consulate might help, Inspector."

"They might indeed. But then again, they might not ... And anyway, why should anyone want to go to all the trouble and expense of sending him a perfectly ordinary Becker violin?"

Sergeant Griffin was bent over the fireplace, trying to coax life into the inspector's three lumps of coal. Mr Bastman's snide remark about 'a roaring fire' had bitten deep. "He might be sending it to himself, sir. Seeing as he's not at home."

"He might indeed. But then again, he might not."

The sergeant wielded his poker tetchily. It seemed to him that his superior was being unusually difficult. "But at least you *are* assuming, sir, that it's the same violin? The same violin as the murdered man was carrying?"

"Some things we just have to assume, Sergeant." The inspector sighed. "And I must agree with you that the coincidence is strange, to say the least."

Sergeant Griffin straightened his back. It was life, really, that was being difficult. "In which case, sir, we can also assume that the foreign gentleman at the post office is our murderer."

"You must admit it fits. The walking stick, the signet ring ..." Inspector Gradbolt smoothed his forehead with thin, chapped fingers. "Tell me, friend Griffin—tell me how many foreigners you think there are in London at this minute. Big foreigners, in dark coats and tall hats?"

Sergeant Griffin gave the matter due consideration. "Big ones, sir, in dark coats and tall hats? Couple of thousand, maybe. Hardly more."

He caught the inspector's acid eye and turned quickly back to the fire. His breath steamed in the chilly air. Three perfectly good lumps of coal, and he couldn't get even them to burn properly.

That night Mattie Falconer went to bed early. She lay in the dark, listening to the small noises of her sleeping daughter. The fog had lifted at nightfall, and down on the river the foghorns were now silent. Up from the yard next door came faint thudding sounds, as the rag-and-bone man's horse kicked dispiritedly at the door of his stable. While from her mother's kitchen across the landing came a ceaseless murmur of irritable complaint.

Mattie pulled the bedclothes up around her ears. On this day, if on no other, she'd have expected her parents to spare her their endless petty disagreements. Did it really matter, exactly at what moment her father took down the ashes from the kitchen range? Was it really of any significance, how long he spent down in the shop, selling *In a Monastery Garden* to little Miss Fairbairn? And she more than thirty years his junior, and engaged to be married to a handsome naval lieutenant?

Mattie covered her ears. She and Albert—their marriage may not have been ideal, but at least there had been respect between them. It was above all this lack of respect, for themselves and for each other, that she found impossible to forgive her parents. The bitter games they played together, each with its complicated, incomprehensible system for scoring points. They made the whole of their life into a sad jockeying for supremacy. She could not endure to see it. And yet she must. Day after day, week after week, she must endure it.

She opened her eyes, and stared out into the blank darkness of her room. Respect . . . Herr Becker had respect. Respect for himself and respect for others. He had strength too, an unassailable inner power. She shifted uneasily in her narrow bed. Herr Becker had asked if he might call upon her the following day. Her state of mourning made such a proposition totally improper. Yet she had not refused it. He had mentioned a concert of sacred music in the coming week, and she had not refused that either. What her mother would say she could not imagine. And how could she explain? How could she find words for her desperation? How could she tell her mother that Herr Becker represented her only possible release, for the short time he was good enough to spare her, from the stifling atmosphere of the shop on Copperas Street?

And that, surely, was all he represented? Indeed, it was foolish even to ask the question. She was but two days a widow. And he, he was rich, he had a busy, successful life of his own, far away, in a town called Mittenwald. Soon he would return to it. He must. And, until he did so, it was not unreasonable that he should befriend the widow of a favoured former employee. Neither was it unreasonable that she, in her turn, should accept his friendship, his kindly, brief, respectful concern . . .

5

JUMP A SHIP ... Stumpy Miller's advice was proving very difficult to follow. For a day and a night now Midge had been hanging about on the river-front at Greenwich and still this morning he was no nearer to getting on board any of the ships on the river. The real problem was that what few ships there were lay well out in the tideway, moored over towards the Millwall side, and Midge couldn't swim. Indeed, the very thought of all that water made him shudder. At the best of times, Midge and water were scarcely on speaking terms.

Admittedly there was a ferry. But it would have cost two of the fast-diminishing store of pennies Stumpy had given him. And anyway, even young Midge was hardly innocent enough to imagine that someone hoping to stow away on board a ship would do well to arrive openly, by public ferry.

So he had spent the previous day lurking among coils of rope and old tar barrels on the quayside, watching the seagulls, and the mudlarks at low tide scavenging the beach below him, and the random comings and goings of the longshoremen. Many lads would have given up after an hour or two. But many lads didn't have Midge's determination. Neither, it must be said, did many lads have London's entire police force after them.

And now, at long last, it seemed that his tenacity was to be rewarded. From a vantage point among the rusty cogs and levers of a disused steam derrick Midge watched attentively as a boat put out from one of the distant sailing ships and started across the river towards him. The tide was high, and on the turn, matching the river's current, so that the boat came on fast, in a straight line, rowed sturdily by two sailors in ragged breeches and dark, heavy jerseys. An oar apiece, they worked in perfect unison, for all that one was a hairy gorilla of a man while the other would have done good work as a racehorse jockey.

Midge leaned forward, peered secretly over the edge of the quay as they came neatly alongside the steps below him. Jockey shipped his oar, took the boat's mooring rope, ran up the steps with it, and looped it through a massive iron ring, knotting it adroitly. Midge retreated into the shelter of his cogs. Jockey perched on a bollard, impatiently swinging his short legs, waiting till Gorilla had joined him. The two of them talked for a moment, laughing and looking back across the river at their ship. Then they hurried off down the quay and disappeared up a narrow alley. Something about their haste suggested to Midge that they would soon be returning.

He crept out to the quay's edge, looked down into the boat where it lay rocking gently on the garbage-strewn water by the steps. He had already seen the dirty brown tarpaulin that was piled untidily in the stern of the boat, behind the rear seat. Now he sized it up. Surely there was room beneath it for one not very large boy to lie unnoticed? And surely there would be ample opportunity, once the crossing was made and the boat safely moored to its parent sailing ship, for that same boy to leave it equally unobtrusively?

He lifted his eyes, gazed fearfully out across the water at the craft to which he would be entrusting himself. Midge was no connoisseur of ships. But it looked stout enough. And it had four masts, while most of the others he could see had only three. And anyway, he didn't really have any very great choice in the matter. Not with Stumpy's advice still ringing in his ears, egging him on: *Go south, boy . . . jump a ship . . .*

A quick glance to left and right told him that the quay was deserted—save for two dark figures far too small and distant to be of any significance. Another moment, and in one slimy, slithering rush he was down the steps and into the rowing boat. It rocked wildly, one of the oars rolling off a thwart and into

95

the bottom with a noise like cannonfire. Midge looked up, appalled, expecting the edge of the quay above to be peopled instantly with angry, staring faces. But nothing moved. Only the seagulls, ceaselessly screaming high above and fighting among themselves.

Midge stumbled aft, unused to the instability of small boats, falling twice, barking his shins. The tarpaulin was heavy, and smelt of rotten fish. He wriggled beneath it, drew in his feet, moulded himself closely to the improbable ridges and projections of the boat's bottom. He lay very still, trying not to breathe, and waited.

The boat stopped rocking, drifted till with a gentle scrape its bow nudged into the river wall. All was quiet, save for the gulls and the soft rustling of the water. Five minutes passed, seeming to Midge like five hours. Somewhere close at hand the gulls now appeared to be going crazy. The boy lay, crushed by the tarpaulin, nearly suffocating, and listened to their wild, fierce screams. He thought he heard a little girl's shrill laughter too, but knew that couldn't be so.

Suddenly the boat lurched and began to move along the wall, banging as it went. There was the sound of voices above, and the heavy tread of feet on wet stone steps. The boat jerked to a standstill.

"Hold her there, matey." Gorilla's voice, horribly loud and close. "Hold her *steady*, I said. Don' want to drop the rum, now do I?"

Then the boat tipped violently as he came thunderously aboard and stood amidships, balancing, the timbers singing their protest in Midge's ears.

"Right now, matey. Down 'ee come, then."

More footsteps, skittering on the slime. Then a different, thudding sound, and a string of obscenities. Uproarious laughter from Gorilla, so that the very planks of the boat seemed about to start from their rivets. Jockey, it seemed, had slipped and fallen.

Scuffling ensued, as the small man picked himself up. Then, at last, a clatter as the mooring rope was thrown into the boat,

96

followed by the final lurch of Jockey's coming aboard.

Gorilla's laughter subsided. "Enjoy yer trip, did 'ee, matey?"

Jockey swore again. "Very funny, I must say . . . Nearly broke me bleedin' leg, I did."

"Tell 'ee what, ol' matey. Steps be for yer feet, not yer backside. Or didn' 'ee know that?"

"Sod off . . . Well? Shall we go, then? Or was yer reckonin' on standin' there all day, boyo?"

"You'm jealous, that's what. Liddle scrimpy ol' thing . . . Bain't no harm in a man showing off his muscles."

Gorilla chuckled, then turned towards Midge, his feet thumping on the floorboards as he approached. "All right, then. Us'll just get thicky ol' barrel stowed away safely, and then—"

A mighty weight descended, from a great height, on to Midge's huddled body. His bones seemed to crack beneath it, and he cried out. The pain was so acute he couldn't help himself. He cried out, and arched his thin little back against its intolerable burden. The weight shifted, rolled to one side.

"Well, I never . . . there's a rum do. Reckon us got mice on board, matey." Gorilla's voice was horribly close above him. "That's what it be. Mice on board, by the sound on it."

The tarpaulin was flung away and a huge hairy hand descended, lifted Midge by the collar of his jacket. He hung in the air, nearly throttled, his feet dangling.

Gorilla advanced his big, red, stubbly face till Midge could see every dirt-engrained pore. "How about that, then?" he called back over his shoulder. "Not mice at all. No, ol' matey, what us got here be a stowaway."

He turned, holding Midge out at arm's length, shaking him till he thought his head was going to part company with his body.

Jockey sniffed. "Don't go for stowaways. Never did."

Gorilla stopped shaking the boy, looked him up and down judicially. "Not that thicky un be all that much on a stowaway. Not all that much on anything, really. Rags and bones, more like."

97

D

"Give over foolin', boyo." Jockey was shipping his oar. "We ain't got all day."

"What, then? Take un back to the bosun, shall us? Show he what us caught?"

"Please yourself, boyo."

Gorilla extended his other hand, twisted Midge's chin sideways between iron-hard finger and thumb. He smiled in an easygoing, friendly fashion, displaying blackened teeth. "What do 'ee think on that, lad? Bosun has the likes on 'ee for his breakfast—when he can get un. Fries 'em, he do. Fries 'em till they'm crisp and brown. Crunches their bones."

Midge closed his eyes. Anything was possible. He imagined his splintering arm bones and shuddered.

Jockey swore impatiently. "If we fool around much longer, boyo, it'll be *you* the bosun 'as for 'is breakfast."

"Him?" Gorilla danced Midge up and down in the air like a puppet. "Sort him out any day—one arm tied behind me back too . . . Tell 'ee what, though." He tweaked Midge's nose and the boy opened his eyes. "Tell 'ee what, lad—ever flown, have 'ee? Y'know, like a birdie. Ever flown, have 'ee?"

Desperately Midge tried to understand the question. What was it the man wanted him to say? He gaped at him, made helpless, strangled noises.

"Don' 'ee fret yourself, lad. Don' 'ee fret yourself." Gorilla winked at him cheerfully. "A first time for everything, there be. A first time for being borned. A first time for dying . . . And a first time for flying, too."

At which he suddenly swung his arm in a wide arc and sent Midge hurtling out across the water. His gargantuan laughter was the last thing Midge heard before he hit the surface, a limp, terrified bundle, and sank instantly. He was dead. He had to be. This was what being dead felt like: darkness, the bitter cold, the roaring in his ears, the fearful pressure clogging his limbs . . .

Abruptly his head broke clear of the water. He could breathe. He opened his eyes, and could see. Frantically he flailed his arms and legs. The river wall towered above him, dripping dark slime. The sailors were watching him from their boat, a few yards away, impossibly distant. Gorilla's mouth gaped wide and, as the water cleared from his ears, Midge heard laughter again.

He tried to cry out. The words were loud in his head; *"Help me. I can't swim. Help me . . ."* But already his face was sinking again as the water sucked at him, dragging him down. Darkness returned. And the terrible certainty that he would never see or hear or breathe again.

Rising for the second time he felt a sharp pain as something struck across his face. He beat it away, gasped for air, choked on the clinging, oily water. And then, just as he was sinking yet again, his threshing hands encountered something hard. A rope. The end of a length of rope. He clutched at it, felt it support his weight. He hung there, his head above the surface, coughing, vomiting black slime.

A woman's voice came down to him, begging him to hold tight. He needed no telling. The rope was his life. He would never relinquish it. He felt himself being dragged sideways, till all at once his little trailing feet struck stonework. His feet, and then his knees. He fell forward, skinning his elbows on the steps down from the quay above. Scrabbling upwards till his body was half out of the water, he rested, panting, utterly exhausted, his hands still in a tight muscular spasm around the end of the rope.

Hands touched him, lifted him gently, held him in softness. He opened his eyes, saw a young woman's anxious face above folds of silky black material. It was a pale face, with wide, dark eyebrows, dark hair falling from beneath a black-ribboned hat. The woman was sitting on the steps and he was on her knee, his wet body pressed tightly against her.

She lifted her face from his and looked out angrily across the water. "You ought to be ashamed," she cried. "A grown man like you—couldn't you find someone your own size to pick on?"

99

If there was a reply, Midge didn't hear it. Only the sound of oars, fading rapidly. He wiped his chin, and began to shiver.

The woman's grasp tightened. "Gracious me, little boy, we must get you home or you'll catch pneumonia." He felt himself being lifted and carried to the top of the steps. "Do you think you could walk now?"

Walk? When he couldn't remember ever being so safe and comfortable in his whole life before? He shook his head vehemently, and clung to the woman's black cloak like a little frightened monkey.

"This won't do, you know. You're much too big and heavy. I really cannot carry you." Firmly he was set down. "Now then. My name is Mrs Falconer. And this is my daughter, Victoria."

For the first time he became aware of a girl standing close by, clutching a paper bag and staring at him with wide blue eyes. Like her mother, the girl was dressed all in black.

The woman ruffled his slicked down hair, dark with river water. "And what's *your* name, little boy?"

He tried to speak, coughed up more dirty water, tried again. "Midge, missis."

The woman was pulling at the muddy, soaking wet folds of her cloak. "Midge . . . that's a nice name. And where do you live, Midge?"

He lived where he was at any given moment. But something prompted him to a more conventional answer. "A . . . a long way away," he muttered, pointing out vaguely across the river.

The woman stared down at him in some perplexity. Then she made up her mind. "In that case, Midge, we shall take you home with us to get warm and dry. What d'you say to that?"

His teeth were chattering now. "I . . . I'd like that, missis."

"Come along then," the woman said briskly. "It's not far. Victoria—you take his other hand. Goodness gracious, Vickie —he won't eat you."

The girl wore warm knitted gloves. The three of them walked slowly away together along the river-front. The woman seemed to be talking to him, but he didn't really listen. He was eyeing the girl Victoria as she trotted neatly beside him, holding his hand. Girls made him uncomfortable. She was almost as tall as he, but not quite. And her face was very pink. Suddenly she put out her tongue at him.

Responding automatically, he kicked her black-stockinged shin. She danced about, trying to stamp on his bare toes, but he was too quick for her.

"Children, children . . ." the woman murmured and, tightening her grip on his hand, began to walk more quickly. Hostilities were suspended as he and the girl struggled to keep up.

They turned away from the river, along a narrow street between tall grey houses. "We were feeding the seagulls," the woman said, "otherwise we wouldn't have seen you. Wasn't that a lucky thing?"

The girl released his hand, rummaged in her paper bag, then held out a bun. He took it and stuffed most of it into his mouth.

Her mother glanced down. "That was a kind thought, my pet. But we'll find Midge something better than that stale old thing."

They walked on, turning on to a street busy with carriages and high-sided wagons. The girl took his hand again and smiled at him, and he smiled back as best he could round the last of his bun.

"You're very wet," she said.

"So would you be, an' you fell in the river."

"You didn't fall. The big man threw you. We were watching."

Midge felt a moment's shame at the indignity of what she had seen. "I arst him to," he said defensively.

The girl opened her wide blue eyes still wider. "Mama—the boy says he asked that man to throw him in the river."

The woman clicked her tongue. "You mustn't call him 'the boy', dear. His name's Midge." And she hurried on, faster than ever.

At last they entered a side street, and turned into the door of a dark little shop with books and shiny trumpets in the window.

101

Midge had a brief, beatific vision of being bought one of the trumpets. He'd never need a broom again, not if he had a trumpet to play on street corners.

Inside the shop there was a high counter, a mouldy smell, and a skinny young bloke with pimples. Midge was bustled through, the bell on the shop door clanging noisily behind him, into a little room, even darker, stacked with dusty piles of books and boxes. There was an old woman also, with a thin cross face, coming down a steep little staircase in one corner. The younger woman, *his* young woman, stopped abruptly, causing the two children to cannon into her like railway trucks.

The old woman halted a few steps from the bottom and raised an accusing finger. "And what, may I ask, is *this*?" she demanded.

" 'This', dearest Mama, is Midge," the young woman answered bravely. "We rescued him from the river, Victoria and I. He needs dry clothes and a good square meal. I—"

"But the boy is an urchin. A positive *urchin*. You surely are not intending to bring him upstairs, I hope."

The young woman put a protective arm round Midge's shoulders. "He's cold and wet, Mama. And I—"

"I utterly forbid it. Really, Matilda, you must have taken leave of your senses. Have you paused to consider what . . . what *unpleasantnesses* he may not bring with him? I imagine not, since you're evidently permitting poor little Victoria actually to hold his hand."

"Please, Mama—try not to be so tactless."

"Tactless, is it?" Midge cowered into the folds of the young woman's cloak as her mother advanced threateningly down the last remaining steps. "And would it also be tactless, I wonder, for me to remind you whose house this is? I will not, I positively will not allow you to bring that filthy little object upstairs . . . And besides, you have that Gradbolt person waiting for you. I hate to imagine what he would think if—"

"He'd understand completely, Mama. He's kind and gentle."

"Whereas I am not?"

102

There was a long silence in the gloomy little room. Midge peered out from the young woman's cloak, saw her frown and bite her lip. She hesitated. Then, "Is Papa in his workshop?" she asked, her voice tightly controlled.

The older woman folded her arms. "That's right, my girl. You run to your poor, weak-minded father . . ." Suddenly her fierceness faded and she began to weep. "You think me a monster, I know. But the struggles I've had, just to keep my home clean and respectable. Your father's friends, the riff-raff off the streets . . . God knows where we'd all have been if I hadn't scrimped and saved, working my fingers to the . . ."

But the young woman was hustling Midge away across the room and her mother's tearful voice followed them unheeded. A door was opened and Midge was thrust through into a long low workshop, deliciously hot, smelling of varnish and wood shavings. An elderly gentleman in check trousers, stooped by a red-hot coke stove with a steaming kettle in his hand, was staring at them anxiously over the tops of small, steel-rimmed spectacles.

The young woman stood behind Midge, her hand on his shoulder. "I'm sure you heard all that," she said shortly.

The gentleman put down the kettle and scratched his chin. "We must not judge too harshly, my dear. At the mercy of the moon, as I told you . . ."

"Yes. Well . . ." The young woman urged Midge forward. "This is my father, Midge. He'll dry your clothes for you. And there might be cocoa too, if you're very good."

Of what had gone before Midge understood very little. Except that the old woman didn't want him. Which was nothing new—few people wanted him, in his experience. But the hot stove drew him. And the word 'cocoa' was a decided attraction. So he edged forward across the sawdust-littered floor.

Behind him the young woman had returned to the door and opened it. "I'll be upstairs with Mr Gradbolt if you want me," she said, "And we'll talk about this young man's future later."

"Indeed, yes . . . indeed, yes." Her father squatted down, held

103

out his hands. "Well now, young feller, what say we take off that nasty wet jacket? And I might have a ginger nut somewhere around, if you think you'd care for one."

Midge heard the door to the workshop close. Slowly, doubtfully, he began to undo the water-stiff buttons of his man's reefer jacket.

Mattie paused for a moment in the store room, waiting for her heart to slow its wild beating. Mrs Skipkin had returned upstairs. Victoria stood where she had been left, washed to one side in the ugly tumult of the last few minutes. Her mother stooped over her, removed the sad black bonnet, kissed her forehead.

"Grandmama gets a bit upset sometimes," she whispered. "You mustn't let it matter."

Victoria looked down at her gloved, starfish fingers. "Why didn't Grandmama want me to hold the boy's hand?"

"His name is Midge, my pet. And Grandmama didn't want you to hold his hand because . . ." Mattie frowned, hating her mother ". . . because she was afraid he'd make your glove all wet."

Vickie examined the glove. "It *is* a bit wet," she said. "But I don't mind."

"There's a good girl . . ." Mattie's attention was already elsewhere. She was thinking of her mother, and of the weeks, the months, the years ahead in the crowded little rooms above the shop. She wanted none of it—neither for herself nor for her daughter . . . Then, sighing, she remembered wearily that Mr Gradbolt was waiting for her upstairs. *Inspector* Gradbolt, that is . . .

He was standing by the parlour window, a lean, slightly stooping figure, looking out into Copperas Street. He did not at first hear her approach, and she had time to observe him. Not at all her idea of a policeman, she decided. More like a . . . a kindly, middle-aged schoolmaster. It struck her that he would be just the person to advise her as to what might best be done about the poor little boy downstairs.

Closing the door, she moved further into the room, and at the sound he turned to greet her. "Mrs Falconer—good day to you, ma'am."

She shook his outstretched hand. Her mother, possibly now a little ashamed at her outburst, has insisted that she went in to see Inspector Gradbolt alone. Mrs Skipkin would see to little Victoria, play schools with her and the doll 'Melia.

The inspector cleared his throat. "No doubt you'll have seen the papers today, ma'am."

"The papers, Inspector? I think not. Should I have?"

"I regret to say, ma'am, that there has been a second murder. Naturally the papers are making their usual fuss. I would have mentioned it to you yesterday, Mrs Falconer, except that the moment seemed hardly suitable."

"Another murder? How terrible . . ." She paled, his grim news driving all other thoughts from her mind. "Are you saying that they are connected, Inspector?"

"I fear so, ma'am. The . . . ah . . . the method is identical in both cases." He went on to remind her of the signet ring lost by the murderer and to explain his theory concerning the subsequent crime.

She sat down, distractedly fingering the stiff black stuff of her dress. "The man must be a fiend. Utterly ruthless . . . It's hard to believe such people exist."

"Hard indeed, ma'am." His agreement, however, carried little conviction. In his world, she realised, such ruthlessness must be all too common.

He seated himself opposite her and leaned forward earnestly. "There's the matter of your husband's violin also, ma'am. You told me it was of little value. Are you certain of that?"

"Albert's violin?" She stared at him, collected her thoughts. "Perhaps I ought to explain. The instrument was a Becker, and all Beckers these days are produced in the mass. Good instruments, but produced in great quantities. And therefore of no very great value."

Inspector Gradbolt frowned, clearly puzzled. "Forgive me

105

for pressing you, Mrs Falconer, but I had to be sure." He sat back, brought out a small note book, opened it, peered at it long-sightedly. "Would a gentleman named Baron Rudolph von Kronstadt mean anything to you?" he asked abruptly.

"Nothing at all. Except that he sounds like a German."

"Lives in Mittenwald, ma'am. Or so we've reason to believe. And you've never heard of him?"

"Wait a moment . . . Albert often spoke of his days in Mittenwald. He might have mentioned a Baron Rudolph. But I cannot think in what connection."

The inspector drummed bony fingers on the open page of his note book. "These crimes, you see Mrs Falconer, appear to have strong Continental associations. The ring discovered near your husband's body—we have made extensive enquiries, and it seems almost certainly to be of German origin. Certain markings, you understand . . . Nothing for you to trouble your head with, of course. But if anything further should occur to you concerning Baron Rudolph, I rely on you to get in touch with me at once."

"Of course, Inspector." Mattie clenched her hands tightly in her lap. "Then you think he may be the man you're looking for?"

"Early days, ma'am. We don't even know if the Baron is in this country. We have asked at the Bavarian Consulate, but they are unable to help. It has to be said that just now they have other concerns. The political situation in their part of the world is hardly stable . . ."

Inspector Gradbolt sighed, then got heavily to his feet. "Few things make the policeman's task any easier, ma'am. And now, if you will forgive me . . . You weren't thinking of changing your address in the near future, were you? Just in case I might wish to talk to you again?"

Mattie made a small, sad gesture. "I shan't be moving, Inspector. Not for a long time."

She rose, and conducted him from the room. In the kitchen her mother and Victoria were busy with slates and squeaky chalks, while the doll 'Melia looked on, her face as blank and seraphic as ever. Not for 'Melia the anxieties of the schoolroom. Inspector Gradbolt gathered up his ulster, bowed civilly to Mrs Skipkin, and started down the stairs. Mattie followed him. Below them the bell on the shop door clanged noisily as someone entered.

As Mattie entered the shop with Inspector Gradbolt she saw with a small lifting of her spirits that the new arrival, a bunch of hot-house roses in his hand, was Herr Becker. He'd promised to call at ten-thirty. She hadn't realised how late it was.

As the two men passed in the narrow space in front of the counter they eyed each other with frank curiosity. Mattie hurried forward. It struck her that this chance meeting might be helpful to the inspector.

She touched his arm. "Inspector Gradbolt—this is my husband's one-time employer, Herr Becker . . . Herr Becker—this is Inspector Gradbolt, who is in charge of the investigations into my husband's death."

The two men shook hands and murmured formal courtesies. Inexplicably Mattie sensed between them an immediate mutual dislike. They were just like two cross dogs, she thought. And babbled on to cover the awkward moment. "You see, Inspector, Herr Becker comes from Mittenwald. So he may be able to help you with . . ." she had no wish to be indiscreet ". . . with those questions you were asking me upstairs."

Inspector Gradbolt coughed, and cracked his knuckles. "This is hardly the place, I suggest, for—"

"But it would be a privilege, Herr Inspector Gradbolt, to help the fine British police in their investigations." Herr Becker's smile was broad. But his bright blue eyes remained fearsomely hooded.

The inspector looked studiously past him, his eye lighting upon, and dismissing, the avid face of Toby Grimble goggling across the counter. "Two small points, *Mr* Becker," he said coldly. "There has been some question as to the value of the Becker violin belonging to Mrs Falconer's late husband. She informs me that all Becker violins are produced in the mass, and are therefore worth very little." He spoke the words with ill-disguised relish.

Herr Becker was unabashed. "Under normal circumstances, Herr Inspector, that would indeed be so." He paused to sniff in leisurely fashion at the bunch of roses in his hand. "In the case of Mr Falconer's instrument, however, there is a small difference. It was, as I recall, an experimental model. Its design was unique."

"Would that make it valuable, Mr Becker?"

"To most people, no." Herr Becker toyed elegantly with his silver-mounted cane. "To myself, certainly not—the designs are at my factory, closely guarded. We may proceed with them yet, if certain production difficulties are ironed out."

"But to a business rival?" Inspector Gradbolt stuck doggedly to his point. "Would it perhaps be valuable to a business rival?"

Herr Becker shrugged. "Who can say?"

"Valuable enough to warrant murder?"

"Men commit murder for the oddest reasons, Herr Inspector ... But I hardly need tell *you* that."

The inspector allowed a short pause. "Would Baron Rudolph von Kronstadt be a business rival of yours by any chance, Mr Becker?"

For the first time Herr Becker appeared nonplussed. "Baron Rudolph? Oh, I hardly think so ... Certainly his family also makes violins. But Mittenwald has many violin factories. And there's room for all of us. Trade is booming, Herr Inspector. Perhaps not always for the Herr Baron, alas—" He hesitated briefly. "But Kronstadts are fine instruments. Baron Rudolph would have little to learn from a humble Becker. Not even from an experimental Becker."

Inspector Gradbolt grunted. "Would you happen to know if Baron Rudolph is in London at the moment?" he asked.

"It is strange that you should say that." Herr Becker frowned. "I met the Herr Baron only last Tuesday evening, outside the Italian Opera House. We were both going to the fancy dress

108

ball . . ." His brow cleared, and he smiled. "A matter of some-embarrassment, in fact, since the two of us had clearly been to the same theatrical costumier—and he had dressed us both as your famous outlaw, Robin Hood . . . That was on the night of the terrible fire, you understand. I did not see him afterwards, but he must have escaped. No one was hurt, I think. But—"

"Do you know where Baron Rudolph is staying, Mr Becker?"

"I fear not. It has to be admitted that the Herr Baron and I are not on the best of terms. A family matter . . . But surely, my dear Herr Inspector, you are not suggesting that—"

At that moment there was a sudden movement in the doorway to the store room behind them. Mattie turned, saw her father peering curiously in, the little boy Midge at his side. They had been attracted, no doubt, by the sound of voices. The boy's clothes were dry now, and scattered with biscuit crumbs, and there was a brown line of cocoa on his upper lip.

As she loked at his face, however, she saw it abruptly transformed. Its contentment disappeared, was replaced by something she could only identify as utter terror. His eyes opened wide, and all the rosy warmth of Towzer Skipkin's workroom drained from his cheeks.

At her side Inspector Gradbolt had turned also, and so had Herr Becker. And in an instant the child Midge changed from a docile, surfeited little boy into a fiercely milling blur of frantic arms and legs. He rocketed forward, dived between Herr Becker and the inspector, scuttled to the door and began hauling desperately at its handle high above his head.

He swung on it vainly, then gave up the struggle and disappeared round the far end of the counter. While Inspector Gradbolt, showing surprising agility, for some reason lumbered after him. And Toby Grimble, still goggling, had his legs knocked away by the boy and fell noisily from sight, directly in the inspector's path.

Now Herr Becker too joined in the chase. The entire scene reminded Mattie of nothing so much as a couple of grown men who should have known better in pursuit of one very small

109

mouse. And through all the confusion one tiny, incongruous point stuck oddly in her brain: the boy's hair, now that it was dry and sticking out in all directions, was clearly of a brilliant, carroty red.

Suddenly all motion ceased. Inspector Gradbolt, panting heavily, with Herr Becker close behind him, was brought up short against the firm little figure of Towzer Skipkin, standing in the door to the store room, one hand raised and placed sturdily against the door jamb, blocking all egress. And beyond him a scuffling of feet and the clatter of the latch on the door to the back yard.

He met the inspector's angry gaze unflinchingly. "He's had enough for one day, the poor mite. Hungry, nearly drowned, and now this . . . I don't like to see kids hounded, Inspector. Life's hard enough on them, without that."

Inspector Gradbolt raised his fist. For one terrible moment Mattie thought he was going to strike her father to the ground. Then he turned to one side, and beat in silent anguish on the wall beside the door. She could understand his frustration, for she knew who the boy was now. But it was no use going after him. He'd be over the wall and through the rag-and-bone man's yard, and a mile off by now, the way he'd been going when she last saw him.

Would her father have acted differently, she wondered, if he'd known just exactly what he was doing? Perhaps he would have, she thought. But then again, perhaps he would not. He seldom saw things quite like other people, did Towzer Skipkin. And he didn't often dig his toes in. But frightened children were more than he could stomach, no matter what.

Frau Gustavia Becker was in the upstairs parlour of the house Graugipfel, playing her violin. The instrument, perhaps unsurprisingly, had not originated in the Becker factory down in Mittenwald. Until the last few years Frau Becker had been too fine an amateur musician to be content with a fiddle produced in large quantities. And although she was now no longer a

110

fine musician, or indeed a musician of any sort at all—and knew it—she still clung to her old instrument: it was at least a Mittenwald violin, a Matthias Klotz, made by the man, a pupil of the great Italians, who had first brought violin building to the town in 1684.

Frau Becker was playing one of her student pieces, a Bach partita that Trude had heard a hundred times. Indeed, it was as if the old woman knew the piece so well that memory filled out for her the fumbled, toneless scraping almost without her noticing it. In her mind, judging from her contented expression, the notes poured forth in a passionate, exquisite cascade, quite independent of her fingers' cramped inadequacies. While her companion, busy at the table with clothes for the dolls she dressed for market, sorted through snippings of satin and lace and closed her ears as best she could. Soon it would be lunch time. And then, *grüss Gott,* it would be time for the old woman's rest.

When the piece was at long last finished Frau Becker laid down her violin and bow, and sat for a while in silence. Trude ignored her. She never wasted time imagining her employer's thoughts. If they concerned her, she'd be told them soon enough.

And today was no exception. Suddenly Frau Becker rapped on the edge of the table to gain her attention. "Trude, my dear—how long have you been with me?"

Trude took her time answering. Certainly she threaded her needle. Since Frau Becker knew the answer to her own question perfectly well there must be something behind it. Probably something nasty.

"Two years," she said finally. "I came to you after the death of your daughter Liesl." The shock of the girl's suicide had struck her mother down. For six weeks she had lain completely paralysed. Recovery had been slow. Only recently had her son Bruno thought it safe to leave her for one of his formerly regular business visits to Paris and London.

Frau Becker smiled slyly. "Two years. So long ... And to think I never realised, never guessed. Not till yesterday."

111

"Yesterday?" Trude's hand jerked, and a scrap of sprigged muslin fluttered to the floor. "What about yesterday?"

"Come now, Trude." The old woman wagged a chilling finger. "You know as well as I do what you saw yesterday."

Yesterday fat, cheerful Herr Zunterer had come up from Mittenwald on one of his regular business visits. Yesterday she had, as usual, quarrelled over some completely trivial matter with the oaf Günther. And yesterday ... "I saw nothing. The sunlight on the lake. I saw *nothing*."

"So you told me, my dear. So you told me." Frau Becker's tone was gentle, as if humouring an obstinate child. She trundled her wheel-chair over to the stove and warmed her bloodless hands on its vivid tiles. When she spoke again the sly manner had returned. "Tell me, Trude, do you have dreams?"

Trude picked up the muslin snippet. Her heart was beating uncomfortably and she was not quite sure why. "What sort of dreams?"

"Everybody has dreams, my dear. Tell me about yours. The dreams you have when you are sound asleep."

"If you don't mind, Frau Becker, I'd rather not." She forced her trembling fingers to crimp the muslin into a tiny over-skirt. A local woodcarver sent her the dolls and she dressed them for a shop in Mittenwald. They sold to visitors, and at Christmas. They sold well, making her feel independent. *Gott im Himmel*, she needed to feel independent of that evil old creature crouched by the stove.

"If you do not wish to tell me your dreams, Trude, can it be they are improper? I won't be shocked, you know." Gustavia Becker paused. "I was a woman myself, once," she added bitterly.

For all that she knew the old woman was baiting her, Trude blushed. "Not in the least improper," she said. Then, feeling a strange need to explain further, "Simply ... dark. Very dark."

The word was pitifully inadequate for the shapeless, nameless horror that sometimes gripped her in the still hours of the night. Frau Becker, however, seemed to understand completely.

112

"The darkness is of your own making, my dear. It is your fear. You hide behind your fear. It cuts you off from your pictures."

Trude stumbled to her feet, spilling pins. "My *pictures*? In God's name, what are you talking about?" she cried.

With surprising kindness Frau Becker held out her hands. "Come here, poor Trude. Come to me ... Two years in this house—two years of those dark dreams—you should have told me ... You really should have told me."

"Dreams are dreams." Trude stayed where she was. "I told nobody ..."

She was shaking all over. It had begun with the simplest of questions—*how long have you been with me?* And now this. Even there, wide awake, in the warm bright room, she felt the darkness hovering.

Frau Becker beckoned with her crabbed, claw-like hands. "Come to me, Trude. Your fear is foolishness. I can take it away."

Trude felt herself drawn. Mechanically, like one of her own dolls, she shuffled forward across the bare polished boards. Her hands reached out, touched the old woman's, were received into an iron grip.

"You see pictures in your dreams, Trude. Pictures you do not understand. So you hide behind your fear. But there is no need." Frau Becker's voice was no more than a whisper, yet it filled Trude's head. "Your pictures are a form of power, my dear. You can use them. You can use them as I do. I *know* you can."

Trude closed her eyes. A word was growing in her mind. A word, a picture. Knowledge. She tried to close her thoughts, but the knowledge wouldn't go away.

She frowned deeply, her jaw quivering. "*Bruno ...*" Somehow the voice was not her own. And the words she must speak, they too were not hers. "*Bruno,*" she repeated, shaking her head from side to side. "*Bruno ... is ... is going to ... Bruno is going ... to ...*"

Suddenly her soul rebelled, the unextinguished spark of con-

113

sciousness that was still she. With a supreme effort she wrenched her hands away, out of Frau Becker's grip. Instantly her mind cleared, and it came to her with blinding clarity—the last time Frau Becker had held her so. Yesterday, standing by the lake, when she had seen ... She backed away, blundering into the corner of the table. She had seen nothing. A trick of the light. Nothing.

She burst into tears. She, tough Trude, ugly Trude, who never wept.

Composedly Gustavia Becker adjusted the rug around her useless legs. "It doesn't matter, child. There is no hurry. Already we have accomplished much. There will be other times." She dragged at the wheels of her chair, spun it across the floor to the table. She picked up one of the finished dolls. "Gracious me, Trude, what fine stitches you make, my dear. And with such big hands. I really do compliment you."

She looked up, a strange, unknowable smile on her withered lips. "You were going to tell me," she said calmly, "that my son Bruno is contemplating marriage. You were going to say that he must be prevented. And I must admit that for once I quite agree with you, my dear. Liesl would never forgive him." She paused. "Or us, if we stood by and let it happen."

Trude sank down on a chair, hid her face in her hands. She'd been going to tell Frau Becker nothing. Bruno? Bruno was in England. What did she know of Bruno? The old woman was mad. Dangerous. *Wicked* ... She should be shunned, abhorred. Her money, the inheritance Trude had planned for, counted on, it was worthless in the face of such evil. And yet, appalled to the depths of her being, Trude felt there nevertheless to be a bond between them now, an unwilling alliance that only death would break.

6

MATTIE FALCONER WAS in urgent need of a job, some sort of employment. Anything ... In the first place, she wanted to contribute towards domestic expenses. Although her father had said not a word, she was painfully aware that the sudden arrival of herself and her daughter strained the shop's meagre earnings well past breaking point. And in the second place, she was desperate to get away from the household for at least some part of every day. Her mother's fractiousness, her ceaseless complaining, bore heavily upon her spirit. And the more so because often—certainly in the matter of Herr Becker's attentions—her mother's comments were wholly justified.

Red roses, indeed. Not to mention the walk together in Greenwich Park. Thoroughly unsuitable ... It mattered not at all that Herr Becker himself had insisted that they take little Victoria with them. Neither did it matter that Herr Becker was clearly a most honest and upright gentleman. Such attentions towards a widow of such very short standing were disgraceful. Heaven only knew what Mrs Skipkin's friends and neighbours would think.

All of which, Mattie admitted to herself, was perfectly fair and reasonable. Indeed, she was not at all sure what the widow herself should think. Except that Herr Becker was kindness itself, and his behaviour never anything but totally proper. And that, as her late husband's one-time employer, he might perhaps be said to enjoy certain strictly limited privileges. Which she, lonely and depressed as she was, had neither the strength nor—it must be conceded—the inclination to deny him. He was so purposeful, so many, so determined ... Mattie also

115

recognised in her dealings with her mother a regrettable lack of tact, even a wilful desire to shock—a desire, so long as she might believe herself to be in the right, to upset the older woman whenever possible.

It must be so. Otherwise, she thought afterwards, thoroughly ashamed of herself, otherwise why should she have chosen breakfast time the following day, Saturday, to tell her mother of her planned visit with Herr Becker on Wednesday next to a concert of sacred music at the Egyptian Hall? She knew perfectly well, did she not, that it was at breakfast time that the malign influence of her mother's own private moon was most powerfully to be felt?

"A *concert*, Matilda? With a *gentleman*?"

The two words, thus spoken, had taken on the aura of ultimate sin.

"But the concert is to be of sacred music," Mattie had protested, well aware that the nature of the programme was quite irrelevant. "Handel's setting of the hundred and ninth psalm, Mama. To be followed by—"

"I totally forbid it. You are in mourning, child. It is out of the question for you to be seen in public alone with Herr Becker."

"But of course you are invited too, Mama. Did I not say so?"

"That is hardly the point. I say again, you are in mourning. And besides, you know very well that the state of my health does not permit of evening excursions."

"Then I shall ask Papa to come instead."

"You shall do no such thing. Are you quite heartless? What of poor Albert?"

"I am sure Albert would not disapprove." In this, at least, Mattie had been innocent of prevarication. Until something prompted her to add, inflammatorily, "He was very fond of Handel's music."

Which also had been neither here nor there, as she well knew.

And so they had wrangled on, till finally her mother had risen dramatically from the table, one hand pressed to her bosom. "Do you wish to kill me, child? Do you wish to see me in my grave?"

"Certainly not, Mama." So calm, so reasonable. "I simply believe that I am old enough to decide for myself which concerts I should attend and which I should not."

"Oh. Oh . . . a viper—that is what I have nurtured. A positive viper . . . You will do as you please, of course. You always have done as you pleased." Mrs Skipkin had staggered to the parlour door and dragged it feebly open. And then the final denunciation. "You're a wicked, ungrateful girl, Matilda."

With which judgment—as soon as the parlour door had closed and the heat of the moment cooled—Mattie had regretfully been forced to agree. Her small daughter's unblinking gaze, too, had disconcerted her. The spectacle she had presented could hardly have been edifying. Children saw through you so—right through to the pettiness in your heart.

It was in this mood of sad self-disapproval that Mattie had set out shortly afterwards, leaving Victoria in her father's willing care, to walk alone in the streets and decide what must be done. Certainly there was wickedness in her. And equally certainly her mother, as none other could, brought it out. Therefore the two of them should not remain cooped up together, day in, day out.

This conclusion, even after only four days in the parental home, was hardly new. Nevertheless, reaching it seemed to give Mattie fresh hope. She lifted her eyes from the pavement and saw instantly, as if it had been meant, a hand-written notice in the downstairs window of the house she happened to be passing: *Female Assistance Required.* And beside it, on the wall by the door, a large brass plate, only slightly tarnished, announcing: DR MOGGRIDGE. SURGEON-DENTIST AND APOTHECARY.

Surgeon-dentist? Dear Lord, anything but that! Still, she was in no position to be choosy. Allowing herself no time for hesitation, she was up the short flight of steps to the door in a flash, and ringing the bell. Even then she might yet have turned

117

and fled, had not the door been opened almost instantly.

A short, red-faced gentleman in riding breeches and a loud check jacket stood on the threshold. He slapped his hands together and rubbed them cheerily. "Painless excavations a speciality," he briskly announced. "And no hot metal fillings for me, madam. My anodyne cement is the finest in London. Extractions only as a last resort . . . chloroform ten shillings extra."

Mattie stepped back a pace, gestured hastily towards the notice. "I saw your sign," she said through firmly closed teeth. "Is the position still available?"

"The position? My word, yes. My sainted aunt, yes indeed." He moved to one side. "Come in, miss. Pray do come in."

She sidled past him. "My name is Mrs Falconer," she said, detecting an unnecessary sparkle in his eye. "*Mrs* Falconer, you understand."

"Charming, ma'am. So young, and so decorative . . . Do you faint at the sight of blood?"

"I . . . I never have."

"I thought not. Sensible as well as decorative. The position is yours." He urged her on down a short passage and into his surgery. "Now, as to terms—"

Mattie stopped short. "Dr Moggridge, you have not yet told me my duties. I might not be—"

"Trifling, ma'am. Quite trifling. I'm not one of your jaw-breakers, you know. Haven't suffered a fracture in . . . oh, in six months at least. Look about you, Mrs Falconer. See the style of it."

Up to that moment Mattie had been doing her best *not* to look about her. Now, fearfully, she raised her gaze, saw a room with a large bow window, in front of which was an arm-chair covered in clean chintz. The walls, hung with elaborate certificates and testimonials, were lined with glass-fronted book-cases. Facing the chair was a stand with hot water jug, glasses, and several stoppered bottles. Mattie read their labels: creosote, oil of cloves, tincture of myrrh . . . On a nearby table lay four

118

satin-lined morocco cases, their contents rather less reassuring. A corkscrew-like instrument of polished steel with an ivory handle. Various suspicious-looking hooks with serrated edges. Any number of forceps, scalpels, chisels. On the table there were also books containing gold and tin foil, and two small bottles of metallic fillings, labelled 'mineral succedaneum' and 'quicksilver'. While away on top of a bookcase leeches squirmed in a tall glass cylinder.

Mattie shuddered slightly, and took a deep breath. "I'm afraid I need to know the exact nature of my duties, Dr Moggridge," she said firmly.

"Your duties, ma'am? Of the simplest, I assure you." He strode across the room and flung up the window sash. "I operate alone, you understand. Patients prefer it that way." He paused to inhale several lungsful of chilly March air. "You show 'em in, I do my stuff, you show 'em out . . . Not, however, before accepting due payment."

The doctor did four rapid knees-bends, then turned back from the window. "In my profession, Mrs Falconer, one needs to keep fit." He struck himself resoundingly on the chest. "There *is* blood, of course, but only in the strictest moderation . . . As to the rest of your duties, I expect you to promote the sale of my patented toothbrush—an excellent article, by the way. My word, yes. Also, ma'am, the exercise of your more womanly virtues."

Mattie tensed, edging nearer to the door. "And what might they be, Dr Moggridge?"

"The reassuring word, ma'am. Firm but gentle. Either you have it or you don't. And you do, Mrs Falconer. Depend on it, you do." He rubbed his hands again. "No hot poured fillings for me. A nice line in tooth renovators, undetectable from the real thing. And extraction only as a last resort."

Mattie relaxed. Dr Moggridge might be eccentric, but he was clearly no monster. And her duties seemed hardly onerous. "Perhaps I might be engaged for a trial period," she suggested. "Shall we say six weeks?"

119

"A capital notion. My sainted aunt, yes." He slapped his horsey thigh. "Nine till six, Sundays excepted. Half an hour for lunch. Twelve shillings per week."

Mattie hesitated. She knew little Victoria would be well enough cared for, mostly by her father, but she'd scarcely see her. "An hour for lunch?" she ventured. "I shall be going home, you see."

"Done. Capital. Start on Monday. Six weeks' trial."

Behind them the doorbell pealed dismally. Dr Moggridge tilted his head. "Aha! A patient . . . Be good enough to smile, Mrs Falconer, as you leave. Smile widely, hmm? They need what encouragement they can get, poor souls."

Obediently Mattie smiled, all the way down the short passage and out through the door, past the wan and tremulous young man waiting on the step. Behind her she heard Dr Moggridge clap his hands briskly together. "Painless excavations a speciality," he announced. "And no hot metal fillings for me, sir. My anodyne cement is the finest in London . . ."

A hundred yards down the road she paused, clung briefly to the railings. What, dear Lord, had she committed herself to? Assistant to a *dentist*? With blood in only the strictest moderation? Still, twelve shillings a week were not to be sneezed at. And the job was only for a trial period, just until she could find herself something better.

That Saturday morning Midge too, though rather less willingly, found himself employment. Indeed, as things turned out, he had no choice whatsoever in the matter.

His flight the previous afternoon from the sudden horrors of that dark little shop had taken him blindly on till sheer weariness forced him to a shuddering standstill. He crouched by a lamp post in a shabby little street, his chest heaving, his knees smarting now from the walls he had flung himself recklessly over in his panic. He no longer remembered the river, the ships upon it, Stumpy's words . . . everything was driven from his mind by the appalling narrowness of his escape. If he closed

120

his eyes the picture of those clutching hands rose insistently before them. And if he opened them it was simply to gaze back, terrified, over his shoulder.

After a while his breathing eased, and he staggered on. He seemed to be safe. No one was pursuing him. The street was crowded with people all far too busy even to notice him. His little world improved. He remembered the nice old man in the check trousers—Uncle Towzer, he'd said his name was. Midge had never had an uncle before. He remembered the cocoa too, and the brown, crisp biscuits. And the sixpence that had gone to join the pennies left over from the small hoard Stumpy had given him, clinking in the bottom of his jacket pocket.

He wandered on. His child's native optimism asserted itself. Life wasn't really so bad, not if you kept your wits about you.

He came to Blackheath, walked on till he saw a pond with ducks. Two were sitting on the grass and he chased them, chased them mercilessly as he had been chased himself. They ran foolishly, flapping and quacking. A small brown dog appeared from the bushes, and joined in the fun. Suddenly Midge felt sorry for the poor ducks. He flung himself down on the grass and, for no reason he could understand, began to cry. He cried with quiet, desperate intensity. The dog came up to him, puzzled, and licked his ear. He rolled over, and sat up. The dog let him hug it. They were friends.

The dog stayed with him all that afternoon, fetching sticks, panting. When he climbed a tree the dog stood at the bottom and barked anxiously. It seemed to want to look after him. Then, as darkness began to fall, suddenly it wasn't there any more. One moment it was dancing round, watching his every movement, and the next moment it was gone. Midge wasn't surprised. Dogs were like that.

Beside the heath there were big, grand houses. Midge raided several of their dustbins—there was no point in spending money when there was good food just there for the taking—and passed a comfortable night on some sacking in a coal shed. A scullery maid scarcely larger than himself came in the morning with a bucket while it was still dark, saw something moving and screamed, and ran away. He was out of the shed and off down the path long before she could return with some large, angry grown-up.

He was idling down Lewisham High Road, smelling the bakery smells and waiting for the shops to open, when all at once he heard a small husky voice calling to him. He froze, instantly afraid, and turned at bay.

"Here, little lovey—don't be feart. It's only Alfie Scattermole. Nothing to be feart of, not in Alfie Scattermole."

There was a barrow over on the far side of the street, a high-sided, home-made box of a barrow. And a skinny little old man, wearing upon his head a red spotted handkerchief knotted at the four corners, sat on its edge, swinging his legs between the shafts.

"Here, little lovey. Want a penny, does yer?"

Midge stole a glance up and down the empty street. A slaughter-house wagon crossed it, piled with bloody carcasses, followed by a herd of yowling cats. "I got a penny," he said defensively. He trusted nobody, not after the trap nice Uncle Towzer had led him into.

The old man sniffed. "No offence meant, I'm sure." He lapsed into silence, contemplated his swinging feet.

Midge edged forward. He and the little old man were the only two people in the whole world. The emptiness of the street seemed to draw them together. He approached to within a few yards. "What yer doin'?" he asked.

"Sittin'." The old man scratched his stubbly chin. "Just sittin'."

"Did yer mean it, 'bout the penny?"

"Mean it, little lovey? Bet yer braces I meant it." He produced a penny, opened his toothless old mouth, popped the penny in, swallowed it. Then, with terrible groans and grimaces, he removed the penny carefully from his ear. If Midge hadn't seen it with his own eyes, he'd never have believed it possible.

122

The old man polished the penny on his sleeve, then tossed it to Midge, who caught it neatly. "Thing is, little lovey, Alfie Scattermole always means what 'e says. Matter of principle."

The boy lingered, keeping his safe distance. Possibly there'd be other pennies.

"Want ter see me yellow canary bird, does yer?"

When Midge nodded the old man hopped down and began to rummage secretly in his barrow. He really was unusually little. Finally he brought out a small wooden box with slatted ends. Midge peered warily, saw a yellow bird inside.

"Why ain't it singin'?" he demanded.

"Too cold, that's why. Canary birds likes it 'ot. Can't say as I blames 'em." He shook the box violently, making the bird lurch and flutter.

Midge sidled closer. "Wotcher keep it for, then? If it don't sing, wotcher keep it for?"

"On account of it's me little bit of sunshine." The old man put the box down in the road between him and Midge, then turned back to his barrow and began sorting through large dirty sacks. Midge squatted down on his haunches and looked in through the end of the box. The yellow bird clung to its perch, watching him first with one bright eye and then the other.

"What's its name, mister?"

"Don't got no name ... Wanter feed it, does yer?"

Midge looked up. The old man had a paper bag held out to him at arm's length. Midge took it, looked inside. It was full of little brown seeds. He tasted a couple. They were gritty and dull, and he spat them out. Then he pushed a handful of them in through the slats. The bird stayed on its perch, watching him.

"I don't think it's 'ungry," he said.

"What's that, little lovey? Course it's 'ungry. Let's 'ave a see." The old man approached and stooped over the box. He clicked his tongue. "Kitchie-kitchie-kitchie ..."

Midge felt the old man's hand on his shoulder. He tried to squirm away, but the little fingers dug in like claws. He tried to stand up, but the old man's other hand had taken his arm and twisted it up agonisingly behind his back. The old man might be little, but he was horribly strong. Midge cried out and fell forward, his face in the gutter. The old chap released his shoulder, holding him down easily by his twisted arm.

"That's the way, little lovey. Sing yer little 'eart out. Set me canary bird a good example."

He tightened his grip. Midge let out a second faint cry, his cheek pressed hard against the kerb stones. Above him the old man was grunting as he struggled with something outside the boy's narrow line of vision. Suddenly Midge was lifted by his bent arm, the joints cracking, and lowered into a gaping black sack. As it came up round his face the old man let go of his arm and deftly thrust him down, tying the sack above his head.

It was dark inside the sack, with a stifling smell of soot. Midge screamed, and kicked out in all directions. Something hit him a sickening thump. He screamed again. And was hit again. He subsided, huddled in smothering darkness.

"That's nice, little lovey. Singin's all well an' good, but we wouldn't want to go callin' attention to usselves. I likes a lovey what learns quick."

The sack was dragged along the ground, then heaved up and dumped, driving Midge's little remaining breath from his body. He felt the canary's box flung in beside him. His sack tilted, and a rattling rumbling began. He was being trundled away in the barrow.

When he screamed yet again the barrow was stopped and put down, and he was thumped systematically from head to foot. He hid his head in his arms, sobbing wretchedly. When the beating was over the old man's voice came to him faintly, muffled by the folds of filthy sacking. The words were quietly reasonable, even plaintive.

"Thing is, little lovey, I'm not an 'ard man. Nobody could call me an 'ard man. But we got to 'ave a bit of 'ush. Yer me assistant, see? An' it don't go for a bloke's assistant to go 'ollerin' all the time. Yer got to learn, little lovey. Yer just *got* ter learn ..."

124

Midge learnt. He lay quietly beside the canary, and as wisely silent, in the bottom of the barrow while it clattered away down the Lewisham High Road. The little old man kept up a good pace, whistling breathily between toothless gums. He was a perky figure, his spotted handkerchief a welcome splash of colour in the grey light of morning. And on the sides of his barrow were painted in cheerful red letters, for all to read who were able, the words: *A. Scattermole. Chimney Sweep.*

Midge had much else to learn also, besides the virtues of silence. And quickly. For Alfie Scattermole, although not in his own estimation a hard man, was a forceful teacher. And the chimneys of the gentry were no place for the slow-witted. And Midge, for his part, was not only as sharp as two pins, but also a born survivor.

In the lonely house on its cliff-top high above the white roofs of Mittenwald Trude had hesitated for three long days, profoundly afraid yet unable to bring herself to a decision. She had gone about her duties like an automaton, aware all the time of Frau Becker's watchful gaze, of the faint, calculating smile on the old woman's lips. Her employer had made no further reference to Trude's dreams, nor to the terrible moment, wide awake and in broad daylight, when Herr Bruno had seemed to stand before her, and in his passionate embrace a young woman dressed sombrely in black. No mention of this was made, and none was needed. For it haunted Trude, sleeping and waking.

And worst of all was the certainty that Frau Becker had shared in her vision. That somehow she and the evil old woman were united, as if in some mutual act of obscenity. Her mind had been intruded upon. Her most secret thoughts, nothing was her own any more.

Trude knew she must get away. And yet, afraid of she knew not what, she lingered. In her few free moments she paced her room ceaselessly, pausing only at the window now and then to stare distractedly out at the white-laden trees, and at the track

that led invitingly away down between them, down to Mittenwald. How easy, just to step out on to the long balcony, descend
the outside staircase and walk away, never to return. How easy
simply to walk away, and yet how appallingly difficult.

And then, on Sunday, it snowed heavily all morning, and the
path through the trees disappeared, and the house was cut off
till Günther could dig a way through, and Trude swung wildly
between relief that no decision could be expected of her and
horror at the trap which had closed about her.

Monday was fine again, and by early afternoon Günther's
path met the men digging up from the valley. For Frau Becker
was a person of some local consequence, and the *Bürgermeister*
would never allow her to be inconvenienced any longer than
was strictly necessary. So Trude was free to go again, and
locked in an agony of indecision.

But today, Tuesday, her mind was at last made up. In the
early hours of the morning she had had a nightmare and, waking, had found the nightmare to be reality. She had dreamed
that Frau Becker was in the room with her, candle in hand,
leaning over her bed, ghost-like in her long white nightdress.
And the old woman was indeed there, watching and crooning
softly to herself as she swayed to and fro. Somehow she had
got herself up, and into her wheel-chair . . .

Now, seeing Trude wake, Frau Becker simply smiled her
small secret smile and gently patted her hand before wheeling
unconcernedly away out of the room, taking her candle with
her. Trude called after her, angry and afraid, but received no
reply: only faint disappearing laughter. She knew then that
she could not spend another night in Frau Becker's house.

Trude made her plans. She would leave quietly, after Frau
Becker was in bed, taking no more than a small attaché case,
for the journey down through the woods was long and steep.
The moon would be up by eleven o'clock to light her way. She
could send for the rest of her belongings later. She would go to
her cousin's house on the Untermarkt, by the church. Cousin
Friede might not be pleased to see her at such an hour, but she

126

could hardly turn her away. And as soon as she had all her things she'd set out down the valley to the next village, Garmisch-Partenkirchen. She had money put by. She'd not starve.

The day passed with painful slowness. After lunch, while Frau Becker was resting, Trude took down her heavy snow boots and hid them behind the stack of logs by the side door. She must go down through the darkened house shoeless, so as not to make the slightest noise. Doubts crowded her mind, but she put them from her. Not even the thought of the legacy she had worked so hard to deserve could sway her. Besides, the old woman was made of sterner stuff than she had at first supposed, seeing her that day two years ago, seemingly at death's door. The way she was going now she'd live to be a hundred.

The long hours of the afternoon and evening dragged by. Trude played her part well, allowing no hint of what was in her mind. She made plans with Frau Becker for the morrow, when Günther would have cleared the path up to the lake and they could take their morning constitutional.

At last it was time for her to make the old woman ready for bed. When she was comfortable Trude lit the scented nightlight and blew out her lamp.

"*Gute Nacht, Frau Becker. Schlafen Sie wohl.*" She turned away. As she reached the door Gustavia Becker called to her. She froze. What now? she thought. In spite of everything, had the old woman somehow guessed the truth?

"Trude my dear . . ." Frau Becker's voice was drowsy, scarcely more than a rustling of leaves. "I'm sorry, my dear, if last night I frightened you."

Trude relaxed. Up to that moment neither of them had referred to the incident. "It didn't matter," she said brusquely.

The old woman sighed. "I couldn't sleep . . . and you're very precious to me, Trude. You do know that, don't you?"

Trude opened the door. "It didn't matter," she repeated. "*Gute Nacht, Frau Becker.*" She went out, closing the door behind her. As she moved quietly to her room the clock in the downstairs hall struck ten.

It was only a minute's work to pack the few things she would be taking with her. She waited then in a chair by her uncurtained window, watching in an agony of impatience for the moon to rise.

It came up almost imperceptibly, silvering first the icy tips of the distant mountains, then spreading its beams till finally the clearing round the house, and the whole valley, was bathed in its singing brilliance. Only then did Trude rise, put on cloak and gloves, pick up her case, and stealthily open the door to her room.

The house was silent. Trude crept along the passage, keeping close to the wall for fear of creaking boards. Moonlight from the window lay in a long oblong across the floor. Outside Frau Becker's room she paused, heard nothing. The stillness beat against her ear drums. She moved on down the passage, skirted the huge linen press, painted with faded scrolls and roses, and came to the head of the stairs. She peered down. Nothing moved. No sound, save for the dusty ticking of the clock.

She descended quickly, her stockinged feet soundless on the polished stair treads. She crossed the entrance hall, went through the kitchen to the heavy oaken outside door. The bolts slid smoothly, their movement scarcely audible even to her close, straining ears. She eased up the latch and swung the door open, feeling the night air like cold fire on her face.

It was then that the music began.

Trude took a firm pace forward, then stopped dead as if turned to stone. The music seemed to fill her head, her whole body, running through her veins like ice. A thin, plaintive melody, slurred and discordant, yet freezing her will. With a terrible effort she dragged her hands up from her sides to cover her ears. Her case fell unnoticed to the ground beside her feet. But the effort was in vain, for the music went on and on, entering her soul, its flow unstoppable, calling her back.

128

Woodenly she turned. The door swung to behind her, closing on the moonlit trees, on her forgotten attaché case, on her freedom. She climbed the stairs as in a trance, drawn ever upwards by the reed-like music, wistfully haunting. *Ach du lieber Augustin, alles ist hin . . .*

When she came to her senses she was in Frau Becker's room. The music had stopped. Gustavia Becker was sitting up in bed, her violin tucked clumsily beneath her chin. Now, smiling gently, she held the instrument out.

"Take it, Trude. You play so much better than I. Take it . . ."

Trude advanced into the flickering circle of candle-light, then halted bewildered, shaking her head. "I cannot play. You know I cannot."

"Nonsense, my dear." Frau Becker spoke briskly. "Now, take off that cloak and those ridiculous gloves. You are young and strong. Your grip is steady. Of course you play better than a foolish, crippled old woman."

"But I cannot."

"But you *can*, my dear. Take it and see. We shall play together. We shall be strong together. There is Bruno, child, to be thought of. Together we shall do great things." She picked up the bow and offered that also. "You shall be my hands, Trude. And we shall make such music . . ."

Slowly Trude took off her cloak and then her gloves, pulling the fingers carefully one by one. Then she moved forward and put the garments on the foot of Frau Becker's bed. She looked at the violin, its rich red varnish glowing in the dim light, beckoning her. And the bow, a thin dark line against the white counterpane. Listlessly she reached out and accepted them from the old woman.

Wednesday came, the day of the concert in the Egyptian Hall. By then Mattie had had three whole days of the cheerful Dr Moggridge and she was a great deal wiser, both concerning him and concerning the grisly trade he practised. Wise, indeed,

129

to the point of excess. Extractions, for one thing, rather than being the last resort he claimed, were in fact almost the invariable rule.

"But it wouldn't do to tell 'em so, Mrs Falconer. Not slap bang on the doorstep. My sainted aunt, no. And besides, it's mostly their own silly faults. I'm no butcher, ma'am. With my anodyne cement I'm a positive artist. But they ought to come to me sooner. With a molar that's four-fifths carious it's the key and the forceps, and artistry flies out of the window."

Perhaps he wasn't a butcher. But he was certainly an extraordinarily fast worker. No extraction, she learned, took more than two minutes. Longer than that and the amount of chloroform necessary had often been known to prove fatal ... And anyway, sitting in her little outer office she soon discovered that to the mere outside listener extractions were infinitely preferable to most other forms of treatment, for which chloroform was not considered suitable.

Dr Moggridge also had a disconcerting line in graveyard humour. He bought teeth in by the gross, for mounting in terrometallic plates. On Tuesday morning, between patients, she had caught him picking over his latest consignment and speculating on their former owners. "Paupers every one, ma'am. And destined for some of the noblest mouths in the land. There's a moral in that somewhere, wouldn't you say?"

And when she remonstrated with him he grinned at her sideways, quite unabashed. "At least they're not *French* teeth, ma'am. After the battle of Waterloo there was a positive deluge of French uns. Not good for the trade, that sort of thing, once it gets about. Not good at all."

Six weeks, Mattie had given herself. And already she was seriously wondering if she would stay the course.

So it was that the concert at the Egyptian Hall took on an added significance, as a precious respite in the grim procession of her days, a brief interlude of artistry other than with scalpel and lancet. She would go, as her mother had rightly surmised, whether that poor lady approved or not. And Mrs Skipkin, making the best of a bad job, had experienced a sudden improvement in her health which enabled her—rather than Mattie's lackadaisical father—to chaperone her daughter. The fact that music of any kind was utter purgatory to her made not the slightest difference. If nothing else, she knew where her duty lay.

The concert began at eight-thirty and, the journey from Greenwich being lengthy, Herr Becker arrived in his carriage for the two ladies at shortly after seven. The hour since Mattie had got home from work she had put to good account, making time for a quick supper as well as putting little Victoria to bed and reading her a story. At least, with only one black dress, no great changing of clothes was necessary. Her mother however, although similarly situated, was pinning herself together up to the very last moment. Indeed, her outfit was still suffering last-minute adjustments as the carriage turned smartly out of Copperas Street into Creek Road.

Herr Becker was an excellent host. He had brought with him nosegays for both his guests, snowdrops and purple spring crocuses in little mossy twists of silver paper. He chatted charmingly, of the dismally seasonable weather, of the music they would be hearing, and of his home in Mittenwald. His house, built in the chalet style, he told them, was called *Graugipfel*—meaning 'Grey Peak' on account of the granite rock on which it stood. Which rock at that moment would be snowy-white, its surrounding pine trees bending low beneath their wintry burdens.

Listening to him, Mattie was reminded sharply of her dead husband, and of the tales he'd told her. But she set the thought firmly aside. Such brooding was morbid. Her whole life, if she were to let it, would remind her of Albert. And the past was past. It was the future that counted—as he himself, in his distant, kindly way, would have been the first to remind her.

It seemed harsh. Looking out at the lamp-lit streets, half-hearing Herr Becker's description of his mountain home, Mattie buried her nose in the snowdrops and wondered how she could be so pragmatic. And her man scarcely more than a week dead. Unless ... She saw suddenly, with painful, blinding clarity, that she had never loved him. Been fond of him, yes. Respected him, yes. Needed him, also. But loved him, never.

This revelation was unpleasant, appalling even. It shocked her deeply. But Mattie was a young woman accustomed to being truthful with herself, and she faced it. She even faced the unwelcome possibility that—had she loved him—then his honeymoon assaults upon her body might have brought him some measure of satisfaction. She knew they were supposed to. She even suspected that some wives found them pleasant also. Her friend Aggie Templeton, for instance, back on Bacon Street ... Surely it could not be right, she thought, with sudden aching intensity, that the procreation of children should be such a brief and joyless affair.

She stole a glance sideways at Herr Becker. He was still conversing animatedly, but it was the movement of his lips, rather than his words, that fascinated her. His entrancing lips, and the fine masculine sweep of his blond moustaches. Her mind, unguarded, wandered down dangerous, unfamiliar paths.

Abruptly she looked away again. Her heart was beating in a manner that disturbed her profoundly. There were longings, too, that must not be countenanced. Truthful as she was, there were still admissions that she dared not make. Instead she forced herself to concentrate on the fusty black folds of her dress. She was in mourning, she reminded herself. She had a child. Responsibilities. She had a mother and father also, to whom she owed a certain propriety of thought and deed ... For the rest of the journey she sat staring resolutely out of the carriage window, scarcely answering Herr Becker even when he spoke directly to her.

They arrived at the Egyptian Hall in good time, with ten minutes in hand before the beginning of the concert. Herr Becker alighted first, then handed Mrs Skipkin and Mattie down. Beneath the flaring gas lamps the pavements were crowded with fellow concert-goers, while across on the other side of the road a swarthy Italian turned the handle of an

132

ancient barrel organ, its busy clatter clearly audible above the shouting of coachmen and the rattle of carriages and horses' hooves on cobbles. Mattie paused, making out the organ-grinder's tune with difficulty under its weight of mechanical trills and flourishes. It reminded her of something, something that hovered at the back of her memory. But Herr Becker whisked her and her mother away into the concert hall foyer before she could be certain of what. She had a vague recollection of an old blind beggar, and black iron railings, and fog, and sadness . . .

The foyer was brightly lit, and packed with London's gentry. Herr Becker elbowed a path for his two guests expertly through the crush. He took their cloaks and was back in a flash, three elaborate, gold-edged programmes in his hand. Mrs Skipkin's cheeks were pinker, her eyes brighter, than Mattie had seen them in years. In the excitement of the outing it was obvious that her delicate health was completely forgotten. Privately Mattie vowed that she would get her mother out more often. It warmed her heart to see the older woman so cheerful and animated.

As they waited in the line slowly edging forward into the auditorium, suddenly Herr Becker stooped in Mattie's direction. "Now that's a strange coincidence," he murmured. "Just over there, ma'am, is Baron Rudolph von Kronstadt—in whom the good Inspector Gradbolt was so interested."

Mattie craned her neck, saw only a confusion of heads.

"Though not really such a coincidence," her companion continued. "The Herr Baron is well known for his love of music. And there are not that many good concerts in London for one to go to."

At that moment, briefly, the heads parted, and Mattie saw at once the man to whom Herr Becker had referred. It could be no other. He was young, as sturdy and Teutonically straight-backed as Herr Becker himself, but clean shaven, with leaner, more distinguished features, and his long dark hair combed silkily back above his ears. A bright crimson sash with the jewelled star of some honourable order lay diagonally across

133

his gleaming white shirt-front. He was, in fact, the perfect German aristocrat. Yet there was little arrogance in his bearing. Indeed, as she watched he stepped politely to one side, allowing a couple less civil than he to push themselves forward in the waiting line.

Mattie stared. Could this be the man Inspector Gradbolt suspected as her husband's murderer? Could she not detect a clear hint of ruthlessness in the firm set of his mouth? And cruelty in his watchful eyes? She frowned, reproving herself—such speculation, she knew, was foolishness. The blandest of outward appearances could mask a most brutal spirit. All too easily one saw what one looked to see ... Nevertheless there was here an excellent opportunity to discover, on the inspector's behalf, Baron Rudolph's London address.

As the Baron's head disappeared again in the throng Mattie tugged at Herr Becker's arm. "Could you introduce us, please?" she whispered.

He began to protest, then smiled and shrugged his shoulders. Moving forward a pace, he waited until the crowd parted again and then raised his voice above the general hubbub, *"Ein Moment, bitte. Baron Rudolph, ein Moment—"*

Hearing his native tongue, the other man turned and his eyes searched in their direction. He saw her companion, inclined his head in the briefest of bows, but made no move. Herr Becker called out again, clearly insisting. With ill-disguised reluctance the Baron came forward through the jostling throng.

"Guten Abend, Herr Becker," he said coldly. *"Was wollen Sie jetzt?"*

Herr Becker touched his arm, spoke firmly in English. "Baron Rudolph, I would like you to meet two very dear friends of mine ..."

Introductions were made. Mattie found her eyes drawn with horrid fascination to the gold signet ring upon one of the fingers of the Baron's surprisingly square and capable hands. But this too was foolishness. The majority of gentlemen wore such rings—why, even Herr Becker himself had one. And any-

134

way, the murderer had lost his, had he not?

Maud Skipkin, flustered by the Baron's title, curtseyed deeply. He urged her gently up. "I am delighted, Mrs Skipkin, to make your acquaintance. You are clearly, like myself, an admirer of Frederic Händel's beautiful music."

His English was excellent, but he pronounced the composer's name *Hendel*, in the German manner, so that at first Mrs Skipkin did not understand. And when she did, she could only fan herself, murmuring something discreet and suitably inaudible.

A pause ensued, the Baron staring politely at the points of his immaculate patent leather shoes while the press moved appreciably nearer to the inner doors of the concert hall. All Mattie wanted to discover was his London address. But she could not for the life of her think of a way to broach the subject.

Herr Becker cleared his throat. Mattie felt sorry for him— after all, this meeting had hardly been his idea. "Mrs Falconer is the widow of Mr Albert Falconer," he offered at last. "I think you met him in Mittenwald, when he was visiting the Becker factory."

The Baron inclined his head. "Certainly I remember. He gave a small recital in the *Rathaus*. A fine musician ... And now you tell me he is dead." He turned to Mattie. "You have my sincere condolences, Mrs Falconer. The world will be a poorer place without your talented husband."

She lowered her head, but watched him keenly all the same, detecting no hint of falseness in his voice or manner. They were almost at the doors now. "Shall you be sitting near us?" she asked hopefully. "We are in Row K."

"And I, alas, in Row C."

She smiled, feeling a little frantic. Another moment and he'd be gone. "Perhaps we could meet again, after the performance," she suggested.

The Baron glanced briefly in Herr Becker's direction. "Unfortunately, no. I must return to my hotel immediately."

A possible opening? Surely not. Yet they were through into

135

the auditorium now, and moving quickly down the aisle. It might well be her last opportunity. Very well then—now or never. Let him think what he would.

"And which hotel is that?" she asked baldly.

"Brown's Hotel, ma'am." He was looking at her oddly, but she did not care a fig. His address—she had it. "But I have to tell you," he went on, "that in the morning I shall be—"

"Row K, I think." Herr Becker halted, losing for ever what the good Baron might have been doing in the morning. "At last we have reached our destination."

Mattie met his eye, saw that he understood her ploy and was gently mocking her. She blushed, hardly noticed the Baron's stiff little bow, his polite words, his rapid departure. Herr Becker led her and her mother along the row to their seats, arranging himself between them. For a few moments he devoted himself entirely to Mrs Skipkin, discussing with her the handsome interior of the concert hall, arranging her shawl about her shoulders. Then, as the orchestra and chorus began to come on to the platform, he turned to Mattie.

"I must congratulate you," he whispered. "The inspector would be proud of you, I'm sure."

Mattie blushed again. "The Baron must have thought me very strange."

"It is of no consequence. To Baron Rudolph most people are strange. He is a very solitary person, you understand." He allowed himself the liberty of patting her arm. "It will be your wish now that the Herr Inspector Gradbolt should be informed of your discovery. Leave it to me, Mrs Falconer. I shall call at his office in the morning."

All around them applause began at the arrival of the conductor.

"But how will you know where his office is?" Mattie asked anxiously.

"My dear Mrs Falconer, all the world knows of your Great Scotland Yard. He will be found there, you may depend on it."

He settled back in his seat. Silence descended on the packed auditorium as the conductor raised his baton. Still anxious, Mattie searched the rows in front of her till she was sure she could see the sleek hair curling at the back of Baron Rudolph's head. It comforted her, knowing where he was. And in the morning Inspector Gradbolt would know also. She held her breath, waiting for the drum roll that would bring the audience to its feet for the National Anthem . . .

"Talk to me, Griffin. Confide your thoughts."

It was two days later, a fine sunny afternoon, and Inspector Gradbolt and his sergeant were sitting uneasily on a buttoned leather bench, rather like two schoolboys outside their headmaster's study, in the corridor that led to Police Commissioner Richard Mayne's office. It was in fact the inspector who had been summoned, but Sergeant Griffin had opted to go with him, at least as far as the great man's door, by way of providing moral support.

At the familiar request, the sergeant blew out his cheeks in a characteristic gesture and earnestly studied the top of his tall black hat held carefully on his knees. "I was thinking about that feather, sir. That green feather what we found in the old knife-grinder's hut."

Inspector Gradbolt removed his eyeglasses, breathed on them. "And making the connection, no doubt, between the feather and the two German gentlemen, both attired, strangely enough, in fancy dress representing Robin Hood."

"It did cross my mind, sir, that *if* we could find the costumier what rented out the suits, and *if* he'd noticed one of the hats returned with a missing feather, and *if* he could remember which of the two gentlemen it was that had—"

"Alas, poor Griffin. Too many ifs, I fear." The inspector broke off, waving his eyeglasses somewhat distractedly. "I . . . I seem to have left my handkerchief down in my office, Sergeant."

Reluctantly Sergeant Griffin produced what was clearly a piece of worn sheeting, none too expertly hemmed. "Allow me, sir."

137

The inspector accepted the fragment without comment, and applied it to his misted-over lenses. "The feather, by the way, is no longer there," he said, with a fine attempt at casualness. "I sent a constable to look. I did not tell you what I had done because . . ."

He faltered. The reason was obvious. It was the good sergeant who had found the feather. And he, his superior officer, who had dismissed it as being of no importance. He sighed. "Children, the constable reported. They were using the hut as some manner of military fortress."

Sergeant Griffin averted his gaze. "Gets in everywhere they does, sir. Can't keep 'em out. Little imps of Satan."

"Which is no excuse, friend Griffin. None at all . . ."

Inspector Gradbolt lapsed into silence. He knew only too well why Police Commissioner Mayne had sent for him. And he did not relish the coming interview. Which came all too soon, in fact at that very moment, with the opening of Mr Mayne's door and the appearance of his secretary in the passage.

"Commissioner Mayne will see you now, Inspector."

"Thank you." Inspector Gradbolt got to his feet, absent-mindedly patted his sergeant's shoulder as if offering the reassurance he himself needed, and went slowly forward into the Commissioner's office.

Mr Mayne was an impressive figure, a man in his early forties with a darkly sensitive face and long, well-trimmed side whiskers. He sat at a fine mahogany desk, his back to the window through which could be seen Whitehall's imposing sunlit façade. A vast fire burned in the grate, making the room, in Inspector Gradbolt's opinion, unhealthily hot. Its walls, like a miniature museum of iniquity, were lined with the Wanted notices for criminals past and present—a constant reminder to the Commissioner of his force's successes and failures.

"Come in, Inspector Gradbolt. Pray sit yourself down."

The tone was kindly, the expression, as always, faintly quizzical. Unlike Colonel Rowan, his fellow-commissioner,

138

Richard Mayne was no military man, and he dealt with his subordinates in a patient, softly-spoken manner. And was no less readily obeyed and respected for that.

Inspector Gradbolt sat down opposite the desk. "No doubt you wish to discuss the Falconer case, sir."

Mr Mayne nodded. "Or the Case of the Demon Swordsman, as our more sensational rags would have it." He smiled thinly. "Perhaps you would care to bring me up to date, Inspector."

The inspector did so, omitting nothing, least of all his own inadequacies. His sergeant featured in the narrative, and always to advantage. When he had done there was silence briefly in the room as Mr Mayne stared thoughtfully at the copious notes he had been making. Finally he looked up, his dark eyes sharp beneath their sensitively curved brows.

"This signet ring engraved with the golden oriole—has the Royal College of Heralds been able to establish *no* possible family connection?"

"None at all, sir. Also, in view of the ring's probable continental origin, I had a man check the *Almanac de Gotha*. No trace there, sir, either."

"And the Kronstadt coat of arms?"

Inspector Gradbolt was ready even for this. "A lion *couchant*, sir, upon an azure field."

Mr Mayne tapped his fingers. "Exactly how much time elapsed, Inspector, between your learning of Baron von Kronstadt's London address and your visit to Brown's Hotel?"

"Hardly more than an hour, sir. The other German gentleman—Mr Becker, that is—was here shortly after nine yesterday morning, sir. Sergeant Griffin and I were at the hotel by half-past ten."

"And?"

"The Baron had already been gone for two hours, sir. The hotel staff informed me that he left for Bavaria after an early breakfast." Inspector Gradbolt fingered his collar. The room's heat was growing more and more oppressive. "I sent on to

139

Dover, sir, but the Baron must have used one of the other channel ports."

"A hasty departure?"

"Apparently not, Commissioner. He had booked for two weeks, and his time was up."

"The purpose of his visit?"

"Business, sir. It seems that he comes to London at about this time every year. So far we have established three musical wholesalers on whom he called during his recent stay."

"You have a description of this man?"

"Passable, sir. Certainly he is tall enough to have been the individual seen by Mr Bastman in the General Post Office. The slight German accent fits also. And the dark coat. But apart from that, as I've already told you, sir, the man at the Post Office was too well muffled for a positive identification."

"In other words, Inspector, no identification at all."

"Not without the boy, sir."

"And the less said about him the better, I imagine."

"Quite so, sir." Inspector Gradbolt bowed his head. To have had the boy twice within his grasp and still let him escape was shaming indeed. He felt sweat trickling down inside his shirt. "But we're still keeping a sharp look-out, sir."

Mr Mayne stroked his silky side whiskers. "The police force in Bavaria is unlikely to be helpful ... Indeed, it can scarcely be said that they have a police force. Not as you or I understand it." He leaned back in his chair. "And anyway, even if it *was* Baron von Kronstadt who despatched the violin to his home in Mittenwald, we have no idea why he should do such a thing."

"It was an experimental instrument, sir. And he might not have wanted to risk being caught with it."

"I have to remind you, Inspector, that you have produced no evidence whatsoever that it was the murdered man's violin."

Inspector Gradbolt kept silent. Certainly the coincidence was remarkable. But Commissioner Mayne was not a man who set much store by coincidences, no matter how remarkable.

140

"Equally, Inspector, it is possible that the entire Post Office episode was designed as a diversion. A red herring, as it were."

"The thought had struck me, sir."

"And?"

"It seemed hardly a profitable line to pursue, Commissioner."

Abruptly Mr Mayne straightened his back and inclined forward across his desk. "Forgive me for saying so, Inspector, but the entire investigation seems to have been somewhat unprofitable."

"I have to agree, sir." Inspector Gradbolt hunched still further down in his chair. "Unless we find the boy, there is little—"

"Let us be frank with each other. One wretched street urchin among so many—what are the chances? He's probably not even in London any more."

"A city child is unlikely to seek refuge in the country, sir. They prefer the familiar."

"True ..." Mr Mayne stared once more at his notes. "Two murders, the second clearly stemming from the loss of the ring during the commission of the first. Two murders only—so it's not simply a homicidal maniac we're dealing with."

Inspector Gradbolt nodded. He knew only too well where the Commissioner's thoughts were leading him.

"The papers," Mr Mayne continued, "have already begun to lose interest, I'm glad to say. Therefore, taking everything into account—" He broke off. "You have no dramatic new line of enquiry in mind, I suppose?"

For a second the inspector considered reminding Mr Mayne of the feather. But it was hardly new, and certainly not dramatic ... If only he could get out of his mind his picture of the murdered man's young widow, so brave and so alone. Her parents, from what he had seen of them, would be of little comfort in her bereavement.

"No new line at all, sir."

"In that case ..."

Inspector Gradbolt had known it all along, right from the

141

moment when he had first received the message summoning him to Mr Mayne's office. The investigation was to be suspended, pending further developments. Not yet one for the Unsolved Crimes file. But no longer one for the Active file either. People would soon forget. It wasn't as if murder was such an unusual occurrence in the city.

As Inspector Gradbolt rose to go a new folder of documents was thrust into his hand. They involved a suspected case of embezzlement, in connection with one of the more recent and fly-by-night railway companies. He took them warily, and departed.

Sergeant Griffin was waiting outside in the blessed cool of the corridor. He also did not need to be told Commissioner Mayne's verdict. Together the two men plodded up the stairs to Inspector Gradbolt's eyrie. They spoke little. But the same picture lingered in both their minds: of a young woman, cruelly widowed, left with a fatherless child, so brave and so alone . . .

Mattie Falconer sat forward over the table in her little outer office, her hands pressed to her ears, trying not to hear the sounds of one-sided battle that came from Dr Moggridge's surgery. Six weeks she had promised herself. And then what? Jobs for a young female person such as she were not easily come by. Except in service, and she could not bear to be so totally parted from her daughter. And her father, for all his protestations, had finally accepted her contribution to the housekeeping with ill-concealed relief. Ten shillings she was giving him, for herself and little Victoria. Certainly it was ample. But God alone knew how she would have managed if she had not had her parents to turn to.

She thought of Herr Becker. She had not seen him since the night of the concert, but he would be calling again on Sunday in his carriage, to take all of them for a ride in the country out beyond Lewisham. She knew he would have kept his promise to tell the inspector of Baron Rudolph's London address. Vaguely she wondered what would come of it all. But it seemed

142

really to be of very little consequence. She wasn't a vengeful woman. Albert was dead, and nothing would change that.

And surely the Baron, despite his coldness, was no murderer . . . Indeed, he and Herr Becker—although there was admittedly an estrangement between them—appeared to have much in common. They were both so *German* . . .

The sounds from Dr Moggridge's surgery had abated. Possibly the doctor's anodyne cement was taking effect—Mattie knew now that it was composed entirely of gum mastic and morphia . . . She thought again of Herr Becker. How curious it was that she should ever have imagined him to be remote. He was really the most accessible of men. And so good with Vickie. And with no mention at all of when he might be returning to Bavaria. How kind he was. And how attentive. It was almost as if he—

She shook her head, firmly dismissing the improper thought. There were so many practicalities to be considered . . . and a decent interval would need to elapse, of course . . . but Victoria did like him, she was sure of that . . . and her parents, once they had got used to the idea, would certainly be relieved . . . and at least she'd never have to listen to Dr Moggridge's 'painless excavations' again . . .

Momentarily she had removed her hands from her ears. Now she replaced them, in a second, vain attempt to shut out such unsuitable notions. She could scarcely believe that it was she who was entertaining them. She who had always had her emotions so tightly controlled. It seemed, however, that she could no more control the urgings of her heart than she could order the rising and setting of the sun. She did not understand what was happening to her, and she was afraid. Afraid . . . yet at the same time bewilderingly ecstatic.

The truth was that at twenty-four years of age Mattie Falconer had never, before that moment, been in love. Therefore she did not recognise the painful joy, the delirious folly, the single-mindedness for good or ill, of her condition.

Part Two

1

MATILDA ANNE FALCONER and Bruno Gottfried Wilhelm Becker were married on November 23rd of that same year, 1856. The ceremony took place quietly in the Catholic Church on Farm Street in Mayfair, and the small reception afterwards was held nearby, in the tiny slot of a house Herr Becker had rented for the duration of his stay in London. That same evening he and Mattie and her daughter Victoria left for Folkestone on the first stage of their long journey to his home in Bavaria. He was naturally anxious for them to be on their way as soon as possible since, although he never complained, he had already been away from his business there, and from his mother, far longer than was suitable.

Mattie had done her best down six long months to follow his patient example. But she felt the delay keenly, being for the first time in love and filled with new and powerful longings. The interval was unavoidable, however, both for reasons of respectability—and even then her period of mourning was only barely enough—and also to allow time for the course of instruction necessary before she could embrace the Roman Catholic faith of her future husband. Accordingly she accepted this ordering of her life as docilely as she accepted much else in the world, and did her best to turn it to good account.

Her conversion, it has to be admitted, was somewhat a matter of convenience. As long as her kindly old instructor allowed her to keep intact her simple belief in God and in the fundamental goodness of His creation, the outward trappings of that belief were of little importance to her. But the six months also provided a valuable opportunity for her properly to get

147

to know Herr Becker. And for Victoria to get to know him also, and he her. The relationship between stepfathers and step-daughters was notoriously difficult, and Mattie hoped very much that her child would, given time, be able to share in her own happiness at having a man in her life again.

Luckily for the three of them, Herr Becker and the little girl got on well right from the beginning. Not that they shared any very great intimacy of affection, but that was hardly to be expected even between men and their natural daughters. But Herr Becker offered a gentle stability, and occasional discreet presents, and was soon providing a sturdy pair of trousered legs which could be grasped unobtrusively whenever the child's small world became unduly threatening.

All in all, Mattie found him completely marvellous, and grew more in love with him with every day that passed. While he, for his part, seemed equally besotted.

In all the excitements of that time, however, there did come one small, sad reminder of the immediate past, making Mattie —for all her strenuous self-justifications—momentarily very ashamed of her happiness. A few days after the outing to the concert Inspector Gradbolt called upon her late in the evening. He came to tell her that the investigations into her late husband's murder were being for the moment set aside. The boy Midge could not be found, enquiries about the ring engraved with the golden oriole had proved fruitless, and Baron Rudolph von Kronstadt had left England before Inspector Gradbolt could get to him.

The inspector seemed depressed, guilty even, peering at her in his lugubrious, school-masterly fashion over the tops of his eyeglasses, and she did not quite know how to set his mind at rest. To tell him baldly that she did not care, that the past was past and best forgotten, would have seemed to him inexcusably heartless. But she could hardly explain to such as Inspector Gradbolt that whatever heartlessness there might be was indeed of far earlier origin, her sad failure down six full years of marriage properly to love her husband. Neither could she ex-

148

plain, both because it would have been scarcely becoming and because anyway she did not herself yet fully understand it, the new, blissful delirium that possessed her.

So she was forced back on to platitudes, and a measure of dishonesty for which she did not admire herself.

"I know you have done your best, Inspector." A mournful, downcast glance. "No man can do more."

"A motive, ma'am. I feel sure that things would have been different if only I could have hit upon a motive."

She shrugged bravely. "Perhaps there was none. It is even possible that my husband was killed by mistake, in the place of another. After all, the night was very dark."

This, in fact, was the decision she herself had decided upon. Bitter as it was, it spared her the thought of premeditated brutality towards someone as kind, as self-effacing, as harmless as Albert.

"You may be right, ma'am. You may be right ..."

But she knew he did not believe it. And he departed as bleakly as he had come, stooping away down the narrow stairs, his voluminous ulster furled tightly about him. She pulled aside the parlour curtains to watch his progress down the dingy street. Poor man, she thought. I hope he doesn't get into trouble on Albert's account ... And then experienced a moment's guilty relief that now, even in official terms, the past was past and best forgotten. And she could therefore live again, and be free.

Within a few weeks of the concert at the Egyptian Hall Bruno Becker was seeing her every day, waiting outside Dr Moggridge's painful establishment at lunch time to walk with her back to the shop on Copperas Street, and dropping in there most evenings also, sitting in the upstairs parlour and making himself totally agreeable to her parents. Mr Skipkin, of course, was enchanted, for the moment apparently seeing the visits as prelude to a massive investment of Becker capital in the retail music business. While Mrs Skipkin, never slow in such matters, recognised at once which way the wind was really blowing. And, although she naturally could not bring herself to approve, she

149

was far-sighted enough never actually to endanger her daughter's eventual happy departure from the parental home.

In particular Mrs Skipkin noticed, and chalked up as a very good sign, the pains Becker was at to make her daughter acquainted with his family situation. One evening, apropos of nothing very much, he even went so far as to announce that he looked forward enormously to the day when Mattie might meet his mother.

"Mutti sees so few people these days, you understand, being without the use of her legs and confined to a wheel-chair."

"Oh, the poor lady!" Maud Skipkin knew only too well the burden ill health could be. "Has she been long afflicted?"

"Two years or so. Since her stroke . . . Up to then she had been the most vigorous of women. Ever since the death of my father when I was only a boy she had been deeply involved in the running of the family business. But now . . ."

He shrugged his shoulders sadly and lowered his gaze, absent-mindedly turning the gold signet ring upon his little finger. Although she knew she was in no sense an inquisitive woman, Mrs Skipkin had long ago made it her business to spy out the design upon the ring—a heraldic emblem, for example, would have denoted some aristocratic connection. To her slight disappointment, however, there were simply initials, too overlapping and ornately gothic to be readily distinguished. All the same, he was undeniably prosperous—and in these progressive days merchants of wealth constituted their own aristocracy.

Herr Becker looked up again, turned to Mattie. "I have to confess to an unfortunate family tragedy, Mrs Falconer. I had a sister, Liesl, three years younger than myself. She took her own life. Drowned herself in a lake close by our house. Such a beautiful lake, set in a hollow in the mountains . . . It was the shock of this that caused my mother's illness."

Beadily Mrs Skipkin observed her daughter's hand reach out and rest briefly upon Herr Becker's knee. But she let it pass. It was a gesture excused by the solemnity of the moment, she decided.

150

"How terrible for you both," her daughter murmured. "To suffer such a sudden double affliction."

Herr Becker nodded quietly. Then he brightened. "But time passes. And dear Mutti has come wonderfully to terms with her condition. Her biggest grief is that her hands are now weakened so that she can no longer play the violin as she would wish. She used to be a considerable musician, you understand . . . But she has an excellent companion these days. And our factory manager comes up to the house every week, and keeps her in touch with business matters."

He smiled. "Mostly she's very cheerful. Her spirit is as strong as ever it was. But Graugipfel is a goodly distance up from town, and she is inevitably lonely. It would be a great joy to her if . . ."

He tailed off, suddenly confused. Mrs Skipkin saw clearly that he had realised too late the implication of his words, their unsuitable boldness. How could he possibly expect Matilda to travel with him to Mittenwald alone, as an unattached young woman?

She decided to rescue him. "Loneliness is very hard to bear, Herr Becker," she said quickly, ignoring her daughter's blushes. "I know it myself. You see me here, in the heart of a populous city. My life, you imagine, is one long round of social gaiety. The truth, however, is somewhat different. You would hardly believe this, I know, but . . ."

She went on to outline at some length—and as tactfully as she might, with Mr Skipkin mercifully occupied downstairs in the shop—the daily trials of her existence and how bravely she bore them. The other, the circumstances necessarily attending upon her daughter's presence in Mittenwald, must wait upon a later, more timely season.

And Mattie, who recognised only too well what her mother was up to, could only sit, patiently smiling, and hope against hope that Bruno Becker would not judge her by the tedium of her mother's conversation. And wait, equally patiently, for that same later, more timely season.

It was in fact on a fine Sunday afternoon in early May—

Mattie would remember it all her life—that Herr Becker first spoke openly of his feelings for her. Their Sunday walks in Greenwich Park had quickly become an accepted ritual, and on this particular afternoon, the daffodils thick in the grassy hollows, it seemed the most natural thing in the world for them to pause a while on a secluded bench beneath a plane tree vivid with the tiny, yellow-green leaves of spring. And, although their conversation was to have its disturbing aspects, the outcome was all that Mattie could have hoped for.

They sat down. Victoria, perched on the bench between them, wriggled boredly for a minute or two, and then got down and wandered off. Mattie watched her fling herself down on hands and knees in front of a clump of daffodils, and for once she said nothing about green stains on best Sunday stockings. Neither did she mention the possibility of being stung when she saw her daughter engrossed in the activities of the bees as they drifted among the nodding flowers. There were times, surely, when the duties of motherhood could be overlooked, with advantage to all concerned.

Herr Becker stretched his gay, tightly trousered legs and tilted his jaunty, wide-brimmed spring beaver on to the back of his head.

"What a beautiful day it is," he said. "How quickly one can forget the miserable London winter ... In Mittenwald, you know, the winters are so bright, so white and sparkling."

Which information was hardly new to her. "I think you love your home very much, Herr Becker," she murmured.

"Please—" He turned to her suddenly across the discreet gap left by Vickie. "My name is Bruno. A strange name to your ears, no doubt, but could you not please use it?"

Her heart missed a beat. It really did. For such an opening could have only one end, profoundly desired, profoundly feared. She edged away, shaking her head. "It would not be ... proper."

"Proper? What is this English word *proper*? You must explain it to me."

"You know very well what it means, Herr Becker." She spoke

152

quite sharply. His English, she knew very well, was up to such an elementary definition. "I am in mourning. For me to call you by your Christian name would be unsuitable, to say the least."

"I hurry things, perhaps. But we are already such good friends, you and I. Are we not good friends?"

"Certainly we are friends. But—"

"And more than friends, even?"

She knew she should deny it. But the words stuck in her throat. She looked away, took a deep breath. "You have been kindness itself to my daughter and me, Herr Becker."

The prevarication would have fooled nobody. Herr Becker smiled.

"Then you must call me Bruno."

"I . . . I cannot."

"Of course you can." He stared at her, his blue eyes appealing to her. Mocking her a trifle also. In spite of herself she smiled back at him. How ridiculous this was!

Bravely she let her gaze meet his. "Very well then—Bruno."

He gave a great shout of laughter. Victoria looked up briefly, then returned to her bees.

"Most proper. *Bruno*—you say it most pro-per-ly." It amused him to separate each syllable. He sat back, folding his arms. "And I—it is only fair, is it not?—I shall call you Matilda. Such an English notion, this *fair*. But I like it."

Mattie frowned. Certainly it was fair. But since when had anything approaching fairness been allowed between men and women? She changed the subject.

"Are the winters in Mittenwald really so hard?" she said coolly. "If that is the case then I do not believe I would much like it."

He was disconcerted. But only for an instant.

"Ah, but the spring, Matilda. When the spring comes it is so much worth waiting for. Such blue skies, the green fields so beautiful . . . and such a quantity of wild flowers as you have never seen, *meine liebe* Matilda."

153

Somehow, in German the use of her first name did not seem so forward. "I would like that," Mattie allowed. "Living in London I know little of wild flowers . . . Does your mother write to you often, telling you of your home?"

"My *mother*?" At once his face grew thunderous. The sudden transformation appalled her. "At such a time as this, why do you speak of my *mother*?"

Mattie trembled before his inexplicable onslaught. "I . . . I was only wondering if she—"

"Dear Mutti—" his tone was bitter "—she does not write, I tell you . . . Yet, *du lieber Gott,* she has her own ways to communicate."

"Her ways? I'm afraid I don't understand."

With an effort he recovered himself. "It is not important. I speak foolishly." He leaned forward, took her hands anxiously in his. "We . . . we have always been close, Mutti and I. It is in my thoughts, you understand, that she speaks to me. I know her so well—it is as if she is always with me."

Such an explanation was hardly convincing. Yet Mattie wanted desperately to believe in it. She looked down at his hands, so broad and strong that they engulfed hers entirely. A new thought occurred to her. "And you think she would not perhaps approve of—of . . ."

She tailed off, feeling a sudden coldness round her heart. She dared not ask if it was she herself of whom his mother would not approve.

He raised her hands till they were held tenderly against his breast. "I am thirty years of age, Matilda. Time for me to make my own decisions, I think. What sort of man would I be, at such a great age to be thinking only of my mother?"

But his words no longer signified. She could feel his warmth, and the beating of his heart. And her own matched his until they were as one. And all misgivings melted away in the wonder of the moment. How could it matter, then, what his mother thought or did not think?

"Matilda . . . ? Matilda . . . ?"

He was calling to her, as from a great distance. She had

154

closed her eyes, and her lips were parted. Her breath came shallowly, her whole being tuned to his.

"Matilda . . . *mein Liebling* . . . ?"

Consciousness returning, she dragged her hands almost angrily away. He had robbed her of self, intruded into the very core of her existence . . . But she could not maintain her anger, for it was an intrusion she longed for above all else.

Yet the charade of propriety must be played out. She was, indeed, grateful for it, since without it all would have been chaos.

"All the same," she said, making a brave try at good sense, "I do not think one's parents can be wholly disregarded."

"Which is why, *meine liebste* Matilda, I intend to speak to your father this very evening."

"Speak to my father? I don't know what you mean."

She knew very well what he meant. But the formalities, even of love, must be observed. And Bruno—to her intense joy, and to her intense embarrassment also, there in the public park—observed them. Removing his hat and hitching up his trouser legs, he got down on one knee on the gravelled path. She looked for mockery in this dramatic posture, and found none. Suddenly, now that it was needful, he was totally sincere, and oblivious of everything but the golden moment. The charade was over, the formalities were transcended.

"I love you, Matilda. You are beautiful and gay. Your daughter, too, is a little enchantress—and she likes me a little, I think. As I believe you do too . . . I have little to offer you both. But what I am, what I have, is yours for ever."

He paused. "You have reminded me that you are in mourning. I know it. But I am bold, for I do not believe that the emotions of the heart can be ruled by such outward displays. Your clothes may be in mourning, Matilda. But you are young, and the sun is shining, and to refuse happiness would be a sin. I do not ask for a decision now, *meine Liebste*. Simply for the hope that one day, if I prove worthy, you might consent to be my wife."

It had been a long speech, and extravagant, and she should

155

have interrupted it a dozen times. Her failure to do so told its own story. As did her additional failure to mind in the least the sensation his attitude was causing among those park-goers close enough to notice it.

Gently she stretched out her hands and lifted him to the seat close beside her. Then she hesitated, collecting her thoughts, determined to give him the solemn, truthful answer he deserved. There would be time enough later for laughter and folly.

"Let us not speak of who is worthy and who is not," she said at last. "Neither let us hide behind talk of hope, but rather begin as honestly with each other as we intend to go on. I give you my decision now, and gladly. I love you, Bruno. Nothing else matters. I would become your wife tomorrow, this very moment even, were it possible."

She was indeed young, and the sun was indeed shining. And happiness was a flower that bloomed fervently beneath such a dual benificence. And if her words seemed a trifle earnest, a trifle self-important, the times in which she lived were earnest and self-important also. Times, blessedly, in which such a declaration was neither lightly given nor lightly received.

Laughter and folly came quickly upon its heels. First, however, she must lift her face to his and receive his kiss. And she knew then, if ever she might have doubted it, that her decision was the only one possible. For the warm fondling of his lips and tongue roused a passion in her that was a freeing of mind and soul and body, almost frightening in its intensity.

At last he released her. For a moment she felt bereft, horribly vulnerable in this sudden breaking of the total bond between them. Then he was on his feet, and holding her in his arms, and spinning round and round and round in the dappled spring sunlight. His feet crunched the gravel, and his laughter at the sheer joy of living, and her laughter too, sounded in the air like dawn, like a whole new world's awakening.

He put her down, breathless now, and they ran together through the soft grass, among the tumultuous, teeming daffodils. Somehow her bun had come unpinned, and her dark hair

156

flowed out behind her like a silken cape. Little Victoria looked up then from her solemn study and saw them run, and ran after. So they waited, and hoisted her between them, her shiny Sunday shoes trailing, and ran on, laughing still. On and on, like giants. Till they tumbled finally in a gasping, breathless heap on the side of a mossy hollow and lay there, puffed and happy, staring up, all three, at the blue vastness of the sky.

And the mere mechanisms of life that inevitably had to follow, even they were imbued with the same childlike spirit of joy and adventure. The walk down the hill and home through shabby streets all somehow bright and shining new. Bruno's interview upstairs with Towzer Skipkin while Mattie stayed down in the dark Sunday fustiness of the shuttered shop, playing ridiculous jumping-out games with her daughter, and giggling, and trying to compose her face for the moment when she must be called upstairs. Which moment, when it came, soon dissolved her frivolity into inexplicable tears, both her own and her mother's. While even Towzer Skipkin's eye was undeniably moist. And Bruno looked on, his arms folded, a rock of proud, delighted masculinity in the surrounding sentimental sea.

So it was that Mattie Falconer, within the family circle at least, became engaged to be married, with the date for the wedding decently set some six months distant. Which seemingly interminable period of waiting often drove her almost to desperation. Especially at night, alone in her narrow bed in the cramped back room she shared with her daughter.

But at least, now that she and Bruno were engaged, custom permitted them more often to be alone together. And, now that her six weeks with Dr Moggridge were over and done with, opportunity permitted also. The good doctor had been astonished, indeed, positively desolated, that she should wish to leave—had she stayed she could readily have learned the trade herself, his sainted aunt yes, and such an up-and-coming profession. But she had kept to her decision notwithstanding: her daughter needed her, she said. Which was true enough, though hardly the entire truth of the matter.

157

And so she and Bruno were frequently, blissfully, alone together. Alone together for the tender words, for the precious intimacies of lovers, the laughter, the fond quarrels, the instant reconciliations. And the kisses . . .

Alone for good sense also, and for the sober assessment of responsibilities. Her future life in Mittenwald, the need for her to learn the German language, which Bruno at once began to teach her. Her daughter also, and the German governess that must be found as soon as the child was properly settled. A *governess* . . . the word, spoken by Bruno so lightly, brought home to Mattie for the first time the great changes in store. Bruno was a wealthy man. Little Victoria, therefore, would grow up in a household where only the very best was good enough. And it was this realisation that brought the final completion of her happiness.

There was in addition, less comfortably, the question of Bruno's mother. Ever since the day in the park when the mention of her had so strangely distressed him, Mattie had been reluctant to question him again. But it was a matter that had to be dealt with. She would, after all, be sharing her home with the old lady. She needed to know where she stood.

She finally found the courage to raise the subject one hot June evening, when they were walking on Blackheath.

"I've been meaning to ask you, Bruno," she said lightly, "does your mother speak English?"

It was an approach she had worked out carefully beforehand, and to her relief he seemed quite unconcerned by her question.

"Of course she does. She has been to this country often—with my father when he was alive, and then afterwards with my sister and me. Principally on business, of course, but she has come to know and like England very much." He paused and turned to her, suddenly curious. "Why do you ask?"

"It's just that . . . well, you've written to tell her about us, I suppose?"

Again the prepared speech. And sounding, she feared, so stilted. But he didn't appear to notice.

"Of course I have, *mein Liebling*. How could I not?" He looked down, puzzled, into her eyes. Then, as always, he understood. "And she has not written to you? You have been expecting a letter, and it has not come?"

At her timid nod he burst out laughing. "*Liebling*—to speak English is one thing—to master its positively idiotic spelling is quite another. And Mutti is a proud old lady—she would not wish to appear foolish and ill-educated in your eyes. Of course she has not written to you. But she has spoken most kindly of you in her letters to me."

Mattie frowned. "But you should have told me," she chided gently. "I have been so afraid that she ... she ..."

"That she is not pleased for me to have found myself a beautiful young English bride?" He laughed again. "Of course she is pleased. If I am happy, then so is she."

He took her arm then, and they walked on together. But she knew him well enough by then to sense a shade of disquiet behind his ready assurance ... Faintly there came to her the summery click of a cricket ball and the sudden excited appeal of a bowler to the umpire. It was a relief to her that Bruno took no interest whatsoever in cricket. To have stood with him and watched the game would have been too painful: a reminder of those afternoons so long ago, up here on the heath in the days of Albert's courtship. Those days from another life, sad and best forgotten, when she had believed in her childlike ignorance that she was in love ...

"Not that it will be easy for Mutti, you understand—"

His words jolted her back to the present. His words, the admission of his disquiet.

"To accept another woman into her home, to be no longer its mistress ..." He struck angrily at the grass with his stick. "Also to know that she is no longer the only woman in her son's life—it will not be easy."

Mattie squeezed his arm. "Of course it won't. We must both do everything we can to help her."

"My wise little Matilda ..." He stooped and lightly kissed

her forehead. "And it will not be easy for us either. Mutti is no meek little *Hausfrau*—she can be very fierce, and for a long time now she's been used to getting her own way. But you'll win her over. So beautiful and so wise—how could you not?"

They strolled on then together, his arm about her waist, pressing her tightly to him, across the joyous summer green of the grass, beneath the limitless, breathtakingly blue dome of the sky. And if Mattie allowed his words to linger in her mind, it was only with fond amusement at their apparent contradictions. Of course his mother was pleased—except that things wouldn't be easy. And of course anything that made him happy made her happy also—except that she'd no longer be the only woman in his life . . . So where did that leave Mattie? No worse off, and no better, than virtually every new daughter-in-law since the beginning of time.

It certainly never occurred to her that Bruno, for all the reservations he admitted to, might still be being less than honest.

And so the months of summer and autumn passed, months of excitement and happiness, and of a painful expectancy bearable only in the certainty of its ultimate fulfilment. Until, at long last, it was the night before her wedding.

Bruno had been away about the final arrangements and she had not seen him all day. She had walked the November streets with her little daughter till she could walk them no longer. Then she had huddled over the range in the upstairs kitchen, listening to her mother's distracted chatter—the morrow would be positively the death of her, although in fact Bruno had so contrived things that Mrs Skipkin had no responsibilities whatsoever, other than those of getting herself ready for the carriage that would arrive at nine to take the entire family to the church. Mattie sat and stared at the flames, silently willing the hours to pass.

Finally, Victoria safely in bed with hot milk and a book and her doll 'Melia, Mattie wandered restlessly down into the darkened shop and positioned herself at one of its windows, watching the meagre activities of early evening out on Copperas

Street: children's squabbles, the return of the rag-and-bone cart to its yard next door, the passage of a muffin man, tray on his head, ringing his bell ... These were the sights and sounds of her childhood—of her whole life, it now seemed. And to-morrow she would be leaving them, probably for ever. All at once the thought appalled her and she closed her eyes, cling-ing with symbolic tenacity to the little brass rail that bounded the rear of the window display. She belonged in Copperas Street. It was the only place in the world where she was truly safe ...

A sound at the back of the shop roused her, and she turned. Towzer Skipkin had entered from his work room, carrying a candle. He put it down on the counter, eased himself up beside it and sat there among the piles of sheet music and boxes of wax piano lights, swinging his legs.

"Mattie, my pet, I'm glad to have this moment. Tomorrow is a momentous day. I should perhaps have spoken to you before. But—"

"The fault is mine, Papa." She spoke quickly, fervently, sud-denly aware of the shameful six-month gap in her relationship with him. All her time, all her thoughts, had been for Bruno. She moved now quickly to her father's side. "You've scarcely seen me—what chance have you had? And tomorrow I'll be going away ..."

"As is only right and proper. Your place is with Bruno. You're in love, my pet." He took her hand. "And for the first time, I think?"

She nodded, blushing deeply but still meeting his gaze.

He smiled at her sadly. "I always knew your marriage to poor Albert was a mistake. But what could I say? You could hardly be blamed for taking any chance that offered ... Any-way, that's all over now and done with." He swung her hand fondly to and fro, just as if she were a little child again. "And I'm so happy for you. So truly happy."

Profoundly moved, she stopped his hand's swinging and brought it up to her lips. "I don't want to leave you," she whispered.

161

F

"Of course you don't. We understand each other, you and I." He put one arm round her shoulder. "But there's just one thing you've got to remember . . ."

With his other hand he lifted the candle and held it high above his head, enclosing them in a warm circle of light. "See that, my pet? Well, I dare say if life were as small as the glow from this candle, you and I could be happy as sandboys together for ever and ever. What more could we need, as long as we had each other?"

She moved closer to him, feeling strangely safe, his arm about her, staring out at the shadows as they sidled close along the shelves around them.

"But life isn't small," her father went on. "It's huge. Quite gigantic. At least, it *should* be so. . . And it's up to you to make sure it is. You and Victoria, you have the whole world at your feet." He squeezed her tightly to him for a moment, then released her. "I'll miss you, of course. But you'll be in good hands. I know you'll be in good hands . . ."

There was, however, something in his tone that suggested he had his doubts. "Of course I'll be in good hands," she cried. "Bruno is so dear." She sought for words that would convince him. "And so rich and clever too."

"All the same, Mattie, if I ever thought for one moment that he didn't love you . . ."

"But he does love me." So her father really *did* have his doubts. How dare he? "Would he have waited so patiently all these months if he did not love me?" she demanded fiercely.

"Only you can answer that, my dear. And I must trust your judgment." He touched the tip of her nose lightly with one finger. "So Bruno *does* love you. And I'm just an old fuss. But you should not blame me for caring. You know how dear you are to me."

Troubled still, she racked her brains for things that might be worrying him. "If he's been a bit distant recently, a bit absent-minded, it's only because he's so tired these days. He hasn't been sleeping well, he tells me."

"That's it, then." He patted her cheek, made a great show

162

of being reassured. "And it's natural enough, you know. Before marriage men are restless creatures ... Forgive me if I embarrass you, my pet. I realise it's not for a father to say such things. But—"

"You don't embarrass me, Papa." She meant it. "I'm no longer a child, you know. I do realise that marriage is far more than simply keeping house together."

"Good. Good ..." He paused. "It grieves me, though, that your mother and I have been able to give you so little—not even the fine wedding that should be by rights our duty. But ..." Ruefully he shrugged his shoulders. "There are the presents, of course. I warrant you won't be disappointed. All the same—"

She reached up to kiss his cheek. "Hush now, Papa. You've given me so much. You know you have."

"All the same, my pet, I had thought that something a little more personal ..." He dipped into a pocket, brought out his watch to which a small sticky paper bag was adhering. He peeled the paper off. "I'd like you to have this watch, my dear. It was your grandfather's."

"But Papa—"

"No buts, my dear." He unclipped the chain from his waistcoat buttonhole, polished the watch on his sleeve, then pressed it into her hand. "Take it, Mattie. It's little enough, God knows. Look at it sometimes, when you're far away, in your new home."

His voice broke. She hugged him then, feeling the watch's warm, comforting presence in her hand. It was, she knew, his most treasured possession. And she must not refuse it.

They stayed for a while in the dusty, shadowed dimness of the shop, speaking little, simply savouring the sweet sad pleasure of their closeness. Storing up their remembrance of it. Then her father slid down off the counter, picked up the candle, and together they went slowly up the narrow stairs, fortified against the anxieties of the coming night, and of the day that would follow.

As things turned out, the day of Mattie's wedding passed

163

without even the smallest hitch. The carriage fetching them was on time, Mrs Skipkin was ready for it, Vickie looked enchanting in her bridesmaid's dress of blue velvet, and there was even a little wintry sunshine to grace the occasion. Mattie herself wore silk of the same blue as her daughter's velvet, with a paler over-skirt scooped up in bows at either side, and a low wide bodice to show off her neck and shoulders. And on her head a cascade of pale blue veiling, held in place by a simple fillet embroidered with pearls.

The ceremony was quiet, and the reception in Bruno's tiny Mayfair house that followed it. He had invited his few London friends, mostly business associates, and Mattie had an uncle and aunt up for the day from Southend, and Aggie Templeton, her closest neighbour back in her Bacon Street days, and of course Toby Grimble, and also her mother's friend Mrs Wassnidge from the shop on the corner of Creek Road. The party was small, therefore, but very happy. And Bruno was, as always, an excellent host. So that the entire occasion constituted a most perfect beginning to what everyone agreed was the most perfect of marriages. The prettiest of bridesmaids, a delectable bride, a handsome, considerate groom . . . and the three of them so clearly united in love as to warm the hearts of everyone present.

It seemed a pity, certainly, that the ill-health of the groom's mother had prevented her from attending. Also, so some thought, that her wedding gifts were being kept for the bride's eventual arrival in her new home. But it was of course thoroughly sensible not to ship costly goods all the way from Bavaria, only to transport them immediately back again. And Germans were always such sensible people, were they not?

As for Mattie herself, she cared nothing about such matters. She moved through the events of the day in a daze of purest joy. And it was, secretly, a relief to her that her new mother-in-law was not present. There would be time enough in due course for that particular meeting . . .

And so the party ended, and the farewells were made, and

164

the cab set out for London Bridge Station, trailing a veritable kite's-tail of nuptial old boots and rusty tin cans. By way of further tokens of good fortune, they happened to pass a chimney sweep en route, wheeling his barrow. Lettering on it proclaimed his name to be A. Cattermole, and he had a sooty-headed young assistant trotting by his side. Bruno let down the cab window and laughingly gave Vickie a penny to throw to the boy.

From the station a first-class compartment was booked through to Folkestone, where one night would be spent before the Channel crossing to Ostend. There the Hotel Metropole had reserved the bridal suite, and a room immediately alongside for the third member of the party.

In some ways it might have been better for the couple if Vickie had stayed in London with her grandparents, to be sent over later with a suitable travelling companion. But Mattie had decided, and Bruno had agreed with her, that such a separation would have got her little brand new family off on quite the wrong footing. And anyway, the child's excited presence on the train journey was a gentle diversion, sparing Mattie and Bruno the usual awkwardness of a relationship made new in the eyes of God and man, yet remaining for the moment substantially the same.

For there was still a certain shyness between the wedded pair. And a diffidence also, now that the moment of their love's consummation was so near at hand, that made haste both unsuitable and unnecessary. So that even after the hotel was reached, and supper eaten, and little Victoria put to bed and sat with until she was contentedly sleeping, Mattie still lingered with her husband in the strange grand private sitting room, fascinated by its painted ceiling, its thickly swagged curtains and massive gilt furniture. As Bruno's wife she supposed she would soon get used to such magnificence. But for the moment she could only tiptoe softly about the room, touching things and peeping timidly at the reflection in a dozen gilded mirrors of the dark-haired, richly-dressed stranger

165

that was she. And of the fine, handsome man who sat quietly watching her.

Until at last, when the moment was right, Bruno rose from his chair and came to her, and took her in his arms. He kissed her then as he had never kissed her before, with his whole being, openly acknowledging his passion, and un-ashamed, secure in the certainty of her acceptance, of her whole-hearted welcome. Which she gave him gladly, for it was her only desire.

They parted by common accord, moving hand-in-hand to the big, brocade-hung fourposter in the next room. And there, standing in golden lamplight, he undressed her gently, with infinite tenderness, till she turned to him finally, quite naked, and looked up into his eyes trustingly, proudly, knowing that they were on her body, and that he found her beautiful.

He too, quickly as naked as she, was beautiful. And sud-denly shy again, so that it was she now who turned down the lamp and led him forward, drawing him down on to the bed beside her, beneath its covers, between its silken sheets. Then his hands touched her, and at once the fever of their shared need possessed them fiercely.

It raged long, for it had been long in the making. A secret world, all-consuming and all-fulfilling, beyond words, beyond thought itself, where none but the lovers themselves should trespass. And in its aftermath there came to Mattie the purest contentment she had ever known. Also, in the awareness of her husband's peaceful, drowsing presence by her side, a new confidence, that the depth of her love should have been tried and not found wanting. And finally, not shocking her at all, the warm, tranquil knowledge that she and Bruno would make love again, that a whole married lifetime of love-making lay before them.

Soon Bruno slept, his head on her shoulder. She listened to his gentle breathing, and her heart was filled with a protective-ness as old as humanity itself. He was her husband, her lover ... and her child. She would guard and spare him always.

It was a dear determination, but vain alas—for, as she was to learn all too soon, there are perils from which no man can be spared, and no woman either. Mysterious perils, that only the sleeping mind is prey to.

She had lain for perhaps half an hour, dozing contentedly, when she was jerked suddenly into full wakefulness by a violent movement at her side. Bruno moaned then, his limbs twitching convulsively as he slept. She leant up on one elbow, gazed anxiously down at him. In the dim light she saw his face strangely contorted, the sinews of his neck iron-rigid as he wrenched his head from side to side. He moaned again, then cried out loudly, confusedly, words in his own language that she could not understand.

She stroked his brow. "Hush, my dearest," she whispered. "I'm here, my precious. Hush now . . ."

But his nightmare held him fast and he cried out again, and his arms beat feebly at her in his sleep. She saw sweat start out upon his forehead, and the frantic rolling of his eyes beneath their closed lids.

Now she was frightened. She shouted at him, and shook his shoulders. "Wake up, Bruno. For God's sake, wake up!"

He shouted also, the one word, unmistakable, *"Mutti!"* then lay transfixed, trembling horribly, so that she feared a fit had come upon him.

For a moment she was aghast, not knowing what to do. Then, acting upon blind impulse, she slapped his face as hard as she was able. At once his trembling ceased. He opened his eyes, reared up in the bed, gazed wildly about him.

"Mutti?"

"You were dreaming, Bruno. Your mother is not here. It is I, Bruno. It is your wife . . ."

He stared at her. Fleetingly his eyes focused. "Matilda?"

"You've had a bad dream, my dearest. But it's over now."

"A dream . . . Yes, a dream . . ."

His head fell back on the pillow and he seemed at rest. But he made no move towards her, and when she tried to cradle

167

his head again she felt his whole body tense against her. So she let him lie. His eyelids flickered, and a moment later he had gone back to sleep. Indeed, as she now realised, he had never been properly awake.

His rejection had hurt her. But it was of no significance, she told herself, being only a part of his dream. Poor man, she thought drowsily, to have his sleep so troubled. But it wouldn't happen again. Her love would protect him from his nightmares in the future, and bring him peace. And so, comforted by this thought and by the many recent proofs of his passionate devotion, she soon could let her own mind, healthy and inviolate, return to dwell on happier, more sensual matters, dismissing his brief distress as the merest passing fancy. So that her own sleep, when at last it came, was without fear, calm, and filled with soft delight.

While her husband, on some mysterious level aware now of her defencelessness, granted her his outward peace as the most precious gift remaining to him, and slept by her side like a stone, mutely fighting dreams of darkness.

2

BEFORE SETTING OUT on the final stage of their journey, the
two-day ride by diligence across the monotonous plain to the
foothills of the Bavarian Alps and then up the winding valley
of the Isar to Garmisch-Partenkirchen and at last to Mittenwald, the Beckers rested for a couple of nights in Munich.
Mattie thought it a welcome relief simply to be spared for a
while the ceaseless lurching of the stage, the noise and the dust
and the boredom. Vickie too was glad of the break, having
found travel hardly broadening to her mind: since she was
too small to see out of the windows of the coach unless she sat
bolt upright, she had spent most of the time slumped between
her mother and some strange German, invariably fat, either
dozing or struggling with intricate string cat's cradles that never
seemed to come out right.

Munich however, for all its jolly marching bands and noisy
beer halls, was a grey, unwelcoming city, its narrow streets
lined with enormous, barrack-like houses, its sky sagging
darkly above steep rooftops and countless thickly smoking
chimneys. November in these parts was a bitter, joyless month.
The clouds were heavy with snow, yet so far none had fallen.
Instead the streets were scourged with harsh flurries of grit-
like hail, blown horizontal in the icy wind. Where, Mattie
wondered, was the bright, wintry beauty Bruno had promised.

They set out again on December 2nd, skirting Starnberg
and the wooded shores of Lake Würm, which was indeed as
large and picturesque an expanse of water as Mattie could
have hoped to see, and then on across a seemingly endless,
wind-swept plain. They travelled all day, the prospect ahead

169

of them shrouded continually in heavy mist. Till suddenly, just as twilight was falling, Bruno leaned out of the carriage window and pointed excitedly.

"Matilda, Vickie—look there. At last the mountains!"

Mattie looked, and saw nothing. Nothing but the dreary plain, and beyond it the mist. She was on the point of drawing her head in again when a curious darkness high up in the sky caught her attention. She raised her eyes. And there, impossibly vast, towering range upon range above the mist, snow-streaked and merciless, were the mountains Bruno had promised. She stared incredulously, craning back her head. The sheer size of their dark immobility took her breath away. They were not mountains, they were gods, petrified, infinitely menacing.

Vickie pushed her head out too, her impatient protests quickly silenced as the awesome beauty of the spectacle bore in upon her. She gazed, struck dumb, and her mother beside her, until their eyes, streaming with tears in the icy wind, could gaze no more.

They ducked back into the carriage and Bruno pulled up the window on its leather strap. He smiled proudly. "The people here call them the sleeping giants. What do you think of them, eh?"

Mattie wiped her eyes. "They're very beautiful," she gasped. "But rather frightening."

"Good ... it is good that you should feel it." He nodded. "Otherwise you might not give our giants the respect they deserve. If you are to live among them, *mein Liebling,* it is important always that you feel respect. Do that and you will come to no harm." He turned to Vickie. "You must think of the mountains as your friends, child. They are always there, and they never change. They see when you are good and when you are not. And still, like all true friends, they never judge you ..."

He laughed then, and ruffled the child's hair. "So you can tell them all your secrets. And maybe—if you're very lucky—

170

they'll tell you some of theirs in return."

Mattie looked at her daughter, saw her wide, thoughtful eyes. She wasn't sure that this sort of magical talk was good for a little girl. But it was Bruno's way never to make it quite clear when he was joking and when he was serious. And certainly Victoria seemed to love to listen to him.

There were other aspects of Bruno's behaviour, too, that troubled Mattie. During the nine days of their journey he had become increasingly distant, increasingly moody. There had been times, indeed, when he seemed totally absorbed in some private, inner disputation, and scarcely aware even of her presence at his side. Times also when she thought she had caught upon his face a brief look of distaste, almost of loathing ... though whether it was directed at her or at the direction of his own thoughts she had not cared to discover.

Not that these moments lasted beyond a short second or two. And when they had passed he was at once his old self again, amusing, tender, endlessly thoughtful. But she knew they were growing more frequent, the closer he came to his home. It was almost, she thought, as if he secretly dreaded the approaching reunion with his mother.

Then again, his dreams had continued to plague him. On their second morning, in Brussels, after the joy of their love-making had been followed once more by the same anguished nightmares, she had thought to mention them over breakfast in the hotel dining room. His response had been to deny all memory of them—and with such forcefulness as to convince her, if not that he was being wholly truthful, then at least that she should enquire no further. If his sleep before their marriage had been as troubled as this, it was little wonder that he had become so tired and over-wrought that even her father had commented on it.

And so night had followed night, her fear at what his sleep would bring so looming over her as soon to taint the happiness of what came before. So that a desperation had come to their

171

caresses, a frantic cleaving of the one to the other, as if in a vain attempt to build defences against some nameless, unacknowledged horror . . .

Now Mattie raised her eyes to her husband's face across the carriage, and rejoiced to see it at peace. It was always the same when he spoke of his home, or of the mountains. The very thought of them seemed to exercise a calming magic. Now he hummed contentedly as he hunted in his pockets for his pipe, and took it out, and began to fill it. Mattie smiled to herself. He had not smoked at all in London. But here in Bavaria, where every man puffed upon some elaborately swooping pipe, even the man up on the box who drove their diligence, Bruno had fallen in enthusiastically with the local custom. He was indeed becoming more Bavarian, redder of cheek and brighter of eye—and brusquer too, it must be admitted—with every mile they traversed.

He lit his pipe and sat back, puffing luxuriantly. "The mountains are not as near as they seem," he said. "It will be tomorrow morning before we are truly among them. And late tomorrow afternoon before we are actually in sight of *das Haus Graugipfel*."

"It stands on a cliff above the town, does it not?" Anxiously Mattie pushed pins back into her wind-disordered hat. "I'm so looking forward to seeing it. And—" she faltered only very slightly "—and to meeting your mother."

He leaned forward. "*Meine liebe* Matilda, let us be honest with one another. You are doing nothing of the sort. Rather are you dreading the encounter."

She admitted it, timidly nodding her head. Already, after such a short time married, she was unsure of him. But on this occasion all was well, for he laughed and slapped his thigh.

"She will give you a bad time, Matilda. It would be foolish to pretend otherwise."

"But you'll stick by me, Bruno. You *will* stick by me?"

"*Natürlich*." He blew her a kiss. "*Siehst du—bald wird alles gemütlich sein.*"

172

She smiled a little doubtfully. He'd spoken very simply and clearly, so that she'd understand. But would things really so quickly be comfortable in the house Graugipfel?

"*Ohne Zweifel hast du recht,*" she managed bravely. "*Aber—*"

"*Aber was*? But what, my dear? Mutti is no monster. You'll win her heart as easily as you won mine. *Das Mädchen auch* —who could resist your little Victoria?"

He leaned back in his seat, happily surveying the two of them. At that moment, however, little Victoria was tugging urgently at her mother's sleeve.

"Please—I feel a bit sick, Mama," she whispered.

Mattie looked down. The child's face was deathly pale, and she was swallowing nervously. And the explanation, unfortunately, was clear enough, for not only was the coach lurching abominably but the atmosphere inside it was rank with the smell of Bruno's tobacco.

Mattie cleared her throat. "Bruno—could we have the window open, please? And could you perhaps not smoke your pipe for a while?"

He raised his eyebrows. "I'm sorry. I did not know it troubled you."

"Not I," she murmured hastily. Then she raised her voice. It was ridiculous that she should be so fearful. "I'm afraid Victoria is feeling unwell. Your pipe is ... well, it's very strong, don't you think?"

His jaw hardened. He stared at the child, coldly considering. "I see ... But if your daughter and I are to get on together, then she's going to have to get used to my pipe, is she not? And the sooner the better."

"But Bruno, it is not simply your pipe—it is the motion of the carriage also. The child cannot help it."

"There I must disagree with you, my dear." He smiled calmly. "She must learn to help it. I am her stepfather—do I not deserve some consideration?"

Mattie straightened her back. She was no longer afraid, she

was furious. "I shall not argue with you, Bruno. If you cannot see the difference between consideration and the unpleasant need to vomit, then I have nothing further to say to you."

"But I, Matilda, have a great deal to say." His icy smile was now an insult. "I am not, I tell you, an English husband—one of those 'gentlemen' always so polite, always so nice, because in their hearts they are afraid of their wives—these are the laughing-stock of Europe. And I am not one of them. It is I who will be master in our home, I who will receive the consideration ... Do you understand?"

Mattie stared at him, appalled. Certainly he had been brusque with her during their journey, but never before so harsh and unreasonably domineering. In this present mood he was an utter stranger to her. A cruel, unpleasant, stupid stranger. She'd not waste time wondering why he had become so. Neither would she argue with him. Instead she leaned forward, firmly lowered the window, and leaned out.

"*Halten Sie, bitte,*" she called up to the coachman.

Abruptly the diligence came to a halt, bouncing on its springs. Mattie had the brief, triumphant thought that her husband must be regretting even the small amount of German he had so far taught her—he would hardly care to humiliate himself by arguing with his wife in front of the coach driver. Then she quickly opened the door and bundled her daughter out.

The poor child was paler than ever, and near to tears. Mattie walked with her a short distance down the road, then they leaned together on a gate. The coach had stopped near the edge of a forest, and the bitter wind brought with it a fresh sweet smell of pine needles. Mattie spread her cloak over Vickie's shoulders.

"Feeling better now, my pet?"

Vickie nodded. Indeed, colour was already returning to her cheeks. Then she bowed her head. "I want to go home," she muttered.

174

Mattie clenched her jaw. She had at that moment been thinking the identical thought. "You won't feel like that once we get to Mittenwald," she said brightly, speaking to convince herself quite as much as her daughter. "It's the strangeness of everything that's so upsetting. But once we get settled, and the snow comes ... it'll all be so beautiful once the snow comes."

She stared out at the grey plain, the dark, menacing line of the trees, a distant group of houses clustered round the unfamiliar, stumpy onion dome of a church. What a bleak, wretched landscape it was ...

She gave little Vickie a comforting squeeze. "We'll make the very best snowman," she said, "once the snow comes."

Behind them footsteps sounded on the stony road. Bruno had left the coach and come slowly after them. He cleared his throat. "How is the little one?" he enquired awkwardly.

Mattie kept her back turned to him. "Better, thank you," she replied briefly.

"I'm ... I'm glad to hear it." He moved forward to lean on the gate at Mattie's side. "I must tell you that I suffered from travel sickness myself as a child. I should have remembered sooner how unpleasant it can be ..."

Then, suddenly, he pointed with his stick to where there was a quick flash of red in the bare hedgerow. "There, Victoria —do you see that robin? He's just like the robins you have in England, is he not? You can see how he fluffs out his little feathers against the cold."

He was, Mattie realised, doing his best. And his best was good enough, for in a moment Victoria, blessed with childhood's happy resilience, had forgotten her griefs and was watching the bird as it hopped closer, its eyes as bright as little jet beads. Mattie relaxed, felt her husband's arm steal softly about her waist. He lowered his face till his lips brushed her ear.

"Forgive me," he whispered. "I am not myself. The journey has been long ... And perhaps, also, I am a little afraid to

175

arrive at our destination. *Meine Liebste*, I want you so much to like it." He nuzzled the side of her neck. "Please forgive me, Matilda."

She leaned towards him, her heart pounding. When he spoke to her so, she could forgive him anything.

Victoria too, looking up at him now, seemed to bear no grudge. "Will the little bird understand me, Step-papa, if I talk to him in English?"

Bruno smiled. "He looks a wise little bird. Why don't you try him and see?"

Just then, however, one of the horses behind them snorted loudly and pawed the ground, so that the robin was startled and flew away, swooping in long low curves across the field. Victoria waved it goodbye, and called "Grüss Gott" after it, the way she'd been taught. Then the three of them turned, and walked slowly back to the carriage. And Bruno's pipe was not produced again for the rest of the journey, either on that day or the next.

They spent the night in a roadside tavern, warm and cosy, smelling of mulled wine and wood smoke. It was a big square building beneath wide eaves, with a long wooden balcony and white plastered walls, and a big gaudy picture of St Christopher painted on the plaster. Many of the houses now had paintings on them, of girls in bright dresses dancing, of cows in green meadows, of men wearing strange short trousers held up with braces. They were simple, happy pictures, and Mattie began to feel that the countryside wasn't really so bad, and that the people who lived in it must be simple and happy also.

They came to Mittenwald, as Bruno had promised, late the following afternoon, having left the tedium of the plain and climbed steadily all day through the mountains. It was a large village, set beside the narrow, swiftly-flowing Isar, at the bottom of a valley deep in the midst of towering, snow-capped peaks. Its streets were colourful, lined with houses all with carved wooden shutters at their windows and the same wide, red-tiled roofs, and in the centre stood the strangest, prettiest little church, its walls pink-washed, its tower decorated with bright statues and marble pillars and vivid ornamental stonework, all painted on to its simple plaster with such skill as to deceive the eye at a distance entirely.

Twilight was falling as they clattered through its busy, cheerful streets. Looking from the carriage, Mattie seemed to see violin workshops on almost every corner, and men in green aprons hurrying between them. In the window of a passing bakery there were rich brown loaves, handsomely plaited, and tray upon tray of the little star- and moon-shaped *Kuchen* that looked so tasty but that she had already discovered were really rather dry and uninteresting.

Suddenly Bruno ordered the carriage to a halt, and pointed up between a gap in the houses. "Your future home," he said. "*Das Haus Graugipfel.*"

Mattie craned her neck anxiously, saw a hill rising steeply at the edge of the village, its top surmounted by an abrupt granite cliff upon which, set among thick pine trees, a lonely house rested massively, looking out across the valley. It was a house typical of all the others in the district, but somewhat larger, foursquare, with two ranks of balcony surrounding it, sheltered beneath darkly-overhanging eaves. From several of its chimneys pale columns of smoke rose, slender and straight in the still evening air, and yellow light shone out from its windows, warm and bright and welcoming.

It was a sight far happier than Mattie's chill imaginings, and she turned eagerly to Vickie, craning beside her. "See, my pet —that's where we're going to live. Isn't it pretty? Just like a cuckoo clock?"

Victoria, however, had her reservations. "But it's so high up, Mama. What if it tumbled, all the way down to the bottom?"

Bruno heard her and laughed. "It's not going to fall," he told her. "My grandfather built it. It's been there a long, long time."

Mattie hugged her daughter, and laughed also. But she under-

177

stood the child's doubts. Obviously the house wasn't going to fall—but there *was* a fearsome, almost menacing aspect to it, perched there on its cliff-top. Sinister somehow, not really like a cuckoo clock at all. Just now the windows were bright, but she could easily imagine them darkened, blankly staring. And the trees that crowded so thickly about it were mysterious, and very black against the mountains beyond. All this the child had seen, and not been able to find the words for.

Mattie shivered slightly, then laughed again, firmly banishing such eerie fancies. "I wonder what Grossmama Becker has ready for our supper," she said. And then, comfortably, "I'm sure it will be something good. And I'm so hungry."

The carriage moved on, soon leaving the village behind and starting the climb up a narrow track on the wooded hillside. The track wound steeply to and fro so that, close as the house had seemed, it was nearly twenty minutes before they finally reached it. Darkness was close, and as the carriage stopped a man in shirt and breeches lumbered out with a lantern to greet them. He opened the carriage door and held out a massive hand to help Mattie down. She accepted it shyly, her few words of German suddenly deserting her. Bruno leapt out after her, bringing Victoria with him. They stood together in a small awkward group on the paved terrace at the side of the house.

Bruno rubbed his hands. "Matilda, *mein Liebchen*, this is Günther. He looks after everything while I'm away—and when I'm here too, for that matter." He turned to the other man and said a few quick, unintelligible words.

Mattie swallowed. "*Guten Abend, Günther*," she said carefully. She was unused to servants and suddenly felt horribly out of her depth.

Günther bowed stiffly. "*Grüss Gott, Frau Becker*," he muttered, his eyes on the ground. She could not be certain if his manner was resentful, or simply embarrassed. He was not a tall man, but enormously broad, with a great barrel chest and arms like a blacksmith. A shock of dark hair grew low

178

upon his forehead, giving him a slightly simian appearance, but his eyes beneath their heavy brows were by no means un-intelligent.

Bruno thrust Victoria forward and introduced her also. Politely she held out her tiny hand. *"Grüss Gott,"* she piped. *"Wie geht es Ihnen?"*

Günther shuffled his feet, briefly took the offered hand in his huge fist, mumbled a reply, then swung quickly away to help the coachman with their luggage. Mattie did not catch his words, but evidently the little girl did, for she nudged her mother and giggled.

"He called me Fictoria," she whispered. "He called me Fräulein Fictoria."

Mattie frowned. "Hush now," she chided. "It's the German way. And it's very rude to whisper." But she was secretly very proud of the child, who had managed the German for "How d'you do" in a way that shamed her grown-up mother.

Bruno moved them on towards the house. "Vickie's made a friend there, I think," he murmured. "I'm very pleased. If Günther likes her then there is much she can learn from him. Well done, both of you."

He put an arm round each of them and led them forward, into their new home.

Just inside the heavy oaken front door two more servants were waiting: the cook, Magda, and a girl, Paulina, scarcely more than a child herself. Mattie found that she was trembling, but greeted them in their own language as best she could. The moment when she must meet her new mother-in-law was almost upon her. Bruno helped her and Vickie out of their travelling cloaks, then questioned the serving girl.

"My mother is waiting upstairs," he said, turning to Mattie. "She lives on the first floor mostly, you understand. The view out over the valley is a great consolation to her."

Mattie nodded, then followed him in silence past an ornate grandfather clock and up the broad, polished stone staircase.

179

She had never seen a house so spotless, so formidably clean. In the hallway behind her there was a stamping of feet as luggage was brought in from the waiting carriage.

Upstairs corridors led away in four directions from a broad, uncarpeted landing, its plain white-washed walls hung with guns and hunting trophies. Lamps stood on ornate wooden brackets, and there were sturdy little rustic chairs, their backs decorated with simple, brightly-painted posies. The whole house smelled powerfully of soap and lavender-scented beeswax. Bruno took Mattie and her daughter down the left-hand passage, paused outside a varnished pine door, knocked upon it, and entered. Mattie followed him in, peered anxiously past his broad back, into a large, plainly-furnished sitting room, well-lit, with a big square wood-stove in one corner, covered with vivid tiles.

"Matilda! *Endlich kommst du.* At last you come. Welcome, my dear."

The voice was strong, strangely deep and husky, almost that of a man. Mattie looked round, saw a tiny shrunken figure in a wheel-chair by the window, huddled beneath a multitude of embroidered shawls. It seemed scarcely possible that the voice she had heard could belong to this small, wizened person. Yet the little old lady was moving towards her now, one trembling, mittened hand outstretched.

"Come in, come in ... Welcome! And the little girl too. *Ach, wie schön* ... so pretty she is. Do not be afraid, *Bubli.* See—I am almost as little as you are."

Mattie stepped forward quickly, feeling she needed to protect Vickie from such determined benevolence. All the same, if this was to be the extent of the 'bad time' Bruno had promised her, she'd have little grounds for complaint. "Good evening, Frau Becker. I hope I find you well. We ... we are a little late, I fear. The journey today took longer than—"

But her mother-in-law ignored her, manoeuvring her chair expertly past and bringing it to a halt in front of Victoria.

180

"You, then, are the little Victoria—named in honour of your fine English queen, *nicht wahr?*" She nodded approvingly. "And as for me, you shall call me Grossmama ... I sit in this chair because my legs are not strong like yours. But I get about very well all the same, *siehst du.*" Neatly she spun her chair in a complete circle on the spot. "Is that not clever? *Ja, ja*—and I have a violin too. Perhaps one day I will let you play it."

Now Bruno intervened, laughing as he stooped and tenderly kissed his mother's forehead. "Not so fast, *liebe Mutti.* The poor child won't know what to think. And besides, in a moment you will have me jealous. I am your son, Mutti. Am I not welcome also?"

"Pfui." The old lady snorted. "*Sons*—they are nothing but trouble ..." She paused, craned up to look into Bruno's face. "But of course you are welcome. *Immer wilkommen*—" Briefly her voice broke and her crabbed hands sought his in a sudden fierce gesture of possessiveness. "A son is always welcome," she muttered.

Then she turned to Mattie, her voice strong again. "Is that not so, Matilda? Men are nothing but trouble, yet we poor women would be useless without them?"

Mattie, scarcely knowing how to answer this extraordinary old creature, made vague affirmative noises. She had been prepared for almost anything—a grudging welcome, even downright rudeness, anything other than this strangely hectic wish to please. Could it be, she wondered, that Bruno's mother, like herself, was actually *nervous?*

While all this time Victoria, not at all as overcome as Mattie would have expected, had been watching her grandmother with wary interest, seriously, not in the least amused by the old lady's antics. Now, suddenly, "I had a papa of my very own once," she declared. "He was killed dead, you know."

In the awkward silence that followed Mattie stared at her daughter, quite bewildered. The child's ears must be longer than she'd thought. Certainly she herself had never said a word about the brutal manner of Albert's death. Obviously Victoria must have overheard some grown-up conversation. But why should she bring it up now, of all times? When everyone about her was clearly doing their best to make the occasion a happy one?

It was the old lady who recovered first. "I'm sure you loved your papa very much, my dear," she said gently. "But now you have a new papa. He is good to you, is he not?"

"No." Vickie clenched stubborn little fists. "No, he's not good."

Mattie started forward, appalled. "What a dreadful thing to say, Victoria. Of course he's good."

"No, he's not. Sometimes he doesn't like me one little bit. He smokes his nasty pipe at me, and ... and ..."

"Be quiet this instant." Mattie was horrified. Usually her daughter was so biddable, so eager to please. Such ungraciousness was quite unlike her. And inexcusable. "You're a wicked, ungrateful girl."

She glanced despairingly at Bruno, then turned back to the child. "You'll say you're sorry, Victoria. At once, now."

Vickie glared obstinately at the floor, saying not a word. And again it was Bruno's mother who intervened. "Perhaps Victoria is right. Perhaps her new papa does not always like her, not all the time. People do not *always* like people. I'm sure she knows that. Perhaps she does not always like her new papa either."

The simple justice of this seemed to appeal to the child, for she shifted her feet and had the grace to appear ashamed.

Frau Becker leaned forward, put a hand on her shoulder. "And as for the nasty pipe, I know it well. And I too do not like it. But men smoke pipes and we women must put up with it. For that, *Bubli*, is what life is like."

Bruno had walked away to the stove, his brow thunderous. Now he swung round. "*Genug ist genug, Mutti.* Enough is enough. Victoria has been a very rude, naughty little girl." He folded his arms. "Well, everything is strange here, and she is perhaps upset, so we will say no more about it. But it is wrong for you to appear to take sides against me."

"*Sides*? You talk of sides?" His mother glared at him, then launched into a spate of rapid, incomprehensible German. Mattie looked wretchedly from one to the other, locked in sudden mutual bitterness, then at her daughter, the unhappy cause of it all. Vickie was weeping now, and hunting piteously in her pinafore pocket for a handkerchief. Dear Lord, only a quarter of an hour in the house, and already there were dissensions. Mattie went to her, took her in her arms.

Abruptly the old lady checked her tirade. She stilled the angry jerking of her hands and carefully composed them in her lap. "I forget my manners. Also, this talk of sides is *dumm*, stupid. A family should not have sides ... And we are all one little family here, *nicht wahr*?"

Bruno scowled at her, still furious, but didn't speak. Silence descended, uneasy, watchful. Mattie found her daughter's handkerchief for her and helped her blow her nose. For all that Frau Becker's words had been a salutary reminder, a reproof to herself as well as to her son, Mattie wondered why she did not wholly believe in them. Possibly she was trusting Victoria's judgment above her own—and Vickie had clearly remained unconvinced by the old lady's great show of goodwill. Certainly children often saw things that their elders missed.

Or was it not perhaps simply the Continental effusiveness that had seemed false to her?

Mattie straightened her back. "Frau Becker, I—"

"Please, my dear. If we are to be friends then you must call me Gustavia. And we are going to be friends, I hope?"

"You're very kind." Mattie lowered her gaze. Kind indeed —but embarrassing also. Which was foolishness really, for had not Bruno once laughingly described embarrassment as 'the British disease'? And if the old lady truly wanted to be friends, then why should she not say so? How difficult life was ...

183

"*Gut, gut* ... so that is settled, then." Seemingly Mattie's awkwardness had gone unnoticed. Frau Becker turned her wheel-chair and moved briskly away to the table. "You must all be very hungry. I shall ask for dinner to be served in half an hour." She picked up a little silver cow-bell and rang it. "And first Bruno will show you to your rooms. Just to begin with I have put you on the valley side, where the view is best. When you have been here a little while and got to know the house you will be able to choose for yourself, of course."

Bruno's anger had passed. He moved away to the door, then turned, clearly uncertain. "You mean the rooms that were Liesl's?" he queried.

His mother met his gaze. "*Ja gewiss*—I mean the rooms that were Liesl's. Günther has made them ready. They have stood empty long enough."

For a moment it looked as if Bruno were going to argue. Then he relaxed. "You're right, of course."

Just then there was a knock upon the door and the girl Paulina entered. Frau Becker gave her rapid instructions. She bobbed a curtsey, then left. Bruno looked at his watch.

"Dinner in half an hour. And what of Trude? Will she not be eating with us?"

"If she gets back in time." Mattie detected a certain coldness in his mother's strangely baritone voice. The old lady turned to her. "Trude is my companion, you understand. She went down to Mittenwald this afternoon with a basket of her dolls. She dresses them for sale in the shops. She should have been back long ago. But she has a cousin in the town, and she stays to gossip."

The disapproval now was unmistakable. Bruno smiled, reproving her gently. "You should not blame her, Mutti. It must be lonely for her, up here. She's still young, you know."

"Trude? Young?" Frau Becker laughed shortly. "I do not believe that Trude was ever *young*."

Bruno frowned. Then he looked over his mother's head at

Mattie, shrugging his shoulders in mute apology. "Shall we go, my dear?"

Mattie took Vickie's hand and joined him at the door. Behind them the old lady's chair squeaked restlessly on the bare polished boards. "You're very pretty, my dear. You and your daughter. I approve my son's choice. This house has much need of pretty faces."

Mattie halted, embarrassed again. But Bruno spoke up quickly, sparing her confusion. "Mutti, you must know, is a great connoisseur of pretty faces. She herself was once the prettiest woman in all Bavaria."

They made their escape then, and Bruno took them back along the passage to the landing, and then on to their rooms. The prettiest woman in all Bavaria? Mattie tried to imagine it, and could only see a wizened old creature with wrinkled, in-drawn lips, huddled in a wheel-chair, immobilised, sustained only by some bright fire of indomitable inner energy. And what might be the force, the motive behind that fire she could not think . . .

She was grateful, however, that her mother-in-law seemed well disposed towards her. She hated to think what it would be like to have such a powerful old lady as an enemy.

There were three rooms, a large central living room and two smaller bedrooms leading off on either side, in which their luggage was already waiting. Hers and Bruno's room contained a dressing table, a wash-stand, a massively carved wardrobe and, beneath great mounds of feather quilt, two single beds. Mattie had been prepared for these—Europeans, she knew, considered the English double bed to be a barbarous piece of furniture, thoroughly unhygienic. But she looked away quickly, reminded uncomfortably of the coming night. Double or single, it would make no difference to the unspoken fear, the desperation of their coming together.

The furniture in Vickie's room was brightly decorated, like the chairs on the landing, but equally simple: a bed, a chest, a wash-stand, a cupboard. Indeed, to someone accustomed to Victorian well-filled rooms the bareness of the entire house was very strange. But at least it was relieved by vivid, hand-stitched rugs upon the floors, and richly-carved surrounds to the doors and windows. In Vickie's room, also, there was a fine doll's house standing in one corner and, on top of the chest, a magnificent musical box, its lid open to display the shining brass cylinder inside, and a battery of other little bells and cymbals, each with its own complicated mechanism.

Bruno stood in the doorway, suddenly quiet, watching Vickie as she wandered listlessly about the room, touching things, peering in the corners. "The doll's house was Liesl's," he murmured, a sudden spasm of pain crossing his face. Then he shook his head, as if to get rid of unwelcome thoughts. "It will be good for it to be played with again. Liesl would have liked that."

He took Mattie's hand and they went away, leaving the child to her anxious exploration. Briefly they stood by their sitting room window, staring out at the lights of the town far below them in the dark valley. Mattie found it a prospect curiously unreal, dream-like in its black immensity. Perhaps Bruno shared her feeling, for after a moment he opened the window and leaned out to pull the shutter firmly across. At once the room seemed warmer, its lamplight more golden. As he crossed to stir the logs in the big tiled stove there was a knock upon the door and Paulina came in, bringing hot water in great gleaming copper jugs.

Fifteen minutes sufficed—by her father's watch laid in a place of honour on the dressing table—for Mattie to wash and change out of her travel-stained clothes. Bruno was still busy shaving, so she left him and peeped in on her daughter. The child was sitting on the bed, sulkily kicking her legs. She had made no attempt at all to get herself ready for dinner. Her portmanteau had been opened, but its contents simply lay in untidy heaps on the floor. Mattie controlled her irritation, seeing it was no time for reproaches. Vickie was obviously tired out—she'd be herself again in the morning.

Mattie bent down and picked up one of the expensive dresses Bruno had bought in London. "Shall you wear this one, my pet? Grossmama would like to see you looking your best."

Vickie hunched her shoulders resentfully. Suddenly she slipped down off the bed and darted past her mother, across the sitting room and out into the corridor. Mattie ran after her. The poor child must be caught, and brought back, and somehow made presentable. It was almost dinner time—already there were savoury smells in the air, and the distant clatter of plates and cutlery.

As Vickie reached the head of the staircase a woman was coming up from below, carrying an empty basket. The little girl halted abruptly. Mattie caught up with her, took her arm, looked down at the woman's head, tight blonde plaits pinned severely around it.

Mattie cleared her throat. "Good evening," she said, then remembered, and began again. "*Guten Abend. Ich bin—*"

But the other woman had stopped dead, recoiled back against the wall, and turned up to her a face that was the ugliest she had ever seen. A broad nose began some distance below massively lowering eyebrows that joined in the middle. The mouth was wide and coarse, the chin heavy and deeply cleft. And the eyes, startlingly blue, that might have been the woman's redeeming feature, distilled such violent emotion that Mattie found herself cowering away, dragging Victoria with her.

Was this then Trude? Bruno had mentioned that she was not beautiful. Kindness, no doubt, had moderated his judgment. Certainly he had not prepared Mattie for such as this.

The woman recovered herself, advanced up the few remaining stairs. She put down her basket, stretched out a thick, raw-boned hand, and laid it on Mattie's arm. And all the while her expression did not change, and her eyes burned with the same terrifying intensity. Mattie tried to back away, but was held fast.

The woman began to speak, almost in a whisper, glancing

187

furtively back down the stairs as she spat out the words in urgent, incomprehensible desperation. Mattie gaped at her, tried to interrupt, tried to say that she did not understand. But the woman took no notice. She was pulling at her now. Was she angry? Was she pleading for help? Or was it a warning she was trying to give? Mattie could not tell. And still the gutteral flow of words continued.

Until suddenly, for no apparent reason, it ceased. The woman let go of Mattie's arm. Her whole body sagged and she stood, head drooped, staring listlessly down at the ground. Her feet scuffed the boards, like those of a girl caught out in some childish wickedness.

Mattie looked away, over the woman's shoulder. And saw Frau Becker, sitting quietly in her wheel-chair outside the door to her room. She was gazing at the woman's back with a curious fixity.

For a time the tableau was maintained, nobody moving. Victoria clung to her mother's skirt, faintly whimpering ... Then, abruptly, Frau Becker propelled her chair forward down the corridor and the spell was broken. She spoke a few soft words to the woman in German, then turned to Mattie.

"You must not mind Trude, my dear. She means no harm, and she serves me well. But her mother was frightened by a *Hase*—how does one say ... by a *hare*, I think. So she is strange sometimes. But not dangerous. Never dangerous."

She touched Trude's back slightly and the other woman stiffened, then swung round and walked silently away, leaving her basket where she had put it down, by the head of the stairs. Frau Becker waited till she had gone. Then she smiled calmly up at Mattie.

"Shall we go to dinner, Matilda? Bruno will be joining us in a moment, I'm sure. And Trude too, when she has composed herself. I want you and Bruno to tell me all about London ..."

She did not wait for an answer, but led the way firmly in the direction of the faint clatter of dishes. And Mattie followed her, holding tight to little Vickie's hand. She no longer cared whether the child had washed and changed her frock or not. Neither did she care to enquire what had so distressed the pathetically ugly Trude. The day had been long enough, and complicated enough, and worrying enough, without that.

3

IT SNOWED THAT night. Not a great deal, but enough so that when Bruno got out of his bed in the morning and opened the shutters, their bedroom was filled with a pure pale radiance. And along the top of the balcony rail outside the window Mattie could see a thin layer of white, like sugar icing. She lay, snug beneath her mound of feather quilt, and fondly watched her husband as he stood in his long nightshirt before the open window. Everything, she thought, is going to be all right. He's a fine man, broad-shouldered, handsome, dependable.

And his mother too—accepting a strange young English-woman into her home couldn't be easy, yet the old lady was going out of her way to be pleasant, and to make her feel welcome. All through dinner the previous evening she had plied them with eager questions, about London, about Mattie's family, about the wedding. And afterwards she and Trude had brought out the presents: silverware, fine linen, and a beautiful diamond necklace, a family heirloom, for Mattie herself. When Trude had first come to the table, inevitably there had been some small awkwardness, but the companion had quite got over her earlier distress and had done her best to take an interest—albeit remote on account of her complete lack of English—in the proceedings.

Only little Victoria, tired out and grumpy, had refused to share in the general goodwill. And Gustavia—by the end of the meal Mattie had been calling Bruno's mother by her first name as if she had known her all her life—had seen this and sympathetically suggested an early night for all three of them.

Even Mattie's own bedtime, which she had been dreading, was unanxious, spared the painful conflict between delight at her husband's touch and dark forebodings. For she and Bruno, exhausted after their long day, went by common consent to their separate beds, and slept almost instantly. Certainly it was not good that, so soon after her wedding day, she should have been relieved not to make love. And the passion itself, the ecstatic sharing of their bodies, she still profoundly desired. But the peace, the simple animal contentment that should have come after it, without that ... As it was, she was simply content in the knowledge that on this occasion Bruno's sleep had apparently been untroubled the whole night through.

Thinking of Bruno's dreams reminded her of her own. She stretched luxuriantly, and sat up in bed. "I had the oddest dream last night, Bruno," she said, yawning.

He didn't reply, but continued to stare out of the window. Yet it seemed to her that his attitude had become strangely rigid.

"Don't you want to hear my dream, then?"

He turned to her then and she held out her arms, wanting him to come to her. She felt warm and happy, and very loving. She wanted him in the bed beside her. Surely there, in the bright joyful light of morning, they could make love without fear?

He stayed by the window. "Tell me your dream then, *meine Liebste.*"

Her hair was falling forward over her face. She pushed it languorously back. "I dreamed that I had woken up. I lay here, in this very bed. And someone, somewhere, was playing a violin. I knew the melody, too." She began to sing it to him, a bittersweet, hurdy-gurdy little tune.

She had hardly sang five notes before he interrupted her. "It wasn't a dream," he said shortly, turning back to close the windows. "My mother does not sleep very well. Sometimes, in the middle of the night, she seeks consolation in her violin. No doubt it was she whom you heard."

191

"Oh, the poor thing. How sad for her."

He frowned. "Sad for those who hear her also. She plays very badly."

He crossed to the bed and stood looking down at her. She tilted her head up, lips parted, expecting his kiss. Instead he lightly touched her on the shoulder. "It is time you were getting up, my dear. Mutti is an early riser. And she does not like breakfast to be kept waiting."

He looked for his slippers, put them on, and his dressing gown, and padded out of the room.

For a moment she was angry, disappointed. He had rejected her. He did not love her any more . . . Then common sense came to her rescue, and she smiled wryly. A long married life lay before them, all the time in the world for love-making. And besides, there was Vickie to think of. The child would be awake by now, and eager to start the first day in her new home.

Bruno stuck his head back round the door. "The tune, by the way, is '*Ach, du lieber Augustin*'." He smiled at her. "An old Viennese folk tune. It's one of Mutti's favourites." He blew her a kiss, and was gone again.

Mattie was content. He'd realised his abruptness, and tried to make amends. Humming the tune once more, she got out of bed and, going to the dressing table, began to brush her hair. She looked in the mirror. Suddenly, in the room behind her, a shadow seemed to move. She swung round, the notes dying on her lips. The room was unchanged, still and silent, bathed in soft snow-light . . .

But she remembered now when she had first heard the melody. *Ach, du lieber Augustin*—Albert had sung it to her, all those years ago, when they were newly married. And again, the old blind beggar had played it at his funeral.

She shivered. Even now there were memories that had the power to disturb her. She hurried to the wash-stand, splashed icy water on her face and hands. All at once she wanted to be dressed before Bruno returned. She did not examine her reasons, she simply knew that she did not wish him to see her naked.

She was in her morning dress of soft grey wool and standing at the window, when he entered. And all her strange, uneasy thoughts had been banished from her head by the view that presented itself there. She was looking not at the snow-covered, picture postcard rooftops of the town below, but rather up at the breath-taking mass of the mountains that towered blackly opposite, on the far side of the valley. They soared literally up to the sky, their peaks hidden in the clouds, their sheer faces seamed with jagged fissures, snow-encrusted, rising in gigantic up-thrust splinters of rock from the trees below. Awesomely silent, timeless. A group of sleeping giants indeed ...

Bruno came to stand behind her. "The Karwendel mountains," he murmured. "Not a presence to argue with, I think. But a protection also. In their shadow no great harm can come. They were here when the world was created. And they'll still be here when we poor humans are long forgotten."

For herself, Mattie found the thought hardly comforting. But she could understand now the fascination this place had for her husband—to be brought up beneath such mountains must make the world outside seem pitifully tame and unimportant.

She turned away. "I must see how Vickie's getting on," she muttered, seeking the reassurance of small, everyday matters. Then, at the door, she remembered something she had been meaning to ask him, and paused. "Trude's a strange woman," she said. "I first met her yesterday, before dinner, on the stairs. She behaved in the most extraordinary fashion. She seemed to be trying to tell me something terribly important—you wouldn't have any idea what it might have been, I suppose?"

Bruno took off his dressing gown and threw it on the bed. "Trude's been here alone with my mother for a long time— and I'm sure Mutti isn't the easiest of employers. She's probably got all manner of strange ideas in her head ... I'll ask her what it was, if you like."

193

G

His manner was casual. Mattie wondered if it was too casual. If he did question Trude, Mattie found herself doubting if he would report the outcome truthfully. "It's not important," she said. "We hadn't been introduced—perhaps she didn't even know who I was."

It was a poor excuse, for who else could she have been but Bruno's new wife? And Vickie his stepdaughter? But she hated not to trust him, and did not want to put it to the test.

She left him then, and went slowly across their sitting room. It was pretty by daylight, warm and spacious. Why, she thought, do I suddenly not trust my husband? Is it because ever since he came into this house he has been different, watchful in my company? Yet there was really no one aspect of his behaviour that she could point to and say, this, this is what has changed between us. So she shrugged, and told herself she was imagining things, and went on into her daughter's bedroom.

Vickie was up and dressed, talking to her doll 'Melia on the broad window seat. Mattie saw how small she was, and vulnerable, and was filled all at once with a fierce protectiveness. Whatever happened, Vickie must not suffer as a result of the new life her mother had chosen for herself. Mattie ran across the room and hugged her daughter tightly.

Vickie wriggled away. "I've been telling 'Melia what steppapa said about the mountains. How they will see if she's naughty, and come down and punish her."

As far as Mattie could remember, that was not at all what Bruno had said. Somewhat the opposite, in fact. Nevertheless, glancing up at the dark, threatening mass that loomed outside the child's window, Mattie could sympathise with the reinterpretation. Sleeping giants, perhaps—but what if the giants should ever wake?

Discreetly she changed the subject. "I hope you slept well in your nice new bed."

"Very well, thank you Mama."

"And isn't it grand, having a fine big room, all of your very own?"

"Very grand, Mama."

"Then you think you're going to be happy here, my pet?"

Vickie had been fussing with the doll's dress. Now she looked up. "Mama," she said, "why is your voice all funny?"

Mattie gaped at her. "Funny? In what way funny?"

"As if you were talking to a baby. I'm not a baby, Mama. I'm six."

Mattie relaxed and laughed. So her anxiety had really been so obvious. "If you're as old as that, my pet, then it's high time you learnt how to plait your own hair. Come over to the mirror and I'll show you."

Which was no answer at all to the child's question. But served very well to distract her suspicious little mind.

Breakfast was served by the window in Gustavia's sitting room—a meagre meal of coffee and rolls and butter that was the European way, and that Mattie and her daughter were just going to have to get used to. The sun was well up by now, bathing the Karwendel mountains in its friendly, pinkish glow. They looked far less menacing, almost approachable.

After breakfast Bruno had to go down to the factory in Mittenwald, and Mattie was eager to go with him. If the making of violins was his principal interest, then she wanted to learn about it as soon as possible. She was determined to be a good, useful wife to him. Gustavia suggested that Vickie might prefer to stay up at Graugipfel, and help Günther feed the chickens and collect eggs from their houses up in the woods. To Mattie's surprise, the child agreed. So Günther was summoned, and seemed willing, and Victoria went off with him, her tiny hand in his huge one, chatting happily, ten words of English to one of German, which he appeared to understand perfectly.

"You don't have to worry," Bruno told Mattie. "I said she'd made a conquest. Besides, all Bavarians love children. He'll be chopping firewood and sweeping snow off the paths later, and Victoria can help him. And there's always Mutti here if she should need anything."

Mattie watched the child go, quelling her misgivings. Her daughter was quite right: she wasn't a baby any more, she was six.

Outside on the terrace at the side of the house a pony and trap were waiting, harnessed and ready. Bruno handed Mattie up, then climbed in beside her. "There's not enough snow yet for the sledge," he explained as they set off, bells jingling brightly in the frosty air. "We'll get along fine if we go carefully."

The morning was perfect, sunlight striking diamonds off the thin layer of white on the trees all around. Mattie sat up very proud and straight beside her husband, warm as toast in the snug winter coat and fur hat he had bought her, breathing deeply, every breath like champagne, ecstatically savouring the excitements of the journey. If her new life was to be like this, then she was well pleased with it.

In about ten minutes they came to the outskirts of the town. Everybody seemed to know her husband, and welcome him. A dozen times or more his "*Grüss Gott*"—God be thanked—rang out. To be answered by a cheerful wave and, "*Der für uns gestorben ist.*" Mattie asked him what it meant.

"They're saying, 'Who died for our sake'," he told her. "We're a very pious folk, we Bavarians. And none the worse for that, *siehst du.*"

They clattered into the centre of the town, where the snow was already turning to slush and dripping from every shutter and window ledge. On many rooftops Mattie now noticed great logs lying across them, tied at either end, dark against the melting snow. Always eager to learn everything she could about this strange new country, Mattie pointed them out to Bruno, and asked their purpose.

He smiled. "They stop the roofs blowing away in the autumn gales. And when the snow is thick they stop it sliding in great quantities down into the streets below. A big slide could be dangerous, you see."

Soon they came to the Becker violin factory. It was a long low building, set beside a mill stream off the river, its machinery powered by a small water wheel. As Bruno turned into the courtyard a boy ran out to hold the pony's head, quickly followed by a stoutly smiling gentleman with waxed moustaches, his head totally bald, wearing a long green overall. Mattie liked him at once—he reminded her so strongly of the bandsmen back in London, in Hyde Park.

Rapid German followed, to and fro, of which Mattie caught almost nothing. Except that they were once more being made welcome. Until Bruno suddenly turned to her. "Forgive me, my dear. This is Herr Zunderer, my factory manager. You'll be glad to hear that Herr Zunderer has a little English ... Herr Zunderer, this is my wife."

He jumped down, helped her after him. Herr Zunderer took her hand, bowed deeply over it. "How do you do, Frau Becker. A peautiful day, iss it not?"

"Very beautiful, Herr Zunderer. And Mittenwald is beautiful also. I'm very happy to be here."

They stood for a moment in the courtyard, and she quickly discovered that Herr Zunderer's English was limited virtually to the few words he had already spoken. It scarcely mattered, however, for what he lacked in language he amply made up for in goodwill.

They went forward into the factory, and at once Mattie's nose was assailed by a multitude of powerful, exciting smells. There was wood, of course, the sharp tang of pine sawdust. And glue also, which bubbled cheerfully over countless burners. And, growing stronger as they progressed from room to room, the rich, pervasive odour of varnish; linseed oil, and turpentine, and gum arabic, and certain other ingredients that Bruno told her were a closely guarded secret.

"It's principally the varnish, my dear, that gives an instrument its tone. The colour, also, helps to sell the instrument.

The British like their fiddles brownish-red. The French prefer a more orange shade. We may not be making Stradivarii, but at least we do understand the international market."

In the first room they came to, violin bodies were being cut to templates, tops and bottoms, six at a time, from great sheets of seasoned pine. Bruno picked one up, sighted along it, held it to his cheek, then had a few words with the man operating the machine. Then he explained to Mattie, "Early winter is a bad time—the air is damp, you see. In a few weeks, when the really cold weather comes, you can pick up a piece of wood out in our store yard and see the dampness frozen out of it. You can wipe it off in fine white crystals."

They went on then into the other rooms, where massive presses curved the newly-cut tops and bottoms, where the bridges were made, and the S-slots cut, and the bass-bars fitted under the tops of the instruments to improve their resonance. The scrolls and pegs, it seemed, were carved elsewhere, and brought in every week. And then the assembly benches, thick with steam, where the sides were miraculously bent, the centre posts fitted, and the purfling added. This last, Mattie learnt, was the name given to the decoration around the violin's edge. In the great violins this purfling would be minutely inlaid—ebony and satinwood, and sometimes even mother-of-pearl. The humbler Becker, however, made do with applied designs, incised and stained.

"But at least," Bruno told her, "our finger boards are still made of expensive ebony. Some manufacturers use birchwood. They make a cheaper instrument—and after a while the players get splinters in their fingers."

And so, finally, to the varnishing rooms, the vapour in them so heavy that it caught Mattie's breath, and made her eyes smart. Here the previous day's batch of violins hung in rich, golden-red rows, drying. And here, as everywhere else, Bruno was continually alert, his glance taking in the smallest detail, while Herr Zunderer anxiously hovered a pace or two behind, always ready with a quick, incomprehensible word of comment or explanation. In the owner's absense he had done his work well, it seemed, and Bruno was pleased.

The inspection over, Bruno paused at the foot of a steep little staircase leading to the offices overhead. "And now, *mein Liebchen*, the real work begins." He smiled and rubbed his hands. "The accounts, the letters, the order books ... I have been away a long time—there will be much to catch up with. Perhaps you would care to walk in the town for an hour or so. There is a coffee house on the Hochstrasse, near to the church. Come back here at twelve, shall we say?"

He kissed her forehead, then went away up the stairs with Herr Zunderer, at once deep in earnest conversation.

Mattie did not mind being so dismissed. Her husband was an important man. He had his work to do, of which at the moment she knew next to nothing. A walk round the town would give her a chance to practise her German. And besides, her head was so full of strange sights and new impressions that she needed a time on her own, just to sort them all out.

She wandered away, down narrow cobbled streets, the houses on either side adorned with baroque frescoes, mostly angels here, and smiling saints, and blue-gowned Madonnas. Certainly the inhabitants of Mittenwald were a pious folk. She paused to look in shop windows. They reminded her that Christmas was near at hand, for decorations were on sale, silvered pine cones and little centre-pieces of fir twigs and bright red berries. In one shop there was a display of beautiful wood carvings, and tiny dolls dressed in the national costume. Perhaps these were Trude's, Mattie thought, and marvelled at the minute stitches. So plain a woman, and so awkward, to be such an artist.

At last she came to the church. Outside it there was a monument, a fine bronze statue of Matthias Klotz, the man who had first brought violin making to the town. She stooped, tried to make out the wording on the plaque. She had a pocket dictionary but it was sadly of little use, for the letters on the plaque were ornate and quite defeated her. She sighed crossly, and

199

straightened her back. And was addressed suddenly, in English, by a man she did not at first recognise.

"Frau Becker, I believe. So you have reached Mittenwald in safety." He caught the blankness of her gaze and bowed. "Baron von Kronstadt. We met in London, at the Egyptian Hall."

"Of—of course," she stammered, blushing deeply. It was his clothes that had confused her. At the concert he had been every inch the aristocrat, immaculate in evening dress, with a crimson sash across his gleaming shirt-front. Now he wore waistcoat and breeches, and a coarse green apron speckled with wood-shavings. And he carried a spokeshave in his hand.

"Of course—Baron von Kronstadt. I'm delighted to meet you."

They shook hands. "I see you have been admiring the good Herr Klotz," he said. "We're very proud of him. They say he worked under Nicolò Amati in Cremona. Now we call Mittenwald the German Cremona. It is self-flattery, perhaps. But many of our fiddles are nothing to be ashamed of."

From him, as from Bruno, she noticed the ever-present undertone of slight apology for their new factory methods. It seemed to her foolishness, for this was the second half of the nineteenth century, and had not the Great Exhibition in the Crystal Palace only five years before proved to the world that this was truly the age of factory production, and proud to be so?

"I'm sure you yourself make very beautiful violins, Herr Baron," she told him.

He spread his hands in mild self-deprecation, indicating his spokeshave. "I like to think so. As you see, I work at the bench myself—whenever I can get away from tedious business matters, that is. I carve the scrolls. And I have a studio also. I learned wood-carving under Meister Hansen. But I'm only a dilettante, really . . ."

He smiled, and ran fingers through his untidy shock of dark hair, raising a small cloud of sawdust. Mattie remembered his unfriendliness back in London—here he seemed almost boyishly open, eager to tell her everything about himself. Whatever coldness there might be between him and Bruno was clearly on her husband's side alone. She must ask him about it later. Meanwhile it would be better if she did not appear too friendly.

And besides, although Inspector Gradbolt had given her no reason, this was a man he had once wished to question about Albert's murder ... What a long time ago that now seemed.

"Bruno is at the factory," she said, glancing uneasily back along the street. "I was taking a walk round the town before returning to him."

"How pleasant." He inclined his head. "And forgive me—I should have congratulated you on your marriage. I am sure you will both be very happy. You were married only recently, I believe?"

"Eleven days ago. We came out to Bavaria immediately afterwards."

"And such a journey ... But it will be many years, I fear, before the nations of Europe forget their squabbles and establish a civilised train service."

She felt happier, seeing how quickly he had taken her lead. Their conversation now was safely impersonal.

"I hope I'm not keeping you from your work, Herr Baron."

"Not at all. My position does bring with it certain privileges." He bowed. "Among them the chance to speak with a beautiful young woman."

She lowered her eyes. So he paid a pretty compliment too. Yet still Inspector Gradbolt's suspicions lingered to disturb her.

"Herr Baron," she said suddenly, "my first husband—you said you heard him play. He was often in Mittenwald, I think. Did you get to know him well, by any chance?"

Her companion stiffened. "Not well at all," he said coldly. "I spoke to him, of course, but only in the most general way. Why do you ask?"

201

"Well ..." Dismayed by the sudden change in the tone of their meeting, she hardly knew how to answer. "Well, he always spoke most kindly of Mittenwald. I ... I wondered who his friends might have been."

"He had many, I feel sure. But I, alas, was not one of them."

For a moment they stood in silence. Then he cleared his throat. "Normally I would have been happy to ask you to take coffee with me, Frau Becker. Or a cup of chocolate. But ..." He fumbled with his watch, though the clock on the church above them was clear for all to see. "But as it happens I—"

"Pray think nothing of it, Herr Baron." If he wanted to get away she certainly would not keep him. "As I told you, my husband is expecting me very shortly."

"Ah. Yes, of course." He bowed again, stiffly, and took her hand. "Till we meet again then, Frau Becker. *Aufwieders'n.*"

"*Aufwieders'n*, Herr Baron."

He turned, and walked quickly away down the Obermarkt. She watched him disappear from sight, her brow creased in a puzzled frown. How curious it was, the transformation that had been wrought by the mere mention of poor Albert. Disapproval, was it, that she, so soon remarried, should have dared to bring up the subject of her first husband? Or had Inspector Gradbolt perhaps been right, and it was something else, something more sinister?

She continued her exploration of the town, but her enjoyment of it was spoiled, and she arrived back at the factory well before the hour Bruno had appointed. Her thoughts were in a turmoil. More than anything else she had wanted to leave the past behind her. Yet now, through her own foolish questioning, it was all fresh in her mind again.

She waited in the courtyard till noon, ignoring the curious glances of the factory hands who came and went, carrying in wood and huge drums of varnish from the outer store rooms. Only when she heard the church clock strike did she go in, and up the stairs to Bruno's office. She was determined to be

202

a sensible wife, and punctual, and not intrude upon his working hours.

She found Bruno and Herr Zunderer still immersed in ledgers, huge red-bound books, their pages crowded with row upon row of spiky German writing. But her husband willingly laid them aside, and called for the pony and trap to be made ready, and questioned her cheerfully about her morning's adventures. She answered as well as she could, keeping the matter of Baron Rudolph von Kronstadt until they were alone together, embarked upon their journey home.

Then, as the pony plodded up the track between the trees, its breath little puffs of steam in the clear, sunlit air, she turned to Bruno. "You'll never guess whom I met in the town," she said lightly, gaugingly. "The man who was at that concert in London—Baron von Kronstadt."

"Oh yes?" Bruno flicked irritably at the reins. "Dressed as a common workman, no doubt."

Her love for her husband did not entirely blind her to his faults. One of which was snobbery. "It seems he's a wood-carver," she said primly. "In which case his clothes seemed really quite sensible."

Bruno should be careful—her own father, after all, had been happiest in his little room behind the shop, working with his hands.

Bruno snorted derisively. "Artistic nonsense! Mere self-indulgence. And it's brought the family business almost to the point of ruin."

Mattie raised her eyebrows. Certainly in London the Herr Baron had hardly seemed to be almost at the point of ruin. Nor that morning either—he radiated such confidence, such an air of unquestioned prosperity.

"*Siehst du*," her husband went on, "he comes of a very ancient and noble line. Yet he plays at life. Plays at it ... It's the despair of his poor sister."

His 'poor' sister—the word suggested to Mattie that Bruno's

203

quarrel was with Baron Rudolph himself, rather than with his family. Unless . . .

"And the despair of his wife too?" she queried.

"Wife? I ask you—what family would allow a daughter of theirs to marry such a *Dummkopf* . . . such an idiot? He thinks himself so superior, so different, so much wiser than other men. A wood-carver, indeed! His father would turn in his grave, I tell you . . . Frankly, Matilda, I would rather you did not speak with him again."

He flicked the reins once more, sharply, in his disgust. Which the sensible pony ignored completely.

Mattie decided to take the bull by the horns. "Bruno," she said, "please tell me what is the cause of this quarrel between yourself and the Herr Baron. If I am to support it then I should surely know the reason."

"The man is a fool. Is that not reason enough?"

Mattie shook her head. "No, Bruno. It is not enough."

Abruptly he pulled the pony to a halt. "In that case, Matilda, I shall have to tell you the story. It is not pretty, so perhaps you will remember that you insisted."

He paused, stared down at the snowy ground, his expression so brooding that already Mattie was regretting her curiosity. But it was too late now. And anyway, if there was not truth between them then there was not anything.

"You must know," he said at last, "that I had a sister. *Schön wie eine Blume*—beautiful, and innocent too. And the Herr Baron bewitched her. Liesl was eighteen years old. They met in the woods in secret . . . I need not spell out to you what happened at these meetings. She was innocent, as I have said, and he was quite without conscience. The match was impossible. Mutti knew that. But by the time the affair came to light the damage was done. So Mutti resigned herself to the inevitable."

Mattie caught her breath. "You mean—?"

"No, not that. At least the good God spared us that. But the association was the subject of common gossip all over the

204

town. I was only sixteen at the time, but I remember it well. The sly glances, the laughter ... So Mutti sent for the Herr Baron, and put it to him. When was the wedding to be?"

The pony shifted its feet and he broke off to swear at it angrily. Mattie waited, knowing only too well what was to come.

"And the noble Herr Baron pretended not to understand her. And when she made herself clearer he denied everything. They were friends, he and Liesl, nothing more—*Du lieber Gott*, if only my father had been alive! Or I myself had been older ..." He beat his gloved fists together. His fury was terrible, like nothing she had seen in him before.

Timidly she touched his arm. "Perhaps the townspeople were wrong," she said. "Perhaps he spoke the truth."

Bruno swung round on her. "And you'd call my sister a liar too, would you?"

She subsided. The confrontation was vivid before her eyes —the philanderer and his victim ... an old, old story, but none the happier for that.

"But he stuck to his denials," Bruno went on bitterly, "so what could we do? After all, he was the noble Herr Baron, and we mere merchant upstarts."

Mattie held her peace. There were levels to this quarrel that only now were becoming clear. *Le droit de seigneur* ... A dilettante, Baron Rudolph had called himself. The high-born dilettante and the serious, hard-working commoner—

"At least they never met again," Bruno concluded. "Of that we made quite certain. And in time the talk died down. It does, you know, even in a town like this. But Liesl—her pain did not fade so easily. Which is why—"

He stopped, muttered savagely in German under his breath. Then he whipped up the pony, and they started their slow climb again up the winding path through the woods.

He hunched his shoulders. "So now you know, Matilda, why it is that I would rather you did not become a friend of ... of that man."

205

She did indeed. Bruno had every justification. But there was still, she realised, none for Inspector Gradbolt's suspicions. The Herr Baron would scarcely have murdered poor Albert, a virtual stranger to him. Unless of course he had lied when he said he'd hardly known him. Even so, to wait six years, and then pursue him to London and cruelly do him to death ... it made no sense at all.

No, the inspector was wrong. Her common sense confirmed what in her heart she knew was true. A philanderer Baron Rudolph might well be, but a merciless killer, never.

The rest of the journey was passed in an uneasy silence. Only as they were turning on to the terrace, swept clear of snow now in long, even brush-strokes, did Bruno again acknowledge his wife's presence.

He twisted round on his seat. "Do not tell Mutti of your meeting with the Herr Baron, if you please," he said coldly. "The very mention of his name distresses her. And the doctor has been most insistent that she should not be upset."

At that moment the clatter of the pony's hooves brought Vickie running from the house, her eyes bright with excitement.

"Mama, mama—ich habe die Hennen besucht, und viele Eier gefunden!"

Mattie stared at her blankly, then turned in despair to Bruno. He smiled thinly. "She says she's been to visit the hens, and found many eggs."

Vickie looked up at them, hopping like a little bouncing ball. "Did I get it right? Günther told me what to say—I did get it right, didn't I?"

Bruno swung down out of the trap. "Quite right, my child." Absently he patted her head, then went round the trap and offered Mattie his hand. "What did I tell you? Günther will be good for her. Children learn so quickly—in a few weeks she'll be speaking German like a native."

Mattie stepped down, laughing. "But it's a fine thing," she said lightly, "when I can't understand my own daughter—"

206

"That is nobody's fault but your own, my dear. The language is simple enough, if you will only apply yourself to it."

Which bitter remark Mattie chose to ignore, she could do no other. But it hurt her. It was Bruno's fault that her German progressed so slowly—recently he had become so impatient with her stumbling attempts that she had been forced to give them up.

She squatted at Vickie's side. "What else have you been up to this morning?" she asked fondly, shutting Bruno's unkindness from her mind.

"We . . . we bundled up sticks." Vickie's hands moved busily in the air. "And I helped sweep the snow away with the big broom. There isn't quite enough yet for a snowman, but Günther says there soon will be."

"Does he so?" Mattie was quite fascinated by the apparent ease with which the little girl and the great lumbering Bavarian were able to communicate.

Vickie hopped some more. "And then Magda gave me hot chocolate and *Kuchen* in the kitchen. And then . . . and then . . ." She wrinkled her brow, trying to remember. Suddenly her excitement evaporated. "And then Grossmama sent for me," she said, becoming strangely quiet.

Feeling Bruno's watchful presence, Mattie prompted her. "What did Grossmama want, my pet?"

"I . . . I don't know. Nothing, really."

"I expect she just wanted to see how you were getting along." Mattie stood up, anxious now to be on the move. "Shall we go in, Vickie? I've been to see Step-papa's violin factory and I want to tell you all about it . . ."

They walked together into the house. Even as Mattie talked, however, she was painfully aware of Bruno's following close behind, his disapproval hanging over the two of them like a dark cloud. It was useless, she knew, to expect tact from a six-year-old child. All the same, Vickie did have a depressing way of making everybody's life just that much more difficult . . .

Things became easier over lunch. Gustavia was at her most charming. And Bruno's mood gradually lightened as the meal progressed. Mattie decided that she'd chosen a bad time to ask him about the Herr Baron—if he was anything like her, by the end of the morning he must have been quite frantic with hunger. The tiny breakfasts here made a wretched start to the day.

Gustavia was telling them about her own morning "... And then, at eleven, I had the little *Bubli* up to visit me. She'd been playing in the snow—you should have seen how pink her cheeks were."

Bruno looked up from his plate. "What did you do together? Did she behave herself?"

"Behave herself? *Aber natürlich*—of course she did. I got out one of your old books, Bruno, and we looked at it. The *Strewelpeter*—what that is in English I do not know."

"Shock-headed Peter." Bruno made the translation. "I remember well how I loved that book."

His mother nodded. "It must be said, I think, that Victoria did not. I do not blame her—the German in it is not easy. I feel sure it was all a great puzzle to her."

Mattie froze. Shock-headed Peter was one of her daughter's favourites—they'd had the book in London and she knew it almost by heart. Why then should she pretend ...? Mattie risked a glance across the table at Vickie: the child was looking straight at her, a curiously wicked smile, almost triumphant, upon her angelic lips. It seemed that whatever her grandmother did, she was determined to be awkward. Quickly Mattie looked away again. And wisely said not a word.

In the afternoon Bruno had to return to the factory. Gustavia suggested that since the weather was so beautiful perhaps Mattie and Victoria might care to accompany her upon an outing to the lake. A ten-minute walk, no more—and they could see if the water was freezing over again. It had been frozen a few weeks earlier, but then there'd been a sudden thaw.

Mattie agreed, firmly, for the two of them. The sooner that Vickie learned that she must get on with her grandmother the better.

Günther carried the old lady downstairs, managing in his bluff way to bring a certain dignity even to this humbling business. Trude followed with the wheel-chair, and Gustavia was installed once more, beneath an even larger number of blankets and shawls. They set off up the path, Günther pushing the chair, Mattie and Victoria hand-in-hand at its side, Trude trailing listlessly behind. Mattie found the ever-silent presence of Gustavia's companion faintly disturbing. Naturally she was silent, having no English. But need she have given up so totally her earlier attempts, in spite of this lack, to be a part of the family group?

As they climbed the snowy slope, suddenly, quite unexpectedly, the lake came into view beyond a low rise, gleaming darkly between the trees. Mattie stopped dead, entranced. It was like a scene from a fairy tale, the water still and mysterious, ringed with forest, beneath towering cliffs of white. And far above, sparkling in the afternoon sun, the breath-taking peaks of yet another mountain range.

Vickie disengaged her hand and ran on ahead, leaving tiny, precise footprints in the virgin snow. Mattie called after her anxiously, but was ignored.

Gustavia shaded her eyes with one cramped, mittened hand. "Let the child go," she said peaceably. "She can come to little harm. Even if she falls in, the water is very shallow at the edges."

Mattie did as she was told. But she didn't wholly share the old lady's complacency—in even the shallowest of water a little girl could manage to get extraordinarily wet and cold. Nevertheless, her mother-in-law's calm good sense impressed her—and saddened her also, on account of the contrast it made with the permanent near-frenzy of her own mother.

Victoria, of course, did not fall in. When they came up with her she was standing on a strip of shingly beach at the water's edge, throwing pine cones in and watching the ripples. Günther left them then, his work done, and returned to the house. Gustavia shifted herself painfully into a more comfortable position beneath her blankets.

"What a pity—it is not yet cold enough for the water to freeze, I see. Later there will be ... I do not know the English word—*Schlittschuhlaufen* ... ?"

Mattie hazarded a wild guess. "Skating?"

"*Ja, ja* ... skating. Do you skate, Matilda?"

Mattie admitted that she did not. In the London she had lived in there had been little opportunity.

"Oh my dear, it is the best thing. You are so free. It is like ... like flying!"

Mattie stared out across the water. She could imagine herself, curving effortlessly across the ice, swooping like a bird in the bright cold air ... And realised with a sudden pang of sadness that her mother-in-law, who loved it so, would never skate again.

"I shall learn," she said stoutly. "And then, if it is safe, I shall take you out upon the ice with me. It will be as if we are skating together."

She turned suddenly to the old lady then and, catching her unawares, saw her face transformed by a look of the intensest loathing. Baleful. Utterly malignant. It passed instantly, so quickly that Mattie felt she must surely have imagined it.

Gustavia smiled. "That's very kind of you, my dear. But I think not. Even with the good earth beneath me I do not always feel secure. One is so vulnerable, you understand."

Mattie stared at her. No, she had not imagined the loathing. What then had she said that was so wrong? Her suggestion had been the kindest, the most generous she could think of. Could it be that the old lady secretly resented her youth, her vigour? Or simply that she sometimes found the kindness of others a burden?

She moved away, leaving Gustavia to herself, a lonely, defiant figure. Trude, she noticed, was keeping her distance, back among the trees, almost as if for safety. Yet she could not have understood their conversation. And there was nothing else in this beautiful place to be wary of.

Mattie went to her daughter. They stood together, listening to the stillness, scarcely daring to breathe. Not a branch stirred, not a bird sang. Just the silence of the mountains, pressing in on their ears ... Feeling a sudden urgent need to break the spell, Mattie stepped back off the beach, bent down, scooped up a handful of snow, formed it into a wet little ball, and threw it at Vickie. The ball hit Vickie's arm, fell dully on to the shingle, its white imprint still on the child's sleeve. And still Vickie did not move.

Until slowly, as if in a trance, she turned. And, waking from it, was instantly animated, her eyes bright, her smile ecstatic. "It's the most beautiful place in all the world, Mama. It must be. It *must* be."

And Mattie laughed, and agreed that it probably was, and thought herself foolish to have been momentarily so panic-stricken, and ran with the little girl back to her grandmother's wheel-chair. Children had their own magic, their own secret places.

They talked for a while, the old lady telling them of skating parties, of picnics on the ice—a happy, uncomplicated family again. Then Mattie took the wheel-chair and they started back down the path. Only then did Trude emerge from the trees and roughly grasp the chair's handles, easing Mattie wordlessly to one side. Which Gustavia noticed—as she noticed everything—and shrugged at resignedly.

"We must be patient," she murmured. "If people cannot be beautiful, then at least they like to be necessary."

A perceptive remark, Mattie thought. Yet, beneath its show of tolerance, needlessly cruel and bitter.

It was not until much later, when she was alone in her room with Vickie, waiting for Bruno's return from Mittenwald, that its probable reason occurred to her. For Liesl, according to Bruno, had been extremely beautiful. And yet clearly had

211

thought herself so unnecessary that she had taken her own life. And in the lake too ... Mattie was no longer surprised at the abrupt change in Gustavia's mood. The wonder rather was that she could ever bear to look upon the lake again.

What, Mattie wondered, had been the cause of Liesl's tragic despair? Hardly the treachery of her lover, Baron Rudolph, for she had suffered that, and recovered from it, ten years before at least. What then? Obviously her brother had worshipped her, and her mother also. What then had prompted her to do such a terrible thing? Mattie sighed. Certainly the subject was too painful for her to ask either Bruno or the old lady. And nobody else in the household spoke any English. And besides, it was really none of her business.

Mattie sighed again, then turned her attention to little Victoria, who was vainly trying to tie skates made of hairpins on to the feet of her long-suffering doll, 'Melia.

"Shall I fetch the musical box from your room?" Mattie suggested. "We could wind it up and listen to some tunes."

Vickie bent closer over her doll. "I'd rather not, Mama," she said, her tone affable yet curiously positive.

At which her mother, understanding her reasons in a sudden moment of shared experience, was silent. And closed her eyes, trying to shut out the bright little nursery tune, hauntingly pretty, that echoed eerily down the dark corridors of her mind.

4

Ach, du lieber Augustin ... the musical box had played scarcely four notes before Mattie knew she had been right to trust her intuition and not insist that her daughter listened to it. Although a couple of days had elapsed before she could contrive to examine it alone, without Victoria in earshot, when she finally did lift the lid and start the mechanism she recognised the tune instantly. She stood for a while, looking down through the box's glass inner panel, watching the long brass cylinder revolve, the little hammers rising and falling as the melody was embellished with a great number of unsuitable drum rolls and cymbal clashes. What a harmless little oom-pah-pah tune it seemed, there in the bright light of day. Yet her daughter, obviously unable to resist playing surreptitiously with the box, had heard it the once and clearly never wished to hear it again. Thoughtfully Mattie fingered the ornate veneering, and wondered what could possibly be Vickie's reason.

For Mattie herself there was a simple enough explanation to her unease, since the tune held unhappy associations. It reminded her unavoidably of the past, of the many times Albert had sung the tune to her when they were first together. But for the child there could be none of these—by the time she was old enough to remember such things her father unhappily had long since ceased to be a singing man ... Unless perhaps she recalled the blind man's penny whistle piping out of the fog at her father's funeral.

Mattie stretched out her hand and stopped the mechanism. That of course must be the reason. Children were sensitive, and they noticed far more than adults gave them credit for.

Clearly the tune reminded Victoria of a day she would rather forget.

On the inside of the lid of the musical box there was a list of the other tunes in its clockwork repertoire, handwritten in spidery gothic script, the black ink faded to a rusty brown. Vickie would not have known it could play other melodies. Mattie shifted the lever, restarted the cylinder, found she had selected a gentle lullaby. She wound the mechanism, then stopped the music in mid-phrase and left it so. Perhaps her daughter would be tempted to play the box again some time. It was so beautiful, and such a store-house of magical delights that it would be a shame if she were put off it for ever.

Mattie turned away, noticed the dolls' house standing neglected in a far corner. She had tried unsuccessfully to interest the child in that also. It was magnificent, a positive mansion, furnished down to the smallest detail, and complete with a family of tiny dolls, the sort of toy to gladden the heart of any little girl. Yet Vickie had scarcely given it a glance. How strange the child was.

Mattie wandered pensively away into the sitting room next door. She wondered if the reason for Vickie's almost aggressive lack of interest was the fact that the dolls' house had been Liesl's. The thought of a haunted dolls' house, however, seemed positively ridiculous. Mattie herself was not in the least superstitious. Anything that was not brand new must at some time have belonged to someone else—and there was always a fair possibility that that person might now be dead. And the manner of that death was surely neither here nor there. These very rooms, for instance, had once been Liesl's—yet it would be foolish to think them any less comfortable on that account...

Vickie too, even if she had gathered enough from the grown-ups' conversation to understand the truth about poor Liesl, had still not been prevented from sleeping soundly in the bed that had presumably once been Liesl's, nor sitting on Liesl's window seat and looking out of Liesl's window.

No, the objection to the dolls' house was simply another sign of Vickie's awkwardness ever since they had come to *das Haus Graugipfel*. And Mattie, to be honest, didn't blame her for being awkward—she'd have been awkward herself, uprooted from her home without a by-your-leave and dumped down in a strange country.

Mattie sighed then, and caught herself doing so, and decided that she was sighing far too much these days. And with precious little justification. She'd never expected that her life in Bavaria would be easy. Admittedly she was lonelier than she had anticipated. The house was isolated, and so far none of the townspeople had come to call. Her mother-in-law, it seemed, had become something of a recluse since her illness. While Bruno, for the moment, was totally absorbed in the affairs of the Becker violin factory. He'd been away in England for a long time, and there were a thousand matters needing his urgent attention. If he seemed moody and preoccupied, therefore, that was perfectly understandable.

And this would not continue. In London he'd been the liveliest, most sociable of companions. And anyway, if she would only work at her German she could set about finding friends on her own account. Her German ... she only wished that she dare ask for lessons from the old lady. But she felt so foolish, so inadequate. It was not that her mother-in-law had turned out to be at all the bogey she had been prepared for. If anything, Gustavia was in fact *too* charming ... Nevertheless, she was not the most patient of women, and hardly one to suffer fools gladly.

So if Mattie seriously wanted to improve her German she must work at it on her own. A challenge, certainly, but not insuperable. So why all the sighs? And why the bleak feelings of listlessness that possessed her at the beginning of each new day?

Vickie, too, had little to complain of. For the last few days she had been busy most of the time with the affable Günther, or downstairs being spoiled by Magda in the kitchen. And the language barrier obviously did not trouble her in the slightest —as Bruno had predicted, her German was progressing faster than Mattie would have believed possible. Shamingly so.

In fact, taking all in all, they were both exceedingly lucky. After the greyness of London, and the genteel poverty, it was a good life they had come to. And soon it would be Christmas.

Mattie crossed briskly to the stove, and made it up with logs from the tiled alcove. Already the house about her hummed with suppressed excitement. Günther, she knew, had been secretly up in the woods, choosing the Christmas tree. It was the Bavarian custom that it should be a surprise, supposedly brought by the Christ Child on Christmas morning. She was familiar with Christmas trees—under the Prince Consort's influence they were becoming the fashion in England—but Vickie had never had one in her own home before. She would remember this first Christmas in Mittenwald all her life.

Only one thing was lacking: the Christmas pudding. Discreet enquiries had revealed that Magda was preparing a special *Torte*, with spices and dried apricots. It sounded delicious, but it wouldn't be the same ... Suddenly Mattie knew what she must do. At last she had a useful project. She would go and ask Gustavia if she could make a Christmas pudding and stuff it with treasures, the bachelor's button, the lucky silver thimble. Gustavia would never refuse—she would understand Mattie's wanting this link with their old life, hers and Victoria's. Magda would sympathise too, if she was very tactful.

And so the days passed busily and happily, and Mattie was able to disregard her unease, her loneliness. And the disquieting fact that, since they had come to Mittenwald, she and Bruno had not once made love.

Then, a week before Christmas, the skies clouded over in the morning and by the middle of the afternoon snow had begun to fall. At first it was new and exciting, and Vickie ran about on the terrace at the side of the house, shrieking like a

216

steam whistle, her face tilted up to the sky, trying to catch the falling snow-flakes in her mouth. And Mattie stood in the open doorway, watching the gay white feathers as they whirled and eddied.

"Mother Carey's certainly shaking out her pillows today," she called to her daughter.

But it snowed and went on snowing, so that Bruno came home early in the pony and trap from the factory, and even then had to lead the pony most of the way up the hill, and arrived in a thoroughly bad temper. "*Ach, dieser verfluchter Schnee!*" he muttered angrily, cursing the weather, and banged upstairs to his mother's room, to play piquet with her till dinner was ready.

It snowed all night also, the wind howling dismally in the chimneys, the trees all around murmuring restlessly and scraping their branches. Mattie got up once and went in to Victoria to see if she was all right, and found her sleeping the sleep of the young and innocent. Which her poor Grossmama evidently was not, since Mattie heard her playing her violin for a long time that night, its thin notes mingling eerily with the wailing of the wind. Mattie lay rigid, her candle wavering by her bed, her father's watch held close against her breast for comfort, and counted the minutes. And counted her husband's fierce snores also, until she thought she would go mad.

By morning the wind had died down and the snow seemed to have abated, so Bruno set out with Günther to see if a path could be cleared down to the town. But he returned within an hour, sweating and angrier than ever, with the news that the snow was soft and drifting, and he needed more help. The two women of the household turned out then with shovels, and Mattie with them, and Victoria, greatly over-excited, getting in everybody's way. Until all at once it started snowing again, harder than ever, and they gave up the unequal struggle.

Bruno's game that afternoon was chess, played again with his mother. Mattie couldn't blame him—they played very well

217

while she herself scarcely even knew the moves. But she wished there might have been *something* they could have done together. At least Vickie got her snowman, however, dug by Günther in the lee of the house, a fine stout fellow with black pebble eyes and a carrot for a nose. And Vickie's own red knitted scarf about his neck until the snow fell on it so thickly that Mattie had to make her go and bring it in.

Darkness came early. Shutters were closed, the curtains drawn, the lamps lighted. Clocks ticked, logs settled softly in the stoves, people went placidly about their business. Upstairs Bruno and his mother were still absorbed in their chess, smoke from his pipe drifting thickly about them. Trude was working on a new batch of her dolls and Vickie was painting innumerable pictures of snowmen, intended to be surprise Christmas cards for everyone in the household. While downstairs in the kitchen Günther was laboriously reading aloud from a week-old newspaper to Magda and Paulina, both busy pounding almonds for the marzipan that would be coloured and fashioned into tiny apples and pears and bananas for Christmas comfits ... The house, in short, was a tiny self-contained world, warm and comfortable and industrious.

Yet for Mattie, depressed and unable to settle to anything, it was hardly better than a prison. Wretchedly she drifted from room to room. Everywhere, it seemed, she was the outsider. Isolated from the servants by her lack of their language, the pudding finished days before and stored away in the larder, she could only smile at them and stumble out a few brief commonplaces, and notice how relieved they were when she turned to go. And even Gustavia was only willing to spare her a moment of her attention, to look up from the chess board and murmur, not unkindly, "You really ought to find yourself something to do, Matilda. In the chest there is some *petit point* I didn't finish. I never will now, so why do you not finish it for me?"

Mattie thanked her—certainly she would feel better if her

hands were busy. And tried not to notice, for surely she had imagined it, the tiny, pitying smile that passed between mother and son.

She got out the embroidery, stared at it. Patchwork she could manage, but what did she know of such ladylike accomplishments as *petit point*? She wasn't like them—she'd been helping in her father's shop by the time she was twelve. Surely they must realise that she'd never had the time to sit around learning the finer points of needlework?

She was being shamefully pettish, and she knew it. Good heavens, if she felt like this after only one day of bad weather, how would she be by the end of the winter? But she'd been alone long enough—ever since she and Vickie had arrived in Mittenwald, if the truth were told. She needed her husband. She needed his love . . . Irritation burned in her body, making her fingers twitch. Irritation, and boredom, and jealousy of his mother . . . and something else that she did not care to recognise.

She stood up, paced to the stove and back again. Neither the chess players, nor Trude and Vickie, busy at the big table, took the slightest notice of her. She felt like screaming. Drawing a deep breath, she took a grip of herself. It was as if this were some obscure test she was being subjected to. If so, then she was determined not to fail it. She sat down, firmly took up the half-finished embroidery again, telling herself that one could accomplish almost anything if one really set one's mind to it . . .

The hours till dinner passed surprisingly quickly. Then there was Vickie to be put to bed. And afterwards, back to her stitching. She was using the old lady's work as a guide—long horizontal stitches with little diagonal ones over them, in a pattern of roses and bright blue cornflowers—and was even beginning to enjoy herself. While Bruno placidly smoked and read a book in his high-backed chair by the stove, and Trude worked on yet another knitted shawl for Gustavia, and the old lady

219

herself nodded gently in the lamplight, dozing away the last of the evening.

Mattie looked about her, thought what a pleasant, peaceful, *normal* family group they made. And told herself she'd been making a lot of fuss over nothing at all.

Finally it was time for all of them to go to bed. Briefly Mattie stood in her nightdress by the open bedroom window, looking out. The snow had stopped at last and the sky was clear again, tingling with stars. The day's wind had driven snow on to the sheltered balcony, heaping it against the wall of the house, almost up to the window sills. At intervals along the top of the balcony rail there were long wooden troughs, intended for summer flowers, each banked now with its own little snowdrift. And beyond, down in the valley, she watched as lights went out all over the town. The people of Mittenwald were making ready for bed, young and old, married and single.

Smiling gently to herself she leaned out, closed the shutters, then the windows. She drew the curtains shut and turned back into the dim, candlelit room. Turned back to her husband.

Bruno was sitting in his nightshirt on the edge of his bed. He yawned, then looked up at her. "Tomorrow we'll clear the path," he said. "Workmen in the town will be out at first light. The Bürgermeister never lets us be isolated up here for long ..."

She went to stand by him. Impulsively she reached out and ruffled his short, corn-blond hair. Its feel was nice, like one of his silky shaving brushes. "I do love you," she whispered.

He ducked away. "There are advantages to being a Becker," he said. "Once there was a winter when our well froze over—they sent the water cart up every day."

She stooped, picked up his bare feet and swung them on to the bed. "You should have worn your slippers," she told him. "You poor darling—your feet are like blocks of ice."

He reached for his quilt. "The Bürgermeister's a wise man," he went on doggedly. "There's a saying in these parts, you know—what is good for the Beckers is good for Mittenwald. And it's very true."

She watched him spread the quilt and pound it vigorously down around himself. Then he lay back on his pillow.

"Snuff out the candles, Matilda. Tomorrow's going to be a busy day."

Silently, sadly, she did as she was told. In the dark she heard him heave himself over on to his side.

"*Gute Nacht*, Matilda. *Schlafe wohl*—sleep well."

"*Schlafe wohl*, Bruno."

She got into her own bed and lay very still, staring with wide eyes at the blackness about her. In a short time his breathing told her that he was asleep. She wept then, softly, into her pillow. She had been as open with him as she dared, yet still he had rejected her. She thought of the families down in the town, happy and loving. The Beckers, for all their importance, were neither ... It was the first of many lonely nights in *das Haus Graugipfel* when she would cry herself to sleep.

In the morning, when she awoke, she felt cold even beneath the great mound of her quilt. Cold, and strangely weary. Bruno was already up and gone from the room, and sunlight streamed brilliantly in between the open curtains, mocking her wretchedness. Slowly she dragged herself out of bed. But the mountains burst in on her gaze, and the day was waiting for her, pure and radiant, and she was young, and it would have been a sin to resist its sparkling promise.

She remembered then that in four days it would be Christmas. Only four days. Quickly she washed and dressed. Then she hurried in to Victoria.

"We must do our Christmas shopping," she announced. "Step-papa will be going down to Mittenwald today—you and I shall go with him."

It struck her that she should have asked his permission first. But she discarded the thought—in the circumstances it was unlikely that he would refuse her she decided, calculatingly.

He didn't. All the same, when she and Victoria met him in

221

the corridor as they were going to breakfast and she told him her plans, he was markedly unenthusiastic.

"*Natürlich* you may come," he said, glancing impatiently at his watch. "But once you are in Mittenwald you must look after yourselves. I shall be far too busy to come to the shops with you."

"It really doesn't matter." She smiled at him with cold brightness. "If I get into difficulties I'm sure Vickie's wonderful German will come to my rescue."

She stepped round him then, and went on in to the breakfast table in Gustavia's sitting room. And, when it was too late, regretted her sarcasm. If once she and Bruno descended to sniping at each other, then really there was no hope for them.

Gustavia had already left the table, and the room was empty, the coffee keeping warm over a little spirit burner. They ate breakfast quickly, happily talking Christmas secrets. As a sop to her conscience, Mattie concentrated on what they might buy Bruno. Vickie should have an advance on her pocket money. Animatedly they discussed the relative merits of a penknife over a new ornamental feather for his hat.

They were just finishing their breakfast, still undecided, when they heard Gustavia's strangely masculine tones calling from her adjoining bedroom. They went in to her, found the old lady in front of an ornate dressing table, Trude brushing her hair. It hung down her back in thin silvery strands, almost to her waist.

She looked at Vickie in the mirror as they stood behind her. "A penknife or a feather," she said, "both are pretty thoughts. But I tell you one that perhaps would be better."

Mattie was confused. Her mother-in-law did not seem to mind in the least admitting that she had overheard their conversation. It was a mercy, she thought, that it had been so innocent.

"Really," Gustavia went on, "you should buy your steppapa a fine new pipe. To show him that all is forgiven."

What a long memory the old lady had. The quarrel over

222

Bruno's pipe had occurred during their very first evening in the house. Mattie herself had quite forgotten it.

"An excellent idea," she said quickly, speaking up on her daughter's behalf. She had learned enough of Vickie to know that otherwise, left to herself, the child might very well protest that all was *not* forgiven. "Vickie shall choose a carved meerschaum. Bruno will like that."

"*Gut, gut . . .*" The old lady's head jerked to Trude's vigorous brushing. "And while you are in town perhaps you could make some small errands for me. Christmas is not easy, you understand, when one cannot leave the house. You will need money, of course." She turned her head. "*Trude—meine Handtasche bitte.*"

While her companion was fetching the handbag Mattie had a chance to look about her. It was the first time she had been in Gustavia's bedroom, and she was astonished to see that almost every inch of wall space was taken up with an enormous collection of violins, large and small, dark and light, row upon row of them. The whole room seemed to glow with their rich colours.

Gustavia accepted the handbag from Trude, fumbled at its clasp with cramped, awkward fingers. "First I would like you to get for me some—" She looked up, caught the direction of Mattie's gaze, broke off. "I was forgetting," she said. "All these are my dear friends, these fiddles, and you have not yet met them."

She abandoned the obstinate clasp of her handbag, wheeled away from the dressing table, reached up and lifted an instrument from its mount on the wall. "This one now . . . this one belonged to the Emperor Maximilian. He liked to possess things, but he was no musician. You can see from the fingerboard—it has scarcely been played."

She held it out and Mattie took it cautiously, turned it over in her hands. The workmanship was superb. She peered through the S-slots, trying to see the label.

Gustavia nodded delightedly. "*Ja, ja*—it is a Becker. A

very special Becker. The Emperor would not have an Italian fiddle. He detested everything Italian, you understand."

She took the violin back, cradled it affectionately to her breast. "Every fiddle here has a story. That one in the corner went all the way to Moscow in the baggage of a French officer. He was killed in the retreat, poor man. *Ach*, the adventures that fiddle has seen ..." She hung the Emperor's violin back on the wall. "They are not all Beckers, of course. By the window there is an Amati. So beautiful. I played it myself at a concert in Vienna once—it was an amateur performance, of course, but the music was very well received ... The fiddle was my father's—it came from the household of *il maestro* Donizetti."

Her eyes were bright, her hands trembling. Never had Mattie seen her so animated, her wrinkled old face so transformed by excitement. Mattie wished her own father could be there—he too would appreciate such an exquisite collection.

"All are not famous, of course," the old lady went on. "But all are *sehr geliebte*—very precious to me." Her voice grew even deeper, and husky with emotion. "This one here—this one is my baby. This one is my treasure." She took down a child's violin, tiny, almost a miniature. "On this fiddle my Liesl learned to play, when she was no bigger than your little Vic—"

She choked, was unable to continue. Tears welled in her eyes. For a moment there was silence in the sunlit room. Then her expression changed, and she stiffened her thin, crooked back as much as she was able. She lifted the violin, and Mattie thought she was going to offer it to Victoria. But she held it out to Trude instead.

To Mattie's surprise the younger woman backed fearfully away, her heavy brows creased in an anxious frown.

Gently Gustavia insisted. *"Komm', Trude. Nehmen Sie es, bitte."*

Trude shook her head, backed away still further. Gustavia's

224

voice grew menacingly silky. *"Nehmen Sie es, Trude. Stellen Sie es zurück."*

There was a brief tussle of wills. Mattie watched uneasily, not daring to intrude. Finally Trude gave in, took the violin, holding it gingerly, as if it would burn her, and quickly returned it to its place on the wall.

At once the old lady relaxed, turned triumphantly to Mattie. Her small victory seemed to have given her curious pleasure. "Poor Trude—she is so shy. She thought I was asking her to play for you, you see. But the fiddle is much too small, of course ..." She leaned forward, spoke confidentially. "You would not think it, Matilda, but the woman plays well, and with genuine feeling."

Then she looked up at her companion, smiling wickedly. *"Sie spielen gut, nicht wahr?"*

Vehemently Trude shook her head, her big red hands tightly clutching the folds of her apron. *"Nie, Frau Becker. Ich spiele nie."*

Mattie looked from one to the other, utterly bewildered. She did not understand how, or why, but clearly Gustavia was taunting the poor woman. She had told Trude that she played very well. And Trude had denied the suggestion with quite inexplicable violence. And now, suddenly, the atmosphere in the room was charged with menace. Vickie felt it too, and moved closer to her mother, holding on to Mattie's skirt for reassurance.

For a full minute Gustavia's eyes were locked on Trude's, seeming to mesmerise her. Then, abruptly, she gave one of her deep, mannish laughs, and shrugged her shoulders, and the spell was broken. Trude moved resentfully away to the dressing table, picked up the hair brush again, waited. Mattie saw that her hands were trembling.

And Gustavia laughed again. "Poor Trude—she is so *bescheiden*, so modest ... It was not kind of me, perhaps, to insist."

H

Not kind at all, Mattie thought. And besides, she knew enough German now to be sure that there had never been any suggestion that Trude should play. Only that she should hang the violin back on the wall. Also there had been more than modesty in Trude's refusal. There had been naked fear.

Just then, to her profound relief, there came sounds from below of jingling harness, and an impatient shout from Bruno. He was waiting to go down to Mittenwald. She moved back a pace, Vickie following close. "I ... I really ought to go now," she stammered. "Bruno is ready ... Thank you so much, Gustavia, for showing us your beautiful collection."

She went to the door, anxious to be away. She had been witness to an intensely distasteful confrontation. She did not understand it, and she did not want to. But she knew now, as she had long suspected, that her mother-in-law's nature was not all sweetness: there was a devious, obscurely cruel side to it also. And she was reminded painfully of her first evening at Graugipfel, her meeting with Trude at the head of the stairs and the mysterious way in which the old lady, sitting in total silence at the far end of the corridor, had somehow made her presence known. There were undertones in the relationship between her and her companion that disturbed Mattie deeply.

At the door, however, duty compelled her to pause, her hand on the latch. "You mentioned errands, Gustavia. If I can help in any way, then—"

Downstairs, Bruno called again. And his mother, hearing him, made cheerful little shooing gestures. The evil little scene with Trude might never have taken place. "Go now, Matilda. My errands are not important. And husbands, *siehst du,* must not be kept waiting." She tilted her head slyly. "And besides, I have changed my mind. Trude shall make the errands for me later. She is upset, I think. It will make her happy to go down into the town.

Mattie opened the door and backed out into the passage. She did not believe in the old lady's sudden change of heart

226

and she felt almost guilty, leaving the two of them alone together, the wretched, ugly Trude withdrawn and tense by the
dressing table while her employer smiled secretly to herself
and drummed crooked, speculative fingers on the arms of her
wheel-chair. Still, Mattie told herself, Trude was a paid employee. If she did not like the job she could always leave . . .

Hastily Mattie went downstairs and bundled herself and
Vickie into warm outdoor clothes. On the terrace at the side
of the house a wide path had already been dug in the snow,
and upon it the sleigh was waiting. The sight of it lifted her
spirits: brightly painted in panels of red and blue and yellow,
it rested upon long, polished-steel runners that curved up in
two graceful scrolls at the front, hung with little silver bells.
The pony too had bells upon its bright new harness, and a
bobbing silvery plume between its ears. It was the first time
out that year for this wintry equipage, and clearly Günther
had been determined that it should look its best.

Bruno was standing by the sled, impatiently stamping his
feet. He grumbled at her for keeping him waiting. She made
her excuses, which he didn't listen to, then climbed up on to
the seat, lifted Vickie up beside her. He joined them coldly,
offered a blanket for them to tuck around their knees.

She stared at the snow, heaped in great mounds on either
side of the cleared path. "Will we really be able to get down
to Mittenwald?" she asked.

It was, perhaps, a foolish question. But his answer was unnecessarily sarcastic. "I would hardly be so anxious to start,
Matilda, if I did not think it possible." He settled himself
irritably. "*Natürlich* I sent Günther down the track first—
there is some drifting, of course, but yesterday's wind has
cleared much of the way. He's down there now, working on
the drifts. They should be clear too, by the time we get there."

It seemed to Mattie that if it had not been she who had kept
him waiting, then the snow would probably have delayed him
instead. She forebore to point this out, however. Things were
bad enough between them, without that.

The sled moved slowly off, Bruno leaning heavily on the brake as they began the descent through the trees. It was a journey into fairyland, the sun brilliant, the snow sculpted by the wind into fantastic shapes on either side of the track, the tree branches bending low beneath great capes of sparkling whiteness. Occasionally, as the sled passed, one of these would slip free, falling piecemeal through to the ground below, gathering others as it fell, raising exquisite crystal clouds that hung like fine silver veiling in the ice-still air.

In the presence of such magical beauty Mattie could not bear for petty dissensions to linger between herself and her husband. The salutary thought had come to her that if there was blame to be apportioned, then surely it might as well be hers as his. Rarely, she knew well, was the end of love a one-sided matter. So she spoke to him gently, fondly, praising the glorious scene before them, the valley, the mountains, the town spread out below, telling him in all honesty the things he would most want to hear.

They traversed several cuttings through deep drifts, the snow sliced through and stacked up in neat, blunt spadesful on either side, and came in due course to the sturdy Günther, standing at the side of the track, mopping his brow. He waved them on, shouting words that Mattie interpreted to mean that from then on the path was clear. And gradually, as she kept up her eager chatter, she felt Bruno begin to respond. So that by the time they reached the outskirts of the town he was as enthusiastic as she, pointing out details she had missed, the footprints of a running fox, a tiny waterfall, frozen whitely, spilling like wax down the dark rock of the exposed hillside. They were together again, and happy, sharing small, innocent pleasures. And Vickie too, her cheeks pink, her eyes shining with wonder, making Mattie's happiness complete.

Truly in such a place, beneath a sky so radiantly, so limitlessly blue, it would have been a sin not to be joyful.

It was with unmistakable regret that Bruno left them on the Obermarkt and drove on alone to the Becker factory. Mattie watched his jingling progress away down the snowy street, her heart full of the hope that a new start had been made, and love reborn between them. He rode the sled proudly, like a prince. He was handsome, well respected. And he was her husband.

Excitedly she and Vickie went from shop to shop. Sometimes, admittedly, her stumbling German got them into difficulties. But Christmas was in the air. Everywhere there was bustle, there were smiling faces. On many streets men were still busy clearing snow with shovels and strange wooden scoops with long handles. But they always had time to pause, and smile at little Victoria, and shout a cheerful greeting.

First there was the difficult question of a present for Grossmama. Handkerchiefs were considered, embroidered with silver Christmas bells. Then Vickie rushed off to examine little arrangements of dried flowers, dyed in improbable shades of red and blue. Finally a pomander was decided upon, spiked with cloves and smelling—so Mattie told her—of all the scents of Araby.

Then it was Step-papa's turn. And, on such a day, no hesitation at all that Grossmama's suggestion was best. The pipe shop had so many pipes to show them that the choice might well have taken all morning. Until suddenly, mercifully, Vickie spotted a meerschaum carved—so she declared—in the exact likeness of her beloved Günther. So that was that. And although Mattie had to dig somewhat deep into her purse to pay for it, she wasn't worried. Whatever else he might be, Bruno was never grudging with money.

Next there was a present for Günther himself to be bought, and ones for Magda and Paulina. And even, so much was Vickie fired with the Christmas spirit, one for Trude—who had never even, as far as Mattie was aware, offered a single word in the child's direction ... And so, finally, to the anxious moment when Vickie had to go off alone, her money held hotly in her pocket, to choose a present for her mother. While Mattie discreetly did the same for her little daughter, buying

229

a pretty mirrored kaleidoscope for fun, and a dress in fine Christmassy red with white lace collar and cuffs for use.

Presents for Mattie's own mother and father had been bought while she and Bruno were still in London. The idea had been his, and also the strict injuctions that they should not be opened until Christmas day. She smiled to herself, recalling the pleasure they had had, choosing them in the big London shops. Her presents for him and Gustavia, she decided, would have to wait till later. Her feet, even inside her boots, were icy cold, and she planned to warm them, and have a cup of hot chocolate with Vickie, in the shop on the Hochstrasse.

And this, when at last Vickie returned to her bearing a large and mysterious parcel, was what she did. They sat together in the crowded shop, at a table close by the steamed-up window, and were served hot chocolate and cream cakes by a fat blonde waitress in a black dress and starched white pinafore apron. And Mattie felt her feet thaw out while Vickie drew faces on the steamy window pane and tried to make her mother guess what was in the mysterious parcel. Which, since Mattie obligingly guessed impossible things like umbrellas or roast chickens, was a game of limitless delight.

Limitless certainly, but only to the extent that Mattie's patience was limitless. So that it was bound to be brought to an end either sooner or later. And frequently in life it is upon these unconsidered sooners or laters that matters of the greatest moment depend. For, had Mattie and her daughter left the coffee shop either a minute sooner or a minute later, then ... Such speculations, however, are hardly profitable. They left the shop when they did. And walked a short distance down the Hochstrasse, looking in shop windows as they picked their way round big piles of snow shovelled on to the pavement from off the road.

Suddenly Mattie heard a curious rumbling, rolling sound. And in the same instant a loud cry of warning from across the Hochstrasse. She stopped dead, looked anxiously about her. And was cannoned into violently by a man's heavy body,

230

moving so fast as to be hardly more than a blur. She staggered painfully back against the wall of the shop, scattering parcels and dragging Vickie after her. The child stumbled and fell. And the man also, prostrate at Mattie's feet.

While close in front of her a massive weight of snow thudded to the ground at the very spot where she and Vickie had been standing not ten seconds before, followed by a mighty baulk of timber, followed by more snow, in a seemingly endless cascade.

Finally the air cleared. In a daze Mattie pushed herself upright, away from the wall. Vickie was on her knees beside her, weeping bitterly. And Baron Rudolph von Kronstadt was climbing stiffly to his feet, rubbing ineffectively at his sodden apron and breeches, a rueful smile upon his face.

"*Entschuldigen Sie mir*—forgive me, Frau Becker. A desperate remedy, I fear." He was still breathless. "But I saw the log begin to move—I saw its fastenings break—so what else was I to do?"

And what else was Mattie to do, in spite of her husband's fierce injunctions, but offer him her heartfelt thanks? And even stay talking with him a while? For clearly the Herr Baron had saved them both from serious injury at the very least. The situation might be trite, but it was no less difficult for all that. Here she was, forced into a position of profound indebtedness towards the one man Bruno had expressly forbidden her to speak to. The function of the log, she knew very well, had been precisely to prevent just such a fall. It was hardly her fault if the ropes holding it had been allowed to grow rotten, so that they parted under the first trial of their strength that winter. Neither was it her fault that the man who had seen the danger, and saved her and Vickie from it, had chanced to be the Herr Baron.

She hid her confusion in picking up their various belongings and attending to poor little Vickie, never a child to cry without good reason, whose knees—even through the leg of her

231

long frilled pantaloons—had been badly skinned when she fell. It quickly became clear, however, that Mattie's tiny lace handkerchief was hardly adequate to the task. The child's wails increased, while her knees remained horribly grimed and bloody. So that when the Herr Baron, deeply solicitous, insisted that they go to his house, only a few doors away down the street, Mattie—once more through no fault of her own— had no alternative but to agree.

Putting on no airs, Baron Rudolph took them at once through the house and into a warm kitchen, hung with hams, and strings of onions, and gleaming copper pans, where they met first his housekeeper and then his sister, Friede. The two women set Vickie gently upon the table, and bathed the knees carefully with borax lotion. The child's crying subsided, helped by a sticky crystallised apricot in each hand, and the adults were able to take stock of one another.

Friede von Kronstadt was a handsome young woman, as dark-haired as her brother, firm featured and self-possessed, with alert, humorous eyes and a generous mouth. Her English, though heavily accented, was more than adequate. And she seemed, contrary to Bruno's words, to be devoted to her brother.

"I am so pleased that dear Rudi brings you here," she said. "Not for the accident, you understand, but for the chance to meet you both." Her gaze was disarmingly frank. "I will be honest," she went on. "There has been for too long unfriendliness between your husband's family and ours. It is my hope, perhaps, that through you, through this day, the quarrel may be mended."

The words were formal, but unmistakably sincere. Mattie hesitated. Certainly Baron Rudolph's sister had wasted no time getting to the point. "You've both been very kind," she began doubtfully. "And I—"

But the Baron interrupted her, laughing comfortably. "*Sei ruhig,* Frau Becker—be calm. My sister, you see, has never been to England. She does not know the English, how much you do not like to be hurried. There will be time enough to talk of reconciliations later, when you have got to know us."

And that, Mattie thought, was just the point. There was no chance at all of her getting to know them. Why, Bruno would be furious if he ever got to hear even of that morning's innocent meeting. And besides, the way Baron Rudolph had behaved towards Bruno's dead sister was unalterable. No amount of getting to know each other would change that.

Wisely Mattie decided to return frankness for frankness. "I'm afraid my husband feels the past very keenly," she said. "And naturally I must—"

"The past?" Fräulein von Kronstadt cast her eyes expressively up to heaven. "You mean the wicked story that poor girl Liesl told to her—"

"That is enough, Friede." Her brother rounded on her, suddenly angry. "Let us have dignity, if nothing else. Liesl is dead. She was sick, and now she is dead. Let her rest in peace, *die arme Jungfrau* ..."

Brother and sister confronted each other. Helplessly Mattie watched them—for herself, she had always recognised the possibility that Liesl, for reasons she could well understand, had not been speaking the truth. But it would be quite useless to try to convince the dead girl's mother, or her brother, of such a thing ... At that moment, providentially, Vickie finished the last of her sugared apricots and decided her knees were sufficiently recovered for her to get down off the table. So the moment's embarrassment passed and they were able, with due expressions of gratitude, to begin to take their leave.

"It is a pity," Friede said, moving to the door, "that you cannot stay longer. We could have shown you the violins, and where they are made. It is different, I think, from the Becker factory. But there is a new method we are using that—"

"Frau Becker is still a newcomer to our town," her brother cut in smoothly. "She will hardly be interested in such matters."

233

Mattie hesitated. "Truly, Baron Rudolph, I'm very interested," she said wistfully. "And it would have been very nice to . . ." She tailed off.

"Another time, perhaps," he murmured politely.

Too politely, Mattie thought. And knowing perfectly well, she realised, that—things being as they were—there would never be another time. But she did not argue, for clearly the Herr Baron had no wish to show her the Kronstadt workshop. Possibly he was ashamed of it. Possibly, as Bruno had suggested, it was indeed on the brink of ruin.

The baron and his sister led them back through the house and out on to the Partenkircher Strasse. It was, Mattie saw at once, an establishment very much of a size with *das Haus Graugipfel*, but furnished in complete contrast, principally in the French style, with gilded candle sconces on the walls, and elegant green and gold furniture. No sign of financial ruin here, certainly.

On her way across the white-paved entrance hall Mattie caught a brief glimpse into a room, presumably the baron's study: a velvet-seated chair was set at a fine bulbous desk, its back and sides a maze of intricate marquetry, while over by the window, uncomfortably dominating the entire room, there stood the carved wooden figure of an old man, almost life-size, his body so gnarled and twisted as to be positively ugly. It was a sinister piece, strangely threatening. If the work were Baron Rudolph's then Mattie thought it was perhaps a good thing she would not be visiting him again. He was gifted, undoubtedly, but with a disturbingly wayward talent.

They stood together for a moment on the doorstep. Fräulein von Kronstadt held out her hand. "I am sorry we cannot be friends," she said. "It is such foolishness. And all because of some—"

And again her brother brusquely interrupted her. "If we cannot, Friede, then we cannot. And that is all there is to be said." He turned to Mattie. Suddenly his sternness passed. "You must not think, Frau Becker, that I was not happy to

234

be of assistance. We have no quarrel, you and I. Quite the reverse ..." He smiled then, aware perhaps that he had said too much. But he went on, all the same. "And please remember this. If ever, in the future, you should need ..."

"*Aber natürlich*," his sister put in. "Frau Becker knows that. Always we are here. Always."

Mattie was confused. "You're very kind," she said, holding out her hand.

The Herr Baron took it, gave a small formal bow. "*Guten Tag*, Frau Becker. And a happy Christmas to you both."

At which Vickie, on her own account, piped up with her own happy Christmas. "*Fröhliche Weinachten*, Baron von Kronstadt."

He laughed, then politely, seriously, returned the greeting.

They went slowly away down the street, and out on to the Hochstrasse. Vickie walked cautiously, holding her skirt away from her sore knees. After they had gone a short distance she looked wisely up at her mother.

"Shall it be a secret, Mama, where we've been? I don't think Step-papa would approve."

Mattie sighed, smiled sadly down at her. "I don't think he would, my pet."

She hugged her daughter briefly, thinking—and not for the first time—how much more children understood than their elders gave them credit for. Then she set off for the shops again, for her own remaining purchases. And tried to put the morning's encounter behind her.

It was not until much later that day, in the late afternoon, when they were back in *das Haus Graugipfel*, their presents safely hidden, that certain of the Herr Baron's words, spoken in haste, returned to her. And by then she had discovered, devoutly wishing it were not so, that at some quite recent time all the windows of their rooms, the rooms that had once been Liesl's, had been securely barred. Barred from top to bottom, at close intervals. And that the door to the rest of the house had once had heavy bolts upon its outer face.

"Liesl is dead," the Baron had told his sister. "She was sick, and now she is dead." *She was sick* ... Wretchedly, incredulously, Mattie shook her head from side to side. Liesl had been sick. And of a sickness, she now realised with a sad heart, that had forced her family to confine her forcibly within these three rooms. Bars at the windows, bolts on the door—these rooms had been poor Liesl's prison.

5

MATTIE SAT BACK on her heels, leant unhappily against the wooden wainscoting, and stared at the door jamb. The marks were there on its surface, and on the door itself: carefully filled and smoothed over, but unmistakable once one knew where to look. There had been marks on the frame of the bedroom window also, small unevennesses, regularly spaced, that had first caught her attention some moments before, as she leaned on the sill, thoughtfully gazing out across the valley.

She had fingered the indentations idly, her hand moving along the woodwork, her mind far away. She was thinking of London, of her childhood, and of Christmas preparations in the rooms above the little shop on Copperas Street. The dusty tinsel brought out from the box in the cupboard under the stairs, the sugared almonds, the handsome tin of Mazawattee tea bought at Mrs Wassnidge's shop on the corner and used as a caddy on the kitchen mantelpiece for the rest of the year ... And her fingers had wandered, noting the neat depressions, moving on, finding more—until at last, her curiosity roused, she had looked down and seen the screw-holes, in pairs, at four inch intervals, along the bottom edge of the window frame. And, when she had looked up, along the underside of the top of the window also, exactly matching those below. Filled, smoothed, thickly varnished, but still unmistakable.

With a sinking heart she had gone from window to window in all the three rooms of their suite, the rooms that had once been Liesl's. Each one bore similar markings. And the markings, she realised, all suggested the same thing: that at some time in the not-too-distant past the windows had been barred, closely, securely, from top to bottom.

The conclusion was obvious. But she had stood awhile, reluctant to accept it, trying desperately to think of some other, less tragic explanation. Certainly no other windows in the house were barred. Perhaps, however, Liesl had been of a particularly nervous disposition, afraid that some night intruder might come up the outside stairs to the balcony and attempt to force an entrance. At least that was a possibility ...

A possibility that was made nonsense of, though, when she went to the door through to the rest of the house and found clear traces on its outer surface of heavy bolts top and bottom, with sockets matching them in the surrounding door-frame. She had knelt down then and examined the lower set carefully, just to be certain. There could, unfortunately, be no doubt at all: a bolt had been mounted there, its only possible purpose to make the rooms within a place of confinement, an unbreachable prison.

Now, sitting back on her heels, she considered the implications of her discovery. And suddenly remembered Baron Rudolph's words: *Liesl is dead. She was sick, and now she is dead.* Sick . . . such a neutral word, discreet, uninformative. While, in the light of what Mattie now knew, another word, painfully exact, came instantly to mind. She was reluctant to frame it. Until, recalling the manner of Liesl's death, she realised that no other word would do. Mad. Liesl had been mad; her family had been obliged to place her under restraint. Until somehow, one fateful evening, she had managed to escape, and had found final, unequivocal peace in the tranquil waters of the lake.

All Mattie could feel was the profoundest compassion: for the girl herself, and for her unhappy mother and brother. She couldn't blame them for never speaking of that tragic time in their lives, nor for trying to remove all physical reminders of it. She herself, she felt sure, would have done the same. The past was past. And the dead were dead.

Did this explain still further the full extent of their bitterness against Baron Rudolph? Surely not, for Liesl had not killed herself until two years before, when she was nearly thirty years of age. While the Herr Baron's involvement with her had ended when she was only eighteen. And Mattie remembered Bruno mentioning that his sister had travelled with his mother and himself on several of their visits to London after that time. So it could not possibly have been the pain of her lover's rejection that had caused Liesl to lose her reason. No, there must clearly have been some more recent cause, some—

"So, Matilda! So this is how you reward us."

Mattie started. The words, harshly spoken, cut through her thoughts. She lifted her eyes, saw first the foot-rest of Gustavia's wheel-chair, then her blanket-swathed legs, then finally the old lady's face, twisted and shrunken yet utterly terrifying in the intensity of its rage.

Mattie shrank away. "Gustavia, I—"

"*Schweige!* Be silent, I say. Have you no shame? Is nothing sacred to you? Is there nothing in our lives here that you will not poke your nose into? There, on your hands and knees, poking and prying—is this how you reward all our kindness to you?"

Mattie scrambled to her feet, backing away into the room. "Please, Gustavia, I meant no harm. I only—"

But Bruno's mother pursued her inexorably. "You meant no harm? You are not a child, Matilda—you have imagination. *Du lieber Gott*, have I not welcomed you? Have I not taken you into my home, you and your daughter? Shared with you everything? Everything but this one small secret? And now you must take even this from me?"

Desperately Mattie tried to stem the angry flow of words. "It happened quite by chance. It was an accident, I promise. I did not mean to—"

"Oh yes—*natürlich* it is an accident that you are on your knees by my Liesl's door." The old lady's sarcasm stung back at her instantly. "*Natürlich* it is an accident that you poke in your nose. You think I am a fool, Matilda, but I am not. I understand this *so-genannte* 'accident' very well."

She lifted a wasted, trembling finger and pointed it at Mattie, fixing her with a malignant gaze that seemed to penetrate into the innermost places of her mind. "It was *him*. He told you. He told you, and perhaps you did not believe him. So he told you then what you must look for. Do not lie to me, Matilda."

Mattie blushed scarlet, for she knew only too well whom the old lady meant. "That is not true," she protested. "He said nothing. The Herr Baron told me nothing at all. He—"

"So. Now you admit it. You have been seeing that ... that wicked man."

Gustavia sat slowly back in her chair and folded her arms, regarding Mattie with open, malevolent triumph. And Mattie saw she had been tricked. Of course Bruno's mother had not seen into her mind. She had simply made the wildest of guesses. Which had led Mattie, in her wish to clear Baron Rudolph of blame, into a dangerous admission. An admission which now must be explained. *Must* be explained, if she were not to lose for ever the good opinion of both her husband and his mother.

Mattie straightened her back and held her hands in front of her waist, clenched tightly together. "Frau Becker, it is true that I met Baron Rudolph this morning. But—"

"No, Matilda. *Genug ist genug.* Enough is enough. For my son's sake I have done my best to make you welcome. In spite of everything I have even tried to like you. But enough is enough. You trapped my Bruno. A widow with a pretty face —you won his pity. Men are such fools. So he married you and now you are here. But—"

"Please, Frau Becker, you must listen to me." Mattie was shouting now, the tears streaming down her face. "You must—"

"I think not, Matilda. It is you who must listen to me. There are many things you do not know. Many things that should be explained to you. Unpleasant things. Unpleasant but necessary." The old lady paused, evilly savouring the moment.

"*Zum Beispiel* . . . for example, the reason my Bruno came to your father's ridiculous little shop. Surely you do not believe it was really because—"

"*Liebste Mutti,* I'm very cross with you." The voice was Bruno's. "Have you forgotten already what the doctor said? That you should not excite yourself?"

Gustavia spun her wheel-chair. Her son, appearing suddenly in the open doorway behind her, now stood calmly surveying her and Mattie. "Not to mention," he went on, "what poor Magda and little Victoria must think, down in the kitchen, with all this shouting."

He closed the door and came forward into the room. Mattie longed to run to him, but dared not. Ever since the morning's inadvertent meeting with Baron Rudolph she had felt uneasy. Even during hers and Vickie's happy drive home with Bruno after their Christmas shopping, her deceit had lain heavily upon her. Yet their relationship had been too precarious, and too precious, for her to dare confess it. And now, under the worst possible circumstances, the wretched little secret must be revealed.

So Mattie kept her distance. But she spoke up quickly, and as firmly as she was able, anxious to present her husband with the truth before his mother offered him her own distorted version. "I am afraid I have not been completely honest with you, Bruno. This morning, when we were down in the town, Vickie and I quite unavoidably became involved with Baron Rudolph von Kronstadt. He—"

"He saved your lives." Bruno interrupted her, also cutting off the beginnings of mocking laughter from his mother. He folded his arms. "You need not look so surprised, my dear. Mittenwald is a very small town—your foolishness was to suppose for one moment that I would not get to hear of the Herr Baron's gallant rescue."

Gustavia began angrily to protest. He raised a hand, stopping her short. "It is true, Mutti. Old Eberfeldt saw the whole

241

incident. The details, I know, will not interest you. But it is undoubtedly true that the Herr Baron very probably saved the lives both of Matilda and of the child, Victoria."

Mattie stepped forward a pace. "If you knew this, Bruno, then why did you not tell me?"

"I was waiting, my dear." His smile was cold, his eyes as icily blue and remote as she had ever seen them. "I was giving you the chance to be open with me, and truthful. You did not take it."

Resentment flared in Mattie. And whose fault was that? she thought. Who was it who had so distanced his wife that she *dared* not be open with him, and truthful? Another moment and she would have found the courage to say these things, but his mother could be silenced no longer.

"Well, Bruno? What now? What are you going to do?"

"Do, *liebe Mutti*? What should I do?"

"This girl you have married—" the old lady's voice was heavy with disgust "—I find her on her hands and knees, like some inquisitive servant, examining the door to these rooms. I presume that already she has examined the windows. And not content with that, *ohne Zweifel* she will soon be forcing the lock on my desk, reading my letters ... And you ask me what you should do."

Mattie watched, outraged but powerless, as Bruno went to his mother and took her two hands gently in his own. "Liesl was a lost soul, my dear. For four long years we managed to save her from herself, but she got what she wanted in the end. She is dead now, and we have done everything that was necessary. *Everything that was necessary, Mutti.*"

"*Aber—*"

"She is dead, Mutti. And now, at last, nothing matters to her, not Matilda, not even you and I. The doings in this house are no longer of the slightest concern to her."

"*Nein, Bruno. Nein—das ist nicht wahr!*" Fiercely the old lady wrenched her hands free, poured forth a vehement flood of German, far faster than Mattie could keep up with. Her son listened to it patiently, nodding, putting in the occasional sympathetic word. . . Abandoned to her own devices, Mattie sank down wretchedly in a chair by the stove. The clock on the wall reminded her that it would soon be Victoria's bedtime, and her mind fastened gratefully on this thought to the exclusion of all others. Soon it would be Victoria's bedtime and somehow Gustavia must be got out of the room before Magda arrived upstairs with the child. Mattie could not, *would* not subject her daughter to the old lady's terrible vindictiveness. Somehow Gustavia must be got out of the room . . .

It was Bruno himself who unwittingly solved her problem. He turned from the wheel-chair, spoke to Mattie through his mother's still urgent protestations. "You have distressed my mother very much," he said coldly. "She will be dining in her room, and I with her. I shall tell Magda to serve your food, and Victoria's, in here."

He bowed to her then, almost as if she were a stranger, and, taking the handles of his mother's chair, walked slowly from the room, opening the door with care and shutting it discreetly behind him.

For a while Mattie sat quite without movement, staring miserably at the closed door, feeling the very fabric of her life in ruins about her. What could she do? She was Bruno's wife, his property, totally at his mercy. If he sided with his mother, as seemed certain, then her existence here would be quite unendurable. Yet where else could she go? Alone with her daughter in a foreign land, with only the sketchiest knowledge of the language, what could she do?

Gradually her common sense returned. And with it, her anger. For him to treat her thus, to leave her with hardly a word, waiting as it were in limbo, was outrageous. At the very least, he should have waited to hear her side of the story. She was after all, in spite of anything his mother might say, in every significant respect completely innocent. And as for

Gustavia herself—if Liesl had been mad, then so, undoubtedly, was she. Such fury, and with so little cause, was beyond all reason. As was the wildness of her talk, blurting out what were clearly the first hurtful things that came into her head. Mattie knew perfectly well why Bruno had sought her out in London. It had been out of respect for Albert, for his one-time employee. To suggest any other motive was ridiculous—mere mindless trouble-making.

If it did nothing else, at least Mattie's anger helped to restore her spirits. So that by the time Magda brought Vickie up to her, she was calm again, and totally in control of herself. If her marriage were really a thing so easily destroyed, then it was hardly worth the saving. She would be well rid of it . . . Of her love for Bruno, of the heartache in store for her, she did not choose to think. Not with the eventual, unavoidable confrontation with her husband still to be faced.

She and Vickie had dinner together, quietly, in their sitting room, the lamps bright, the stove crackling cheerfully. And if Vickie thought their lonely meal strange, she wisely made no comment. She had spent the afternoon helping Magda with the cream cheeses, pressing the curds into muslin bags and waxing them, and her excited explanations were so full of German words and phrases that poor Mattie was often hard put to understand her. The need to concentrate on something other than her own problems, however, brought her a useful sense of proportion. Ultimately it was Vickie who counted. And she knew that nobody, and nothing, would ever be able to take her daughter away from her.

When the meal was over she told Vickie a story, then put her to bed, sitting with her for a while in the darkened room till she was safely asleep. Then Mattie tiptoed away, past the exquisite dolls' house, still untouched in its corner, and out of the room, closing the door softly behind her. She sat down then in the painted rocking chair by the stove, folded her hands calmly in her lap, and waited for her husband.

The night was still, the house silent about her, contained tightly in the deathly hush of the surrounding snow. And the silence began to work on her imagination. She thought of Liesl, of the long years the poor woman had spent, confined in these three rooms. She pictured the endless, restive pacing, and her eyes seemed to follow Liesl's monotonous path, from window to door, from door to window, from window to door, like a caged animal. Shadows crept and flickered. And it was as if Liesl's wretchedness hung massively in the air, tangible, oppressive.

Abruptly Mattie got to her feet, strode to the window, flinging it wide, and the shutters also. At once the shadows stilled and the atmosphere lightened. Not true, she told herself—for the movements had been only her foolishness, and the weight of misery also. She leaned out, drawing in great breaths of the cold night air. The window was unbarred, and the room behind her was a room like any other room. Liesl, poor, sad, demented creature, was dead.

It was there, standing at the window, her head flung back, her mind free now of all morbid imaginings, that Bruno found her. She heard him enter, turned slowly to face him. Without defiance. But without fear either. For she had fought with a fear far deeper and more potent: fought with it and conquered.

He held the door open, pointed down at it. "Mutti says you claim you discovered these marks by accident."

"She misunderstands me." What a mean-minded, unimportant business this was. "It was the marks of the bars at this window that I discovered by accident. When I guessed what they were I went to the door, looking for confirmation."

He closed the door without comment, moved across the room towards her. She stood to one side while he examined the window-frame, ran his hands over its woodwork. Then he looked up at her. "I believe you," he said.

Much of the stiffness, the hostility, went out of him. He closed the shutters, the window, the curtains. There was still,

245

however, a leaden formality about him as he gestured her to a chair by the table, then seated himself opposite.

"We will not speak of your visit to the Herr Baron's house," he said. "Perhaps you could have avoided it, perhaps you could not. In the circumstances I shall assume that any debt of gratitude this family might bear for what he did has now been paid. And we will never refer to the matter again."

His coldness, his terrible self-righteousness, appalled her. How, she wondered, could this be the man who had danced with her in Greenwich Park, who had shouted for joy beneath the sun-dappled trees? Yet she recognised also in his words the nearest she would ever get to an apology. And for that, since she was after all his wife, his property, she was wise enough to be grateful.

She lowered her gaze. "Thank you," she whispered.

"*Gut. Gut . . .*" He leaned back in his chair. "Next we come to the matter of my poor sister. You know now that Liesl was insane. Her sickness took the form of a suicidal melancholy. We consulted the finest Viennese doctors, but they could do nothing. It broke my mother's heart." He paused. "And when Liesl finally escaped from these rooms and killed herself, it broke my mother's body also."

Mattie lifted her gaze, saw the pain this bald recital had cost him. So that, for all his arrogance, for all the unfeeling treatment she had received at his hands, her heart went out to him. He was a man who had suffered terribly. She should not judge him, let alone condemn.

Sitting forward, she reached out to him across the table. "Bruno, I—"

But he evaded her grasp. "Let me finish, please." His voice was harsh now, his face rigid with controlled emotion. "For there is more to be said, you see. I . . . I know now that I should not have married you, Matilda. I should not have brought you here. It was not . . . fitting. We are not as other people, Mutti and I."

He choked briefly. "I want to ask your forgiveness, my dear."

The room seemed to reel about her. "*Forgiveness,* Bruno? But we love each other. How can you talk of forgiveness when—"

"Love?" His lips curled in a wry grimace. "*Siehst du,* it is not, I think, a word to set much store by. The excuse for much of the folly of this world . . . I tell you, Matilda, if I had truly loved you then I would have done anything rather than bring you to this place."

"But it is your home. You belong here."

He sighed deeply. "You speak more truth than you know, my dear. *Das Haus Graugipfel* is indeed my home. I do indeed belong here."

And there was such anguished bitterness in his tone that she could only stare at him. Desperately she tried to collect her thoughts, to understand what lay behind his strange reply. It seemed to her that a great deal, possibly their entire future together, hung upon her next few words.

"Bruno my dearest," she said at last, "you must tell me the truth. Is it because of your mother that you say these terrible things? Has her kindness all been a pretence? Does she really hate me?"

There was a long silence. Slowly Bruno stood up, turned away, covered his face with his hands. "My mother," he whispered, "hates everybody. She hates life itself." His shoulders convulsed. Suddenly he lowered his hands and swung round on Mattie. "And do you blame her?" he hissed. "Seeing what she is, what she has become, do you blame her?"

For a moment neither of them moved. Then Mattie was on her feet, her arms tight about him, her head against his chest. "Oh, my love . . . my poor, poor love . . ."

She held him close, feeling him begin to yield. His body bent to hers, his lips brushed her hair. "Matilda . . . *ah, meine Liebste* . . ."

They stood together, timelessly, murmuring soft endearments. Mattie's heart sang. Relief flowed through her veins like wine. All that really mattered was that Bruno loved her.

No manner of adversity, nothing his mother could say or do, could take that from her. Certainly there were difficulties ahead —she did not delude herself that her life at Graugipfel would be easy. But she knew that, with the certainty of Bruno's love to sustain her, anything was possible. So she embraced him joyfully, secure and content against the warmth of his body.

Until at once, to her utter bewilderment and alarm, he stiffened again and broke from her arms. Silently, grimly, he strode to the door, flung it open, then stood transfixed. Over his shoulder Mattie saw Gustavia sitting impassively in her wheel-chair outside the corridor, as motionless as if she were carved from granite.

She and Bruno faced each other, neither of them speaking. Mattie could read nothing into her expression, neither anger nor disgust nor scorn nor pity nor shame. Just her flinty regard, and the thin, unrevealing line of her puckered old lips.

Finally, still without a word, she turned her chair, its wheels squeaking faintly on the polished boards, and vanished from Mattie's sight, back along the corridor, the way she had come. And Bruno, meekly, inexplicably, without a backward glance into the room, followed her.

Mattie remained where she was, frozen into immobility by the sheer horror of the moment. Finally, with leaden limbs, she went forward, looked briefly down the deserted corridor. Its emptiness pressed against her like an impenetrable wall, filling her with cold despair. Slowly she closed the door and returned to her place by the stove, to its false warmth and the delusive security of the flower-decorated rocking chair.

She sat there, without movement, almost without thought, until far into the evening. She was lost, powerless, her confidence in herself, in life itself, totally destroyed. For she knew now that in any conflict with Bruno's mother her weapons— honesty, tenderness, love—were pitiful irrelevancies. The old lady wielded the darkness of nightmares, the silence of a heart that was without mercy.

It was after midnight when Bruno returned for the second time. He came easily, almost casually into the room.

"I am glad you are not yet in bed and asleep, Matilda. I have to tell you that Mutti and I have come to an understanding."

She looked up at him dully, not speaking. His manner was strange, even his face. He was a stranger to her.

"A helpful understanding, I think ... For one thing, my dear, I have convinced her that you were completely innocent in this morning's unfortunate incident."

She managed a pale smile. "Good news, Bruno."

He moved restlessly about the room, paused by the book-shelves, took out a book at random, read its title, replaced it. "Secondly, Matilda, I have shown her that we were wrong not to be completely open from the very start about Liesl's ... sickness. You were bound to discover the truth for yourself, sooner or later."

She shrugged. "It's really not important, Bruno."

"That's *exactly* what I told her." He beamed. "Between you and me, *mein Liebling,* it has become something of an obsession with poor Mutti. You must be patient with her—she sits and broods, you understand. It does not always do to take what she says completely literally ..."

He paused again in his wandering, drew a finger tentatively along the joins in the stove tiles. "It is the same with me, I fear. We are not British, *siehst du.* There is a tendency to passion, to excess."

He laughed self-consciously, looked awkwardly down at her. At the back of her mind hope sparked faintly. "You mean it was not true? Your mother does not really hate me? Does not really hate everybody?"

"What a thought!" He tilted his head and rubbed the side of his jaw. "A fine, tragic-sounding phrase—nothing more, I promise you." He held out his hands, lifted her to her feet. "Today, I grant you, Mutti was upset. Very upset. But you, Matilda—you have known her now for long enough to be able

249

to judge for yourself. *Ich stelle dir die Frage*—I ask you, has she behaved to you as if she hated you?"

Dumbly Mattie shook her head. Her thoughts were in turmoil. She no longer knew *what* to believe. He put his arm gently about her shoulder, and began to lead her away towards the bedroom. "So there you are, my dear. Of course Mutti does not hate you. Tomorrow you will see it was all what you English call 'a storm in a teapot'."

She smiled then, too weary to correct him.

In the bedroom he drew away, bent his knees to look squarely into her face. "Am I forgiven, then?"

"Oh, Bruno . . ."

"And Mutti, is she forgiven also?"

A split second's hesitation. Then she sighed. "There's nothing to forgive," she murmured.

"*Gut. Sehr gut* . . . I shall tell her you said that." He turned away and began to get ready for bed. "It will make her very happy."

All Mattie knew, or cared, was that her emotions had been totally drained by Bruno's 'storm in a teapot'. So that it was an inexpressible relief, a few moments later, to accept his dutiful kiss upon her forehead and sink mindlessly down into her bed as he busied himself about the room, tidying the clothes and blowing out the candles. She was asleep before he had finished patting his feather quilt down around himself.

Weary as she was, she did not sleep long. Hardly more than an hour later she was jerked into instant wakefulness. She sat up in bed, gazing wildly into the darkness all about her. And the blood chilled in her veins as she realised the reason for her waking. As faintly, in the aching silence of her room, she heard the sound of distant tinkling music. The tune of which, for all its trills and ornamentations, was horribly familiar.

She fumbled frantically for a lucifer, and lit her bedside candle. But the light, for all its familiar warmth, brought little comfort. For the music box continued its plaintive, tinny refrain. The music box that she had set with her own hands to another melody. The music box that was in her daughter's room. The music box that now played, on and on, round and round:

Ach, du lieber Augustin, Augustin, Augustin;
Ach, du lieber Augustin, alles ist hin ...

With a trembling hand she took up the candlestick. Bruno had not stirred. He lay with his back to her, the quilt rising and falling peacefully to his noiseless breathing. And the ghostly music beckoned. She swung her feet down on to the floor, stood up, and went to the dressing table. By her father's watch the time was nearly two. Briefly her attention was caught by her reflection in the mirror on the dressing table, wild-eyed, scarcely recognisable. What was happening to her—could that haggard apparition really be she? But the music played on and on, and she turned quickly away.

As she opened the bedroom door the music swelled. Guarding the candle flame with her hand she padded across to Vickie's room, pursued by stealthy shadows. There she paused, her fingers on the door latch. Beyond the door all was silent, save for the sweetly innocent, beckoning melody ... She pressed down on the latch and the door swung gently open.

She saw at once that her daughter's bed was empty. Anxiously she hurried forward into the room. Tripped. Nearly fell. And, looking down, cried out softly in uncomprehending horror.

Instinctively she recoiled from the spectacle before her. While the music played on and on, round and round ... Then, recovering herself, she dropped to her knees, the candle lurching crazily. She tried to take her daughter in her arms. But Vickie resisted her, her stiff little body wrenching away as she resumed her briefly-interrupted game: the game she had been playing, silently, and in total darkness, when Mattie had come into the room.

Mattie crouched beside her, watched as her daughter, pale

251

as a ghost in her white nightdress, moved the tiny dolls and their furniture from here to there with unerring fingers, while her lips fluttered in wordless, smiling, imagined conversation, and her wide blue eyes gazed sightlessly down at the miniature world she had created in front of the open dolls' house. And the music played on and on, round and round ...

Cautiously Mattie leaned forward and touched the child's arm. "Victoria ... Victoria—you must wake up, my pet."

But Vickie heeded neither her words nor her touch. Just went on walking the dolls hither and thither, talking to them silently all the while.

"*Victoria*—" Mattie checked, took a grip on her precarious self-control. Abruptness was dangerous—her daughter must be woken gently. She got to her feet, picked up the candle, moved instinctively to the musical box on the chest of drawers. There she hesitated, filled with an unreasoning, primeval fear. Then, suddenly bold, she rested the candle on the top of the chest by the musical box, bent forward, and firmly stopped the mechanism.

Total stillness descended instantly, pressing in on her ears. She turned back to Vickie, saw the child motionless now, kneeling, her head fallen limply forward on her chest. A moment later she slumped, face down, on to the floor, scattering the tiny toys, crushing many of them. Softly she began to moan. And the sounds grew until they became an unearthly wailing.

Mattie darted forward, lifted Vickie in her arms, cradled her tenderly. "Hush, my pet, my dearest. Hush you now ..."

Gradually the wailing faded. Vickie stirred, opened her eyes. "Mama?" She clung to her mother. "I'm so cold, Mama. So cold ..."

She began to shiver convulsively. Mattie carried her to the little rose-painted bed and laid her down, tucking the quilt tightly about her. "You'll soon be warm now, little one."

The child's bright, anxious face stared up at her from the pillow. Her lips moved. Finally she spoke. "Where did the lady go, Mama? Where did Auntie Liesl go?"

The words brought terror clutching at Mattie's heart, impelling her to lift her eyes, gaze fearfully round the room. The candle flame burnt steadily in the calm air. Nothing moved. The bedroom was empty save for the two of them.

Mattie forced a smile. "There's been no one here, my pet. You had a dream, that's all. Just a dream."

Vickie frowned, drowsily puzzled. "But the lady—"

"A dream, Vickie. Just a dream."

The child sighed. Her eyelids fluttered, closed. She turned her head sideways on the pillow, hunched the quilt about her fragile shoulders, and slept.

And her mother stood guard beside the bed, out-facing the elemental dread that tingled her nerve-ends. A dream. No more than that. Just a dream. Vickie had dreamed. Walking in her sleep, she had dreamed that Auntie Liesl had come to play with her. Walking in her sleep, had started the musical box. Walking in her sleep, had selected the old, familiar melody ... That was the obvious, the only possible explanation. Anything else was mere superstitious nonsense. For Liesl was dead. Auntie Liesl was dead. *Dead* ... her body rotted to dust and her poor demented spirit safe and at peace now in God's merciful care.

It was this unshakable belief, burning as strongly, as steadily as the candle flame above her, that finally banished the dark terror in Mattie's soul. So that in the end, with a calm mind, seeing that her daughter slept soundly and tranquilly, she could turn away from the bed and retrace her steps across the room. She took up the candle, glanced briefly down at the music box, closed its elegant, softly-gleaming lid. Then, before leaving the room, she stooped and tidied away the dolls and their furniture, the whole and the broken, and closed the beautiful front of the dolls' house upon them. She wanted no reminders of that night. Some dreams were best forgotten.

She returned to her room, where Bruno still slept on, undisturbed. At one time dreams had plagued him also. But they had passed, as was their way. And they signified less than nothing. She got into bed, blew out the candle. Only then did she realise how bitterly cold she had become during her silent vigil. She curled up into a ball. And, as warmth slowly returned to her body, she too drifted off into sleep, deep and dreamless.

6

MORNING WAS ANOTHER day. Mattie had decided to tell nobody of her interrupted night. What was the point? Before breakfast pacing her room, engulfed in sudden panic, she had found herself seeing Vickie's dream as yet another step in the eerie sequence of inexplicable events that seemed to be gathering momentum all about her. A malign vortex, leading her inexorably to the still centre of ultimate horror. She felt herself utterly alone, in an evil, unhappy household, at the mercy of unknowable forces ...

Then she turned to Vickie, anxiously watching her. The child herself, making no mention of her nightmare, had clearly forgotten all about it. Could it then really have been so important, so sinister? While reassuring sounds came up from below, the cheerful stamp of Günther's boots in the hallway, the comfortable clatter of breakfast plates? While the air was rich with the scent of fresh coffee? And while, once again, the sun shone joyously, filling the room with a dazzle of snow-light, making nonsense of such morbid imaginings? No—a dream was no more than a dream. And Bruno loved her. And he had made her peace with his mother. And now, this morning, Mattie's main concern must be to be ready with Victoria to go in to breakfast in his company, since she would prefer—for the first time after yesterday's unpleasantness—not to face the old lady alone.

It was a small concern. Manageable. And, in the event, unnecessary. For there was, after all, no one better able to be agreeable (when she so desired) than her mother-in-law. Or at least to *appear* agreeable, which in the circumstances was probably the most that could be hoped for.

"My dear ... *guten Morgen* ... come in ... sit down ... see what a beautiful day it is again! You slept well, I hope?"

Mattie swallowed. "Very well, thank you, Gustavia."

"*Sehr gut* ... that is very good. Bruno—call Paulina for more coffee. Matilda my dear, you have been strong and have behaved most sensibly. You are very British, I think. And I —I am much ashamed of myself ..." She fiddled briefly with her cup and saucer. "But enough. Yesterday was yesterday and today is today. Let us think of something special for you and your little daughter to do on this so beautiful morning."

Bruno cleared his throat. "For myself, I'm afraid I have a busy day ahead of me. I shall not even be home for lunch. There are the last-minute Christmas orders to be got ready for the city and the wagon leaves at three."

His mother flapped her hands. "When, I ask you, was it not so? Business is business, *natürlich* ... Matilda must simply make the best of her day without you."

Various suggestions were discussed. Finally it was decided that a short expedition should be made to see an unusual snow cave that Günther had reported finding in the woods below the house. He would go with them to lead the way, and take a small toboggan for Vickie to ride upon should she become tired. Mattie was delighted—on such a morning she was glad of any reason to get out of the house, for even today, with sunlight in its rooms and Gustavia at her most charming, it oppressed her. It was as if the misery it had known could never be scrubbed away, no matter how determinedly Paulina might labour.

And indeed, shortly before the end of breakfast this feeling Mattie had was strangely reinforced. As always, Trude was at the table, a silent, watchful, disturbing presence. She ate and drank as stolidly as ever. Until suddenly, as if some hidden inner well of anguish could no longer be contained, her great ugly face crumpled, and huge tears began to flow soundlessly

256

down her cheeks. She closed her eyes, shook her head slowly
from side to side. She cried like a child, without shame, without concealment. Nobody moved or spoke. Until at last, still
in total silence, she rose with clumsy dignity from the table
and walked stiffly from the room, closing the door carefully
behind her.

It was little Victoria who broke the uneasy hush that
followed her departure. "*Grossmama*," she piped, "*warum
weint Trude?*"

Gustavia smiled fondly. "Why is Trude crying, *Bubli*?
Because she is sad, I expect. *Weil sie traurig ist.*"

"But why is she sad?"

"That is a long story. Perhaps because she is not beautiful
like your Mama."

Mattie would have interrupted, but found herself with
nothing to say. Sometimes the simplest answers contained the
greatest truth.

Vickie pouted. "I don't like it when she cries."

At which Bruno flung down the last of his buttered roll and
leaned forward angrily. "That is enough, child—more than
enough. You are a cruel little girl. You should not complain
when poor Trude cries—you should feel pity for her."

Mattie, for once in complete agreement with him, hoped
that her daughter would now have the grace to be ashamed.
Instead she simply hung her head sulkily and kicked at the
leg of the table. While Gustavia stared fixedly out of the window and murmured, as if to herself, "Some people, unfortunately, it is very hard to feel pity for ..."

Mattie stood up, removed her daughter firmly from the
table. Every child was aware that there were undercurrents at
work among its elders. But Vickie should positively not be
encouraged to play on these. She dragged the child off to her
room, and there spoke to her extremely sharply. Vickie wept
then, and expressed regret—but only, Mattie thought, for the
sake of peace, because that was what was expected of her. Her
mother decided there and then that the sooner the German

257

I

governess Bruno had spoken of was engaged, the better. A firm hand was needed—clearly the servants at Graugipfel allowed her far too much of her own way.

Later they went downstairs and saw Bruno off to work in the brightly-painted sleigh. The sound of its bells faded slowly in the frosty air. Then they went back into the house and dressed up warmly for their own expedition.

The terrace in front of the house ended in a low wall. At one end of this a heavy wooden gate led through to the path taking them to the snow cave, across the face of the cliff below. It was a narrow path, but the previous day's sunshine had melted much of the snow from it and they made rapid progress, Günther carrying the toboggan effortlessly on his back and holding Vickie's hand all the way. The two of them chatted easily, Vickie obviously not in the least alarmed by the precipice that fell steeply away on one side. Mattie herself felt rather less confident. She was not, she believed, someone who suffered from vertigo. But the tops of the trees below her on her right hand seemed distressingly far away. And the path was not at all as wide as she would have preferred. So that she was much relieved when the cliff finally ended and they came to a track leading on through trees across a far gentler, snow-covered slope.

The scenery was breath-taking. They had rounded the end of the hill now and were trudging up a small side valley, out of sight of Mittenwald, with nothing but snow and the black striding ranks of the pine trees all around them. They passed a lonely stand of birches, the trunks stripped of bark by hungry deer, the snow beneath trampled and stained. They came to a little mountain stream, still flowing, the pebbles and moss at its edges fringed with tiny sparkling daggers of ice, and stepped carefully across its darkly running water.

Inevitably the sight of the toboggan up on Günther's back proved a serious drain on Vickie's usually limitless energy. So that, when they had been walking for scarcely ten minutes, she began to stumble pathetically, clearly in the last stages of exhaustion. Instantly Günther hoisted the little sled down and, before Mattie could protest, had the child cosily installed upon it. And, looking down at her daughter's shining, wicked little face, Mattie could hardly blame her. The toboggan's runners hissed so pleasantly through the snow. And Günther's broad back, bent so willingly, was an intensely reassuring and manly spectacle.

He had removed his gloves to disentangle the toboggan's traces, and for the first time Mattie noticed the large silver ring he wore on his right hand. She eyed it curiously, suddenly reminded of the ring, engraved with a golden oriole, that Inspector Gradbolt had shown her all those months ago, in London. The ring once worn by Albert's murderer. It was an unhappy recollection and she looked quickly away, shuddering slightly.

But Vickie had noticed her interest. "There is a head on Günther's ring, Mama. A head with a circle round it. Günther says it is *der heilige Kristoph*. He means Saint Christopher, I think."

Mattie didn't answer. She would have preferred to talk of other things. But Vickie, full of superior information, was not to be discouraged.

"He told me all about it," she went on, her head bobbing to the jerking of the toboggan. "He says the men of Bavaria are very brave, and fight a lot, and hit each other with their fists." She demonstrated with her own tiny hand. "They hurt each other with their rings, he says. But because the hurt is made with the good Saint Christopher it is never very bad. And it gets better quickly because it has the saint's blessing. It is like magic, Günther says."

She raised her voice and shouted something in German. Her willing horse looked back over his shoulder, nodded seriously. And Mattie, fascinated by such curious reasoning, smiled quietly to herself and held her peace. And realised, upon consideration, that it was not altogether comfortable to think of a nation of men who could bring matters of religion even into their drunken brawling.

Soon they reached the head of the little valley. And there,

in a narrow defile, the snow cave had formed, an arch above their heads, pearly white, shot with exquisitely iridescent shafts of blue and green. They entered between fantastically sculptured drifts, into a world without shadows, a world that stifled sound, a world of perfect, terrible tranquillity.

Günther stood just inside the entrance, putting on his gloves. *"Es ist schön, nicht wahr?"*

Mattie pulled her fur collar up round her ears. "Yes—it's very beautiful."

Their voices died instantly. And she felt the bitter cold frosting her cheeks with her breath.

Even little Vickie's habitual exuberance was muted. She advanced a step or two, then stopped and held out her hand. *"Komm' mit mir*—please come with me, Mama."

Reluctantly Mattie took her hand, and together they went slowly forward. The cave was wide enough for them to walk side by side. And it seemed without end, a tunnel into the frozen heart of the mountain. In places the sides were bare rock, its surface marbled with screens of milky white ice. And overhead stretched the luminous arch of snow, layered and mysterious.

Mattie looked back half-fearfully towards the cave's entrance. Günther was still in sight, standing against the sky, placidly filling his pipe. He meant them no harm, she told herself. And he'd never have let them go into the cave if he thought there was any danger.

Vickie was in the lead now, creeping on, her eyes wide. "Are we nearly at the North Pole, Mama?"

The moment, Mattie felt, was hardly right for a geography lesson. "I don't think so, my pet," she offered instead.

They tiptoed on. And the next time Mattie looked back the tunnel had narrowed and curved, so that Günther was no longer in sight.

"Vickie—we've gone far enough, I think."

She found that she was whispering. And Vickie too, but full of childish obstinacy. "Come *on*, Mama—I want to find the

North Pole. And I'm sure it's just round the next corner."

Mattie could be obstinate too, however. She stopped dead. "We have gone far enough," she said loudly.

Disturbed by the sound, a few grains of frozen snow sifted down from the arch high above their heads. And, strangely, her daughter didn't argue. She stood for a moment, quite still. Then, suddenly, she had turned and wrapped her arms tightly about Mattie's waist.

"I love you, Mama," she said, her voice strangled with emotion. "I love you so much."

Astonished and bewildered, Mattie held her close. "And I love you too, my pet."

And the child was weeping. Desperately, inexplicably. "So much, Mama. I love you so much." And repeating the words over and over again.

Mattie comforted her as best she could, waited unhappily for the worst of her anguish to pass. Then she squatted down, looked into the child's red, tear-smudged face, kissed her forehead. "Whatever's the matter, Vickie? What—"

"Don't ever leave me, Mama." Through dying sobs. "Don't ever go away and leave me."

Mattie's heart lurched. "Why should I ever leave you? You're my little girl, my treasure. What has somebody been saying?"

"Don't ever go away and leave me."

"Of course I won't. I promise I won't. But you must tell me, my pet, who it is who has—"

"Don't ever go away and leave me."

It was an eerie, heart-rending appeal, there in the echoless whiteness, white on white, all about them. The entire extraordinary episode disturbed Mattie deeply. But she was able to get no other response from the child, and in the end she gave up her fruitless questioning.

"I'll never go away and leave you," she told her daughter earnestly. "I'm your mama, my pet. I promise I'll never go away and leave you."

261

At which Victoria seemed convinced at last, her childish, incomprehensible fears resolved. She mopped her eyes and blew her nose.

"I'm tired of looking for the North Pole," she said brightly, as if nothing had happened. "Shall we go back now?"

So they went back, stepping eagerly out into the sun's welcoming radiance, into reality, into a world that lived and breathed.

While Vickie was reassuring Günther, who had been waiting a trifle uneasily by the snow cave's entrance, Mattie turned and looked again down the soft perspectives of the cavern. She must have been mad, she thought, ever to have agreed to explore them. Certainly they were reason enough for the terror that had gripped her daughter, finding expression in the insecurity, unreasoned but profound, that must exist in every child's mind.

They began the return journey, Vickie—still somewhat chastened—riding again upon the toboggan until the path narrowed and steepened and they were at the end of the trees, beginning again the traverse of the cliff-face below the house. There, where the snow thinned, Günther made the child get out and walk with him, holding his hand. While Mattie followed behind, her eyes resolutely on his broad, confident back, rather than on the emptiness below.

And so they came at last, considerably out of breath, to the house, and to the bright kitchen, where mugs of hot chocolate were quickly provided. And Vickie, her fears now completely forgotten, gave Magda and Paulina a fluent—and, as far as Mattie could make out, greatly overdrawn—account of their adventures.

Mattie was able to leave her, then, and go to their rooms upstairs. In spite of the warmth of their welcome she felt a return of her earlier unease, her vague premonitions of disaster. Nothing, really, had been resolved. Unnerved by her experience in the snow cave, she realised that even the peace that now existed between herself and Bruno could be regarded as no

262

more than a truce. And the same might be said for Gustavia's elaborate cordiality. Her behaviour the previous evening had confirmed all Mattie's worst fears. The friendliness was no more than a veneer, laid paper-thin over such perverse resentments as Mattie dared not imagine.

She leaned by the window, staring sightlessly out across the valley. In the presence of so many tensions it was hardly surprising that Vickie walked in her sleep, felt disturbed, insecure ... She twisted her head from side to side, caught sight of the bright pile of parcels stacked in the corner. In three days' time it would be Christmas. Peace on earth and goodwill to men—what chance of peace had any of them in that accursed house?

She closed her eyes. No, it was not the house that was accursed. It was the people in it. And, among these, herself and her daughter. Common sense told her to take little Victoria and go. But where to? And how—what reason could she give? Premonitions of disaster? When she herself had always viewed such notions as superstitious nonsense?

She went to the stove, clanged the door open, thrust in fresh wood. The mundane act calmed her. Bruno was her husband. She loved him, and he her. The conflict, if conflict there was, existed between him and his mother. The oldest conflict in the world. And one that the passage of time would surely resolve. She told herself she was being impatient. It was, after all, scarcely more than three weeks since she had come to *das Haus Graugipfel*. Time was needed. Just a little more time ...

A thought flashed into her mind: *time is the one thing I do not have.* She quelled it. Childish hysteria. To abandon a marriage after only three short weeks would be wicked and irresponsible.

She sat down in the rocking chair. *It was Papa who told me that the whole of life was mine if I cared to take it. And I must not be afraid.*

The chair's rockers creaked beneath her. *Bruno is my husband. He has shown me, as no other man has, what that word*

263

*means. We have been happy before and we will be happy again.
And if it is necessary that I fight for that happiness, then I will
do so . . .*

She was still sitting in the rocking chair, staring rigidly in
front of her, filled with a strange exaltation, when Vickie burst
in, saying that lunch was ready. And she went to the meal
cheerfully, as if to battle, fortified by a new faith, dangerously
innocent, in her own resources. Earlier that day, she now believed, she had comforted herself with romantic nonsense:
sunshine that would vanquish all evil, the reassuring sound
of Günther's boots. But the Lord, as Aggie Templeton had
been so fond of saying, helped them as helped themselves. And
she was now prepared, soberly, almost exultantly, to take up
the challenge.

Lunch however, perhaps mercifully, provided her with little
opportunity to display her new determination. Gustavia's
affability seemed genuinely unforced and, once the morning's
visit to the snow cave had been dealt with, it was Vickie who
monopolised the conversation. It seemed that Günther had
told her that the ice on the lake was now safe for skating, so
of course she must go and try it just as soon as the meal was
over. Skating, she felt sure, was the best thing in the world.

So Mattie smiled, and wisely kept to herself dire mental
pictures of skinned elbows and twisted ankles. If there were
dangers to be feared, then they were quite other.

"Of course we must go," she said. "But I think we should
ask Grossmama first, my pet."

The old lady shrugged. "If Günther says it is safe then you
need not worry. And he will show you how to tie the skates to
your boots. We have many sizes, you understand. Left over
from . . . other days."

In spite of herself, Mattie felt a moment's sincere pity. "Shall
you come with us, Gustavia?" she asked, remembering too
late the old response with which this suggestion had been received once before.

But Bruno's mother simply shook her head quietly. "*Nein,
danke.* I think not. After lunch I must have my rest." She

264

shrugged again, glancing at her silent, heavy-browed companion. "It's Trude's rest really, of course. But I do not complain. It serves to break up the day. And she deserves a little time to herself, poor thing."

Mattie too looked at the woman, saw her stolidly munching her way through her bowl of liver dumplings. It was difficult, seeing her so, to believe in the morning's violent display of emotion. Or, come to that, to credit the artistic imagination shown in her needlework. It was as if her present lumpish indifference were a defence. And, in that house, with that employer, possibly the only defence left to her.

And there, thought Mattie, but for the grace of God—and my own endeavours—go I.

"You'll fall down, of course," Gustavia went on in her rusty baritone. "But if you are careful, and try to keep your feet together, and lean always forward, it should not be too difficult."

"I'm sure we'll manage."

"Of course you will. You're both of you young. And to the young all things are easy."

Mattie frowned. It was an attractive sentiment, if nothing else. "We lean forward," she said, trying to concentrate, "and keep our feet together?"

"*Ja, ja* ... And turn outwards to push. First one and then the other. As when you are walking. It is really very simple."

It sounded, to be honest, nothing of the sort. But by then Vickie had cleaned her plate and was bouncing impatiently up and down on her chair. So Mattie excused herself from the table and took her daughter off to dress her in her warmest—and most cushioning—clothes.

The skates were kept, carefully greased, hanging on pegs at the back of a big cupboard in the downstairs entrance hall. It was Magda who came out of the kitchen to show Mattie how the fastenings worked, since Günther's duties had taken him away from the house for the moment. Magda had deft fingers.

"*Sie machen so,* Frau Becker. *Und wieder einmal,* so ..."

265

Mattie watched, and quickly understood.

The path up to the lake was by now well-beaten. If they stayed up there long enough, Mattie thought, they might well see Gustavia after all, on her afternoon constitutional. Vickie ran on ahead, swinging her tiny skates by their laces. A slight wind had got up, tweaking at the tasselled pom-poms on her hat. The sun, already past its zenith and descending, lay the shadows of the tree trunks in hard black shadows across the snow. And suddenly the lake was in sight, slate-grey, its surface clouded with silvery particles scurrying in the breeze.

They reached the lake's shore. Left to herself, Mattie would probably never have ventured out on to the ice at all, for the prospect it offered was unrelenting indeed. But Vickie had sat herself down on a fallen log and was already struggling with the fastenings of her skates, and getting them at once into a terrible muddle. So Mattie hurried forward to help her. And then to fix her own skates as firmly as she could to her strong, high-buttoned boots.

Together they teetered forward on to the ice. And—as the old lady had predicted, fell over almost instantly in a hopeless confusion of arms and legs. But they persevered, and—as the old lady had also predicted—with the determination and resilience of youth were soon performing slow jerky circles, hand in hand. Which developed before long into more confident forays, further and further from the lake's edge.

Already Mattie was discovering something of the skater's magical intoxication. Able now to lift her eyes fleetingly from the ice directly in front of her, she became aware of the wind on her face, and the sharp, exciting hiss of the metal blades beneath her feet. And, however graceless her lurching progress would have seemed to someone on the shore, to her it was as free and soaring as the flight of a bird.

She still fell, of course, with disconcerting, unpredictable suddenness. And Vickie too, rather more frequently. But the bumps went virtually unnoticed. For they were skating. Really skating. In the high, pure, sunlit air of the mountains, beneath shimmering crags, between tree-fringed shores, crisp and white, on the ice-grey eye of the lake, they were skating. *Skating* ...

And the trees flashed by, and the sky wheeled above them, as wider and wider they turned, and faster and faster, till their ankles ached with the ceaseless juddering, and the wind brought tears streaming down their cheeks, and they staggered to a halt, coming together far out upon the ice, their laughter echoing back from the cliffs like the frail twittering of a flock of birds.

And it was then, as if Fate had let them play for long enough and was now giving them fair warning, that a small cloud, strangely black, passed slowly across the sun, darkening the eye of the lake for perhaps the space of ten heart-beats. Mattie noticed it, looked round at the distant, sombre, impenetrable trees, was filled with a sense of her own inconsequence, and felt all the joy abruptly drain out of her.

The sun, returning a moment later, did nothing to lighten her dread. She stood, suddenly very still, her shoulders hunched, her arms folded tightly across her chest, her shadow gaping like a narrow, bottomless pit in the ice before her.

With an enormous effort she roused herself, turned to Vickie. But the child was gone, moving stiffly away across the lake towards a cliff on the far side, where a frozen waterfall descended. Moving slowly but with total determination, as if in a dream. And Mattie trembled, watching her progress with new eyes, seeing its ungainliness, its precarious instability. And heard the ice beneath her daughter crack like bones.

"Vickie—come back. *Come b-a-c-k* ..."

She was not surprised when the child ignored her, for she had seen the end of this moment in its beginning. The leaden inevitability of the grave. But she called again, for that too was inevitable. And stumbled forward on aching feet, first one and then the other, in pursuit of her daughter. Summoning her resources of faith. Remembering her brave determination. While the ice clanged in her head like the splitting of teeth.

She saw that the waterfall was beautiful, its veils of ice

seeming to catch the sunlight and fracture it into a million jewels, beckoning the child on. And the frozen surface of the lake beneath it ominously dark, sparkling with crimson fire, and blue, and gold ... Vickie had almost reached it now, staggering, about to fall. And the lake cracked its knuckles in sure anticipation.

But it was Mattie herself who fell. And Victoria who blundered on, past the waterfall and on, unable to stop, the ice somehow bearing her weight, till she came at last to the shore beyond. Where, brought up short among the stones and reeds, she tottered forward on to her hands and knees, safe on the snow-dappled shingle of the beach.

Mattie slithered to a painful halt, cold wetness penetrating even her coat and the looped-up fold of her skirt. She felt the ice lean beneath her. Its surface was brown and mushy. She crouched there, staring down in horror at the slow ripples of water seeping across it. She thought of the impossibility of swimming, the bitter water, the heaviness of her clothes. Courage was nothing, save for the determination to die bravely. For the grave's shadow that she had seen was her own.

Yet she *must* not die. For Vickie's sake, if nothing else, she must cheat the slowly lapping water, the leaning, treacherous ice. Her fingers scrabbled fruitlessly at its surface. She was offering up a desperate prayer when suddenly, incredibly, a man's voice came to her, echoing between the crags and in her head.

"*Still,* Frau Becker. *In Gottes Namen, bleib' still!*"

She lifted her eyes, gazed unbelievingly at the stocky figure who had materialised somehow on the distant beach. It was as if the intensity of her appeal had conjured him there. He had helped Vickie to her feet, and now he was waving frantically.

"*Bleib' still,* Frau Becker!"

She needed no telling to be still, for her smallest movement seemed to start new cracks leaping away across the ice. The man, of course, was Günther. He had a huge coil of rope and he had come to rescue her. But it was not possible. Who had sent him? How had he known of her danger?

The questions revolved in her mind, a shapeless litany of shock and dazed relief, blurring her awareness of the perilous minutes that followed. After a while he was nearer to her, advancing cautiously to the edge of the sound ice. Vickie was away behind him, waiting on the shore. The end of the rope thudded close by. She groped for it, missing it as it skidded away. It was withdrawn and thrown again. This time she caught it. Her weight shifted, and she gritted her teeth as the cracks around her hissed and flashed like lightning.

An enormous weight seemed to come on the end of the rope. She held on blindly, closing her eyes, letting it drag her bodily across the snatching ice. Inch by inch, foot by foot, the long slow journey out of the narrow pit, from death into life. Until all at once the skates were being ripped from her boots and she was lifted to her feet. She stood then, Günther's strong arm about her waist, and walked. And came finally to the shore.

She sat on a tree stump, recovering her senses, comforting Vickie's passionate tears of relief. Günther said little. But what he did say was simple, so that she might understand it, and to the point. He had come to the lake just as soon as he had returned to the house and heard what she and Vickie planned to do. The ice was not safe, he said—certainly not near the waterfall where, until the previous day, the mountain stream had been running freely into the lake. Someone should have warned them. He could not understand why nobody had warned them.

Mattie stared at him thoughtfully. Vickie was edging away, her body curiously stiff and remote. She swung round on her daughter. "Did you lie to us? Were you lying when you told Grossmama and me that—"

The child burst into tears. Mattie felt bewildered, and very angry. "Were you lying," she persisted, "when you told us that Günther had said the ice was safe?"

269

She knew the answer to her question now. But her anger was such that she repeated it, again and again. "Did you lie to us? Did you? *Did you?*"

Her daughter's sobs intensified. "I ... I wanted so much to ... to go skating ..."

"Then you did lie?"

A pause. Then a tiny nod. And a whisper, scarcely audible, "Don't leave me, Mama. Don't leave me ..."

Mattie's anger left her. Instantly she reached up, gathered her daughter into her arms. And thought, wryly, that she had indeed come horribly near to leaving her. For ever.

"There now, my pet. Of course I won't leave you. And you must never, never tell me wicked lies again ..." She kissed Vickie's wet little cheeks. For the child had clearly been punished enough. She got to her feet. "And now, my pet, I think it would be very nice if you thanked Günther for coming to our rescue."

And she joined in Vickie's thanks as well as she could. Words, even at their best, were pitifully inadequate. But at least they were something. And she hoped that somehow the depth of her gratitude would show through the stumbling phrases.

Günther scuffled his boots, his big, weatherbeaten face creased with embarrassment. He turned his head away, his throat working strangely as he sought for a reply. Then, "Pliss," he muttered in painfully halting English, "what I do is nothing. Do not speak, Frau Becker. You bring every day sun in the house Graugipfel. Do not speak ..."

He bent down then, blushing deeply, and began intently to coil in the untidy loops of rope that lay across the snow-spotted shingle. Mattie was deeply moved. This was the first English she had heard from him—the fruit, presumably, of the many hours he had spent in her daughter's company. She only wished that what he had said was true. But as far as she could see, her coming to the house had brought only trouble.

The way round the lake to the path down to the house was

270

marked as if by the plunging of a bull elephant: Günther's frantic dash to their rescue only a few minutes before. She followed him back along it, moving awkwardly in her stiff wet clothes, her daughter, much subdued, at her side. Already Mattie was wondering how best to present the whole sorry affair to Bruno on his return from Mittenwald. The child, she felt sure, had learned her lesson. Yet she could predict only too well his brutal reaction, the damaging harshness of his anger, the violence of the retribution he would think it necessary to inflict. And she could see no way in which these could be avoided.

It was Gustavia herself, Bruno's mother, who strangely enough provided Mattie with a way out of her difficulty. The old lady was up now from her rest and waiting anxiously. After she had been told what had happened and had assured herself, with typical directness, that nobody in fact was seriously the worse for wear, she fell silent for a moment or two, her fingers picking absently at the edge of her shawl. While Trude, apparently as blankly uncomprehending as ever, whistled tunelessly through her teeth as she waited, a blanket in her arms, ready for her employer's afternoon constitutional. It was a curiously unmusical noise, Mattie thought irrelevantly, for someone who, according to Gustavia, played the violin with genuine feeling. What a bundle of contradictions the woman was . . .

"I would prefer it," the old lady said at last, "if my son were told nothing of this afternoon's little adventure. It would only distress him. He has a great fear of the lake, you understand . . ." She looked down, pretended to study her busy hands. "But you are his wife, of course. If you think he should be told of it, then . . ."

"I'm sure you know best," Mattie put in hastily. Even if she had wished to, it seemed inconceivable that she would have dared to differ with the old lady. "And I feel certain that Vickie is truly sorry for what she did."

"*Gut. Gut* . . ." Gustavia folded her arms. "I shall speak to

271

Günther. You went skating. You skated. You came back from skating. *Und das ist alles*—and that is all there is to be said."

Mattie left her then, taking Vickie with her, and went to change her sodden clothes. There were advantages, she realised, in even the harshest of tyrannies.

The rest of the afternoon she spent in her room with Vickie, cutting out paper dolls. In the aftermath of her escape she felt strangely light-headed. Her morning's brave determination to make a new start returned to her, stronger than ever. It was as if all her premonitions of danger had now been fulfilled, and she could indeed begin again, she and Bruno together, finding once more the happiness that had been theirs before they came to *das Haus Graugipfel*.

It was after dark when he returned from the town and she was waiting for him in their lamp-lit sitting room, Vickie tactfully out of the way, down in the kitchen with Magda, his glass of hot spiced wine ready by his chair. He took the wine, kissed her forehead absentmindedly. And went to sit with his mother.

Taking up the wine jug, Mattie followed him quietly, set it by the stove, brought out her neglected embroidery, and settled herself at the table with Trude. She was prepared to be patient. The old days would not return instantly, just because one wanted them. They had to be worked for.

At first Bruno and his mother spoke in German, business matters concerning the factory. That much Mattie understood, and was reassured. Gustavia took a lively interest in the family concern: it was only natural that her son should want to discuss it with her. Then the conversation turned to Christmas, and they spoke in English. Herr Zunderer and his wife would visit on Christmas afternoon. The factory manager had a daughter not much older than Vickie. Perhaps the girls would become friends. Mattie joined in. Vickie needed companions of her own age. She had been with grown-ups far too long.

Gustavia agreed with her. And Bruno agreed with her also. There was, besides, the question of the governess to be gone

272

into. He would make enquiries. In the new year something would be arranged.

At which Gustavia suggested that she consult the priest. He would be coming to the house on Christmas Eve. He was a learned man and might very well know of some suitable person. And Bruno declared this an excellent idea. While Mattie re-filled his glass, and smiled and managed to believe that the contented family she longed for was well on the way to coming true.

Dinner followed, with little Victoria evidently still chastened, and nervous, and very much on her best behaviour. When the child had been put to bed they sat again round the brightly-tiled stove. Trude, a little apart as usual, was putting the finishing touches to some particularly intricate piece of needlework. Mattie felt sorry for her, for the perpetual isolation in which she seemed to live. So she summoned her faltering German and spoke to the poor woman, seeking to include her in the family circle, bravely asking her what she was making.

Trude looked up from her work, a wary expression in her deepset, lack-lustre eyes. Diffidently she spread out the material. It was a white blouse, with neat puffed sleeves and exquisitely embroidered flowers round the neck. Mattie thought it beautiful, and told her so. Even Gustavia joined in with an unstinted word of praise. So that gradually, as if a veil were being lifted, Trude's sullen features lightened. Holding up the blouse, displaying it proudly, she became almost animated. And Mattie saw for the first time past her pathetic ugliness, to the bright, childlike spirit that burned within.

The blouse was a Christmas present for her cousin Anna, Trude said. Anna lived in Mittenwald and tomorrow morning Trude would wrap her present up and take it down to her. Anna had a husband, Hanns—a fine handsome man who worked in the customs house on the outskirts of the town. In the spring, Trude said, her cousin was having a baby. She hoped it would be a boy, so that it would grow up into a fine

273

handsome man like its father ... Trude smiled at this—she herself would prefer the baby to be a little girl. Then she could make it pretty dresses. But, boy or girl, at least for the first few years, thank God, it didn't much matter. Already she was preparing pretty things for her cousin's baby.

Mattie could have wept for the innocence of her pleasure. And for the wistfulness, unadmitted, that surely lay beneath it. For when Trude spoke of the coming baby there was a softness in her voice, a tenderness that tore at Mattie's heart. And, miraculously, not a trace of envy ... Mattie knew then for certain that, when the day came for Bruno and her to have their own baby, the same tenderness and love would be lavished upon it. The thought warmed her. And made her suddenly very hopeful for the future.

So the blouse was admired again, and Trude set to work finishing the last crimson silken rose. And when it was done, and the conversation round the stove had begun to falter drowsily, it was time for the four of them to go to bed.

Mattie sat at the dressing table in her shift, brushing her hair. Before her was her father's watch, her treasure, her promise that life was good, glinting softly in the candle-light. And in the mirror she could see Bruno behind her, shrugging his broad shoulders into his nightshirt.

Now she could reach him. The time, she knew, was right. It would never be righter. The reserve that had grown up between them—if she were ever to break through it then now was the moment. He was watching her, watching the lazy movement of her arm as she brushed and brushed, her dark hair crackling and springing away as if it had a life of its own. Surely he must sense how her whole body cried out for him, for the healing touch of his hands, for his gentle power, for his love?

She put the hair brush down and rose to her feet. Simply, making no fuss at all, she crossed the room to him, reached up on her toes, and kissed him. Lightly. And with the humble confidence of one who has come home after a long journey.

His eyes had followed her approach. Yet her kiss caught him totally unawares. He trembled, stared down at her, his face expressionless, a pulse leaping in the knotted muscles of his jaw.

Suddenly she was shy. She lowered her gaze. "I . . . I do love you, Bruno," she whispered.

She heard the harshness of his breathing, waited. Then, when he still did not move, she lifted her head again. She met his eyes. And, because she must help him, because pride was meaningless, and shame also, because he was her husband, because nothing else mattered except that she be honest with him and he with her, she said, calmly and clearly, "And I want us to be man and wife together, my dear. You want it too, I think. Now, Bruno. Now . . ."

A moment longer he lingered, motionless, their gaze locked. Then he broke away.

"Man and wife?" He gave a strained laugh. "How could we be any other? We were married, were we not? We made our vows?"

His pretence at misunderstanding should have warned her. Did warn her. Yet she persisted. Something was holding him back. If she could but find the right word, the right gesture, he would come to her.

"Love me, Bruno. Please love me."

He frowned. "What talk is this? *Natürlich* I love you. You are my wife."

"Then use me as such." The words were out almost before she knew it. She had not meant to say them. *Use me* . . . it was not what she intended. She wanted tenderness and love. And consummation. But now the words were spoken she stood by them. He should evade the truth no longer. "Use me as your woman, Bruno. Your wife, my dear. Your woman."

She held out her hands to him. It was not a challenge. Neither was she pleading. Rather she called then on all their shared memories, the nights they had spent discovering the fire, the

275

tumult and the subtlety, of their passion. Of their all-encompassing love.

In the silence that followed her hands quivered, then fell back down by her sides. There was anger in his face now, and cold disdain. And she knew that she had dared everything, and lost. But she did not yet know how terribly.

She turned away. "I'm sorry," she said, her body chilled and leaden. "I'm sorry, Bruno. But it really doesn't matter."

"Forgive me, Matilda, but I think you are wrong." His voice, almost unrecognisable, stopped her dead. "It *does* matter. If you can be brazen, then so can I. You will find that even here, in this room that was once Liesl's, I can be—"

She shrank from him, appalled. "Liesl? What in God's name are you saying? Is it that you thought our love so ugly that you could not bring yourself to—"

But he was past hearing her. "So be it, Matilda. If you have no sense of the rightness of things, then so be it. And if I married a whore, then so be that also."

Slowly, calculatingly, he pulled his nightshirt up over his head and stood before her, naked. She cowered away, not from the sight of his body but from the detestation, for her and for himself, that she saw in his eyes. And he came after her, reaching out and tearing the front of her shift with casual savagery. She whimpered, attempted vainly to cover herself. Then he was on her, grabbing her, flinging her back on to the bed, her scream stifled instantly by one merciless hand as the other ripped away what was left of her clothing. His body thrust between her legs, spreading them wide. And his face loomed huge above her, distorted by icy hatred.

"So be it," he repeated. "If I married a whore, then so be it."

She was not a child. She had heard of rape. She had even thought she understood its horror. But the monstrousness of what Bruno did to her that night, her husband, the man she had loved and trusted above all others, the violation of all that had been precious and beautiful between them, was an outrage beyond her most fearful imaginings.

276

And in his final moment of joyless consummation the one word, like a cry from the damned in hell, as he arched his back, his head straining up and away.

"Liesl!" he shieked. And thrust and thrust again.

When he had left her she lay very still and quiet, her eyes closed. There was, in a sense, a terrible justice in what he had done. *Use me,* she had said ... But there had been trust then, and love. And now no more, for the cruelty of that night would stand between them both, irrevocable, as long as the two of them lived.

She did not try to speak to him. Neither did she weep. For the well of her tears lay scorched and dry. And even the sounds in the room about her seemed strangely, comfortingly distant.

She sensed him stand over her, briefly uncertain. He laughed then softly, and pulled the quilt roughly over her. Then he padded away across the room, humming to himself as he snuffed out the candles. The tune was so faint and disjointed that she could almost have chosen not to recognise it. Yet she could not choose so, for she recognised it very well. And retreated still further into the still, cold world of her wretchedness.

He broke off, grunting as he eased his head back into his nightshirt. He got into his bed. Soon he slept.

She did not wonder what he had been thinking, why he had laughed, how he had come to terms, now that the perverse madness of his lust had left him, with what he had done. She simply lay, sleepless, as still as death, shocked into total inertia, waiting patiently till her mind should be ready again to take on the burden of living.

7

I cannot spend another night in this house ...

Mattie laid down her pen and hid her face in her trembling hands. The words told no more than the truth, yet how bald they were, how crudely melodramatic! What would he think when he read them? Would he not dismiss the writer as a foolish, hysterical woman, and read no further? Would he not crumple her letter and fling it from him? What right had she to be seeking his help? Three chance meetings, a kindness shown ... Mattie calmed herself, picked up the pen again, dipped it in the ink.

Vickie and I must leave Mittenwald. Today. Help us, I beg you ...

She was writing to the Herr Baron because she had no alternative. She'd been over and over the possibilities. Ever since waking in the cold light of dawn, with the man who was her legal husband snoring in his bed beside her, she had thought of nothing else. She scarcely knew the Herr Baron. And what little she did know left her with mixed feelings. His wood-carving, for instance ... Yet he had been kind to her. Once he had even offered his help. Where else could she go? What else could she do? Who else would befriend her?

I do not ask you to take us in. Merely to arrange transport. Surely there must be some coach or wagon leaving for the city. Anything will do ...

But perhaps there would not be anything. Today was Christmas Eve. No decent, God-fearing carrier would set out for Munich on such a day. She stared at the page, at her shaky writing. It was scarcely legible, the hand of a stranger.

278

Horses. You could hire a horse and Vickie could ride with me . . .

He would not know that she had never ridden a horse in her life. And she would manage somehow. Just as somehow she would steal the money for the journey. She knew where the key to the chest was kept. If only Baron Rudolph would help her.

Please help us in this. There is no one else we can turn to save you and your sister . . .

An explanation? That was one thing she could not give. Not to him, not to anybody. Not now. Not so soon . . . When Bruno had finally woken she had feigned sleep. She could not bear to hear his voice, even to see him. At breakfast time she had sent word by Paulina, excusing herself and Vickie. He had returned then, found the door locked, beaten angrily upon it. She had told Vickie they were playing a game, and had outfaced the child's wise, disbelieving eyes. Finally he had gone away.

So I beg you to do what you can. The bearer of this note will wait for your reply . . .

Günther. She would send Günther. He would not refuse. He was her friend. He had saved her life, had spoken the only words of true kindness she had heard since she came to *das Haus Graugipfel.* Dear God, how she hated even the name of the accursed place!

She read the letter through, signed it. A foolish, hysterical woman? She hoped not. But even a foolish, hysterical woman might warrant a moment of the Herr Baron's time, if he was the man she judged him to be. And certainly he was not one to fear the consequences of helping her. The choice would be plain, between herself and her husband. And he had no reason to respect the Becker family. Or to fear them.

She sanded the letter, then folded it and dripped sealing wax upon it. She thought of the monogram on Bruno's ring, and of the other, the bird, the golden oriole, worn by Albert's murderer. It was a memory from another life. A life that had seemed to her so sad, so lonely. So sad and lonely that she had

279

abandoned it willingly. Ah, if she had but known then what she knew now.

She rose from the desk, Liesl's desk by the window. All at once it was as if the shadows of bars lay hard and black across it. She shuddered. Poor Liesl. And how terrible the legacy of her suffering. Her brother's love contorted into something vile, unspeakable. And the bars, everywhere the bars remaining.

Vickie was sitting in the rocking chair, cradling her doll 'Melia, talking to her. In German, Mattie realised with a sudden twinge of unease. Poor Vickie too, she thought, to be uprooted again so soon, when she was just beginning to feel at home . . . But that was nonsense. Children hid their feelings well. But beneath her present show of normality Victoria was as anxious as she herself. *Don't leave me,* she had cried.

Mattie went to the door, unlocked it, looked out. The passage was deserted, the house silent. Tucking the letter into the pocket of her skirt, she ventured out. Günther, she hoped, would be in the kitchen. Quietly she made her way towards the head of the stairs. And, rounding the corner on to the landing, was confronted by the impassive figure of Bruno's mother.

She stopped short, her heart pounding. The old lady's hands were folded peacefully in her lap. She was staring straight in front of her. It was as if she had been waiting for something. For someone.

Mattie swallowed. "Good morning, Gustavia."

"*Guten Morgen,* my dear. Your headache is better, I hope?"

Guiltily Mattie pressed a hand to her brow. "Not . . . not very much better, I'm afraid."

Gustavia peered at her. "You are pale, I agree."

She fell silent, smiling quietly to herself. Mattie fidgeted beneath her calm, appraising stare. "I . . . I was looking for Günther," she stammered.

"Come now, my dear." Gustavia leaned back, flicked unnecessarily at the fringe of her shawl. "I am not a fool, *siehst du.* And you can confide in me."

Mattie felt a spasm of pure terror. What did the old lady

suspect? "I don't know what you mean," she murmured.

"This 'headache', Matilda—*ist es nicht diplomatisch*? It is a diplomatic complaint, is it not? I am not a fool, and neither am I deaf. Last night you and my son had a quarrel, I think. So this morning you avoid him. I have been married too—I know these things. Is that not the truth?"

A quarrel ... in her relief Mattie came near to laughing aloud. As if what had happened between herself and Bruno could possibly be reduced to the level of a lovers' quarrel! "No, Gustavia, your son and I did not have a quarrel. I promise you."

"Ah. So I was mistaken. And the headache is genuine. And the sounds I heard ... ?"

There was a mocking, almost prurient edge to the old lady's voice. Mattie stiffened. "You were mistaken in those also," she said firmly. "There were no ... sounds."

And felt suddenly sick. Had they really been overheard? Had her utter humiliation really been so audible?

"So be it." Gustavia shrugged. "And what have you done for this headache? A tincture, perhaps? Some eau de Cologne?"

Clearly she was still disbelieving. But Mattie no longer cared. "I have been resting, Gustavia. Soon it will go away."

"Then we should help it, my dear. I shall send Trude with a preparation. I suffer from headaches also, you understand."

Mattie didn't argue. But she knew she would rather suffer agonies than touch a drop of the old lady's preparation.

"And now," Gustavia went on, "you were looking for Günther, I think. He is not here. He is down in Mittenwald with Bruno. He will be there the whole day."

Despair gripped Mattie so violently that she came near to fainting, Her plan, the only faint hope left to her, lay in ruins. Yet somehow, by a supreme effort of will, she remained outwardly calm.

"I am surprised that Bruno did not tell you," Gustavia was saying. "It is the custom on Christmas Eve for him to visit the

281

families of his workers with small gifts. Günther goes with him. It is the custom."

Mattie cleared her throat. She felt removed from reality, as if she were looking at the world through the wrong end of a telescope. "A ... a pretty custom," she said. "I'm sure it must be greatly appreciated."

If the words sounded false, the old lady did not appear to notice. "*Ja, ja*—he is a good master, my Bruno." She smiled her wizened, toothless smile. "But you must tell me why it is you wanted Günther. Perhaps Magda or Paulina can help."

"Not ... not really." On some miraculous level Mattie's wits were still about her. Rapidly she improvised. "It is Vickie, Grossmama—she hoped to go with him to feed the chickens and collect their eggs."

"*Ach so* ... then she must be disappointed, I fear. He was out before daybreak and the work is now all done."

At last Mattie felt she could escape. "Then I must tell her so," she said. "And we will find something else to pass the morning ..." Wretchedly she felt the letter in her pocket press against her thigh as she turned away.

"Rest some more, my dear," Gustavia called after her. "Trude shall bring you a bottle. Take two spoonfuls. And by lunch time you will be quite recovered."

Under the old lady's watchful gaze Mattie managed to walk firmly back along the corridor to her rooms. Once inside the door, however, her whole body sagged despairingly, and she leaned back against its painted panels. Panic gripped her. With Günther gone from the house there was no escape for her. She was trapped. Powerless. And in the evening her husband would return. He would look at her, knowing her shame.

Vickie glanced up from her doll. "Is someone trying to get in, Mama? Is that why you are leaning there?"

The child seemed not in the least alarmed, just mildly interested. Her comically earnest curiosity sobered Mattie. She smiled. "Of course not, my pet. I'm only resting. My ... my head hurts, you see."

Vickie stared at her thoughtfully. "Grandmama in London always liked lavender water when her head hurt."

She put down 'Melia and trotted away into the bedroom. When she returned Mattie was sitting on the broad window seat. Her daughter fussed about her, pouring the lavender water copiously on to her handkerchief. "Shall we close the curtains, Mama? Grandmama in London always liked the curtains closed."

"Thank you, Vickie. But that won't be necessary."

Mattie felt slightly ashamed. Probably her headache was no more genuine than her mother's had been. She didn't like the thought that she had been brought to the same pathetic expediency. But she had to admit that Vickie's attentions were wonderfully calming.

She could think more clearly now. The obvious course was for her to go down to Mittenwald herself, call upon the Herr Baron in person. She could go on foot—the journey was not far. But what could she say? Explanations would be needed, and she could not bring herself to give them. How much more preferable the letter would have been. He could have read it at his leisure, and come to a decision privately, without the pressure of her uncomfortable presence. And besides, face to face with Baron Rudolph she could not rely on herself not to embarrass him with her distress. She dreaded the interview. Her appeal, his reply—such matters were so much better distanced by the merciful inadequacies of the written word.

A knock sounded on the door. Trude entered, wearing her drab outdoor clothes. And in a flash Mattie remembered the cousin down in Mittenwald, the visit to take Anna's Christmas present. This, then, was the solution to all her difficulties.

Trude came diffidently across the room. *"Guten Morgen, Frau Becker. Ich habe für Sie diese Flasche gebracht."*

Limply she held out the small green bottle she had brought, and Mattie took it. Gustavia's preparation—at least it had served a useful purpose, bringing Trude to her. The woman turned to go then, but Mattie called her back. Carefully assemb-

283

ling the simple phrases, she asked her if she were still going down to Mittenwald that morning.

Trude nodded.

Then would she please perform a small errand for her?

Trude's eyes darted warily round the room. But she nodded again.

Did she know where the Herr Baron von Kronstadt lived?

It seemed that Trude did. Which was unsurprising, for locally Baron Rudolph must be a man of some importance.

Then would she please take a letter to the Herr Baron? And wait for a reply?

"*Wenn Sie wollen.*" Listlessly Trude agreed.

Mattie brought the letter out of her pocket, weighed it in her hand, filled with sudden misgivings. Presumably Trude would do as she was told. But how could she rely on the woman's discretion? Only, she decided, by appearing to be completely open with her.

It was a message from Herr Becker and herself, she told Trude firmly. He had forgotten to take it with him that morning to Mittenwald ... Mattie paused, wondering if she should invent a subject for the message. She looked at Trude, standing incuriously. Better not, she decided. The poor woman would hardly be used to her employers taking her into their confidence.

Instead she handed her precious letter over without another word, as indifferently as she was able.

Trude took it, held it uninterestedly in her hand. Mattie hesitated again. Then she reached for her purse. Herr Becker, she said, would like her to have a small present. A little something for her cousin's baby, perhaps. These were hard times.

At last she had raised a small spark of animation. The letter would be delivered and the reply brought back, Trude promised. Without fail.

Looking at the woman, Mattie believed her. The money for the baby had finally engaged her interest. The only danger now was that she would see Gustavia before she left, and mention the letter to her. But there was small risk of that. Her relationship with the old woman was surely not one in which she would volunteer information unnecessarily.

All in all, Mattie decided, enough had been said.

Trude put the letter, and the money, carefully away in the pocket of her cloak. Then she bobbed a dutiful curtsey. "*Grüss Gott,*" she murmured.

"*Der für uns gestorben ist,*" Mattie replied, watching her leave the room. *Who died for our sake* ... And offered up a heartfelt prayer for the success of her desperate enterprise.

The rest of the morning passed with painful slowness. Vickie, strangely enough, had shown little interest in Trude's mysterious errand. Her sole comment, after Trude had gone, had been curiously oblique in that way children had. Oblique, yet utterly to the point. She had sniffed absently at Mattie's lavender-scented handkerchief. And then, "I *like* Baron Rudolph," she had said with an air of total finality.

Lunch time came. The fiction of the headache was played out, Mattie thought. So she went forth bravely to join Gustavia, reasoning that had Trude mentioned her errand to the old lady there would have been fireworks long before now.

For the rest, the prospect of Gustavia's company no longer deterred her. The vagueness of her earlier forebodings was gone. She knew now that it was Bruno whom she must fear. And Bruno from whom, God willing, she would soon be free.

What must come later, the practicalities of her future life, her grief for a love torn brutally from her heart, all that was for the days ahead. The worst had happened. She knew her enemy. So that the imagined menace of his mother held no further terrors.

One look at Gustavia, seated calmly at the lunch table, told her that all was well. Either the old woman was dissembling consummately well—and for what possible purpose?—or she knew nothing. She greeted Mattie warmly, called for Paulina to bring the food.

Only one further question occupied Mattie's thoughts. A

285

question she scarcely dared to ask, for fear she give herself away. All through Gustavia's bland enquiries after her health, and her satisfaction that the contents of the small green bottle should clearly have been so effective, Mattie struggled to hold her anxiety in check. Finally she could fight it no longer.

"Gustavia," she said lightly, oh so lightly. "Gustavia—when are you expecting Trude back from Mittenwald?"

The old woman prodded peevishly at her plate. "How should I know? I have not seen her since early this morning. She was on her way out when I sent her to you."

Reassuring news. But still no answer. "Surely she will not leave you long alone?" Mattie persisted.

"You might well think that." Gustavia snorted. "But when she and that cousin of hers start to talk, who knows when it will end? She comes when she comes."

Mattie looked away. Somehow she must contain herself in patience. Gustavia was right—Trude would come when she came.

"Why do you ask?" her mother-in-law went on.

The question was inevitable. Wisely Mattie had her answer ready. She hated these lies, the ease with which they sprang to her lips. Not for much longer, she prayed. Dear God, not for much longer.

"I asked her to perform a small errand for me," she replied brightly. Then, sensing her daughter's sudden startled glance, she quickly added, "A last-minute Christmas present. A little surprise." And hated herself the more. A surprise indeed. But how bitter. A mockery ...

Vickie relaxed. And Gustavia mumbled through her potatoes unconcernedly, "I hope the stupid woman does not forget it. Today is her holiday, you understand. Not convenient, with Father Martinus expected. But I shall manage somehow. And I suppose poor Trude must have *some* time to herself at Christmas."

She spoke the words as if she scarcely believed them. Then, suddenly struck by a new thought, she looked up from her food. "And Günther is away also. *Du lieber Gott,* how difficult life is! Who will show the good Father in? One can hardly ask Magda. And Paulina is—"

"Allow me to, Gustavia." It would not be a happy task. She had encountered the priest before, briefly, on one of his earlier visits. And had, to say the least of it, been unimpressed. But today she would do anything—anything to help pass the waiting hours.

She leaned forward. "I would be very happy to help in any way I can. Your rest, for instance—if you need—"

"Thank you, Matilda. My rest I can gladly do without. I've said this before—it's Trude's rest, not mine. But as to Father Martinus ... certainly it is right for you to see him today. He comes at three o'clock to bring the Mass and hear my confession. He speaks enough English so he could hear yours also, if you wished."

"I ... I'd rather not." Mattie lowered her head in confusion. For once her acquired religion lay heavily upon her. A true confession, she knew, was impossible. A priest would tell her that her place was with her husband, no matter what. And she *could* not obey him. "Another t-time," she stammered. "I ... I need to prepare myself."

She felt the old lady's eyes boring into her. But she maintained a stubborn silence. She would make her own peace with God. In her own time. And in her own way.

Finally, "It shall be as you wish, of course," Gustavia murmured coldly. "Perhaps when you have spoken with Father Martinus you will change your mind. He is an excellent man. And not without learning."

He arrived promptly at three. And, as Mattie had suspected, there seemed to be very little about him that might be called excellent. Except perhaps his punctuality. Certainly nothing to make her change her mind. He was a moist-handed, ingratiating sort of person, with a ruddiness of complexion that surely owed more to the schnapps bottle than it did to the rigours of the climate. Learned possibly, but a man well-versed in the expedient, she judged, and possessed of an obliging tolerance of the sins of the wealthy. She greeted him as briefly as she could, suffered his unctuous approval, then showed him up to Gustavia and left the two of them alone together.

She wandered out on to the corner of the balcony that commanded a view of the track up from Mittenwald, leaving Vickie playing with her doll in the room behind her. The sky was overcast. Soon dusk would be falling—surely Trude must return while it was still daylight? If she did not then Baron Rudolph's reply, whatever it might be, would come too late. Mattie leaned on the balcony rail, staring down the track ... But it remained deserted. Away to her left, past Gustavia's windows and the steps down to the terrace, she could see the awe-inspiring view out across the valley and the rooftops of Mittenwald to the darkly brooding crags of the Karwendel mountains. On such a day it was a sinister prospect indeed.

After a long while she heard her name called. Chill to the bone, she went wearily back into the house. She found Vickie gone and, hurrying to Gustavia's room, discovered her there with Father Martinus. And there was something in the spectacle of the three of them together in the lamp-lit room that set her teeth on edge: Gustavia, crippled in her chair, and helpless, yet endlessly watchful, endlessly calculating; Father Martinus, her shadow, black as a crow, leaning forward in beady benevolence; and little Victoria, golden-haired, bright-eyed, innocent, perched on a chair between them like a toy for them to play with.

She tried to be sensible. Naturally Gustavia would wish the priest to meet Vickie. And Father Martinus, if nothing else, knew his duty. There was, after all, the question of a governess to be found for the child. They discussed the matter. Gradually the painful image faded. Father Martinus wrung his clammy hands, and promised to do what he could. There was an admirable woman in Garmisch-Partenkirchen, he said, who was of good family but living now in somewhat reduced circumstances ... And Mattie thankfully reminded herself that in a

288

few hours, God willing, she and the child would be far, far away from *das Haus Graugipfel*.

Then, mercifully, it was time for Father Martinus to leave. He gave them his blessing. Mattie bent her head dutifully. But she couldn't help noticing the arrogant tilt of Gustavia's head, and the half-smile, almost derisive, on the old woman's face as she received the benediction.

The priest, understandably, saw nothing of this. Nothing save the ample stack of coins pressed into his hand as he took his departure.

And then it was dark, and four o'clock, and Paulina was bringing tea and *Kuchen*. And still there was no sign of Trude back from Mittenwald.

Beneath her fragile show of calm Mattie was in despair. The whole day had been wasted. Even if Trude came at once she would still be too late—how could Mattie and her daughter set out for the city now that night had fallen? She did not blame Trude—it must be that the Herr Baron had failed her. Surely, had he been able to help, Trude would have returned long before this. Yet Mattie could scarcely believe it of him. There must have been *something* he could have done?

And still the hours passed. Until it was time for dinner, and Gustavia said she would wait for Bruno, and Mattie ate—did not eat, how could she?—alone with her daughter. And finally, resignedly, put the child to bed.

Her determination to leave the house, she told herself, was as firm as ever. But now she must wait, wait till after Christmas, wait till she could secretly make her own arrangements. And if meanwhile Bruno came to her bed again, tried to force his sick lust upon her, she would ... She closed her eyes. There were scissors on her dressing table, a paper knife in her desk— terrible visions of blood flashed across her mind. She shut them away. He would not come to her again. It was not possible.

She had expected little Vickie to be excited and hard to manage, for tonight was Christmas Eve, when the Christ Child

289

K

came. The tree, she knew, was already set up in a locked attic, waiting for the final touches after Günther had brought it downstairs. And the Christmas presents too: it was the Bavarian custom to give these on the evening before Christmas day, but Gustavia had insisted that they wait until Bruno's return. So Vickie must wait for her presents also.

Yet the child was strangely calm, her behaviour muted. She snuggled down beneath her quilt and obediently closed her eyes. Perhaps she didn't properly understand, Mattie thought. Or perhaps, sadly wise beyond her years, she sensed her mother's wretchedness. Or perhaps she was simply remembering her last Christmas, in London, on Bacon Street, when her father was alive . . .

When she was finally asleep Mattie tiptoed away. At the door she turned, candle in hand, and looked round the shadowy, flower-painted room, the musical box silent on its chest of drawers, the dolls' house disregarded in its corner. Impulse took her back, a sudden cold dread, back to lift the music box and carry it away with her. The thought was irrational: that the box, more than anything else in the house, was Liesl's. And the wish that on this night of all nights her daughter's dreams should be of simple, childish things.

Closing the bedroom door behind her, Mattie set the box down on the brocaded window seat. She stared at it. It was what it was, no more and no less. And Liesl, poor soul, was dead.

She settled herself to watch and wait. Not for Bruno's return. Not even for Trude's, since whatever news she might bear would bring but slender comfort now. There was in fact nothing for her to wait for. Nothing for her to watch for. Yet she waited and watched. And the house waited and watched also.

It may be that she dozed. For it was as if waking from uneasy slumber that she became suddenly aware of a faint sweet tinkling sound. And riveted her gaze, preternaturally acute, upon the musical box where it lay on the heavy brocade of the window seat. And saw that its lid was still closed, its mechan-

290

ism silent. And mocked herself for the foolishness of her fears.

The tinkling sound, she now realised came from outside the room, and was of sleigh bells. Bruno was returning from Mittenwald. Something—habit perhaps, or a terrible foreknowledge —took her down the stairs to meet him. She stood in the open doorway, her shadow sharp against the golden oblong of light stretching out across the beaten snow, and watched as the sleigh came into view. Its lamps were gleaming brightly, bells on horse and curved steel runners jingling like a fairy tale. The thud of hooves came to her, and the warm horse smell rich in the bitter air.

The sledge hissed forward, halted in the light from the open door. And Mattie saw, and knew at once that this indeed was what she had been watching and waiting for, that there was a third person riding on the sledge as well as Bruno and Günther. A square-shouldered figure in a long dark cloak, descending awkwardly. Trude.

Involuntarily Mattie cowered back against the door jamb. In her mind there was only one reason why Trude should be there with Bruno. And the woman's leaden approach confirmed it. Silently, reluctantly, head lowered, she trudged towards her across the snow. As she reached Mattie she lifted her gaze, cast one brief, haunted glance in her direction. Then she passed on drably into the house.

Günther was holding the pony's head while his master removed various packages from the sledge. Mattie watched Bruno, saw the anger, the repressed violence in his every movement. She felt sick with fear. If he had seen her note to Baron Rudolph then there was no knowing what he might say, what he might do. Yet she waited for him, coldly resigned. There was, after all, ultimately nowhere she might go to escape his fury.

He gathered up his parcels, gave curt instructions to Günther, then started towards the house. She stiffened, ready to meet him. She had come to his home a loving, complaisant wife. Now her love for him was dead, leaving only fear in its place. And the fault was his: his the brutality, his the terrible betrayal. He could abuse her all he wished. She would not falter.

He came abreast of her, his rage like a deadly aura in the air about him, looking neither to left nor right, and followed Trude wordlessly into the house. It was as if Mattie had not existed. She stood for a moment transfixed. Far worse than anything he might have said was this silence, this total rejection. Slowly she turned and went after him, moving stiffly, drawn inexorably in his wake.

In the hallway he had paused to set down his packages. Now he was climbing the stairs. Desperately she called to him. "Bruno?" she cried. "I am here, Bruno . . ."

He appeared not to hear her. His stride not faltering, he went on up the stairs and disappeared from sight.

She ran after him, reaching the door of his mother's room just as it was closed in her face. She hesitated. She would not plead with him. But he must acknowledge her. She had been humiliated enough. He owed her that, at least. Lifting the latch, she opened the door again, and went boldly forward into the room beyond.

He was standing in front of his mother, the note to Baron Rudolph held mutely out to her, its wax seal broken. The old woman scarcely glanced at it.

"Trude brought you the letter," she said bleakly. "That is good."

Bruno lowered his hand. "Then you knew of it?"

His mother reproved him. "Certainly I knew of it. But I did not interfere. Trude's mind is like an open book. She brought it to you. She could do no other."

"And you know what is in the letter?"

"Not the words. But they are of no consequence. Your wife wrote it. And she sent it secretly to . . . to that man."

Of Mattie herself they took no notice at all. Yet they must have wished her to understand, for they spoke in English. Behind them in the furthest corner of the room, Trude was huddled like a frightened child, her eyes flicking restlessly here

292

and there beneath their heavy brows.

Bruno offered the letter again. "Read it, Mutti."

Reluctantly Gustavia took it, handling it as if it were unclean, and read it through. Then she smiled. "So. Your wife wishes to leave us. And that man, of course, is to go with her. How romantic."

Mattie could stay silent no longer. "That is not true. That is not in the letter. I scarcely know the Herr Baron. He—"

"Your wife is a foolish woman, Bruno. Foolish and worthless." It was as if Mattie had not spoken. "So what are you going to do, my dear? I asked you that question once before. What are you going to do?"

Bruno paced to the stove and back again. "She must be taught ... wisdom."

"And loyalty, Bruno. How do you teach a woman loyalty? When she does not know its meaning?"

Mattie darted forward. "These words you use are lies. With love there is no need of wisdom, no need of loyalty. And when love is destroyed, then ... then you can only teach fear."

The icy silence sapped her courage. She subsided, waited helplessly.

Gustavia looked past her. "I have helped you before, Bruno. I can help you now."

"I know that, Mutti. But ..."

His mother held up one cramped, mittened hand. "I do not like to say this, my dear. But sometimes you are weak. And you do not listen. If you had taken my advice many months ago you would never have married that worthless, foolish woman. And what misery would we both then have been saved!"

"I know that too, Mutti." He hung his head.

"And what about me?" Mattie demanded, beating her fists against the empty air. "What about *my* misery?"

And once more the total disregard.

"Then you must let me help you, Bruno. Before it is too late and we are publicly shamed." Gustavia paused, a sudden remoteness in her face. "Also, my dear, there is Liesl to be considered. You will want her forgiveness, I know."

A shudder passed through Bruno's frame. He clenched his hands till the knuckles cracked. "There is so much to be forgiven—more than you know." His voice was hardly more than a whisper. "But how, Mutti? *How*?"

And then, unbelievably, he was weeping. Standing before his mother, his shoulders hunched, weeping.

Mattie backed away in horror. This was insanity. Mother and son, locked together in an evil, cruel delusion. The entire discussion about her, in her presence, ignoring her, had been perverse enough. But now this new depth of madness . . .

She watched, terrified yet still incredulous, as the old woman leaned forward and touched Bruno's arm. "Naturally, my dear," she said softly, "there must be a sacrifice. A suitable sacrifice."

The word was drawn out, spoken lovingly, its sibilants lingering in the air. Mattie had heard enough. Sacrifice? The idea was outrageous. Laughable even, had it not been so vile. Calmly she turned away. No effort was made to stop her. She reached the door, opened it, and passed through. Was Gustavia then so confident of her power? Did she imagine that Mattie was like Trude, poor subjugated Trude, with no will of her own left to her? Was she expected to wait, meekly obedient, ready to play her part in whatever macabre drama might be devised?

She closed the door behind her. Only then, in the stillness of the corridor, did she acknowledge her fear. She felt the dark weight of the house press in upon her. She stared around, panic-stricken. Günther—Günther was her friend. She was not totally alone. Günther would help her . . . But help her against what? What could she say to him? In her German, how could she explain? Günther was a simple man, honest and faithful. A scene such as she had just witnessed would be incomprehensible to him. She pressed her palms to her forehead. Behind her, through the closed door, the voices rose and fell. Those people

294

—Günther would return her to them. He would think it only right.

Abruptly the last shreds of her self-control snapped. She ran in blind terror to Vickie's room. Taking up the lamp, she leaned over the little painted bed. Her daughter lay sleeping peacefully. Mattie stood then, for a brief moment undecided. Her instinct was to snatch the child up, carry her away, out of that terrible house ... But the night was icy cold, and Vickie would need to be dressed. She would chatter, ask endless questions, perhaps cry out.

In the room behind her a floorboard creaked secretly. Mattie stifled her horror, ran back to the door. Nothing moved. But the house all about her waited and watched. She could delay no longer. Impulsively she locked Vickie's door and, taking the key with her, fled down the stairs. It was she Gustavia threatened, not her daughter. Vickie would be safe enough behind the locked door till her return. Gathering up her hooded, fur-lined cloak and muff, she staggered out into the singing silence of the night. Her one thought was to summon help. And the only help she knew was down in the valley. Baron Rudolph and his blunt, kindly sister.

Her cloak trailed behind her, the air sharp as needles against her cheeks. The sky had cleared now, and the moon was just showing above the mountains. But the path through the trees was steep, and still in shadow, lit only by the diffused, eerie whiteness of the snow. Gradually her headlong pace slowed. Free now, out of the house, beneath the circling, ice-bright stars, she could collect her thoughts. She could make plans.

It would not be easy, she knew, convincing the Herr Baron of her predicament. She could scarcely understand it herself. Neither would his intervention be easy. But somehow it would be managed. Somehow, this very night, they would get Vickie out of that mad, terrible house. Somehow they would face Bruno and his mother. Somehow the nightmare would end.

She reached the outskirts of the town, flitted like a shadow through the empty, snow-banked streets. On either side of her the houses were shuttered, cracks of light shining through, and sounds of busy, happy people. Tonight was Christmas Eve. Soon the bells would be ringing for Midnight Mass. In the churchyard, as she passed it, tiny Christmas trees stood by the graves, their candles burning steadfastly in the still night air.

She came at last to the house on the Partenkircher Strasse, knocked timidly at its door. Then more loudly, till its panels resounded to her frantic blows. At last it was opened. A grey-haired manservant, stiff-backed and tall, gazed warily out at her.

Mattie tried to calm her laboured breathing. *"Der Herr Baron, bitte,"* she demanded boldly. *"Meine Name ist Frau Becker. Ich muss mit Baron Rudolph sprechen."*

The manservant hesitated. Certainly it was a strange time for a person to come calling, asking to speak with the Herr Baron. The manservant inclined his head regretfully, his hand still on the door latch. But then, mercifully, from behind him came the voice of Friede von Kronstadt.

"Frau Becker—*komm' herein* . . . please come in. What a pretty surprise. *Fröliche Weinachten* . . . happy Christmas . . ." Friede hurried forward, swept the man aside, and took Mattie's hand. *"Wilkommen,* Frau Becker—welcome."

There was, however, in her greeting an uneasiness that Mattie, in her wrought-up state, noticed at once. For she kept glancing back over her shoulder, a slight look of anxiety on her handsome features. The clear suggestion was that, much as Friede was pleased to see her, the visit could have taken place at a more opportune moment.

Mattie clung to her cloak and muff that the man was trying to take from her. "Forgive me," she muttered. "F-forgive me for calling so late, Fräulein von Kronstadt . . ." She cleared her throat, spoke up. "I . . . I was hoping to see your brother. It's very important . . . so important—otherwise I would never have thought of troubling you."

Again the nervous backward glance. "Trouble? It is no trouble. But for a minute now Rudi is busy. He has with him *zwei Besuchern*—two visitors, yes? *Ein seltsames Paar*—a strange couple, I think." She flashed a wary smile, was on the point of explaining further, then changed her mind. "He soon will come, perhaps. But can I not help you myself, instead?"

Mattie looked at her, at her unmistakable discomfort. It was not an attitude to invite confidences. "I ... I would rather talk to the Herr Baron." She hated to insist. But the thought of what she had left behind spurred her on. "Could I wait, please?"

A shade of embarrassed reluctance. Then, "*Aber natürlich* —of course you must wait." She led the way into Baron Rudolph's study. "Please, Frau Becker—make yourself comfortable."

Mattie entered the room, stood stiffly, anxiously by the desk. Friede von Kronstadt waited in the doorway, watching her. She coughed discreetly. "Your little daughter is well, I hope?"

"Very well, thank you."

"And Herr Becker also?"

Mattie nodded, no longer sure that she could control her mounting hysteria. But she must stay. Come what may, she must stay until the Herr Baron was free to see her. If only she could simply be left alone ...

It was as if the other woman had read her thoughts. "I shall go, then," she said brightly. "And I will tell Rudi you are here." She looked hesitantly at Mattie a moment longer, then went out, closing the door behind her.

Restlessly Mattie began to pace the room. The carving of the old man caught her attention. Its distortions worried her. She looked away, her eyes lighting at random on an open violin case, the instrument within it golden against the blue silk lining. She felt sick with worry. How soon would Baron Rudolph come? What were they doing now, up in *das Haus Graugipfel*? Already she had been away too long. Perhaps she should have woken Vickie and brought her. And yet ...

She found herself staring, almost mesmerised, at the violin in its case. Both seemed familiar. But that could not be ... Filled with a new dread, she crossed to the case and picked it

297

up, taking it to the desk where the lamp burned brightly. She laid it down and with trembling hands took out the violin. Yes—there was a chip on the head that she recognised.

Fresh horrors crowded in on her. She had thought of this house as a refuge. She had come here seeking help. She had come here, to Baron Rudolph, because there was no one else she could turn to. And now ... She twisted the instrument over in her hands, let out a cry of outraged astonishment. For the back had been peeled carefully away, leaving the carcase open, its dusty interior exposed. Its secrets also—since had not Albert always said it was unique?

The case too she recognised. There was the stain on its lining where Albert had spilled his brilliantine. And the chip on the instrument's head, which had been caused when the shelf he had mounted on the wall had fallen beneath its burden of music sheets. They had congratulated themselves then that the damage was no worse—his precious fiddle could easily have been destroyed completely.

Albert's fiddle. Abruptly Mattie dropped it, as if it was burning her. Albert's fiddle, here in Baron Rudolph von Kronstadt's study ... For a moment her mind refused to cope with the hideous implications of her discovery. Dumbly she shook her head from side to side. It was Gustavia she had fled from. Gustavia who threatened her very existence. Gustavia and her son. While Baron Rudolph was her friend. She needed him. Needed his strength, the promise of his help.

But the past could not be ignored. London. The desolation of those days after Albert's death. Unwillingly she recalled the grey, stooping figure of Inspector Gradbolt. His words to her. His suspicions. The Herr Baron had been in London when Albert was murdered. And he had left discreetly, before the inspector could speak to him. And now, here was Albert's fiddle, which had been stolen from his dead body.

And she was alone. Quite alone, with nobody she could turn to.

Baron Rudolph, then, was Albert's murderer. What more

298

confirmation was needed? And yet, confirmation there was. For on the leather surface of the desk, where the violin had fallen, there were pens laid out, and crystal ink-stands, a candle and sealing wax, and a seal with a massive silver handle. Frantic now, though still unwilling to believe the evidence of her eyes, she picked the seal up. And turned it slowly over. And saw on its face the neat, crisp outline of a little bird. Just such a little bird as had been engraved upon the murderer's signet ring. A golden oriole.

While behind her the old man hunched his twisted wooden shoulders, mocking her foolish innocence. Carved by a master hand, no doubt. But the hand of a ruthless murderer.

8

MATTIE NEVER KNEW exactly how she got from the Herr Baron's house. Only confused images remained in her mind, of doors snatched open, and a startled manservant staring after her. Indeed, she did not truly come to her senses until the town had been left behind her and she was panting up the steep snowy path between the trees. There were tears on her face and a terrible despair in her heart.

She was returning to *das Haus Graugipfel*. Returning to such horrors as she dared not imagine. Returning to a nightmare. Yet she stumbled on. It was Vickie who drew her. Had it not been for the child she would have gone anywhere, done anything—even thrown herself on the mercy of the unctuous Father Martinus—rather than return to that house on its sombre cliff, that house the very walls of which were permeated with the sinister power of Bruno's mother.

Getting back to her daughter—beyond that point Mattie's mind refused to function. Behind her, in the painted, elegant dwelling on the Partenkircher Strasse, was the man on whom she had pinned all her hopes—Baron Rudolph, Albert's murderer. Baron Rudolph the artist, the charmer ... the cold-blooded assassin. And all to what purpose? For the simple possession of a *violin*? Surely not. Yet the instrument had been unique. And Bruno's words flashed through her head: *He's brought the family business to the brink of ruin.* And certainly the violin was now dismembered, its secrets—whatever they might be—exposed ... Was it really just for this that poor Albert had died? No, she thought. There must be more. There *must* be.

The path seemed endless. The moon was high now, sparking daggers on cold fire. And the shadows beneath the trees as black and blind as death itself. The silence was total. Nothing moved on the bleak hillside. Only her struggling figure, tiny beneath the moon's cold brilliance.

She came at last to the darkly looming mass of *das Haus Graugipfel*. And wrenched at the door latch, and staggered through, the door closing softly, inexorably behind her. And was brought up short, the hot blood of her exertions draining from her cheeks, the beating of her heart abruptly suspended. For there, in the silence of the house, above the faint ticking of the clock by the foot of the stairs, a sound came to her, chilling her to the depths of her soul. A faltering sound of music that drifted sweetly down in the listening air. A violin's notes, thin and sad, bitter sweet, calling to her.

Ach, du lieber Augustin, alles ist hin . . .

The nightmare was beginning again. She knew now what the words meant. All is gone. All is over . . . And they were not true. *Dear God, they were not true.*

She was up the stairs in an instant. The house was hushed, waiting. In her room the lamp still burned where she had left it. But the door to Vickie's bedroom stood wide open: the door that she had closed and locked, taking the key. And beyond it she could see the child's little bed, unoccupied, the quilt flung back, the pillow still bearing the imprint of her head.

"*Vickie!*" The one word, anguished, almost a scream. While the violin's melody wavered on, softly beguiling.

She did not call again. Instead, now hardly with a will of her own, moving as if in a trance, she went slowly where the music beckoned. Out of the room, along the passage, pausing only briefly at a closed door, then opening it and entering. To where the music was loud and pure. To where Gustavia waited.

There was darkness. And then, as Mattie's eyes adjusted, silvery moonlight from the unshuttered windows, and from the open door out on to the snow-covered balcony. It cast its eerie glow over Bruno, hunched forward over the table. And

301

Trude, stiff as a rod behind Gustavia's chair. And Gustavia herself, her skull face smiling as she beat time to the music with one claw-like hand. And over little Victoria also where she stood, fully in its light, a tiny violin, Liesl's violin, tucked beneath her chin, her slender body swaying gently as she played. *Alles ist hin.* All is over. *Alles ist hin* . . .

Slowly Mattie went forward across the polished boards. This was a new horror, unspeakable, beyond her understanding. She faced it. "No," she said with quiet determination. "No, Vickie. No!"

Shadows moved. Her daughter hesitated, then went on playing. Gustavia swung her chair, its wheels rustling like dry leaves. "We've been expecting you," she said.

Mattie ignored the old woman, directed her gaze intently on the child. "Victoria, my pet. It's me. It's your mama. Stop playing now, there's a good little one."

But the music continued.

Gustavia folded her arms. "You've been away a long time," she said. "But we knew you would be back."

The night was in the room with them, chilling the air. Mattie moved to her daughter's side, touched her arm. "Vickie . . . Vickie, my pet, my little treasure."

But the child played on.

"She does not hear you, you know," Gustavia murmured, her tone conversational.

Mattie took little Victoria and shook her. The violin clattered to the ground. Vickie stood, staring blindly. Tears formed in her eyes and trickled unheeded down her cheeks.

Mattie let her go. "What have you done to her?" she cried.

Bruno stirred, lifted his head. "You went to the Herr Baron," he whispered. "You went to the Herr Baron . . ."

"And now I've come back." Mattie squared her shoulders. "And I want to know what you've done to my daughter." Evil hung in the air about her. She fought it the only way she knew. With simplicity. With the sheer force of her innocence.

302

Gustavia laughed. A deep, almost masculine sound. "Just pick up the violin, will you, my dear? Liesl won't like it left there, lying on the ground."

"*Liesl is dead!*" Mattie rushed at her. "You're mad, I tell you. Liesl is dead."

She would have struck her then, had not something in the old woman's strange stillness held her back. And Gustavia watched her, not flinching.

"Was it your daughter, then, playing the violin?" she demanded coldly. "Was it your little Vickie, who has never played a note in her life?"

Mattie shuddered. "It was you. Just as it was you who made Trude go to Bruno with my letter. Just as it was you who—"

"Just as it was I, I suppose, who led you out yesterday across the ice."

Mattie stared at her, struck dumb. It could not be true, what was she saying.

Gustavia sighed. "You should have died then, Matilda. It would have been just. And poor Liesl might now be at peace." She stretched out a crooked, pointing finger. "You must go from this house, Matilda. Go and never return."

"Gladly." Mattie was hysterical now, almost laughing. "Gladly . . ."

It was Bruno who sobered her. "But you must leave Victoria here with us, my dear. You must leave Victoria here in *das Haus Graugipfel.*"

A deathly calm descended on her. The voice was Bruno's, but the words—surely they were his mother's? "You cannot mean it," she gasped. "It is not possible."

He met her gaze. "Indeed it is, my dear. We are quite decided."

"But why? In God's name, why?"

"There was a time, my dear, when Liesl too was six years old, with all her life before her."

Vainly Mattie grappled with his words. "That is no answer.

303

I . . . I still do not understand what—"

"Then understand this, Matilda," his mother cut in sharply. "It is to be your punishment. For what you did to my daughter. It is to be your punishment."

Mattie felt as if she were drowning. Deeper and deeper she floundered. "I did nothing to your daughter. *Nothing* . . . I never even met her."

In the silence that followed she heard a small movement. She turned, saw Vickie jerk into life, stoop, pick up the tiny violin and trot with it across the room, then hang it back in its place on the wall. The bow too she returned to its ledge. Her task completed, she stood motionless again, as if waiting for the next command. The tears on her face were dry now, her eyes blankly staring.

Gustavia shifted in her chair. "You say you did nothing, Matilda. Yet you killed my Liesl as surely as if you had thrust a knife into her heart. You took her lover from her. You took her future husband. You married Albert Falconer."

Softly as she had spoken, her words were like hammer blows. Mattie reeled before them. "Albert? You mean . . . you mean he had spoken for her? He had asked her to be his wife?"

"Do not quibble with me, child." The old woman tossed her head angrily. "Liesl loved him. And he loved her. He would have returned to Mittenwald. He would have married her had you not bewitched him. It was you who killed her, you and he together. The news of your marriage was unbearable. It robbed her of the will to live."

And suddenly the nightmare in which she was trapped became clear, understandable. Mattie could believe that Liesl had loved Albert, and that on this love she had built dreams of future happiness. Just as earlier she had built false dreams upon her friendship with Baron Rudolph. Mattie could believe also that the destruction of these dreams—and for a second time—had brought unendurable pain. To a lonely young woman, isolated here in this terrible house, and with such a

304

mother, life must indeed have seemed not worth living ... But the entire structure was unreal, a love-lorn fantasy. Albert had never loved her. For Mattie knew, as only a woman can, beyond the smallest shadow of doubt, that she herself had been Albert's only love. His first and only love.

Yet of what use was such a certainty now, in this bitter, moonlit room, before this vengeful old woman and her wretched son? And why—dear God, why, knowing what he did, had Bruno married her?

But the time for questions, for argument, was long past. "I shall do as you ask," Mattie answered. Calmly. Grimly. "I shall leave this house as soon as I am able. And I shall take my daughter with me. You cannot keep her here. You have no right."

Gustavia smiled. "A small demonstration, I think." She looked past Mattie, at her son. "Your stick, Bruno. Bring me your stick."

Bruno hesitated, then turned obediently and left the room. Mattie watched him go, wondering what new ugliness was in store. For the moment, she thought, Vickie was safe enough. Gustavia's wish was to possess her mind, not to destroy her. And her power could be broken. Given love, and determination, her power could surely be broken.

Bruno's mother smiled again, and rearranged the blanket more comfortably about her legs. Behind her Trude stood, as stiff and remote as ever, hearing nothing, it seemed. Seeing nothing.

"There now," Gustavia murmured, settling herself. "And as to why my son married you, Matilda, only you yourself have the answer to that ... "

Mattie started. The question had indeed been in her mind. But she'd been tricked that way before. Her thoughts were her own. And she guarded them steadfastly.

"He visited you," the old woman went on, "because the thought of Albert's widow intrigued him. It was not suitable,

305

and I opposed it. Albert was dead, and that was enough. But he chose not to listen. And what happened next only you can tell. You enslaved him, just as you had enslaved Albert. But it is seldom difficult. Men's bodies are weak. And their minds also ... Still, I fancy my son paid a heavy price." She nodded complacently. "I do not give up easily, you understand. And I could reach him. Even after you were married, I could still reach him in his sleep."

Mattie caught her breath. The dreams. Bruno's terrible dreams. And Vickie's also, two nights ago ... She saw then, for the first time, Gustavia's true power, the nightmare darkness of mind she wielded without mercy.

The old woman chuckled bleakly. "I admit that you are strong, Matilda. I could make him suffer, but I could not change him. It was only later, you understand, after he had brought you here, brought you shamelessly into this house, that I was able to teach him his errors. Liesl and I together. We convinced him, *du siehst*. But it was not easy."

Poor Bruno. Now, almost, Mattie could forgive him. Torn between herself and his mother's evil promptings. And Liesl too—his sick reverence for a dead sister's memory ... Behind her the door opened, and Bruno returned.

His mother held out her hand. "The stick, Bruno. Give me the stick."

Docile as ever, he handed it over, a polished walking stick with a gleaming silver handle. Gustavia took it, and twisted the handle, and drew forth the slender blade of a sword. It flashed like ice in the moonlight. Mattie stared at its shifting brilliance, frozen into dreadful immobility. For she knew that she was seeing then what she had seen before, in her grief, in her fevered imagination, thrusting cruelly into Albert's body. Before her was the weapon that had killed him.

She was losing her reason. In this house of the insane she was going mad. What, now of the Herr Baron? For it was Bruno who was the murderer. Bruno who had wreaked a terrible vengeance for his sister's death ...

306

Gustavia pointed the blade, circled it in the frosty air. "He had to wait, you understand. First Liesl's sickness, then my own. He could not leave us. He was a good brother, and a good son ... Six long years we waited." She paused. "And then—" She stabbed into the darkness. The sword blade quivered, held still.

Mattie waited. She's playing with me, she thought. She cannot hurt me. She is old and weak. I could disarm her easily.

Then, chuckling again, Gustavia lowered the sword. She closed her eyes. Suddenly she became still. Inexorably Mattie's gaze was drawn away, to rest in wordless dread upon her daughter. For Vickie was moving now, neatly, carefully, across the room to stand by the old woman. She reached out and, before Mattie could stop her, had taken the sword from Gustavia's hand. It was heavy, and the point drooped. But Vickie held it firmly, lifting it till it was pointing straight at Mattie's heart. She began to walk forward.

"Don't, Vickie. *Don't* ... It is I, my pet. It is your mama. I love you, my treasure. *I love you ...*"

But the child continued to advance. Her eyes were bright, and her pretty lips smiled. And the point of the sword was close to its mark.

Despairingly Mattie stepped to one side. The sword blade followed her, glinting evilly. She retreated. "Listen to me, Vickie. I love you, my dearest. Listen to me ..."

Her words were wasted. The point of the sword came steadily, unfalteringly nearer. Mattie retreated until her back was pressed against the wall. Another moment and the shining blade would thrust relentlessly into her heart. Driven home by her innocently smiling daughter.

In desperation Mattie abandoned her vain appeals. She braced herself, then threw herself sideways, lunged round the sword, caught hold of Vickie's arm, and wrenched the weapon from her puny grasp. It was done with pathetic ease. But it left Mattie trembling, utterly speechless, in a state of profoundest shock. If she had not defended herself the child would

307

have killed her. Killed her own mother at Gustavia's command. She leaned against the wall, appalled, her chest heaving, while Vickie stood a pace or two in front of her, uncertain now, confused, making helpless little thrusting movements with her empty hand. At last it dropped to her side and she was still.

Gustavia cleared her throat. "Merely a demonstration," she said mildly. "Nothing more. You are big and the child is small —there was never any real peril ... But can you always be so certain?" She flicked lightly at the fringe of her shawl. "The world is a dangerous place, Matilda. Will you, for example, ever dare walk beneath those flower boxes on the balcony, knowing that your daughter is within reach of them? Will you lock up your knives, Matilda? Will you rest easily in your bed?"

Bruno had turned away. He was slumped at the table again, his head in his hands, sobbing quietly. His mother ignored him.

"Or would it not be wiser to do as we say? Leave the child with us, Matilda. Admit that I am stronger than you. Admit that you are beaten, and go away. Leave *das Haus Graugipfel* and—"

"I cannot." Mattie pushed herself upright from the wall. Bruno's sword was ready in her hand. How simple, how obvious it would be to ... How simple, yet for pity's sake, how impossible. "*I cannot leave my daughter.*"

All at once Vickie began to scream. Her cries, thin and pitiful, tore at the icy stillness of the room. Beyond her Bruno hunched himself lower over the table, covering his ears, twisting his head wretchedly from side to side. The sound was so terrible it penetrated even Trude's blank immobility. Her whole body jerked convulsively, her hands tightening on the handles of Gustavia's wheel-chair till the knuckles stood out like bare bones. Suddenly she lifted her head, and her eyes beneath their heavy brows burned like dark coals.

"*Alles ist hin,*" she whispered. "*Alles ist hin ...*"

She leaned forward. Slowly, purposefully, the chair began

308

to move. Gustavia caught at the wheels, spoke urgently, commandingly, her voice rising to a shriek as the spokes of the wheels tore through her vainly snatching fingers. Propelled by Trude, ugly Trude, mindless Trude, obedient, silent Trude, the chair rolled towards the open door and out on to the balcony.

Mattie watched, rooted to the spot, as it crunched through the frost-crusted snow and, turning to the left, disappeared from sight. And Trude's broad, grimly determined back also. And Gustavia's voice, fierce now in vehement, incomprehensible protest, fading slowly. Until it broke off abruptly in a brief, terrifying confusion of sounds, above which a single, agonised, heart-stopping cry rent the cold night air, its echoes dying rapidly to silence.

Vickie, too, was silent now, gasping for breath, her hands pressed to her head. For a second longer Mattie stood paralysed, unable to move. Then, in one movement, she was at the door. She saw footprints in the snow, and the double line of wheels, leading away along the balcony. And at their end, at the head of the staircase down to the terrace in front of the house, Trude's still, square, powerful figure. Gustavia, her wheel-chair, these were gone. Sharply Mattie pictured the steep flight of steps, the chair's lurching, headlong descent, the old woman's helpless terror. She shuddered. And thanked God that the nightmare was now over.

Trude was looking out across the valley. Suddenly she turned and smiled, as from the silvery town below there rose a distant tumult of bells. Soon, Mattie realised, it would be midnight. And down in Mittenwald they were calling the people to Mass.

In the room behind her Bruno staggered to his feet. Thrusting past her with a wordless, animal cry, he reeled drunkenly along the balcony and down the staircase. A moment later Victoria joined her mother, clinging tightly to her friendly skirts. Mattie looked down into her face, saw bewilderment there—the wide, half-fearful eyes of someone who had just woken from a deep, uneasy sleep. Bewilderment . . . and trust. And loving innocence.

309

Relief blossomed joyously in Mattie's heart. She embraced the child, whispered soft, tender endearments. Vickie pressed closer, hiding her face. Until a further cry from Bruno drew Mattie forward, her daughter with her, to the head of the stairs. She stood by the unmoving Trude, and stared down. Gustavia lay beneath her, tiny on the snow of the terrace, spread out like a broken doll, black, deathly still. Her wheelchair rested crookedly on its side close by, one of its buckled wheels still turning slowly. And her son stood over her silent body, his arms hanging loosely by his sides, his head turned up to the circling stars. He cried out again, a savage, desolate sound, swallowed instantly in the dark spaces of the night.

Away at the corner of the house, where the track up from Mittenwald joined the terrace, there was movement, a sudden commotion of shapes. But Mattie's eyes were fixed in horror on her husband as his cry turned now to unmistakable, spine-chilling laughter. He lifted his foot and began to kick at the lifeless body on the snow before him. Kick and kick again. While his laughter grew.

Sick with revulsion and pity, Mattie stooped and covered her daughter's face in her skirts. And looked away herself. So that it was left to Trude, calm now and moving with easy assurance, to go down the steps to the terrace and gently take his arm.

"*Was machen Sie,* Herr Becker?" Her voice was strong, yet compassionate. "*Sie ist tot,* Herr Becker. *Was machen Sie?*"

Silently Mattie repeated the words after her. *Sie ist tot ...* she is dead. Gustavia is dead. Is dead ... Suddenly, incredibly, a quick little figure darted across the moonlit snow towards them from the corner of the house, its voice raised in shrill, excited triumph. A voice that caused Mattie to stare, and blink her eyes in total astonishment, and stare again. For she knew that beyond any shadow of doubt she recognised both the voice and its owner.

"It's 'im, mister," Midge cried. "It's 'im what done in the

fiddler bloke. It's 'im! It's 'im, I tell yer . . ."

Mattie's thoughts were in chaos. She saw Bruno stiffen. Slowly he turned as two bulkier shapes detached themselves from dark shadows and began to approach him. One of them, she realised instantly, was the Herr Baron Rudolph von Kronstadt.

The boy Midge had stopped a few yards short of Bruno. "It's 'im," he repeated impatiently. "Mister Gradbolt sir, *it's 'im*!"

With an angry oath Bruno lunged forward, his arms outstretched. And was brought up short by the steely glint of moonlight on the pistol held unwaveringly in the second man's hand.

"Now then, Mr Becker—there's been enough violence one way and another, wouldn't you say?" Inspector Gradbolt murmured quietly.

By now Mattie was past astonishment. These then, the boy and Inspector Gradbolt, were the 'strange couple' with whom Baron Rudolph had been busy when she called. And the suspicions they brought which had caused his sister's uneasiness . . . She watched in a dazed silence as Bruno hesitated, swaying on his feet, then turned and stumbled blindly away across the terrace. He reached the gate to the cliff path, lurched through it. Trude stepped forward, called urgently after him, warning him, but he took no notice. His slithering footsteps faded. Until abruptly, inevitably, they ceased. The path was narrow, treacherous by moonlight. There was a brief, desperate scuffling. Then branches splintered as slowly the sounds of his fall dwindled. And the silence that followed them beat painfully in the listening air.

Mattie closed her eyes, hugged her daughter closely to her. When she looked again Trude was standing alone by the low wall at the edge of the terrace, gazing over. While from below her came men's voices, and the sound of their cautious progress downwards. Behind her Gustavia's body, spread-eagled on the

311

snow. And the chair at rest now, its wheel no longer turning.

At long last the inspector and Baron Rudolph returned to the terrace. And Mattie could tell at once from their demeanour, from the dragging slowness of their movements, that they had found Bruno, and that he was dead. Her husband was dead. Her husband and his mother also ... And the only words that ran through her head, hauntingly, insanely, as she rocked little Victoria gently to and fro, were those of a meaningless children's nursery tune:

> *Ach, du lieber Augustin,*
> *Augustin, Augustin...*
> *Ach, du lieber Augustin,*
> *Alles ist hin.*

The fire in Baron Rudolph's study was burning brightly. Mattie sat in a low chair beside it, Vickie on her knee. Mercifully the child was asleep now, her head resting on Mattie's shoulder. She remembered, it seemed, nothing of her actions before the old woman's death. And of the rest ... It would be foolish, Mattie knew, to expect the night's horrors to pass easily from her. But children survived. And somehow they made peace with their memories.

Baron Rudolph was sitting quietly at his desk, on which the violin case, Albert's violin case, still lay open. The silky hair combed back above his ears was disordered, his lean face sad and thoughtful. In his hand he held the silver-mounted seal, and he was turning it absent-mindedly over and over.

Inspector Gradbolt stood across the fire from Mattie. She looked up at him, saw his shabby Norfolk jacket, his schoolmasterly stoop, his familiar eyeglasses clipped firmly to his nose. His expression was concerned and he had, as always, an open note book in his hand. Suddenly it seemed to her as if somehow she were back in the crammed little parlour above the shop on Copperas Street. As if soon her father would come into the room. As if everything that had happened in between were no more than a dream.

"I went to the Bürgermeister first, of course," the inspector was saying. "But I have to admit that he was less than helpful. My own position, naturally, was not easy. But his principal concern appeared to be with the social standing of the Baron here and Mr Becker, rather than with the crimes one of them might have committed."

Mr Becker ... Mattie was grateful to him for his obstinate Englishness. Never once had he called Bruno *Herr* Becker. Never once, either, had he referred to him as 'your husband'. And this *Mr Becker* was a stranger to her, a man she had never known, never loved. A stranger—which was indeed what poor Bruno had become. An unknowable, monstrous stranger.

Inspector Gradbolt coughed discreetly. "Inevitably that placed me in a somewhat difficult situation. I have no legal standing here at all, you understand. I'm in Mittenwald on my own account entirely. By way of a small holiday, you might say." He removed his eyeglasses and began to polish them assiduously. "Nevertheless, having travelled so far with my young companion I was naturally unwilling to abandon such a worthy enterprise. So—"

"So you came directly to me, you and your small friend." The Herr Baron managed a weary smile. "I was, after all, the nearer, the more convenient. And, fortunately for me, my face proved my innocence."

"I never really doubted it would." Inspector Gradbolt put in stoutly. "From Midge's description I felt sure Mr Becker was the man I wanted. All the same . . ."

"All the same, Herr Inspector, you had to be certain. But that boy is a clever one, I think."

Midge was in bed now, and imperviously asleep, after a nameless, early-hours-of-the-morning feast of hot chocolate, and ham, and more Christmas *Kuchen* than Mattie would have believed possible. She smiled to herself. He was indeed a clever one. Friede was with him now, in case he might wake. But

313

Mattie knew he'd sleep through till the morning. His body was warm, his stomach full. And that, for such as Midge, was all that mattered.

And as to his future—that, she felt, was in her own hands. Something could be arranged. Certainly he need never go hungry and cold again. He was older than Vickie, and far, far wiser. He'd make her a fine companion, a fine new brother.

She turned back to the inspector. "How did you find him?" she asked. "When the case was supposed to be closed, I mean. And after so long a time..."

Inspector Gradbolt held his spectacles up to the lamplight, breathed on them. "Gentleman name of Scattermole," he said. "Chimney sweep by profession. Sergeant Griffin and I were sent to a house where he was working. Matter of a pair of silver candlesticks that had somehow found their way into his sack. A sharp-eyed servant had spotted them. We made the arrest, of course—him and the poor wretched boy he'd been working up the flue. I'd have got him for that too if I could—break your heart, some of these boys would. But the law's the law ... and Lord Shaftesbury's having a hard time changing it, more's the pity."

He sighed, gave his glasses one last polish, and replaced them on his nose. "Still, ma'am, that's neither here nor there. Took them both to the station. Wasn't till we gave the boy a bath that we saw what we'd got ... There's an old saying, ma'am—everything comes to him who waits. Mostly I'd say it's a lot of nonsense. The Lord helps them as helps themselves is my motto. There *are* times, though ..."

He tilted his head and shrugged, self-deprecatingly. "And at least I'd been right about the boy—he *had* witnessed the murder and he was able to give us a very passable description of the criminal ... All the same, ma'am, in my opinion there's no substitute for a positive identification, face to face. So I pulled a few strings, and took my next year's leave a bit early, as it were, and ... well, ma'am, here we are."

"You're a conscientious man, Inspector Gradbolt."

The inspector looked away. "I never did like unfinished business, ma'am," he murmured. "Not that there was much I could do, mind, Bavaria being somewhat out of my jurisdiction. Still, there was your position to think of, ma'am. If the murderer did turn out to be Mr Becker then you had a right to know, I thought."

And now Bruno was dead. She had given the inspector a description of the events leading up to his death—brief and confused, and only half understood, but enough to tell him that he should not press her further. And enough also to tell him that she could feel no grief at her husband's passing. As the man she had married he had ceased to exist. And at least, like that of his mother, his poor tormented spirit was now at rest.

Mattie sat for a moment, gently rocking her sleeping child. "Shall his death mean trouble for you, Inspector?" she said.

"None I can't handle, ma'am. The Baron here is my witness that it was no fault of mine."

"And that of his mother?"

"Clearly an accident, I'd say." Inspector Gradbolt studied his bony hands. "I wasn't there, mind. But from what you've told me it seems the companion was most devoted. The chair must have slipped. She'd never have pushed her mistress intentionally. Not in a million years."

A wise conclusion. Certainly nobody except Trude had seen the old woman fall. And she would hardly insist upon her own guilt, if guilt it was . . . She was with her cousin now. It wasn't, she had told Baron Rudolph, that she was afraid to stay up in *das Haus Graugipfel*. She was, indeed, perfectly calm and composed, almost radiant—a very different woman from the withdrawn, listless creature Mattie had grown used to seeing. But Christmas with her cousin Anna, she said, would be rather more festive. And this Mattie could well believe.

The other servants, having no relations in the town, were to spend Christmas in the Herr Baron's household. So the house now stood empty on its dark rock, abandoned to the mountains and their silence. If Mattie had anything to do with it, it would stay that way. For her at least, even though its evil genius had now departed, the misery it had seen would linger on, clinging to its sombre walls. Though it might well be hers now, and the Becker factory too, she wanted none of it. And the money these represented ... something for Vickie, perhaps, in the distant future.

She would never fully understand, she realised, what had prompted Trude to intervene so ruthlessly, and so decisively. What anguish she had suffered at the old woman's hands, what subtle tortures had been inflicted on her. But she clearly felt no guilt in the matter. It was rather as if a terrible weight had been lifted from her shoulders, freeing her spirit. And Mattie could only rejoice in her soul's liberation.

For she knew that in her own battle with the malign Frau Becker, no matter what the outcome might have been, the real sufferer would have been little Vickie. There were other victims too: Trude, Bruno, even no doubt poor wretched Liesl, till she had escaped into madness ... the tally was horrible indeed. An evil beyond all human forgiveness. Mattie shivered at the thought, and hugged her daughter tight.

Inspector Gradbolt had lapsed into silence. The clock on the mantle at his elbow struck three. In a scant few hours the people of Mittenwald would be waking to Christmas morning. It was a time for joy. Yet there in the Baron's study Mattie sat on, purposeless in the aftermath of terrible events.

At the desk Baron Rudolph abruptly laid down the seal he had been turning over and over. "I blame myself," he said. "If I had not stayed talking, if I had come out to you directly Friede told me you were here, then none of this would have happened." He looked across at her, frowning. "And when I did come, you were gone. We followed, naturally. Friede knew you were distressed. But why did you not wait?"

Mattie roused herself. Awkwardly she explained: the seal, the violin, her suspicions. Even the carving of the old man,

316

its ugliness contributing to her sudden certainty. The Herr Baron heard her out. Then he nodded, slowly, sadly.

"*Nun verstehe ich*—now I understand. The true explanations, of course, are simple enough. You were not to know it, but the seal is that of Mittenwald's guild of violin makers. We all use it ... And as for the violin, it arrived one day from England. No letter, nothing. I had been showing it to the Herr Inspector just before you came."

Inspector Gradbolt crossed from the fireplace, picked the instrument up, its back gaping dustily, and turned to Mattie. "Obviously Mr Becker despatched it by way of laying what I believe is called a red herring. I had suspected as much from the outset." He replaced the fiddle, sighed ruefully. "But the seal is another matter. Scotland Yard failed you there, ma'am. The symbol of a guild—we should have considered the possibility."

"Naturally I was curious about the violin," Baron Rudolph continued. "It was a Becker—yet unlike any Becker I had seen before. So ..." he spread his hands, "I opened it. But there was little to be learnt. New techniques certainly, but nothing my small factory could attempt. And anyway, I suspect, not commercial—they were not repeated, after all, even in the Becker factory ... I do understand, however, your suspicions."

He swung round then, looked back over his shoulder at the wooden carving. "All this I understand," he repeated. "But not your feeling about my work. The old man—surely he is not *ugly*? He is the shape of the tree that grew him. He was there, waiting for me in the wood." Now, suddenly, the Baron's eyes began to flash and his voice became fervent. "Do you not see? He flows upwards, out of the ground. He is like a force of nature. He is nature itself. Not ugly. Surely not ugly?"

And Mattie looked. And saw then, as if through Baron Rudolph's eyes, the movement, the vigour, the ancient wisdom, contained in the old man's twisted body. It stood, as strong

317

and weather-worn as the mountain out of which it had grown. As watchful also, and as silent. The sight was a revelation, and it humbled her.

"No," she whispered. "Not ugly. Not ugly at all. I was mistaken." And felt the inadequacy of her words, and the sudden, irresistible weariness that was possessing her. "I'm sorry," she said. "Not ugly at all. Noble . . ."

Her voice tailed off and her head nodded.

At once the Herr Baron was contrite. He sprang up, moved to her side. "Forgive me. You are tired. You have suffered so much, and I—I talk to you of art . . . It is time for you to rest. Please forgive me."

He stooped forward then, and tenderly lifted Victoria from her lap. The child slept on, peacefully, in his arms. "When you have slept we will talk again," he said. "But it is not necessary to worry yourself. Our house is yours. Friede and I—we are very happy that you stay here as long as you wish."

Mattie got to her feet. As she stumbled towards the door Inspector Gradbolt came to her assistance. Dimly she heard the Herr Baron's words. They sparked a sudden determination in her mind.

"England," she said faintly. "My father . . . my mother . . . I must return to England." She paused in the doorway, straightened her back. "I must return to England as soon as it can be arranged," she told them.

She moved forward then, out into the tiled hall, Inspector Gradbolt at her side. Baron Rudolph followed her, her sleeping daughter held effortlessly in his arms.

"But you will come back," he murmured. "You will come back to Mittenwald."

It was no question: a statement rather. Mattie didn't answer him. Slowly she began to climb the curving staircase. But she knew, somewhere deep in her tired mind, that he was right. She had seen the mountains, lived beneath their awesome beauty. She had seen the old man too, their faithful spirit. And through him had come to understand something of Baron

318

Rudolph, his creator. And she knew now that, in spite of everything, in spite of all that she had endured, she would come back. She and Vickie together. Not to the Becker factory, not to *das Haus Graugipfel*. But to the mountains, and to the town cradled in their midst, and to the Herr Baron. She would come back. And they would wait for her. And, when the time was right, welcome her.